Otaku

Also by Chris Kluwe

Beautifully Unique Sparkleponies:
On Myths, Morons, Free Speech, Football,
and Assorted Absurdities

Otaku

Chris Kluwe

TOR

A Tom Doherty Associates Book
New York

OTAKU

Copyright © 2020 by Chris Kluwe

A Tor Book
Published by Tom Doherty Associates
120 Broadway
New York, NY 10271

www.tor-forge.com

Tor® is a registered trademark of Macmillan Publishing Group, LLC.

The Library of Congress Cataloging-in-Publication Data is available upon request.

ISBN 978-1-250-20393-9 (hardcover)
ISBN 978-1-250-20397-7 (ebook)

Our books may be purchased in bulk for promotional, educational, or business use. Please contact your local bookseller or the Macmillan Corporate and Premium Sales Department at 1-800-221-7945, extension 5442, or by email at MacmillanSpecialMarkets@macmillan.com.

First Edition: March 2020

Printed in the United States of America

0 9 8 7 6 5 4 3 2 1

Otaku: Loosely translated from late twentieth-century Japanese—a person obsessed with a particular aspect of culture to the detriment of their social skills. Otaku primarily began with anime and manga subcultures, but later grew to encompass a wide variety of interests.

—Entry on the Web Archival Project

THE SOUTH COAST PROTECTORATE,
by Global Travel LLC

Hello, and thank you for choosing Global Travel for your world experience needs! Global Travel—if we can't get you there, then it's not worth visiting™!

For our valued customers who wish to see the exotic sights of the South Coast Protectorate, located on the eastern part of the North American landmass (a peninsula formerly known as "Florida"), there are several things you should keep in mind when you visit, in order to ensure a smooth and harmonious experience.

1. Due to past and ongoing hostilities between the western and southeastern portions of the continent, as well as racial tensions within what used to be known as the "United States," we recommend you do not refer to the South Coast Protectorate as such—the locals tend to become upset, and violent, when reminded of their protectorate status. Instead, use the local nomenclature and describe the city as Ditchtown! It'll make you feel like a local, and you can take in the scenic waterscape sights without too much fear of a stabbing!

2. Since the Church of Christ Ascendant, the local governing body, is strictly isolationist, members of the South Coast Protectorate (Ditchtown) do not look on their leaders with much favor. In all cases, they will refer to members of the CCA as "gummies," a local slangword. Anecdotally, it is believed that "gummies" arose from the accents of the CCA when referring to the word "government," which they appear to pronounce "gummint." Strangely, many members of the CCA security forces also refer to themselves as "gummies," so don't feel like you will offend by using the term!

3. Members of Ditchtown refer to the peoples of the Silicon Zone Egalitare as "silkies," instead of using the proper address of "Free Randians" the SZE promotes. Though some members of the SZE live in Ditchtown, it is highly unlikely that you will happen across them, as tensions between the two polities (CCA and SZE) are still high following the aftermath of the Water Wars. As the controlling polity of Ditchtown, the CCA shares anti-SZE propaganda on the regional 'Net on a regular basis, and this manifests in how members of Ditchtown speak to each other about the "silkies." If you *are* visiting an SZE acquaintance while in Ditchtown, remember to travel safely! Global Travel cannot be held liable for any accidents, as stated in our mandatory end user license agreement!

4. Ditchtown's regional 'Net has strict morality features in place, so be careful what you browse! Homosexual material, licentious behavior, and any sort of political questioning of the Theocrophant will result in strict penalties for users without the proper permits. Women are not allowed these permits, so we recommend silence as the best option. Instead, enjoy the wonderful sights of the sea spreading amongst massive towers! Truly, a man-made wonder!

5. In Ditchtown, you will find many veterans of the Water Wars, or "the Dubs," in local parlance. We highly recommend not interacting with such people, as it can trigger post-traumatic stress memories, and lead to an unwanted altercation. If they wanted to get better, they would have availed themselves of the CCA's numerous facilities, so stay safe and don't engage!

**Enjoy your trip to the South Coast Protectorate,
and thank you for choosing Global Travel!**

1

[Newbie]

I pull my dagger from the chimera's eye with a sound like someone sucking soda, leather-strapped hilt molded to my palm. Green blood drips from the chiseled point of the blade, steaming slightly in the dank underground air. One of the beast's feathered hind legs spasms briefly, drumming a tribal tattoo into the rocky floor, which startles Kiro back a few steps. His staff wavers in the gloom, the glowing light at its tip coming close to a few of the oddly shaped stalactites. Shifting highlights momentarily gleam in his brilliantly purple spiked hair.

"Careful," I hiss, trying not to yell, "you hit one of the alarms, and we're gonna be neck deep in flenser worms quicker than you can spit."

"Sorry, Ash, sorry, I swear, it's the inputs. They're not reading my motions right."

"Don't give me that shit. You know the Game can't be hacked. Their encryption's better than the gummies and silkies combined. If you fuck up, it's on you."

"Ash is right." A deep baritone comes from my left, where a thickly muscled woman levers herself to her feet with a large axe. Chain mail drapes her body, and an assault rifle hangs from her back. What skin isn't covered by armor is the deep red of coal embers. "Said you knew encounter. Said you were good."

"I do, I am, I swear," Kiro whines. "I read all the online guides and ran all the sims until I could do it bli—"

"Nashor's balls, you brought a *newbie* on the run, Ash? As *support?*" A high-pitched voice sounds from my right. An anthropomorphic fox with camouflage fur finishes carving off small pieces of the chimera's body with a serrated blade, more short sword than knife. She snarls at me. "Why the hell isn't Brand here?"

"I haven't been able to reach Brand in two weeks. Keeps going to avatar. It was either Kiro or wait for the next reset. High-level supports don't exactly grow on trees, and you know we can't plug in a random. Everyone's a newbie at some point. He knows this is his chance to prove he can handle endgame." I plunge my fist through the chimera's dulling eye, reaching into its brain cavity for the essence jewel I know lies within. My fingers brush aside lumpy brain matter, searching for the hard facets of the jewel, the only currency that matters in endgame—proof an obstacle has been surpassed. "Besides, I know Kiro in the real. He's solid."

"Ugh, I guess, but still . . . a *newbie?*" The fox sighs and lops off the barbed tail, sticking it into a pouch on her waist. The large segment seems to shrink down into the mouth of the pouch, then disappears, defying all expected laws of physics. "It makes my fur itch." She turns and looks at the muscled woman in chain mail. "Also, Slend, you need to change your voice setting. It's freaking me the fuck out. You sound like a guy."

"Stoofoo, Wind. My voice, my mod." The battleaxe comes

flashing down on the chimera's groin, a post-mortem neuter-
ing. Kiro winces again, and I frown. If he can't handle harvest-
ing resources from endgame trash, there's no way he's going
to have the stomach for a boss encounter, especially in the
Everdark facet of the Game. Most people think fantasy and
picture elves, unicorns, other twee fairy shit. Most people never
make it to Everdark, relive the old myths. With a wrenching
twist, I yank the fist-sized jewel free from the chimera's brain
stem and walk over to Kiro.

"You doing okay?" I ask, absentmindedly placing the gem
into one of my storage pouches. Ichor drips from my hand to
the floor in a steaming puddle, the sensation like warm candle
wax bathing my fingers.

"Yeah, yeah, I'll be fine. It's just . . ."

He waves a hand at the scene. The half-butchered corpse of
the chimera lies in front of us, Wind and Slend plucking feathers from its outstretched wings. Viscous green blood pools
beneath its corpse. In the illuminated area around us, writhing stalactites, shaped like giant worms, hang from the ceiling,
fang-filled maws bracketing a narrow path. Disgustingly organic
sounds echo from the darkness, a mixture of slurping moans
and bone-crunching snaps—an atmosphere that reaches down
to the hindbrain and yanks some very primal levers.

Just another encounter.

I nod. "You're right. First time through, it's a bit of a
change from Candyland, huh?"

". . . Yeah. I don't know if I like it. Are all the encounters
like this? In Everdark?"

"Most of 'em. There are a couple that are more logic ori-
ented, but even those have psych-secs."

"Psych-secs?"

"Psychological sections. Fighting's only part of endgame,

and the devs love to mess with people's heads. Better get used to it if you're gonna run with us. If you want endgame trophies, you gotta earn 'em. Psych-sec's part of that."

He grimaces. I can't say that I blame him. It takes a special type of mind-set to run endgame encounters, the toughest challenges Infinite Game's developers can nightmare up. No one knows if they have that mind-set or not until they do their first run. Most of them head back to Candyland, home of the omnipresent computer assist. I decided to stay, the darkness calling to something inside me, a thrill I can't find anywhere else. I'm hoping Kiro stays for a while too, since Brand, our normal support, is away from world somewhere, and supports are hard to find.

I walk back over to Slend and Wind. The wings are bare, lumpy flesh oozing more glistening fluid. I nod in satisfaction. Almost every useable piece of the chimera has been stowed away in limitless bags of holding, one of the few game allowances for convenience outside of Candyland. The remnants of the monster lie sprawled in front of us like a mangled mole rat, pink skin shining wetly beneath Kiro's staff.

"Good job. That'll at least pay for rezzes if we wipe later. Wind, you've got point. Slend, make sure Kiro doesn't walk into a trap."

"Whatever you say, Ash." The fox grabs a pair of nightvision goggles from a waist pouch and walks forward in a crouch. "If you hear me die, assume that something bad happened."

I fall in behind her, adopting the same gliding walk, my boots hitting the ground like falling leaves. "If only we could be so lucky."

"Let Wind watch the newbie," Slend grumbles from behind. Chain mail clinks gently but her feet are whisper quiet.

"Wind has a higher dex, and she's more expendable if we lose someone before a boss."

"Hey!"

Three trash clears, a logic trap, and an hour later, we're standing in front of an ominously glowing cavern entrance. Bloodstains mar the rocky floor, the jagged mouth of the cave exhaling hot air in rancid breaths. Our path leads directly into the flickering opening, impenetrable rock walls to either side.

"Okay, we're at the boss. Last time, this was a Diremoth," I whisper to the others.

"Latest patch notes said that endgame encounters were re-balanced," Kiro whispers back. "Are you even sure it's still the same base type?"

"Oooh, look at the newbie talking about patch notes," Wind mocks. "Next thing you know he'll be telling us what rotations we should be using."

"Newbie has a point," Slend says slowly. "Devs like screwing the ladder. Wipe here, drop at least five. Season's almost over. Losing first would suck, 'specially to Mikelas. Fucker's evil."

"Yeah, he is," Wind responds, her voice subdued for the first time all run. "Him and his boardshits cornered me back when I was still leveling, before I joined Ash. If we had been in the real . . ."

"We've got your back." I pat her on the shoulder, fur silky beneath my hand, trying not to think about my own encounters with Mikelas, some in the real. "Kiro's right, though. It might not be a Diremoth. The devs have kept endgame the same for the last month. They're trying to get more people out of Candyland, give 'em predictable progression, but the league's about to end. That means it's gonna be different. Devs always change things near the end."

I bounce a rock idly in my left hand, thinking, my eyes locked onto the pulsating cavern entrance. The Everdark facet of Infinite Game is designated part of the fantasy spectrum, which means our guns aren't going to be very helpful here— not only are the monsters resistant to any damaging tech more advanced than a crossbow, the encounters themselves are prioritized to punish tech use, like how the frozen flenser worms surrounding the chimeras we dispatched earlier forced us into melee combat, instead of a safer ranged battle. Devs like to make things hard, but not impossible, so whatever's in this cave shouldn't be a permanent flyer.

The key word there being "shouldn't," I think sourly. Not "won't." They could be trying to lull us into a false sense of security with all these melee encounters leading up to a ranged fight. Wouldn't be the first time.

I turn back toward the group.

"Okay, here's how we're going to do this. Standard diamond formation, Wind up front, Kiro in the back. Slend, you take left. If it's still a Diremoth in there, same plan as last time. If not, we'll improvise."

"Uh, what was the plan last time?" Kiro asks.

Wind silently mouths the word "newbie" at me, and I glare at her before answering Kiro.

"If you see its wings shimmer, throw a vortex barrier in front of us so we don't get hit by acid pollen. Other than that, stay out of the fire, try to get some skill shots in if you see an opportunity, and be ready to drag one of us to safety if we take a hit. We'll have to wait for it to land to cripple its wings for phase one. Your trauma skills are near maxed, right?"

"Yeah, I suppose . . ." His voice trails off in a petulant pout.

"There's no suppose about it," I say, glowering at him.

"This isn't Candyland. This is endgame. Trust your training, and we'll make it through just fine, but you gotta react *fast*. There's no room for error here." I put a hand on his shoulder, feeling the sleek fabric of his sigil-inscribed robe. "Look." I go on more gently. "It's okay to be nervous. Everyone gets nervous their first time in endgame. That's why you're in the back, to keep you out of the heavy shit." I wave my free hand at Wind and Slend, both busy checking their equipment. "We've killed hundreds of Diremoths. It'll be fine. You'll get a feel for the encounter, and next time it'll be easy peasy. It's like anything else—the more you do it, the more natural it seems."

"I guess you're right . . ."

Dammit Kiro, I don't have time for one of your sulks, not right now. I punch him on the arm, trying to shake him out of his funk.

"Of course I'm right, stupid. I'm always right. Just try not to cause a wipe, okay? Losing our streak would suck."

He swallows. "Got it."

I pat Kiro's shoulder.

"Let's go get some loot, then. Wind, take us in."

We creep through the twisting passageway, its narrow walls almost brushing my shoulders, even crouched as I am. Ominous light flickers ahead of us, and pulses of rancid air increase the stifling heat. It feels like going through some huge animal's digestive tract, working our way down its throat and into its stomach. Another psych-sec. I look back at Kiro to see how he's handling it, and grin inside. His face is set in a scowl of disgust, but he doesn't hesitate, following Wind's footsteps precisely.

Nice, Kiro, nice. I knew you had it in you. I'll make a raider of you yet. This is just another encounter, something to get used to.

Ahead of me, Wind stops and gently raises a closed fist, fur rippling along her arms and back. I settle onto my heels and wait for her to report, motioning for Kiro and Slend to join us. They crouch-walk forward and we huddle our heads together, cheeks almost touching.

"Large cavern just around this corner," she whispers, breath brushing across my skin. "Light's bad, can't see too far inside. Lots of steam. Looks like magma vents around the edges of the room."

"Okay, that means lava's gonna come into play as an environmental hazard," I whisper back. "What's rule number one?"

"Don't stand in the fire," three voices chorus back, Kiro's slightly slower than the other two.

"Right. Don't stand in the fucking fire. Anything else, Wind?"

"Big pile of rocks near the middle. Might be a rockfall hazard, might be a golemtrap. Couldn't tell. Steam hashed the optics on my rifle." She pats the weapon strapped to her back.

"We'll operate under the assumption that it's rockfall at first," I say, "but keep your distance from it just in case. A golemtrap is really gonna hurt our deeps if we have to split damage. Any sign of a boss?"

"Nope. Visibility's real bad. Can't see much past six meters overhead. Could be a Diremoth in the ceiling; they like damp places." Wind pauses, then continues, her voice pragmatic. "Could be something else too. Won't know until it eats the newbie."

"Great." I rub the hilt of my blade, its worn grip comforting in my hand. "Okay, we'll proceed as planned, ranged weapons first. Diamond formation, watch for lava and rockfall, don't get near the center. Kiro, be ready to solid-shield us the instant something appears—I wouldn't put it past the devs to have the encounter start with a sneak attack from above. We'll react from there. Let's move."

A chorus of whispered assents, and we advance into the cavern, Wind in front, assault rifle snugged to her cheek and gently bobbing from side to side, Slend to the left, chain mail softly clinking. I scan our right flank through the holographic sights of my own rifle, trying to take in everything, knowing that anything could be a warning, or a threat. In the Game, you learn quick or you die. Exhalations of steam billow from gently bubbling mounds ringing the edges of the room, creating a hot, wet mist in the air.

We cautiously advance counterclockwise around the room, keeping clear of the large, shadowed mass in the center. The tension saws at my nerves, every sense hyperalert, waiting for the encounter to begin. Magma vents continue their slow churn. We make it halfway across the room, and then everything goes to hell.

2

[A Smile like an Open Grave]

"Dragon!"

Wind screams the word with an accompanying burst of gunfire, and my head snaps over to the left. The hulking shape in the center of the room, what I thought might be rockfall or a golemtrap, is slowly unfurling a huge pair of wings, delicate purple veins undulating against the leathery skin. A long neck stretches up into the air, tapered scales running its entire length, and perched atop is the dragon's death-cold stare. Malevolent red eyes glitter beneath thickly armored brows, and a crown of horns sweeps back from the top of its head. It opens its mouth, revealing two sets of meter-long serrated teeth, and roars, blasting sound at us like a riot suppressor.

"What do we do? What do we do?" Kiro squawks in alarm, his breath labored. It sounds like he's hyperventilating.

"Stay relaxed. Scatter and ground it." My voice is calm, but only from years of training. Inside, my heart feels like it's going to burst through my chest. It's incredibly rare to encounter a dragon, and the wipe rate against them is close to ninety percent. We've only fought one once before, and that was carefully planned out over an entire month. Even then, if it hadn't been for Brand working miracles in support, we would've failed.

Nothing you can do now, except fight your way through. Just another encounter.

I sprint to the right, keeping away from the magma vents and maintaining my distance from the giant wyrm. Adrenaline surges, the old fight or flight instinct kicking into gear, and I flip my assault rifle up, thumbing off the safety. I focus on my sights and loose a chattering series of shots on the run, aiming for the dragon's wings. Several impact the worm-like veins, but only open small holes—our tech weapons still weakened by the rules of Everdark. Not good. If we don't keep the beast from getting airborne, we have no chance. We learned that the hard way last time.

"Kiro! Ranged buff, now!"

An orange glow suffuses the air around my tactical rifle, but it's fitful and weak, like a sputtering fire. I curse under my breath—Kiro isn't maintaining his forms properly, lessening the effect of the spell, which means I can't afford to miss. I slide to a halt, snug the stock up to my shoulder and cheek, the movement second nature by now, and take a deep breath. Slowly exhale, pause, then gently squeeze the trigger.

Chattering barks fill the air, and my bullets slam home, tracers filling the air with bright flashes. Three of the veins I aimed for wink out, spurts of purple blood falling to the rocks below. The dragon's right wing goes limp and ragged, unable to maintain its structural integrity. Short bursts of gunfire from the other side of the room indicate Wind and Slend following my lead, efficient as always, trusting that I can handle my side on my own. After playing for this long together, it's almost like we can read each other's minds. The other wing shudders and falls. Kiro cowers near one of the back walls, fumbling at the safety on his gun with one hand while trying to maintain the complicated finger motions for the spell with his other. He's not doing a great job of accomplishing either. At his feet, his anchoring staff lies forgotten.

The dragon screams in rage, rearing up on two hind legs, thrashing its now-useless wings and sending the mist roiling. A spiked tail comes whipping across the ground, and I vault it with one hand, slapping the pebbled skin to give myself a boost over the top of its mass. Jagged tail spines whistle past my body, but I chose my gap carefully, and I land unscathed on the other side. Suddenly, the beast draws in a huge breath, chest expanding out like a balloon. Scales glow cherry red across the front of its torso.

We have ten seconds before someone gets incinerated. Another fact learned the hard way.

"Regroup at Kiro and get ready to group shield," I yell, integrated comm channel sending my words to the others. The tail comes slashing back in my direction, and this time I tumble underneath. A spike snags my rifle strap, sending the weapon spinning away across the floor, but I use the change in momentum to roll upright and back to my feet.

Thank goodness the quick-release clip worked properly, otherwise I'd be a red smear on the rocks right now.

I dash over to Kiro, huddling fearfully near a vent, the iron sights on his rifle bobbing through a shaky figure eight. He's panting in sharp gasps, hyperventilating, hindbrain instincts exerting control. I slap him across the face.

"Kiro! Drop your gun and get ready to shield! We'll support, but you've gotta initiate it!"

"I . . . it's . . . dragon . . ." His rifle drops back against his chest and he kneels for his staff, clutching it like he's going to be sick.

Wind and Slend run up next to me, breathing slightly

heavier than normal. Slend reloads her rifle, grabbing an armor-piercing magazine from her ammo pocket and slotting it home with smooth, economical motions. Wind pulls a belt of grenades out of one of her pouches, like a magician's trick, and straps them around her waist. She looks away from the dragon and groans, seeing the whimpering form of Kiro huddled on the ground.

"Dammit, Ash, I told you he was gonna be trouble. We're gonna wipe for sure, and on a dragon too. What a useless waste of time. This could've made us rich."

"Shut it, Wind. He'll come through for us. You'll see." I grab Kiro's forearms, trying to get him to look at me. "Kiro. I know this is pretty heavy for your first encounter, but you have to raise a shield. Otherwise, we're toast. We have about . . ." I quickly glance at the enraged dragon. ". . . three seconds before we're charcoal. C'mon. I know you can do this. Focus, just like we practiced."

A moment of silence fills the cavern, the dragon's steam whistle intake of breath suddenly gone. I look over again, seeing the tiniest wisps of flame starting to leak out of the corners of its mouth, and swear. My hands move, seemingly of their own accord, starting the motions of a barrier, but it's pointless. I don't have enough specialization in applied defensive magic to keep us safe if I'm the spell anchor, and Kiro's staff isn't attuned to me. Wind sighs dramatically.

"Fucking newbies . . ."

A broad hand brushes me aside, interrupting my cast.

"No. I . . . I can do this. I can."

Kiro steps in front of us, then slams his staff into the ground. A minor shockwave ripples out, tiny dust waves undulating across the floor. His hands blur into motion, creating the impossibly complex forms required to initiate a max-level group shield spell, the now-unsupported staff floating gently above the ground, a solid pillar of brightening green runes crawling along its length.

"Get in support positions!" My voice is halfway between a yell and a cheer.

Good job, Kiro. I knew you could do it.

Wind and Slend take positions to either side. I run behind Kiro, completing the diamond formation, and prepare for impact. Above us, a massive fireball descends.

Kiro finishes the final hand gesture and crosses his wrists in front of him. We all copy him, bracing one foot behind our bodies. Beams of light flash from us to the staff, and then a shimmering blue wall flashes into existence, between us and the descending torrent of flame. A millisecond later, it hits like a crashing tsunami.

Raw force slams into my arms, the sheer power of the dragon's fire eliciting an involuntary grunt. Straining, I push back against the brutal pressure, keeping my section of the shield firm. My shoulders and core muscles quiver beneath the stress, and I scream out in defiance.

Magic in the Game is reflected by three elements—physical dexterity to create the proper forms; raw strength proportional to the level of the spell being cast; and the force of will to endure the pain for as long as it takes. A max rank shield spell will withstand anything, as long as our flesh doesn't give way. If it does, if we fail to hold the appropriate form against the requisite burden, then the spell crumples, along with our bodies. In situations where a max rank shield spell is required, that means a wipe.

In front of me, the other three push out as well, muscles bulging. Tears are leaking from the corners of Kiro's eyes. As the anchor, he's bearing the brunt of the attack, an onslaught of crushing weight trying to smear him into the ground, and if we weren't sharing the load, the dragonflame would've breached the shield almost instantly. Even the strongest Gamer in the world isn't strong enough to withstand close to a ton of pressure.

Incandescent heat spreads across the pale blue of our barrier, a half dome covering our braced forms. Rock melts and flows in a circle around us, but the shield stays intact, keeping us safe in our tiny island. Sweat pours from my brow, but I ignore it. If I didn't want to push myself, I would've stayed in Candyland. Finally, mercifully, the fire ends, the smothering weight falling away.

"Wind, Slend, draw its attention. I'm going for the tail. Kiro, move! Don't stand in the fire!"

We split apart once more, Kiro narrowly avoiding a magma eruption at his feet by diving out of the way. Hissing superheated rock shoots into the air behind him, a deadly fountain barely missing his leather boots. It cools and solidifies into a new layer on the ground. I shake my head at his narrow escape.

You gotta pay attention to environmentals, Kiro. That's how most parties wipe.

I notice glowing cracks beneath my feet and sidestep a magma eruption of my own, then turn my attention back to the dragon.

The creature is fully mobile now—twenty tons of murderous muscle atop four dextrous limbs, each equipped with an opposable digit and talons the size of a scimitar. Of course there's also the prehensile tail covered in needle-tipped spines, and the flamethrower system in its throat. Dragons don't mess around. Murderous red eyes track my movements, singling me out as the most dangerous target.

I dodge a casual swipe from its claws, waiting for Slend and Wind to get into position. Once they distract it, I should have a free run at the tail. Killing a dragon is a matter of taking away its weapons, one at a time, in a very specific order—wings, tail, claws, throat; gradually wearing it down until all threats are neutralized, with no room for error.

Slend bellows at the creature, taunting it to attack her, and it spins in place, surprisingly agile for such a large beast. She waves her axe at it, drawing its attention. To her side, I can see Wind pull the pin on a flashbang from her grenade belt. The flashbang won't really hurt the dragon, but it'll confuse it for the bare moment I need to sever the nerves at the base of its tail. My blade slides into my hand naturally as breathing, the worn leather grip comforting in my palm. It's nothing special, just a fifty-centimeter piece of metal designed to cut what I want it to cut, but the sharpened steel is an extension of myself, a familiarity earned from years of practice.

Slend blocks a claw swipe, using her axe to beat the scaled mass of the dragon's paw to the side. Behind her, Wind cocks her arm back and throws the flashbang, alert for the opening. The dragon smiles like an open grave.

My eyes narrow. Dragons don't normally . . .

Shit.

"It's a dev! We're being featured!"

Glowing golden runes appear on the walls, cutting away the steam and turning the cavern into a massive arena. Fast-paced music bursts into the air, heavy on the guitar riffs and choral melodies, a thrumming bass line syncopating like a heartbeat. Another rune, this one electric blue, appears above the dragon's head—the sigil of whichever dev has taken over the program that normally runs the monster's reactions. In this case, the twisting lines let me know that it's Hammer. I grimace. He and I have history, and he's been itching to take me down.

Of all the top-tier devs in Infinite Game, Hammer's the best, and he hates letting players win. Especially with an audience. Judging by the runes on the walls, there's at least a million viewers tuning in for the showdown. We must be the first guild to make it this far after the new patch, and I'm sure GameCore has been hyping this on the global 'Net since we started the run. I've been running my personal stream, of course, but that's a drop in the ocean compared to the attention GameCore commands. Ashura vs. Hammer, come one come all, get your tickets at the door. I know without looking that a jade green sigil is floating over my head, the swirling frozen explosion of my guild tag. The SunJewel Warriors.

Fighting devs is always a risky proposition, because they never react like the normally programmed responses in an encounter. It can be a lot of fun in social events, because then you really feel like you're interacting with living beings, but in the combat events it creates a dangerous unpredictability. Even worse, devs are the ones who design program behaviors, so they know the best way to subvert everything a player's learned about a specific encounter. The good ones have a nasty habit of studying previous strats the leaderboard groups use, so they're prepared to counter everything we normally do. The best ones, like Hammer, have an uncanny ability to get inside a non-human skin, and make it do something unexpected.

Lightning quick, Hammer flicks his tail and bats the grenade directly back at Wind, causing it to detonate in front of her face, a move no dragon's ever pulled before. Stunned, she falls to her knees, hands blindly groping through the air. Ignoring Slend's taunts, the dragon swipes Wind with an open palm, slamming her furred body into the cavern wall in a cloud of dust and flying rocks, then grinds its taloned hand in a circular motion against the wall. A bloodied pile of meat slowly slides to the floor, the once agile fox now roadkill.

"Fucker! That hurt! Fucking fuck, I hate fighting devs. Watch the tail, Ash." I hurdle the whipping tail once again,

Wind's high-pitched voice sounding in my head like the voice of a disembodied phantom. Which, essentially, is what she now is.

Dying during an encounter ghosts a player for as long as the encounter persists—able to relay information to teammates, but unable to physically interact with anything. Some games fade the screen to black and mute communications, so the dead player can't call anything out, but in Infinite Game, the devs figure if you lose somebody in endgame, you're going to need all the help you can get.

I dodge a crushing stomp from one of the dragon's back legs and flick my blade out, aiming for the tendon controlling its foot. Metal sinks in deep, but not enough to fully sever the iron-like tissue. It's enough to injure that foot, though, and Hammer roars in fury. I spend the next several seconds weaving between claws and tail whips, contorting my body through impossible poses—katas learned from Mom long ago, practiced religiously every day, like dryburb prayer sessions. Hammer's head darts down away from me, adder-quick, and magma erupts in the background. More runes appear, the music increasing in volume.

"Slend, try and get it off me!"

"Can't, boss. Got et. Fucker's fast."

". . . Shit. What's Kiro doing?" I backflip over the tail, slicing through scales and nerves in a blurring strike. The last third goes limp, but I'm not close enough to get the upper nerve clusters that control the whole length of the tail. Hammer roars and spins again, trying to impale me with concentrated lances of flame from the dragon's mouth. I quickly dodge, bobbing and weaving across the rocky floor, molten puddles congealing behind me.

". . . I'm dead too." Kiro's voice is glum. "Was trying to shield Slend, and I forgot to watch the floor. Magma eruption."

"Fucking *newbies*," Wind says, exasperated. "Well, Ash, looks like you get to one vee one a dragon. Something that's literally impossible. Have fun with that. Oh, and there's only about five million people watching now, so you're doubly fucked. Hammer's gonna get *paid*."

"Great," I groan.

"Why don't you just bail, Ash?" Kiro asks softly. "You'll only drop a couple places. It's a lot safer than trying to take a dev. Besides, there's no way you can beat a dragon by yourself."

"The hell I'm running from a fight, Kiro, and the *hell* I'm letting Mikelas's group of boardshits win this season," I snarl. "Not gonna happen. Don't distract me."

A petulant sigh is his only response.

In front of me, Hammer rears up, planning to flatten me beneath the dragon's bulk, and I sprint forward, aiming between its massive hind legs. His shadow starts descending, and I push my muscles even harder, hoping I don't tear a hamstring. Luckily, my body accedes to my demands, and I dart out from beneath the crushing weight, blade flickering from side to side. This time, I get both tendons cleanly, crippling Hammer's movement. The dragon's torso comes crashing down, causing the ground to shake.

Without breaking stride, I plant my sword in the side of Hammer's tail and use it to swing myself on top of his armored hindquarters, searching for the weak juncture between plates. A quick thrust and twist, and the rest of the tail goes limp. Hammer bellows, shaking his body, throwing me off, but I convert my fall into a dive and spring upright, spinning to face the angry beast rolling around on the floor. Even more runes pop into existence, the walls now almost completely covered with curving glyphs. The music increases in intensity.

"Just another encounter," I whisper, heart thudding in my chest in time with the mantra. "Just another encounter."

Wind lets out a low whistle. "Holy shit, Ash. Not only did you outrun a bodyslam, you turned it into a tail crit. You should've been dead, there."

"'Aten't dead yet,'" I mutter, thinking of one of my few heroines. "What's it look like damage-wise?"

"Closer to even," Wind responds, her voice rising with excitement. "Mobility's gone, bleeding heavy from the wings. Flame breath's still in play, but you should be able to dodge *that*." Her voice goes even higher. "No one's ever soloed a dragon before. Especially not one controlled by a dev. The viewrate is skyrocketing. You pull this off, and we're rich. Fuck, we're already rich from the split, even if you wipe."

"It's not over," I say, spinning my blade absentmindedly. "That was the easy part. Hammer wants to get paid too. He's gonna back himself into the exit and make me come to him. It's what I would do."

As I say the words, Hammer does exactly that, pushing the wounded rear of the dragon into a notch in the cavern walls, talons digging deep furrows in the cooled lava floor. He props his head on his front legs, like a dog resting on a carpet, and stares at me. Waiting. A grin snakes across the crocodile face, revealing long yellow teeth stained with blood, and a pointed tongue licks scaly lips.

"Feeling lonely, Ashura?" The dragon's voice sounds like crumbling bone, Hammer relishing the moment, playing to the crowd. "It's only half your progression if you give up now. You'll still be top three, top five at worst. Save yourself the humiliation of a full wipe. It's the smart thing to do."

"And let you knock us out of first? Go back to Candyland, Hammer. That's more your pace."

I know how to play to the crowd too. More glyphs burn into existence, news of the encounter viraling across the 'Net like a plague, socials close to crashing under the commentary.

"Besides, when I kill you, we'll clinch the ladder for this season. Dragons are worth triple, not even counting the dev bonus."

"*When* you kill me, Ashura?"

Hammer laughs, long and low. My mind races, trying to think of a viable strategy against a monster twenty times my size. I have a vortex grenade in my inventory, but that'll kill me just as quickly as Hammer in an enclosed space like this, and we don't get the win if the entire party's dead. My rifle's too far away to reach cleanly, and Hammer will be expecting that. I still have my blade, trusty tool for so long, but—

"Ash! Look out!"

"Don't distract her, newbie!"

Kiro's voice is shrill in my head, Wind's admonition slightly less piercing, but I'm already moving, deeply ingrained instincts slamming my body into motion.

Smoldering orange-yellow cracks appear beneath the back third of the room, centered where I was just standing. Magma vents shriek and hiss, belching more hot rock into the air, and I leap forward, desperately trying to clear the edge of the fractured lines. My feet barely make it out of the danger zone before a full third of the room explodes into lava, massive geysers shooting from the floor. Heat sears my back—nothing damaging, but uncomfortable all the same.

Diving forward, I tumble once, then push off the ground with my right foot and arm, cartwheeling to the left. A taloned hand slams into the space I just vacated, cratering the rock again and again, always a bare instant behind. I manage to get a couple attacks in on Hammer's paws, but the shallow cuts don't do much more than irritate him. Finally, I create enough room to back out of the threat space directly in front of the dragon.

"Not bad," Hammer says conversationally, "but how long

can you keep it up? Your body has to be getting tired. Wipe timer's counting down too."

Unfortunately, he's right. Another lava eruption behind me punctuates his statement. It's closer than the previous one, lessening the amount of available maneuvering area, and more are on the way. Devs don't let you dick around in an encounter forever. My sides ache from oxygen debt, my muscles are on fire, and the whole chamber is going to be full of boiling magma pretty soon. I have to end this quickly, but how . . . ?

Hammer yawns, exposing the wet pinkness of the dragon's throat.

"Looks like I win this one, Ashura. A pity. You've been worthy prey."

That's when it hits me. The passageway leading in—of course. No one's tried it before, because it's a horrible idea, but it makes sense within the Game's logic. There're always clues to the encounter, for those who pay attention, and there's always more than one way to win. Successfully pulling it off, though, is going to require some finesse, and no small amount of luck.

Time to play Jonah. The gummies are gonna love this.

"Slend," I subvocalize on our private channel. "When the dragon ate you, where were you positioned?"

"Underneath chest. Claws don't reach. Uses mouth."

"Perfect. Any tells when it came down?"

"Black eyes. Shark eyes."

"Got it. Kiro?"

"Yeah?"

"Be quiet. Don't distract me."

Another angry huff.

Lava erupts again, bare centimeters from my spine. Time to move. Above and around, the cavern walls are almost pure gold, glyphs covering us in a dome of brilliance, millions upon millions ignoring whatever grips them in the real, instead watching me in the spotlight. The twinge of nerves and adrenaline hitting my stomach is like the purest high in the world, banishing all sensation of pain. If I make this work . . .

I reverse the sword's grip in my hand, setting the blade back along the length of my forearm, dull side in, chisel point almost touching my elbow. A lone stringed instrument sustains a high note, the entire cavern seeming to hold its breath. My hamstrings and calves tense, muscles coiling, and then, almost unthinkingly, I'm in motion, feet gliding over the rocky ground. My mind falls into the dreamlike state of full combat, at one with my body, reactions coming before my brain even has time to craft a response.

Hammer attacks, swiping with one clawed hand, but he's not fast enough to do more than ruffle my hair with the wind of its passing, talons brushing past my face scant millimeters away. I continue my sprint, then roll to the side, avoiding a swing from his other hand. That one passes by my feet, slicing a thin layer from the bottom of one boot, a sliver of my sole. I plant my left foot and push myself back upright, running directly toward the copper-green chest of the dragon, momentarily left open by Hammer's lunging sweeps. Lava bursts behind me, but it's a distant thunder in my ears. Flame lances blast the ground, cratering explosions nearly lighting me on fire, but the shifting movement pattern I've adopted helps me avoid a direct hit.

It's like running a hundred-meter sprint through hell.

The last lance explodes behind me, and I stagger to a halt directly beneath the dragon's chest, breathing hard. A towering head stares down at me, nearly twenty meters up, swaying back and forth on a supple neck. With a sudden rush, scaly arms slam down behind me, blocking off any retreat. Hammer chuckles.

"Impressive, but now there's nowhere left to run, is there?"

Blood-spattered lips peel back to reveal stained fangs once more.

"I will relish this moment. The mighty Ashura, finally brought low, your reign atop the leaderboards ended. Any last words?"

I smile tiredly, adrenaline high gone, lactic acid burning my legs and arms, cramps threatening to seize my limbs, but my blade steady in my hand.

"Yeah. Eat me, Hammer."

Double rows of teeth shine in the blinding light of glyphs surrounding us.

"With pleasure."

A nictating membrane slides over the dragon's eyes, turning them the dead black of a burnt-out viewscreen. I summon up the last of my reserves, willing my body to obey me one last time, fighting through the toxic by-products of my own muscles.

"Ash!"

Kiro's voice sounds in my head simultaneously with the dragon's strike, but I can only focus on one thing right now, and it has to be the descending maw. Time slows, the gaping mouth growing larger and larger in my field of vision. I suck in a deep breath, lungs pressed to bursting against my chest. Right before the rows of teeth seem ready to close on my upper body, I *jump,* arms extended above me, pushing with every ounce of strength I possess, my own lips pressed tight.

The warm wetness of the dragon's throat engulfs me, closing around my body like a fleshy glove, pressing in from all directions. I feel teeth snap beneath my feet, but Hammer is too slow. With a snarl, I plunge my sword into his ridged gullet and pull myself deeper into the fetid tunnel.

Hot air swirls around me, the noxious fumes stinging my eyes, but I keep going, stabbing the blade in again and again, kicking my feet for purchase, holding my breath to avoid being poisoned. Acid burns along my exposed flesh, corrosive digestive juices breaking down my skin, but I wall the pain away. I can feel the dragon spasm and shake, Hammer frantically trying to dislodge me from his throat, but I go deeper, worming my way forward. Frozen breath hammers my lungs, carbon dioxide starting to build up to dangerous levels, and finally I feel an opening in front of my outstretched hand. Silently, I thank the hours spent learning the anatomy of creatures that live only in imagination.

Not much time left before you suffocate. Stomach's in front, which means the heart should be . . . there.

Two quick cuts, my blade's keen edge slicing an opening in the striated esophagus lining, and I reach through to feel the pulsating wetness of the dragon's heart, a thickly muscled mass almost as big as a child. Another slash opens it up, hot blood gushing out in torrential spurts. The sword's handle grows slick in my hands, Hammer's thrashing death rattles nearly jarring it loose, but the comforting grip doesn't fail. It never has.

I keep cutting and pushing my way forward, metal sliding through muscle, then fat, then finally skin, oxygen deprivation spots flashing against my eyelids, and suddenly I'm sliding wetly from a slit in the dragon's belly—a shockingly violent birth.

The brimstone air of the cavern fills my lungs. It's the sweetest thing I've ever tasted. Sobbing, laughing, shuddering, I stagger to my feet and howl victory at the overwhelming glyphic light, brandishing my sword like a talisman, dragon blood streaming down my arms and face, bathing my body in a gory shroud. I am scalded, burnt, not quite whole, yet wholly alive. Magma explodes around me, triumphant horns making the very air shake, and though I can't hear the roar behind the glyphs, I know it's there nonetheless.

Just another encounter.

3

[Molting a Polymer Skin]

"Fucking *hell*, Ash. I still can't believe you pulled that off. You're nuts, you know that? Absolutely certifiable."

Wind's voice comes drifting from the dragon's corpse, where she and Slend are carving off various useful bits, their bodies restored to life after I successfully took down Hammer. Kiro pokes glumly at the dragon's tail with his staff, his expression downcast, no doubt blaming himself for not being more useful, upset at the chastising Wind and Slend gave him for not maintaining comms protocol, angry at me for bringing him into an encounter he didn't feel prepared for.

I want to tell him to stop whining, but all I can do is lie on the floor, my arms and legs sprawled awkwardly out from my body. Anything more than staring at the mist overhead seems unthinkable at the moment. The glyphs vanished shortly after my triumph, absconding to other featured highlights and taking their light with them. I can feel the sheath of my sword digging into my back.

"Only option I had," I hear myself say, almost disassociated from my body by exhaustion. "No way a standard strat was going to work on a dev like Hammer. He's seen our kills before, knows how we fight. How I fight. Fuck, if he was a player, he'd be fighting us for the leaderboard. Had to try something new."

"Well, it was definitely new, that's for sure," Wind says. "Don't think anyone's ever killed a dragon from the inside before. I'm surprised they even have that coded in as an option."

"Lots of options," replies Slend. "Point of the game. Find unique, get rich. People love watching unique."

Wind giggles. "Heh, that was 'unique,' all right. We *destroyed* the simultaneous view record. Guess how many people were streaming us, Ash."

"How many?" I ask numbly. I want to care, but I'm too tired from the adrenaline crash. I can feel the cramps threatening to overtake my entire body.

"Over three hundred *million*. It viraled like you wouldn't believe—every regional 'Net picked it up. *The* Ashura, champion of SunJewel, leaderboard streak on the line, going one vee one against a dev dragon controlled by *Hammer*? You should've seen the socials. Nonstop wagering; odds definitely not in your favor. When he ate you, everyone flipped their shit, thought that was it. But when you cut your way out?" Wind whistles. "I thought the global 'Net was gonna crash. They're already breaking it down into frame by frame on all the major sites. You made history, Ash."

Wind's voice is gleeful, the shared triumph of success. Behind her, Slend briefly nods at me, the closest she ever gets to a smile, and I try to feel happy for them. One of the main draws of endgame, and the whole purpose of the ladder, is that if you're good enough to be featured, you get a cut of the ad revenue—more if you win. Devs have the same incentive, which leads to very real competition during endgame battles.

Three hundred million viewers is going to result in a significant amount for the four of us, enough to splurge for a few years, or, more likely, go into our savings to buffer against the inevitable shitty day in Ditchtown. Traditional sporting event attendance started dwindling once hapchambers became sophisticated enough, and now Infinite Game occupies the public area once held by the professional leagues. Turns out people love watching displays of incredible physical prowess all the more when there's no actual risk of traumatic long-term injury, no messy cleanup of battered heroes who've outlived their glory.

Unfortunately for me, a significant amount only adds up to another month of treatment for Mom.

"I'm just glad we clinched," I respond. "Means we can relax for the rest of the season. Look, I need to get hydrated, get some rest. You good with finishing up?"

"Yeah, of course, Ash," Wind replies. "We'll put your share of loot in the stash." Slend waves a hand, then goes back to pulling out dragon teeth. Kiro keeps poking at the limp tail, ignoring everyone.

"Kiro, head out with me?"

A mumbled response, vaguely acknowledging.

I sigh, and trigger my logout sequence. Ten seconds later, the cavern dissolves around me, and I'm standing in the comforting space of my home portal, a cheerily lit grotto, fairy-lights hanging from the stalactite ceiling. Knickknacks and collectibles I've discovered over the years, each trinket a memory, fill rectangular glass display cases, bright pillows and beanbags slouching against their bases. Painted trophies of various monsters line the rocky walls, vanquished foes in crystal frames. Stone-arched doors lead to more memorabilia—weapon racks, enchanted items, long lost tomes, piles of gold; the usual clutter any endgame player accumulates in Infinite Game.

A new trophy pops into place, hanging in midair, then another, gifts from the devs to commemorate our achievement.

One is a stylized picture of a woman facing a dragon, sword swept back along her side, its bulk towering over her. The art style resembles a fifteenth-century painting, muted pastels coloring the vast majority of the picture, an electric-blue sigil shining from the dragon's brow, emerald green shining forth from the girl. The sigils glow from within, clearly artificial, but somehow fitting the style. I hang it next to an abstract representation of something in vivid shades of purple and black, composed mainly of teeth.

The other trophy is a glyph with the exact viewrate number of our encounter etched beneath. It slots into place next to a row of similar icons opposite the paintings, a long line of shattered records, more trinkets for my hoard.

I slump into a deep cushioned chair, wincing at the pain in my legs, and reach over to an end table to grab the iron ball festooned with cruel-looking barbs and spikes that accesses my public persona. It's what I use to log into the Game and everywhere else on the regional 'Net. Ashura the Terrible—my avatar. It looks like a medieval morning star, or a metal sea urchin, and the jutting points dig into my skin savagely as I pick it up. Almost a million messages stare back, the number rising every second, surrounded by a pulsating red circle that demands attention.

I start opening them at random, briefly scanning the contents, passing the time while I wait for Kiro. Some are supportive—admirers letting me know how fun it was to watch the most recent encounter. Some are spam—various phishing tactics and get-rich-quick schemes endemic to any grouping of humanity. Most are insults from Mikelas's asshole guild, IonSeal, or boardshits encouraged by him, threatening to track down where I live, wishing the dragon had eaten my stupid whorebitch face and raped my corpse—and those are the polite ones. The socials have never been welcoming for those without a pale-skinned dick. I sigh, run my moderately illegal program that signifies

I've read them all, and place the now-smooth ball back on the table. More spikes immediately start growing from its surface, like blades of grass in a time-lapse documentary.

I ignore it and grab my battered toy cat that the 'Net filters can't see, a vanishing grin on its wide, stuffed face. A small prompt appears, and I rotate its ears twice, then pat its back. The cat disappears, leaving only the enigmatic smile behind, security measures disarmed.

My cat accesses a small private persona that bypasses all the usual 'Net filters, an even more illegal piece of code than the autoreader, and one obtained at a high price. If not for a friend, it would have been an impossible price. Private personas carry a twenty-year sentence in a gummie "reeducation center" for unregistered anonymity. With it, I can escape the world for a little while, run freely through any game or 'Net I want, gummies and adoring/hating public none the wiser. I don't use it often, but without a place to hide I'd have gone insane by now. My portal is set up to automatically forward to the cat any messages that matter—much easier to keep track of important information that way.

Another automated reply from Brand's avatar, letting me know she's unavailable. I frown, delete it. It's not like Brand to be out of touch this long without telling someone. A statement from my bank, new funds deposited—minus their commission, of course. I open it, look at the number. Quite a few zeros. Used to think that was a lot of money. Now it just means I have an additional month to find more. Refile it under "business," along with a couple sponsorship offers that join the stack I'll look at later. Never hurts to get something for free. A message from Hammer, wryly congratulating me on the win, hoping that I'll remember that strat the next time we meet. I grin, face momentarily flushing, then tap out a quick reply, thanking him, and send it off. A couple pings from the few people I've allowed into my inner sanctum, words of encouragement, which I respond to with words of thanks. Friends are hard to come by, even harder to keep.

Dammit, Kiro, where are you?

I wait another minute, but no one triggers the admittance protocol on my portal. Swearing, I log out to the real.

Darkness greets me, the blank nothing of deactivated immersion goggles. I push them up onto my forehead with a shaking hand, groaning at the cramping pain, exactly how I felt in the Game. Dim light illuminates a spherical room, nearly four meters in diameter, oddly gray-colored material surrounding me, like the pixels of a busted monitor. I'm sitting in the rough approximation of a chair formed from the same substance, its surface cool through the thin material of my full body hapsuit. A portal irises open in the curved wall.

"Almost broke the chamber this time, Ash," comes a laconic voice as a curly-haired woman steps into the room. Thin covers surround her feet, like nurse's scrubs, and mirrored silver glasses cover her eyes. "Servos could barely keep up when you went diving around that dragon. Energy bill's gonna be a bitch."

I groan, thinking of the money that could go toward Mom's treatments, now forced to pay for petro from all the power I just used.

"I'm good for it, Sare, don't worry." My voice is muffled by the layer of bodysuit covering my mouth and nose. My reflection in her glasses reveals only a thin strip of visible skin across my eyes, like I'm one of those old anime ninjas.

"Oh, I'm not worried; this one's on the house. That stream was pure gold." Sarah smiles, revealing crooked white teeth.

"My reservations just about quadrupled when everyone saw you climbing out of its stomach. We're booked solid for the next six months. Can't beat advertising like that." She leans down, extending a hand. "Here, you look like you could use some help."

"Thanks," I grunt, pulling myself to my feet. The chair melts down into the floor behind me, electric current shaping the malleable polymer. A thin sensation of static fills the air, the base state of any activated hapsphere, waiting for energy flows to mold it into whatever form the user desires. Gingerly, I walk over to the portal, legs quivering with each step. The slight incline is agony. Behind me, Sarah peels up a section of the floor with a thin multitool that hangs from her form-fitting jeans, creating a seam in the seamless plastic. Intricately folded machinery glitters underneath.

"Hey," I say, pausing at the oval frame, "is Kiro still here?"

"Yeah. Saw him go to the men's locker already." Sarah looks up at me, her fingers adjusting something—no doubt an actuator driven past its limits by the stresses I just put the room through. I'm struck once again by the way her jeans hug her body, but I push the thought aside.

"Make sure he doesn't leave without me, please."

"Mm-hmm. I'll hold the doors. See you tomorrow." She taps her fingers briefly, then goes back to the maintenance chores. "Unless you want it to be tonight."

"Thanks, Sare." I blush at her barely disguised flirting, as I always do. "See you tomorrow."

She smiles and flips a hand, shooing me away.

Outside the room, a brightly lit hallway stretches to either side, high-efficiency glow panels set into the ceiling. More portals, all closed, dot the walls at regular intervals. Sarah's business—renting out premier quality hapspheres with the fib-optic connection to utilize them—takes up the entire thirty-fifth floor of the megaspire we're currently in, but business hasn't been great lately; barely enough to keep her afloat. Another recession rippling through the economy has people less willing to spend on true one-to-one quality rooms, content instead with limited hap and latency from home bodysuits.

It seems like that's what we're all doing. Trying to keep our heads above water, I think bitterly. *Glad some of the viewers realized the quality of Sarah's rooms. They'll keep us swimming a little bit longer.*

I push open a door marked LOCKERS, and walk through the rows of metal cages to my unit, a battered collection of holostickers covering its front. Time to shed my skin.

First off is the immersion viewer, a gently rounded pair of lenses that look like old aquatic goggles with earpieces attached, and a small bulge for my nose. Re-creating scents is one of the hardest things for current haptech to handle, and it's priced accordingly, but I'm not going to take any chances when it comes to success in the Game. The whiff of a monster's odor has saved me from more than one ambush. An adjustable strap keeps the viewer snug against my face, and connects it to the control box at the back, a flexible piece of computing substrate that bends and twists with the motions of my head.

I lay the entire unit carefully in my locker—it's designed for the rigors of full haptic immersion, but only the ignorant rich or fools treat their equipment poorly. That's also why I keep my gear here—I can't afford for it to get stolen out of my room.

Next is the back zipper, starting at the base of my neck and running down my spine to the hollow just above my ass. Unlike traditional metal zippers, this one is actually a molecular lock, forced apart by the catalyst stick lying inside the locker. Exposed metal on a live hapsuit is a quick way to get electrocuted, as the military's first iterations proved so many years ago.

I peel the hood up and over, letting it dangle in front of my neck like someone just flayed my face, the subvocal mic sticking briefly to my sweaty neck. My hair sticks up in short spikes. I'd prefer it long, but long hair can interfere with the EEG sensors in the hood, and that can throw off the brain tracking for the suit's feedback, so short it stays, my bangs the only concession to fashion, a dark blue curtain just above my eyes. Not for the first time I wish I had Mom's thicker, kinky hair, but those genes went to someone else. I got stuck with my father's boring, straighter strands. I shrug my arms out, pull the suit down my body, then off my legs, until I'm standing naked in front of the locker, relishing the cool air-conditioning on my exposed flesh. The suit lies crumpled on the floor, its wetsuit black surface dull. Like I've molted a polymer skin.

Ultrafine specks, almost too small to see, dot the interior of the suit in ordered grids, contact points to transmit nerve signals when I'm in the hapsphere, reinforcing the immersion. The suit mimics almost any possible sensation while I'm inside the room, but quickly grows claustrophobic once away. I hang it up in the locker and trigger the automated cleanbot, then head to the shower.

A thin stream of hot water sluices down, resource rationing always in effect these days, but at least Sarah covers the first minute of charges. An involuntary groan escapes my lips, the momentary heat like a thin slice of gummie paradise. Aching muscles roll and pop like beaded water on a skillet. The dragon tattoo on my right side seems to dance as I move, nanoparticulate scales gleaming iridescently in the single shower light. Its tail wraps around my thigh, body leading up to a head perched on my shoulder, outstretched claws framing my breast.

I wish I could soak here for an hour, but I need to talk to Kiro. A loud grumble from my stomach reminds me that I need food as well, especially after burning so many calories battling Hammer. Reluctantly, I turn off the water and head back to the locker, toweling myself dry with one of the rough swatches of fabric, more like reclaimed carpet squares than towels, that are all Sarah can afford. Almost everything she makes goes to maintaining the hapspheres, as she's grouched more than once.

Back at the locker I quickly dress, throwing on a loose-fitting pair of black cargo pants over my underwear, the polymer fabric scratchy as always, then some gray socks. I lace up my tacboots— the ubiquitous footwear left over from the Water Wars that nearly every native of Ditchtown wears. A lightweight gray hoodie goes on top of my compression bra, a long-forgotten corp logo across its faded front.

Not that you really need the bra, I think sourly, catching my reflection in one of the mirrors. An oval face with high cheekbones, close-cropped brown hair with a streak of blue framing a nose just a little bit too long, brown eyes tilted slightly upward surrounded by browner skin. No one ethnic group claiming dominance, but everyone in evidence—"We're all mongrels these days," as Dad so laughingly put it back when he was still around, before Mom got sick. Thinking of him makes my jaw clench, and I force my teeth to stop grinding.

Under the hoodie's thin shapelessness, my arms are chiseled muscle, legs and butt the same, six-pack abs hard enough to use as a washboard. Not for the first time, I think about getting an augmentation for my chest. Restore some of the burned-off fat with silicone or polymer, remake myself to look like one of the 'Net models. Not for the first time, I reject the idea. Anything that might change how my body moves or reacts inside the hapsuit just isn't worth it. Besides, boobs are overrated, and none of those models would last a minute in endgame.

I know a lot of the guys who play Infinite Game flaunt their physical capabilities, muscles honed through countless hours in hapchambers and gyms bulging out of skintight clothes, but I've always felt like that would hang a target around my neck. Still too easy to be attacked simply for who I am; "put the uppity bitch in her place." Recessions have never been good for women, and this one's been going on for close to twenty years, so hoodie and workout pants it is. Camouflage through shapelessness. Getting called a dyke is just a fun bonus.

I throw on my AR shades, tinted lenses coming alive with information when they recognize my biometric signature, and a lightweight pair of hapgloves to access the glass. AR shades can be operated by eye movement alone, but hapgloves are much faster once you get accustomed to them. Their thin mesh, much more breathable than the suit, feels almost like a second skin.

I tap my fingers together in a quick rhythm to sync the gloves and glasses. The material covering my fingertips briefly stiffens, acknowledging the link, then drops back to neutral. Another series of finger twitches—electrical current turning the polymer in the gloves semisolid to provide the illusion of resistance, like typing on an invisible old-fashioned keyboard—sets my avatar to private mode, cutting off the deluge of friend requests, congratulations, and threats from the socials. Don't really feel like talking to anyone right now.

Last, but most importantly, I strap a long sheath to the outside of my left hip, dull black matching my pants. A worn hilt with leather wrappings sticks out of the polymer covering, and I run a hand over it lightly, feeling the alternating ridges of oil-softened material glide past my fingertips. I check the draw, make sure nothing sticks. The blade slides out smooth as silk.

Normally, it's not legal to carry larger weapons in Ditchtown, but I finagled an exception through the cultural heritage laws, one of the last remnants from before the Split. The fifty-centimeter, single-edged alloy blade is partly for protection—Ditchtown's not like one of the dryburbs, with their hardened encryption secdrones watching all the time, and I've got more than my share of enemies—but mainly because it's a part of who I am after so long in the Game. It's nothing special, just a sharp piece of metal, but I'd rather leave a body part behind than be without it.

Armoring complete, I head toward Sarah's lobby, where Kiro is no doubt waiting impatiently, working himself into an even bigger sulk, wondering why she won't let him leave. I steel myself for the confrontation.

Arguing with my brother always sucks.

4

[Five Steaming Woks on a Four-Burner Stove]

Kiro paces in the small lobby, heavily muscled arms bulging through a thin gray shirt, tight polymer shorts stopping just above his knees, outlining almost comically oversized thighs. He stands a solid half meter taller than me, the top of my head not even reaching his acne-scarred chin, and he has a lot more of Mom's coloring than I do. His petulant expression sours even further when he sees me step through the door, red-tinted hexagonal glasses riding up a pinched brow.

"Hey, bro."

"Sis."

He tries to grunt the word, but it's still the awkwardly high pitch of my younger brother's voice, desperately trying to conceal his youthfulness. I keep my smile hidden—revealing it would only make him angrier.

"Was waiting for you at my portal."

"Didn't want to talk. Can we go?"

"Only if we talk along the way. Let's get some noodles. I'm starving."

". . . Whatever."

Great. It's going to be one of *those* conversations. I tap a message to Sarah, let her know she can unlock the lobby. The door clicks, and I pull it open, motioning with my arm.

"Ladies first," I say, hoping he'll complete our ancient joke, lose some of his sulk.

His mouth twists, and I'm suddenly afraid that he's in too deep, too caught up in himself, slave to the awkward hormones that plague every teenager, insecurities driving entirely too many into the arms of the boardshits. I remember being seventeen, the tugging surges of giddiness and depression hitting on a daily basis. What if he doesn't care about childhood memories anymore?

Finally, the ghost of a grin works its way to his lips.

"Age before beauty," he replies, and my heart sings to see the familiar presence of my laughing younger brother, instead of the permanently angry young man whose metamorphosis he seems dedicated to.

We walk down the dingy hallway toward the lift bank in awkward silence, our footfalls slightly muted on the thinly carpeted floor. Hidden turrets filled with incapacitating gel track us from the ceiling, their jet-black domes disguised as cameras—Sarah knows that some of the people sending me threats over the socials would be more than happy to carry them out, and she's had to "discourage" fanatics before. Kiro has no idea the turrets exist, has never had to worry about some things I've had to worry about. Must be nice having a dick.

"So what did you think about the encounter?"

"Intense." His voice is low, distant.

"Endgame isn't for everyone." He flinches, and I wince. Shaming him wasn't my intention.

"Hey, hey, I wasn't knocking you." I try to keep my voice soothing. "It takes everybody time to adjust. It's nothing to worry about."

"Didn't take you any time at all. I've seen the replays."

Dammit. Of course he's seen the replays. Everyone's seen the replays of Ashura the Great, Ashura the Terrible, every second of my life in Infinite Game saved to solid-state memory for future consumption, constantly replayed late at night on high-light streams and broken down on after-action socials. I stab the old-fashioned analog control button for the lift with my finger—thirty-fourth floor utility room leading to the thirty-third floor skyways. Taking the front door after an encounter like we just experienced wouldn't be wise.

"Yeah, I picked it up quick, but I wasn't top tier right away. Even I had stuff to learn."

"You killed a Gorger, solo, your first hour into endgame, sis. I looked up the records—it takes most people three weeks to pre-pare for a Gorger fight, and that's with a full group." He stares at his feet, arms sullenly folded across his chest. "Hell, you just soloed a dragon. That's *never* been done before, and all I could do was get melted by lava. Why did you even bring me along?"

The lift continues dropping, small bumps and rattles follow-ing our descent. Maintenance is supposed to be annual, keep problems from building up. Last inspection date reads five years ago.

"I brought you because we needed a support, and you're the only person I knew I could trust ingame. Sure, I finished the dragon alone, but I couldn't have gotten there without everyone else. You've seen the bounties on me, yeah? The ones from some of the other ladder players?"

". . . Yeah."

"Then you know why I can't just grab any rando off the 'Net." I playfully punch his arm. "Besides, if you hadn't raised that barrier against the initial flame surge, we all would've wiped, *and* you called the encounter change. Give yourself some credit."

He rubs his arm, as if I actually hit him, and I try not to sigh at his petulance.

"I guess. I still don't get why so many people hate you, Ash. What did you do to them?"

This time I do sigh, frustrated. No matter how many times we have this conversation, we keep having it.

"I didn't *do* anything to them, bro. I just happen to be better than they are at something they think is important, and I'm a girl. There're a lot of boardshits out there living shitty lives, and blaming women's their only escape. Same as it ever was."

"I never see anything like that."

"Yeah, well, maybe you don't want to look," I snap, the familiar anger rising.

Kiro frowns and turns away, shoulders hunched. The lift judders to a halt, doors sliding open, the right one sticking halfway. I heave it the rest of the way to the side, and enter a narrow hallway, half the overhead lights dead. Kiro slowly steps out beside me, still not talking. I lead us over to an unobtrusive door with no nameplate, and tap in a forty-character code on the numpad lock.

A flight of stairs takes us down to a tiny room, not much more than a closet, and I check the viewscreen showing the main corridor outside. I take a moment to gauge the mood of the crowd—the skyways are usually safe during the day, but not always. A month ago, a group of Hajj were lynched up in Northspire, anger over petro prices and fanatics flaring up again. Of course, the Hajj that got lynched had nothing to do with any of it, but they were wearing the wrong clothes at the wrong time.

On the viewscreen, hundreds of people in cheaply printed clothes rub shoulders with each other, walking under a ceiling painted to look like a noonday sky, communication protocols and privacy filters floating over their heads. Most are wearing tinted glasses over darkened skin—AR, augmented reality lenses, synced to the local 'Net. Those few too poor to afford them carry large tablets, which they occasionally hold up to scan for shop information or directions—computer camera eyes translating an invisible world. Several Shinji tourists in natural fabric outfits pass by in a rare bubble of seclusion, anti-crowd fields nudging away anyone who gets too close with a crackling hiss of static. Privacy masks cover their heads, presenting an alien stare to the outside world; faces with no features; the annexed island returning to isolation after the Water Wars and declining population saw them bloodily absorbed by Han. A gummie Preacher scowls at them, the bright golden cross on his stained white robes glowing from incorporated light diodes, full three-sixty sensor halo ringing his temples recording everything it can, AR emitters blaring the good word while his hands are busy shoving a way through the crowds of people. His scowl deepens at the sight of a chattering group of Hajj, head coverings around their shoulders as legally required in public, but then an eddy in the flow of humanity pulls him around a corner.

I take a closer look at the crowd surrounding Sarah's back door, scanning for threats. Most are dressed in standard Ditch-town fare: multi-pocketed cargo pants or shorts, thin printed shirts designed to wick away sweat if their business carries them out into the relentless heat of the ocean surrounding us, ubiquitous tacboots shuffling across the linoleum floor. Some carry signs with my name, or pieces of memorabilia, desperately hoping for an autograph, chatting amongst themselves and trading replays of the encounter through their glasses. Others display the guild tags of other top-ladder Gamers, jokingly trash-talking each other in AR space and commiserating over their shared bad luck. A constant thrum of conversation suffuses the air, like waves lapping against building foundations, and above it all, the small bulges of gummie surveillance spheres swivel silently in their shells.

Good. No riots today.

I slip outside and plunge into the torrent, heading away from the fan club, elbowing aside those in my way and getting elbowed in return. Kiro follows, head down, his solid bulk unfazed by the flow of humanity. A couple people give him disgusted looks, and I glare at them. I know why they look at him that way, recognizing the muscular build of a Gamer, and I hate it.

Not everyone's a fan of the Game. A lot of people, especially here, view us as freaks, wasting our time in a make-believe world, unable to function in the shitty reality we're all forced to share. Wasting water and calories on unreality when every day's a struggle for survival under the gummie boot.

Reflexes itch, demanding I wipe those judgmental sneers off their faces, but this is the real, not the Game. I content myself with an extra vicious elbow into the side of one of them as we pass, aiming for his kidney. A gasp and stumble signifies my aim was true. It almost always is, and the cameras don't care about minor bodily harm, not in this pit. Hell, they only care about murder if it's someone important doing the dying. Finally, we reach Glassbridge, and the crowds thin out a bit.

I pause, entranced as always by the sights.

Glassbridge was one of the first skyways in Ditchtown, back when people realized the water wasn't going away, oceans inexorably rising no matter what last-ditch efforts they tried, and it was built for beauty in an increasingly ugly world. Crisscrossing steel beams hold an arched corridor of translucent panels—heavily reinforced polymer—extending from Highrise to the Brown like a fairytale construction. Below, murky blue ocean glitters in the afternoon sun, small whitecaps cresting with the wind and splashing against the submerged lower stories of every building. Gulls and terns swoop and soar around the bridge, driven away from the clear barrier by micropulse emitters. A winged shape dives into the water below, searching for food. Other megaspires, green vertical farms draping their sides, rise in the distance, more whitecaps dotting their bases. Skyways, ugly structures built for function and nothing else, stretch between them like steel spiderwebs. A dirty smudge on the horizon signals the retaining wall separating us from an Enclave, gummie-operated drones keeping their particular dryland fantasy safe and secure. Above, one of the omnipresent 'Net balloons hangs stationary against the puffy clouds, a rocket contrail slowly fading far behind it. Judging from the angle, probably a Han heavy lifter heading for one of their upper hemisphere orbitals.

I wonder what this place looked like before the waters came. Did the people who lived here ever think they'd have to fight the planet itself? Will any of us ever get a chance to stop fighting and just breathe?

The bird pops back up to the surface, gulping something down its throat in jerky motions. Suddenly, water boils beneath it, silvery flashes of scales and teeth, and it's gone. Tattered scraps of feathers float on the surface.

Needlefish. Great in a food printer, vicious in the wild.

"So what's for lunch?"

Kiro's sullen voice breaks into my reverie, and I turn away from the view, wiping a hand across my brow. The downside of Glassbridge is amplification of the everpresent heat, especially on clear days. The climate control must be busted again.

"Johnny's."

"Awwww, Johnny's is halfway into the Brown. Why do we have to walk all the way over there? Supernoodle's way closer."

"Because Supernoodle's a shitty corp chain run by robots. I

like getting my food from actual human beings, ones I can . . . talk to, if they try and hack my order. Besides, you haven't visited Johnny in a while."

Or Mom, you stupid lump. Not that you'll let me tell you that without flying into a rage.

Kiro sniffs. "When did you become so paranoid, sis?"

It's a struggle not to mention, yet again, the endless stream of abuse filling my public inbox from the socials, or the particularly inventive boardshit who caused a thermal detonation in the drink printer at my favorite caf shop minutes after I stepped away from it, or the gummie crisis squad that showed up at my last known address, killing the current resident's barking pup after they busted down the door but before they figured out they got spoofed. Kiro's my brother, and I love him dearly, but he can be impossibly dense sometimes. I'm just lucky they haven't tracked down my latest living space. Yet.

"Some of us have to deal with the world differently because of who we are, bro," I respond. "Anyway, I'm paying, so we're walking."

". . . Whatever."

We cross over Glassbridge from Highrise into the cooler air of the Brown, currently suffering one of its regular power failures. Emergency red lights illuminate shadowy passageways filled with residents going about their daily business, seemingly unconcerned by the muted crimson. Ubiquitous surveillance spheres rest quietly in their ceiling mounts, vacant eyes staring at nothing. Smaller, jury-rigged spheres twitch and jiggle madly beside their inactive cousins, torn between competing demands from whoever currently controls their open-access protocols, and I try not to smile. In the Brown, everyone watches the watchmen. Even the gummies.

With a quick hapcommand, my glasses switch to lowlight mode, and the narrow halls brighten to a shade approaching normal, the people moving through them shadowed in odd ways as the visual processors strain to keep up. A small 'Net icon appears in my vision, a grinning, pale white mask, but I ignore it—no need to log in yet. A small thud and a muted curse cause me to look over at Kiro, rubbing his head where he ran into an overhanging beam.

"Stupid Brownies. Can't even keep their lights working right." His voice is petulant, whiny. I stop, focusing on him.

"You ever considered that maybe the 'Brownies' know exactly what they're doing with their lights?"

He scowls at me, and I try to keep my temper tamped down. *He's a teenager, he'll grow out of it, don't drive him off, he's your brother, where are you going to get another support, stay calm, don't get into a fight . . .*

I make a conscious effort to relax the muscles in my face. Smile. Everyone's always telling me to smile.

"Take a second to think, Kiro. You see any working gummie cams in here? Any *tourists?* Doesn't it strike you as odd that we came from a fully functioning hapchamber into what looks like a Fundie compound, yet our 'Net connections still function perfectly and the climate control's actually *better?* And the cam problems persist no matter how often the gummies try and fix it?"

"I don't get it."

I repress the urge to shake him.

"We're going to have to work on those deductive reasoning skills. The only reason any of that makes sense is if this is grayhat territory. You *do* know who grayhats are, right?"

". . . Stupid 'Net club."

"Idiot. Grayhats are the last remnant of the old net, the one before it became the 'Net. Back before portals and ID linking, when you could be anyone you wanted. Anonymous."

"Sounds dirty. Why should I care if everyone knows who I am? I don't do anything wrong."

"Jesus, Kiro. Try using your brain outside the Game for once. Follow me." I turn away from Kiro and start walking, making my way through the twisting corridors by memory. "Sometimes it's important for people not to know who you are. To have a place where you can be someone else. Where you can make mistakes, learn who you are and what you believe, what you're willing to fight for."

I nod to a one-legged man propped in a battered chair, eyes shut in his weathered face like he's sleeping. An insignia peeks through the grime on his battered flight jacket, one of the southern drone squadrons from the Water Wars—the Dubs. He nods back, fingers twitching inside his hapgloves. I lead Kiro through another claustrophobic conduit, exposed wiring drooping overhead.

"Maybe you're saying something nice, maybe something mean, maybe it's the right thing to do, maybe not. What matters is that you can say it, and if it's wrong, learn from it, and if it's right, your door isn't kicked down in the middle of the night. As long as it holds, anonymity keeps you safe from those who want to hurt you."

Kiro brushes away a strand of wires, and I wince. Another couple centimeters and he would've channeled some serious voltage.

Then again, maybe that's what he needs.

"But that doesn't make sense. On the 'Net, no one can say bad things without you knowing who they are. Like the people who don't like you, Ash. With portals, and IDs, why don't you just block them?"

I resist the urge to slam my palm into my face.

"First off, I didn't do anything to them other than exist. I shouldn't have to block them; they shouldn't be saying that shit. *They* can get fucked. Second, even if I wanted to block them, the gummies don't give me that luxury."

"What do you mean?"

Dammit Kiro, are you really that blind? That unaware of the world we live in?

"Seriously? Do you even history? Have you bothered to look at any of the archives I sent you?"

". . . No. Been busy playing the Game."

"The Game's important, but the real's important too. You should know this stuff."

"Just tell me, then."

I frown. Kiro still doesn't understand how to learn, how to find information, how to sift the pure from the dross and draw a conclusion. This could be a problem. I try to figure out how to condense decades' worth of history into something that might break through his obsession with ignorance.

"Back before the silkies and the gummies broke the world, the net was equal for everyone. Well, mostly equal; Han already had a prototype regional 'Net. All you needed was a connection. Then the Dubs began, the Split happened, and everything got chopped into pieces. Once the radiation stabilized, we ended up with the regional 'Nets, and the global 'Net. Everyone in power spun it as giving citizens a choice to access content exclusively meant for them, keep them safe from hospital hacks, autocar ransoms, all the scriptkiddy shit, but in the end, it was just plain old censorship. Info from the global 'Net has to make it through regional 'Net filters before we can access it, which means the gummies control everything we see. It's like that everywhere now."

I duck through a rattling bead curtain into a well-lit small restaurant, more a hallway than a room, and wave to the large, balding man standing behind the counter in an old-fashioned chef's apron. He ignores me, madly shifting five steaming woks on a four-burner stove, his skin flushed from the heat of the electric coils and the constant motion, and I smile inside.

I've never seen Johnny not juggling a million things at once. I grab a stool at the empty counter and motion Kiro to sit beside me, turning off my lowlight program and pushing my glasses up onto my forehead.

"Anyway, filtering the information flow was the only thing the silkies and the gummies agreed on, though for different reasons. The silkies wanted their own anarcho-capitalist paradise, everything guided by self-interest and Saint Adam's invisible hand. The gummies wanted to make sure everyone acted the 'right' way—'moral authority.'"

"What happened? What's the difference?"

"Silkies got monopolies, dereg, and now they're ruled by the Big Three, the last corps standing. Their 'Net sucks, and their lives aren't much better. Shit in the skies, shit in the water, shit everywhere that's not an arco, and you gotta be at least mid-level corp to live in one of those. Gummies got the Theocrophant and the Enclaves, lot more green than the silkies, but only if you follow their rules. Pushed the rest of us out here to rot or drown until we convert. Our 'Net's quicker than the silkies', but not by much. Only reason is because the gummies want everyone to know how great everything is under their 'rules,' so they don't throttle access quite so much as the silkies do."

"Sounds like we have it better."

I interject.

"No, bro, *you* have it better, because you've got a dick. Gummies care more about that than they do about skin color, but not by much."

"What does that have to do with what you said earlier?"

"The gummies force those of us they think are women to listen to what they have to say, to 'save us,' and a lot of it isn't very pleasant. Blocking an 'educational message' as a woman is considered a crime. Lots of ways to call someone something awful and still have it meet the standards of an 'educational message,' especially quoting that book they love."

"Sounds like you're getting worked up over nothing. Lots of angry people on the 'Net. Why don't you just ignore it? Stay away from it?"

I swivel and look at Kiro, not even trying to keep the anger from my voice.

"This may come as a surprise to you, bro, but there are things that I have to deal with, because I'm a woman, that you simply *don't*. Things like people saying they want to kill me, and I don't know if they're serious or not."

I flick a couple of my most recent hate messages over to his glasses, ones that appeared in my socials on the walk over. There are plenty to choose from. Some are poorly spelled walls of text, racist slurs in prominent capital letters. Others show more effort, videos with my face replaced on a woman being beaten, a woman being hung, a woman being raped. The scariest are short, measured phrases, a list of things to be done to me, along with former addresses I lived at. Kiro waves them off.

"They don't mean that. It's just talk online. Everyone's free to talk."

"For fuck's sake, Kiro. It's not freedom of speech, it's the gummies forcing me to listen. Women can be *jailed* if we don't read through messages in an 'appropriately timely fashion,' which is insane, but there you have it. You get to block people who say things you don't like, because you're a guy. Lucky you. I have to drown in their hate, and it's horrible. It's not like I can leave the 'Net, now, is it? No one can. It's impossible to make a living without being online. Hell, it's impossible to *survive* without being online. Not unless you know some magic way to make free water appear out of thin air. And don't say rain, because the gummies charge credits for that too."

A door in the back slams open and a torrent of angry

Cantonese spills out, interrupting whatever Kiro was going to say. A young man with dreadlocks and light brown skin ambles through, screaming a parting insult behind him before the door closes. He walks over to the counter, surplus tacvest with its many pockets baggy on his slight frame, and I smile at him, my mood lightening fractionally. At the electric range, Johnny continues juggling his woks, stirring and tossing noodles like he has a pair of extra arms.

"Sup, Jase. Quite an entrance. Another satisfied costumer?"

"Hey, Ash. I tell you, these slantdick scriptkiddy cipherbrains don't listen for shit. I told them, quite clearly, in small words, with an illustrated diagram, *not* to interface the board I gave them with an unsecured line. Naturally, they completely ignored everything I said, and got pissed when it exploded. *Then* they had the nerve to come and demand a refund, like I didn't just save their asses from a spook drone squad knocking down their doors in the middle of the night."

"Fucking scriptkiddies."

"You said it. Nice job on that dragon, by the way. Won me close to a hundred."

He pulls a microfiber cloth from one of his pockets, thin black mesh hapgloves looking like gothwear, and wipes the metal surface of the counter down in economical sweeps. Once I can see my reflection in it, he flips the rag over his shoulder and grabs a couple bowls from below, setting them in front of us.

"Hey, Kiro, big man, why so down? Your biceps shrink from that lava? Or was it from watching your big sis save your ass on a featured stream?"

Kiro scuffs his feet against the counter wall and ducks his head, cheeks flushing. I tilt my head at him, still seething over our earlier conversation, angry he can't empathize with my situation.

"He's sulking because he's dumb. He thinks the lights don't work here because you don't know how to fix them."

Jase laughs and places a pair of chopsticks next to each bowl, scratchy recyclable napkin shielding splintered bits of recycled plywood from the spotless counter.

"Big man, we need to have us a talk one of these days. Get you educated on the real, away from the Game, teach you how to deal with the physical."

"That's what I was telling him, but he obviously doesn't want to listen to his big sister about anything. Not about women, not about grayhats, and especially not about history. No one wants to listen about history anymore."

". . . Doesn't matter." Kiro's voice is low, angry.

"Doesn't matter?" Jase feigns shock, and reaches back to grab one of the woks from the stove without looking, Johnny moving fluidly around him. Another wok instantly takes its place. "Big man, don't get me wrong, the 'Nets are important, but the real is the only thing that matters. Can't eat virtual food." He dumps half the noodles on my plate, half on Kiro's. Steam rises to the ceiling vent, garlic and broccoli and printed protein mixing together into olfactory bliss. I inhale deeply, then start shoveling noodles into my mouth.

"Mmmph. Thish ish great, Johnny."

A brief thumbs-up flashes within the ballet of woks. Kiro stares at his noodles, poking at them listlessly with his chopsticks.

"But we *are* free. We have the Game. We have hap. We can do whatever we want."

Jase's eyes widen.

"C'mon, big guy, that's seriously all you care about? Bread and circuses, just like the rest of the clowns? You don't see how messed up this all is? How far we've fallen, out here in the real, dancing for the tentmasters? Sure, your subs pay for your hap, if you're good enough, but meanwhile everything out here keeps falling apart, and no one's fixing it. Freedom ain't free when it comes with a whip and chains."

"I just wanna play, man. The Game has everything. It's better in there."

"Sheeeeeit. And here I thought you were supposed to grow smarter when you got older. Ash, you sure you two are related?"

"Yeah," I say around a mouthful of noodles. "No doubt about it. He's an idiot, but he's still my baby brother. Had to change his diapers myself."

"Well, if you say so." Jase doesn't look convinced.

"Still doesn't matter," Kiro mumbles. "Who cares about the Brown? Gummies are in charge anyway, that's what you said."

He starts eating his noodles, the chopsticks curiously delicate in his large hands. Jase throws his skinny arms up theatrically, narrowly missing a wok moving through the air.

"Big man, we're probably the last megaspire where it's possible to get something approaching privacy. We're the ones who make things happen, out here in this sunken shithole. You want an embargoed silkie hapsuit with all the latest sensegadgets? You talk to us. An anti-filter board that'll bypass the regional blocks and let you see the global 'Net? Still us. Surveillance programs to track down dissidents avoiding your morality filters?"

Jase frowns.

"Well, you don't talk to me, but there're others here who'll do it for you. That's why the gummies keep us around, why we're gray, yeah? Mix of black and white, good and bad, yin and yang and all that Han philosocrap. We keep the cameras offline here, and the gummies get plausible deniability for the shady shit they do. That's the only reason they leave us alone. They're smart enough to know we're smarter than they are, and that we'll never live in a dryburb without breaking it just to find the cracks. They don't like their people asking questions, but they can use our curiosity, harness it while pretending we don't exist. Especially if they want to hit the silkies without breaking the treaty, or keep themselves safe from Han memetic attacks, or any of the hundreds of other things their shitty Theocrophant can't do because they stifle anyone they catch exhibiting an original idea."

"Doesn't keep them from cracking down on 'hats they don't like," I say bitterly.

"Yeah, well, lots of people like punching down," Jase replies. "Lot easier than punching up."

"Cowards." I motion for more noodles, and Jase grabs another wok.

"I swear, you eat more food than anyone I've ever seen. Where do you put it all?"

"Goes to the Game," I say around another mouthful. "One-to-one fidelity ain't easy on the body. Especially not after an encounter like that. Dragons're bullshit."

The sound of beads rattling interrupts our conversation. Two Han women wearing mechaforce suits walk into the shop, privacy masks retracting into golden plates on the sides of their heads. Both have the straight black hair and tattooed cheeks currently in fashion among the security forces of the Dynasty, but their features aren't the biosculpted symmetry of natives, and one has dirty blond roots barely showing. Must be client-state embassy guards, probably from the NK or Russo protectorates. Small molyblade scabbards hang from their left hips, atop the articulated limbs of the mechas, and their pupils have a slight glassy sheen, likely from the combat cocktail of drugs within their tattoos.

"Great. Razorgirls," I mutter.

The left one glances around, then sniffs haughtily.

"Huh. Looks like ass. I thought you said this was supposed to be some world-class noodle place, Karina."

"The 'Net crawlers must have been hacked. Hey, you, shopboy!" The second one yells at Jase. "We're hungry. Is there an actual eatery around here?"

"You'll need to head back to one of the other spires," Jase responds politely, though his eyes are hard. "I doubt anything here will meet your tastes."

"You got that right . . . wait a minute. Ilya, check it out." She points at Kiro, ignoring me in my baggy clothes. "That one looks delectable."

The razorgirls stroll up to stand on either side of Kiro. One traces a painted fingernail down the outside of his arm, outlining the chiseled tricep.

"Delectable indeed. Why don't you join us, big boy, show us some sights, give us a *personal* tour. We're *much* more fun than this trashpile."

Kiro bows his head and blushes, shoulders hunching in like he's trying to hide. Awkwardly, he shoves some more noodles into his mouth.

". . . Can't."

"What was that?" the second razorgirl asks, running her hand over Kiro's other arm. "I couldn't quite hear you."

". . . Have to practice. Game."

"Oh for fuck's—" The first one backs away, voice scornful. "Forget it, Ilya. He's *otaku*."

"Ugh, you're right. What's the point of wasting all that beautiful flesh on a *Gamer*? Worthless."

The second razorgirl pushes herself away from Kiro, causing him to spill noodles onto his lap, and he cringes, face darkening under already dark skin, trying to wipe his shorts clean. They laugh, cruel mocking sounds.

I realize I'm on my feet, muscles tensing, arms low and to

my sides. The weight of the blade on my hip is solid, reassuring, needing the slightest of wrist movements to appear in my hand. The first one stares at me, letting her hand fall to her molyblade sheath.

"Look, Ilya, a mouse thinks it wants to play. We might have some fun this trip after all. It's been *ages* since my moly sang."

She pulls the hilt free slightly, unwinding the invisible edge coiled inside the sheath. Air molecules hiss and crackle against the barely exposed portion of the blade, creating a light blue glow, and the stink of ozone fills the air. Mentally I prepare myself—molyblades are deadly, but only if they hit you, and razorgirls rely too much on their drugs.

"I think you two better leave, right now," Jase interrupts, his high-pitched voice friendly on the surface. Cold iron lurks beneath, though, like an Arctic anti-shipping mine waiting for the barest touch to detonate. "I think a couple *tourists* might have wandered into the wrong place, and bad things sometimes happen in wrong places."

"Oh yeah? What are you going to do, shopboy? Throw noodles at us? Tell on us to your teacher?"

Jase grins.

"I wouldn't think of wasting them on you, and my school's tougher than it looks. You wouldn't want to meet *my* teacher. He's busy, and he *hates* being interrupted."

Behind him, Johnny continues shifting woks around, seemingly oblivious.

"See, I'm actually doing you a favor. Getting hit with a jolter"—Jase pulls a small black rod from under the counter and waves it in the air—"while you're in those fancy suits would be *really* painful, especially if the jolter happened to be modified with a safety override for mechas."

The razorgirls step back involuntarily, fear momentarily flashing across their faces. Jase continues.

"However, the pain of having your arms and legs swiftly broken while your mecha tears itself apart would be like rainbows shooting out of a unicorn's ass if I let *her*"—he nods at me—"do what she wants to do to you. I don't have nearly enough cleaner on hand to get your blood off the walls, and I don't much feel like shopping right now, so let's say we call this a draw, you two leave, and if you ever set foot in the Brown again, I'll dump your corpses in the blue after she's done." He pauses, looking thoughtful. "But only after I strip out the interesting parts from your mechas. Deal?"

The first razorgirl tenses, like she's going to finish drawing the molyblade, tattoo coiling into motion on her face, ready to inject its aggressive cocktail into her bloodstream. Jase levels the jolter at her, tendrils of electricity forming at its tip. The sound of rattling cookware echoes in the sudden hush, Johnny still cooking industriously, thin curves of hot metal dancing through the air. I feel myself dropping into a combat trance, pushing aside the pain of my aching muscles, time spinning down like an unwinding watch.

Just before it seems the room will explode into violence, the second razorgirl grabs the first one's wrist.

"Forget it, Karina. These filth aren't worth it. Especially not over an *otaku*. Those noodles know more about fucking than he does. Probably stiffer too."

Kiro flushes again, hands trembling in his lap.

The first one licks her lips hungrily, then slams the hilt back home into its sheath.

"You're right. Let's go somewhere civilized and get the stink of monkeys out of our hair. This pitiful little backwater bores me."

They back up to the bead curtain and the second one ducks through, privacy mask rising to cover her face. The first one stares at me for several seconds longer, our eyes locked onto each other.

"I'll remember you, little mouse." She grins, jewel-fronted teeth glinting. "You, your insolent shopboy, and that ball-less lump. Next time, I'll not leave without my fun. See you soon."

The privacy mask turns her face to nothing, and the bead curtains rattle once more. Jase lets out a breath.

"Whew. Thought for sure the needlefish were going to get a second lunch there." He turns the jolter off and returns it below the counter. "You okay, Ash?"

I don't answer right away, trying to calm myself down, quiet the adrenaline coursing through my veins. *It's not an encounter. You're in the real. It's not an encounter.* What I want to do is chase after the razorgirls and end the threat, two quick slices, but this isn't the Game. Cutting down two Han embassy guards in the middle of the street would bring a lot of attention to people who don't need it, and I can't do that to Jase and Johnny. I'll have to be patient, deal with the razorgirls when the time is right if they decide to mess with Kiro again.

". . . Yeah. Yeah, I'm fine."

Jase stares at me for a couple seconds, then turns around to help Johnny with the woks. Kiro shakes slightly, hunched over the counter like he wants to sink into it. A tear rolls down his cheek into the bowl. I put a hand on his shoulder.

"How're you doing, bro? That was pretty intense."

". . . Why do they hate me so much? What did you do to them to make them hate me?"

I can feel my hand tightening, stress and frustration and anger tautening already vibrating muscles.

"What did I . . . ? Kiro, those razorgirls wanted to hurt you because they could. That's what gets them off, part of the conditioning they go through. I was trying to protect you from them."

He stands abruptly, the stool falling with a clatter, and I step back, startled.

"Well, maybe I don't want your protection! Maybe I can handle myself! Maybe I'm tired of getting sucked into all this drama that surrounds you, tired of your victim complex, tired of you blaming me and everyone else for your problems! It's bad enough in the Game, but out here too? I'm the one that gets picked on, every time. I'm sick of it! Sick of *you*!"

Hormones, it's hormones, don't drive him away—

"Victim complex? Kiro, look, it's not your fault—"

"No, it's *your* fault! I'm going back home. Don't bother me anymore, not here, and especially not in the Game. I'll find my own guild. I'm done with you, Ash!"

He walks to the curtain, feet stomping on the polymer floor.

Don't lose your temper don't lose your temper don't lose—

"Fine! I thought you were someone I could trust, a support I could rely on, but you're just like Dad, bailing out when things get tough. Refusing to look at the truth because it isn't what you want it to be. Coward."

Kiro falters midstride, then lowers his head and bulls through the curtain, out into the darkness. One of the bead strands pops loose and falls to the floor, scattering brightly colored balls in a rattling shower. I groan, and slump onto one of the stools.

"Fucking great. Just . . . great. Got any more noodles, Jase?"

5

[His Phantasmal Touch]

"Soooo, that was awkward."

I ignore Jase, pushing more noodles into my mouth, following them with long pulls from a tall glass of water, watching my credits tick down with each swallow. The flat taste doesn't pair with Johnny's cooking at all, a by-product of the fact it's essentially boiled swampwater, but if I don't get some carbs into my system and rehydrate, it'll be full body cramps for sure. The normal savor of Johnny's cooking barely registers on my taste buds at the speed I'm chewing and swallowing.

"Ash?"

". . . We're fine. He's going through a phase. He'll get over it."

Jase's eyes narrow, and he stares at me.

"You sure about that, Ash? Because what I saw was a guy who wants nothing to do with his big sister, and that kind of stuff tends to linger. Sometimes it's permanent. Sometimes it gets uglier than that."

"Wise words from someone barely out of puberty. I said we're fine. Drop it. Anything else?"

"Yeah. Got a job for you. Tonight. Silkie shipment coming in on a container boat out of Industan. Gummies want us to interdict and seize something; no questions, no tracks. Intel they gave, and you can trust it as much as you want, puts three hostiles onboard, specifically tasked with ensuring delivery. Close combat specialists."

I pause for a moment, thinking.

"Why's a silkie container boat coming here? Tariffs are going to eat up all their profit."

Jase shrugs.

"Dunno. All I know is there's a job."

I keep pushing noodles into my mouth, forcing fuel into my body.

"Any guns?"

"Not according to intel."

"What's the payment?"

"Enough for water and another couple weeks of your mom's bills. Oh, and free noodles, of course. You in?"

". . . Yeah. Where?"

"Dinghy'll meet you on the waterlevel of Eastspire. Oh one hundred."

"I'll be there. Gimme some more food."

Jase hands me a third bowl and then disappears into the small storage room at the back of the kitchen. I finish up in silence, Johnny continuing his ballet of woks at the stove, dipping them toward the small mountain of cheap recycled paper cartons next to him, quickly sealing the containers once they're full. He looks at me with one eyebrow raised, then at the cartons, and I nod.

"No problem. I'll hit them on my way home. Send me the locs."

He pulls a faded olive duffel bag from beneath the counter, darker patch where the unit insignia once belonged, and neatly stacks the cartons inside, then slides it toward me. I scoop it over my shoulder, the nylon strap digging into my flesh, and head for the door, gulping down the last of my water. A list of locations in the Brown appears in my glasses, phosphorescent green numerals floating ghostlike in the corner of my vision. Most are less than a five-minute walk, simply requiring me to traverse the lift-and-stair network inside the megaspire to different levels before I head back to my own shabby room.

I enter the murky red light of the main corridor and make my way to a lift bank, blending into the crowd of silently moving figures, blue swatches dotting their clothes. It could almost be mistaken for a prison complex, or deepground mining outpost, if you didn't know to look for the subtle twists and taps of hapgloved hands. I twitch my fingers, hidden inside the pockets of my hoodie, and access the small 'Net icon that looks like a grinning bone mask in front of a spiderweb. A blinking prompt appears, and I enter my fifty-character alphanumeric password, making sure to time my inputs within the standard parameters set to my profile—another, less obvious layer of security, one much tougher for an intruder to spoof. Seconds later, conversations explode into existence around me, a strange mishmash of acronyms, animated pictures, memetic links, and contextual shorthand.

That the Brown has its own personal 'Net, the Web, is an open secret among those who want to know. Actually getting into the Web is much harder. Part of it is the standard grayhat fetish for crypto, but it also serves the gummies' interests to quarantine us away from those who live in the dryburbs, present us as a danger to keep the others in line. They tolerate the anarchic little corner we occupy as long as we keep our firewalls hot, but it's not true privacy. That went away a long time ago, despite the illusory freedom of the Brown.

Besides, it's not like they can't drone the megaspire whenever they feel like it, I think sourly. The shattered shell of the ninety-third floor is proof of that—some arrogant blackhat dumped a few too many secrets about a few too many influential people, and then one night the drones showed up. Only, instead of suppression loadouts, this time they were packing wargear. No one's bothered to rebuild it since.

I glance through what passes for a news network on the Web while I walk to the first address. It's the usual mishmash of conspiracy theories, technical updates, malware ads, and job requests, everything in shades of gray, but nothing looks out of the ordinary. Just another day trying to scrape out a living in a world with no place for dreams.

A gently blinking icon appears—private message—and I smile. I already recognize the sender's encryption key. There are only a few people who I talk to on the Web these days, and almost all are for business.

This is the only one for pleasure.

<<Wanna get together?>>

I tap out a response, hands still hidden in my hoodie's pockets, heart thumping at the innocuous words.

<<Yeah, gimme a few. Gotta run a couple errands first.>>

<<K. Be waiting.>>

<<K.>>

I skip up a flight of stairs, and with a start, I realize I'm grinning like a fool. The expression feels strange on my face, but I relish the sensation for a minute or two, then regretfully let it fade. Walking around in the Brown like that wouldn't be the best of ideas; it's not as bad as some of the other megaspires, but people who feel the future is leaving them behind tend to do dangerous things. I'd prefer not to be a statistic. Stairs pass under my feet, my muscles protesting slightly, but they're already recovering from this morning and it feels good to stretch them out.

After another fifteen flights, my glasses alert me that I'm on the right floor, and I duck through a bead curtain draped across the stairwell exit. It gives off a soft rattle, like dusty snake scales brushing on gravel. Another warning—warnings everywhere, people claiming the illusion of control.

A hallway stretches before me, metal doors on either side. One glows green, outlined in my vision. I check to make sure no one's waiting to score an easy mark, then knock on the door, two quick raps. It opens with a rattle of chains, and I slide the carton into the gap. A whiff of chilled air is my only response— the unmistakable signature of a server farm. As soon as the carton passes the door, it slams shut. Whoever's inside must be working on a particularly difficult coding problem. Makes me glad Johnny insists on payment before delivery, though—don't feel like shaking some techhead down to collect.

I head back to the stairs, my next stop another three floors up. As I slip back through the bead curtain, my glasses blink again—a message from an old working partner, a friend I still talk to occasionally. The last time we spoke, her name was Ryeen. It could be anything now. I tap it open.

<<Sup.>>

<<What do you want?>>

<<Couple clients asking for the best. Rich ones. Your other name still carries a lot of weight, figured I'd see if you were interested. We always worked well together.>>

<<No. You know I'm done.>>

<<It's easy money. Twenty minutes, tops. Unless you want to make some serious creds, and do it in the real. Those rich fucks pay out the nose for that. Send an orbital hopper and everything.>>

<<I told you, I'm out. For real.>>

<<Fine. Your loss. Well, mine too, but I'm just jealous. How's your moms?>>

<<Same as always. Busted, not enough money to fix her.>>

<<That's why I pinged. You sure?>>

<<Absolutely. Stay safe.>>

<<You too.>>

I close out the message and rub my face, trying to keep the memories from rushing back. It doesn't work. Ryeen means well, but I never liked ghosting with strangers. When things got bad, after Mom was in the hospital and Dad left, it was the only way to raise the money she needed, but I hated it. Hated the way it made me feel, meeting a john in hapspace, his phantasmal touch on my body, the feel of his flesh beneath my fingers, even knowing he wasn't really there. Hated having to surrender myself to someone I didn't know, a stranger's groping hands running along my skin, feeling him inside my suit. I was good at it, good enough to pay Mom's hospital bills, good enough to keep me and Kiro fed, but I never enjoyed it, not like Ryeen and the others. I could fake it well enough, lose myself in Ryeen and ignore everything else when it got too intense, but now that I have the Game, I'm never going back. Not unless I'm the one in control.

I trudge up the next two flights of stairs, my earlier energy fading. Several figures dash past me, heading down, a pack of courier boys racing to deliver datasticks, their refurbished tacboots clanging on the metal stairs. The Brown has its own 'Net, sure, but there are some things the grayhats don't want *anyone* snooping on, and the only way to keep them secure is physical transfers to airgapped servers. I wave at the last one, but he's too busy keeping his balance around the turns to acknowledge me. I continue upward.

Another rattling chain, another carton delivered. Busy, busy coders, toiling away in their cells, reliant on drones to keep them alive, hoping drones don't make them dead. My next delivery is on the same floor, on the other side of the megaspire. A waypoint appears in my vision, like a ghostly green will-o'-the-wisp. I chase it down dark corridors, relishing the chance to run free, unencumbered by the Game, my mood rising once more. Climate-controlled air streams past my face, dropping my hood across my shoulders, my bangs whipping from side to side. A smile slowly creeps back onto my lips. Courier boys got nothing on me.

I round a corner and slam into a broad-shouldered figure, knocking the dark black AR glasses off his face. The two of us spring apart, the duffel bag slamming against my back and then the wall behind me, metal clasps clinking dully against the bare steel. I stammer out an apology. "Sorry, sorry, my fault. You okay?"

"Watch where you're going, you stupid bitch. I'm looking for someone."

My eyes narrow at the hostile tone.

"Excuse me?"

I take a closer look, and silently swear. The chiseled features, the tight-fitting clothes, the twisting sneer. Of all the people to run into. I notice his expression harden, and my stomach drops. He recognizes me too, without the hood to shadow my face. I hate this fucking place.

"Well, well, well, and it looks like I found her. If it isn't Ashura, all alone in the Brown. What floor you on these days, girl?" He picks his glasses up, idly polishing them. "I've been up and down this damn tower for a week trying to find you. Me and the boys have been trying to pay you a visit. A shame you moved out of your old place. Greentower was so much nicer than this dump."

Fuck. I *loathe* Mikelas.

"Get the fuck out of my way, asshole. Keep your manshit in the Game."

He makes an ugly sound, halfway between a grunt and a snarl.

"I don't think so, Ash. You just assaulted me. I'm going to need some satisfaction, something to make me feel better."

I feel the anger uncoil. I spit on the linoleum floor, dropping my hands into a combat stance, the weight of my blade comforting against my hip.

"Fuck your satisfaction. You want to make this a thing, you'll bleed in the real. I already apologized, and I've got things to do."

He tucks the glasses into a pocket of his expensive formfitting pants, then spreads his arms, crouching into an offensive pose.

"You don't have anything to do except what I want, whore. I know what you used to do. What you used to be. You're probably still doing it, aren't you? Fucking your way up the ladder? That's how you clinched today, isn't it? Giving some dev a piece of that black ass?"

I force my expression neutral, not letting his words hit me visibly. They still hurt, a lot, but I'll be damned if I'll give him the pleasure.

"I don't know what you think you know, but if you don't get out of my way, you're gonna regret it. Last warning."

A hungry light enters his eyes, ugly and primal. He reaches toward his crotch, blatantly adjusting himself.

"I think it's time I got a taste of what you're selling. It's only fair, right? Let me show you how that cunt should be treated, you fucking slut." He laughs nastily. "And don't worry about the recordings. I'll make sure they don't pop up on *every* chatboard."

My lips peel back. That fucking scumbag would do it too, rape me and post the sensor logs from my glasses like some kind of obscene trophy. I'm sure he'd blur his face—the gummies enforce *some* laws out here—but everyone would know it was him. Wouldn't be the first time either, from some of the deeper boards I've scanned. There've been a couple other local female Gamers on the ladder who've stopped playing unexpectedly, moved somewhere far away.

Not this time, Mikelas. You're just another encounter.

I wait for him to make the first move, so confident in his aggression. Sure enough, he reaches for my arm, meaty hand darting for the wrist I offer slightly ahead of my body. I let him close on it, his palm pressing the thin material of the hapglove into my skin, then I shift my positioning ever so gently so his weight transfers to the front of his feet. Quickly, I cup my other hand behind his elbow and pivot. Hard.

His momentum, already moving forward, suddenly accelerates, and I drop my wrist to pull his head down, his fist still trapping me in an iron grip, only it's an illusion, because his entire body is now mine to control. I take a step, more like a leap, and slam him face-first into the metal wall. His nose breaks, the sound like a branch snapping, and he collapses to his hands and knees, stunned, releasing me from his grasp. Grinning savagely, I walk around behind him, and then kick him in the crotch as hard as I can. He squeals and crumples to the ground in the fetal position, hands desperately covering his groin. Not enough muscles in the world to protect that particular weak spot.

"Stay out of the Brown, Mikelas. Next time it's my steel. Fucking believe it. See you in the Game."

I kick him one more time in the ribs for good measure, savoring the crunch, then steadily continue walking to the waypoint still floating in my glasses. Behind me, Mikelas's snuffling moans fade into the distance. I doubt it'll stop him permanently, but there's always a chance. Once around the corner, though, I have to wait a few minutes for the tremors to subside. Part adrenaline, part fear, all unwanted. Fucking Mikelas. Fucking Ditchtown.

The last few deliveries go off without further incident, dented doors rattling open to accept my offerings, then slamming shut again, the wordless transactions giving me a chance to collect myself. After the last one, I make my way back to my room via a winding path, checking, as always, to make sure I wasn't followed. The last thing I need is to have to move again because someone released my address on the boards. Mikelas knows I live in Ditchtown, same as him, and it looks like he's narrowed down what megaspire I'm in, but he hasn't pinpointed my current bolthole.

Apparently not for lack of trying, though. Dick.

No one's lurking around, so I quickly unlock my door and step inside. After the three deadbolts thunk home, I let out a breath I didn't even know I was holding.

Safe, at least as safe as it gets in this shitty place.

The motion-activated ceiling light comes on, illuminating the tiny three-by-five-meter rectangle I call home. Most of the back wall is taken up by my mattress, a small metal footlocker huddling along one side. Several hooks dot the walls alongside the bed, various articles of clothing hanging from them—mainly hoodies and workout clothes. No reason to own anything fancy. It's not like I'm going ballroom dancing in the real anytime soon. The space between the bed and the door I keep empty for my katas—it's not enough room to practice all of them, but it's enough to practice most.

I sit down on the bed with a groan, leg muscles still sore, and start unlacing my boots. One foot slides free, then the other, and I fall back onto the mattress, wiggling slightly cramped toes inside thick socks. It feels good to finally get off my feet. I tap open my messages again, debating whether or not I feel up to it after the unpleasantness with Mikelas.

After some internal debate, I decide that I do. Something nice to balance out the bad, take my mind away from the dark places it's all too easy to fall into.

Sometimes you have to force yourself to be happy, until you finally believe your own lies.

<<Hey. I'm free now if you wanna hang.>>

<<Sure. Usual spot?>>

<<brt.>>

I feel the irrational grin steal across my face, but I don't care. No one can see it in here, not even the surveillance spheres. One of the perks of living in a glorified closet in the Brown instead of a bunkroom, and it's worth every extra cred.

I reach over to the footlocker and punch in my security code. It pops open with a hiss, and I pull out a neatly folded hapsuit. It's not the same as my Game suit back at Sarah's, but it's just as advanced, if in its own specialized way, and there's only one person now I'll wear it for. It only takes me a second to strip down naked and slide the suit on, a thin rectangular box resting on top of my mons amidst the baggy folds of fabric. I plug in the power cord to one of the wall outlets, then slide my glasses over the integrated haphood and sync everything up. Fabric tightens and smoothes, touching my body with the familiar hapsuit tingle. Last is a jammer cable from the footlocker to connect my glasses to the dataport next to the outlets.

The jammer cable, one of Jase's, provides an additional layer of security—it'll bounce my info through a couple million relays in case anyone decides to come sniffing around digitally, then hit them with a nasty shock once they're good and lost. My personal life is going to stay mine, away from the gummies and boardshits, no matter how much it costs. The glasses go fully opaque, connection established, and I log in to my portal. It's not the full three-dee of the immersion goggles, but it's close enough.

I pilot my viewpoint over to the stuffed cat with its vanishing grin, and go through the ritual that accesses my private persona. Seconds later, I'm standing in a shadowed lobby, delicate black dress draping my shoulders, train stretching behind like a midnight tail, a small cat in profile on a thin chain around my neck. Muted conversations drift from tables that stretch away in endless rows if you know how to look at them a certain way, each one barely illuminated by a flickering candle in its center. I try to listen in, but, like always, the words hover tantalizingly just out of reach—hashed and salted into incomprehensibility. A gothic figure in jester's motley with four arms materializes in front of me, face simultaneously the florid health of the incurably sick and a death's head skull. It bows.

"Joining us for . . . ?"

I rattle off a string of gibberish, fed to me by the necklace—my half of the entrance key. The gatekeeper bows again, arms spread wide.

"Welcome. Your table is ready."

Without warning, I'm seated at one of the tables, the chair across from me empty. For now. I light the candle with our agreed-upon cipher. Only someone who knows what to look for, and knows the appropriate complement, can interact with me now. And that's *if* they make it past the gatekeeper.

One of the few things that the gummies and silkies agree on is that crypto-rooms shouldn't exist, and they enforce that agreement. Lethally. Anonymity, in their minds, means loss of control, and that is the one thing they cannot abide.

Naturally, a thriving black market exists to supply crypto-rooms to those willing to accept the risks of using them. Some in the Brown are part of that market, and I hope I never learn their names, nor they mine. A secret known to more than one person is no secret at all.

A figure appears in the chair opposite me, wearing a formal tuxedo, and I feel my heart beat faster.

Some secrets are worth sharing, though.

"Hey."

"Hey yourself."

I reach across the table, and we intertwine fingers, the sensation reproduced faithfully in my suit. His hands, so unlike mine, free of any calluses or scars. Hands that tried to crush the life from me earlier, hands that reached for my wrist, my neck, my vitals, hands that tried to rend and rip and tear. I force down my memories of the past, of johns grasping instead of caressing, taking instead of giving. I'm going to be happy, dammit, happy with this man who loves me. My anchor.

He grins momentarily, shaking his head, setting shaggy dark hair swinging across his pale face, green eyes twinkling, and I find myself grinning in response, unsure of the joke but delighted to see him smiling.

"What's so funny?"

"Oh, just remembering the encounter earlier. It's been two years, and you're still surprising me."

"It was the only chance I had. You're too good. The rest of my team never saw it coming."

He shrugs. "I cheated. We normally don't wait to reveal ourselves. It's kind of an unspoken internal agreement, otherwise it'd be too easy to wipe a group, and that gets boring. People don't want to watch boring."

I feign outrage, trying to keep a stern look on my face and failing miserably.

"You monster!"

He laughs, running a thumb over mine. Goose bumps ripple across my skin.

"Well, technically a dragon, but yeah, I guess you got me. However, if I'm good, you're better. I don't know what else we can do to try and knock you off. Hell, you soloed what everyone else thought was impossible. QA about had a collective heart attack when we did the after-action report."

My voice turns serious.

"Well, if you think of something, you make damn sure you keep it to yourself. That's the last thing we . . . I need. I haven't even told the others we're together."

He nods soberly.

"I hate that we have to play it that way, but I think you're right. There's no way the boardshits wouldn't scream 'collusion,' try to stir up another witch hunt." We both look down, thinking of the past. Of noncommittal responses, corp-speak, and suicides. A relentless typhoon of hate swallowing up another imagined siren and spitting out her bones. He looks back up. "But enough shop talk—how was your day?" he says, faking the cheerfulness I need; his hand reaching up to trace my cheekbone with almost inhuman grace. I sigh.

"The usual. My brother hates me for saving him from some razorgirls, I won't get enough sleep tonight doing another grayhat job for Mom's bills, and Mikelas tried to assault me while I was running noodles for Johnny." I caress his cheek in return. "Just another perfect day in Ditchtown."

His hand drops back down to the table and pounds it once, a restrained motion.

"Wait, what? Mikelas attacked you? Out there?"

This anger is unlike him. I briefly recount what happened in the hallway. His face turns grim, and he hits the table again, as if it's someone's face.

"You need to report it. We can ban him from the Game if

it's an official complaint, or at the very least suspend him for next season. Everyone knows you don't take conflict outside— that's rule number one. Not to mention morality laws are one of the few things the gummies try to enforce. Even *I* know that."

"Yeah, they try in the dryburbs, but this is Ditchtown," I respond sourly. "Most likely scenario is some gummie bishop dismisses it for 'lack of evidence,' Mikelas comes back angrier than ever, and then he'll just try something worse. Besides, I handled it. I kicked him in the balls. Hard. His kids might end up sterile, assuming he ever cons one of those boardshits into sleeping with him."

He shakes his head.

"Yeah, like groinstomping a monster is going to stop him. He's not going to let it go. He's going to make it personal. His type always does. Let me file a report."

"I told you, I can handle it. I don't need help from the gummies, or your people. No one gives a shit about us out here, and you either learn to take care of yourself or you die. I'm not some damsel that needs saving."

His lips turn down.

"*I* give a shit. I'm serious, you should say something. You have the visual evidence to back it up. I can probably help, I've got some pull."

I feel my voice harden.

"And then I'm the one that gets everyone digging into her personal life, along with the inevitable 'What did you do to make this happen?' as if assholes unable to control their dicks are somehow *my* fault. Shit, I get that enough from Kiro already. I've told you what I had to do before, to survive. If someone digs deep enough, knows enough to ask the right questions to the right people, they'll find it. Then I become 'the slut who slept her way up the ladder.' Mikelas suspects *something*, but luckily his boardshits haven't found anything concrete. Yet." I exhale forcefully, trying to calm myself down. "Thanks, but no thanks."

"Well, it's your choice." His fingers tighten on mine. "I just want you to be safe, and I hate that there isn't anything I can do. I feel like I should be more; like I'm letting you down."

I smile, his words somehow softening the anger in me, like always.

"Just be you. That's all I've ever wanted. I know it isn't easy to watch someone else deal with shit while you're helpless, believe me." I pause, thinking of Mom, then banish it from my mind, forcing myself to recapture the earlier feelings of happiness. "But right now, I'm here, you're here, and I don't want to think about anything else. I just want to be with you, in this place, where we don't have to worry about the horribleness of the world for a while. Can we do that?"

"Of course," he responds gently, reaching back up to cup my face. "Whatever you need, Ashley, if it's in my power to grant, I'll make it happen. Just ask. I love you."

"I love you too, Hamlin." I blow out the candle, shifting us to an opulent room filled with a massive bed, sheets so soft you could drown in them, pillows ringing every circular edge. A muted glow suffusing the air provides just enough light to see by. I run a finger down his now bare chest, feeling muscles forged in the same crucible as mine, body like a Greek god. Old memories flare up, but I quash them mercilessly. This is for me. This is my choice.

I push him onto the bed and grin wickedly.

"Now, I believe you mentioned something about 'remember that strat the next time we meet'?"

6

[Eyes like Melted Wax]

The ocean spray is cool against my face, at least what little of it remains uncovered by the skintight silkie infiltrator suit covering my body. A crescent moon gleams on the shifting wave-tops, small sparkles reflecting like lightning bugs. The infsuit copies the dancing light, small sensors constantly sampling the surrounding visual information, turning me into another patch of choppy water indistinguishable from the rest.

Behind me, Ditchtown's megaspires rise up into the night sky, a forest of shining lighthouses, windfarm blades spinning shadowy webs across their surface. A drifting shape briefly eclipses the moon, another 'Net balloon, one of the thousands keeping everything connected. Beneath the waves, murky domes beckon like underwater wisps—subsurface farming spheres filled with almost extinct crops used to growing on now-submerged land, now shielded from tornados and cat-sixes by a thick blanket of water. In front lies a half-kilometer-long cargo ship, like a megaspire turned sideways and placed into the sea.

My target.

The view is strangely barren without my AR glasses, but other than the infsuit, I'm running totally dark. Gummies pay for plausible deniability, and that means no identifiers, espe-cially tech. I kept the suit from a previous job—told the gum-mies that it'd be less risky if they only transferred it to me the one time. Sawyer didn't like it, but I don't like him, so I guess we're even. At least I'm spared from the constant stream of hate for a bit. A minor blessing.

Did some solo work in the Game after my rendezvous with Hamlin—daily social quests, restocking supplies for raiding, some unscheduled light PvP when a group of boardshits tried to jump me in Arthuria. Something ironic about seeing five knights in full chivalric armor screaming "DIE WHORE-CUNT!" as they tried to ride me down. Unfortunately for their egos, they were nothing but mid-tier wannabes, so all they ac-complished was dropping a couple rungs after I cleaned them out and junked their gear. Almost felt bad for them, mistaking enthusiasm for skill.

Almost.

I motion to the shape behind the dinghy's steering wheel, a wizened grayhat whose name I don't know and doubt I'll ever learn. He nudges the small inflatable craft toward the massive bulk of the container ship.

Up close, the size of it is staggering, a wall of metal stretch-ing overhead, seemingly insurmountable. The grayhat keeps us from being crushed with consummate skill, a job he's clearly done before. Time to get to work.

I sling a bullpup rifle over my back, loaded with tranqdarts, and make sure the combat knife is secured to my forearm. It's different from my sword—lighter, smaller, covered in the same material as the infsuit—but a blade is a blade. The Game requires familiarity with a variety of weapons. I'm not sure where the grayhat got the rifle. Not my business.

A pair of geckgloves go over my already covered hands, hydrophobic aerosol applicators curling around the wrist sections like spongy bangles. Another piece of wargear drifting around Ditchtown. I make sure to keep them well away from my eyes. The left glove's base bulges over the old-fashioned mechanical watch wrapped around my wrist, covering its durable chunkiness beneath springy rubber, timer counting down the hour I have before the grayhat leaves.

I place one palm against the side of the ship, and trigger a small burst from the aerosols. Water flees from the glove, repelled by the hydrophobic particles. Immediately, my hand feels anchored to the ship, van der Waals forces bonding the microfine tendrils on the gloves to the now dry metal. I lift myself up, abdominal muscles crunching together, and slap my other hand onto the ship, repeating the process. I give the aerosol time to dissipate, then peel my lower hand away and pull myself up again.

Slap. Twist. Peel. Slap. Twist. Peel.

Halfway up, pain shoots through my right shoulder, muscles cramping and twitching, still not recovered from my first encounter with Hammer, but revived a bit by the second. It's been a long day. I ignore it and continue on.

Slap. Twist. Peel. Slap. Twist. Peel.

The climb seems endless.

Reaching the deck railing feels like a minor miracle, like I just soloed three top-tier combat zones simultaneously. I squat briefly and shake out my arms, trying to flush the lactic acid, then pull the geckgloves off and roll them into a leg pouch. I check the watch. Two hours until docking, one hour until dawn, forty minutes until my ride leaves. Tight, but doable.

I unsling the rifle from my back, snugging the polymer stock to my shoulder. It blends into the surroundings, outer casing shifting to match the infsuit's camouflage. All around me, shipping containers rise up like slum apartments, corrugated metal sides painted with corp marks and graffiti. The magnetic grapples of a crane sway slightly overhead, drifting with the motion of wind and waves. I set off toward the bow, moving slowly, deliberately, giving the infsuit time to adapt its coloring to the environment.

Gummie intel put the target container in the third cluster from the front of the ship, on mid deck level. Easy access to clear out before customs arrives, whatever happens to be inside. Intel didn't say much more than it would be a box, slightly larger than my head. Hopefully they weren't wrong.

Aisle coming up to my left, a gap between containers. Gently, I peek around the edge, staying low. Nothing visible. Hold for a ten count, barely breathing. Sweat trickles down my back, hot and prickly.

Brief movement from one of the containers, a shifting swirl of blue into red, then back to blue. Great. Gummie intel didn't mention infsuits on the other side. Typical.

Another swirl on top of the containers, patches of starlight rotating as if seen through a gravity lens. That makes two. Both impatient, undisciplined. Where's the third?

I force myself to wait, track the brief signs of their movement, visual spoor. Still just the two, one monitoring the deck level, one on top of the containers. Either the third is somewhere I can't see, or he's practicing much better opsec than his companions. Regardless, I'm running out of time.

Burn that bridge when you get to it.

I draw a bead with my rifle, and it burps softly, once, twice, followed by the scraping thuds of two bodies collapsing. No guns appear, so it looks like at least that part of the intel was accurate. Slowly, making sure my infsuit has time to adapt, I stalk over to the container door, a metal slab designed to hinge out when unlocked, its only security an antiquated padlock. I pause by the door, waiting for the third guard to come to his partners' aid.

Nothing.

I re-sling the rifle across my back and pull out a pair of lock-picks, thin metal lengths with oddly hooked ends. Two seconds later, the padlock clicks open in my hand. Gently, I lever the door open enough to look inside, hinges moaning softly.

Shadowed rows of boxes stacked neatly atop one another greet me, each one slightly bigger than my head, some sort of artwork on their side.

Ugh. Intel didn't say which box to grab. Fucking gummies. Guess they'll have to make do with one at random.

I pull a box out into the dim light of the ship and halt, momentarily frozen, now that I can see the art.

These . . . are haptic hoods, the new Golgbank models. Sarah was talking about upgrading to them. What do the gummies want with a silkie *product? They've proscribed silkie tech in the drybur—*

Pressure on my shoulder. I drop the box and twist, reflexes moving me without conscious input. A line of fire explodes from the side of my neck and down my back. Cool air mixes with the warm rush of blood from my skin, and I tumble away, combat knife leaping into my hand, tranqrifle clattering off across the deck, shoulder strap snipped in two. Color shifts and fractures in front of me, emerging from the container door. My own suit flickers, then freezes in hashed gray static, my body tuned to a dead channel, suit integrity too badly compromised.

Fucker. Was hiding in there the entire time. He almost got . . . no, she *almost got me.*

Blood drips from a thin, curved blade in the slender figure's right hand, spattering the steel deck. With a flourish, the inf-suited guard whips her weapon down, spraying a thin line of red across the deck, and tenses into a fighting stance, one hand slightly in front, knife hand clenched behind. Her blue eyes stare at me from the kaleidoscopic swirl of the suit, but they're the empty blue of a crashed server.

Wait . . . I've seen that movement before . . . No. That's impossible.

". . . Brand?"

She charges at me soundlessly, knife diving for my throat, swirling patterns shimmering like nouveau abstract art. I eel around the strike, trapping her arm between my chest and right forearm, my blade pointed down her arm, hers safely pointed away from me. Our feet dance through blow and counterblow, heels blocking shins, thighs blocking knees, insteps sweeping outsteps, hooking ankles catching air. All the while, she tries to yank her knife hand free, surging motions I barely contain.

"Brand! It's Ash, Brand! What are you doing out here?"

Her only answer is a series of palm strikes with her free hand, trying to break my nose, cheek, orbital socket. I redirect each one, my hand flowing around hers, guiding her vicious blows safely away, then twist her trapped arm up over my shoulder, putting us back to back, trying to get her to drop the blade. I feel bones grind, but her grip doesn't loosen.

"Brand, you need to drop the knife. I'll have to dislocate your elbow if you don't. You know what that'll do to your—"

Suddenly, she wrenches her body down, levering her arm out of my grasp. The pops of ligaments snapping in her elbow and shoulder fill the air, her blade tumbling out of nerveless fingers, but she twists and rolls, grabbing the falling knife out of the air with her remaining hand. I flip away from a slashing swing at my Achilles tendon and Brand springs to her feet, right arm dangling loosely at her side, weapon angled at me once more. Through it all—silence.

"Brand . . . ?"

Another lunging strike, keen edge once again coming for

my throat. I lean back slightly and let my own blade fall, then trap her wrist between my hands. I continue her forward momentum, keeping her off-balance, then spin and drive her into a container. Her head hits the metal with an audible clang, and she falls to the ground, convulsing. Sparks rise from her skull.

"Brand!"

I rush over, peeling off the infsuit top. Pieces of a haphood fall away, but then stop, like they're anchored to her scalp. Underneath, a gently rounded face spasms and shakes, the cracked hood components spitting electricity into the chill predawn air. Fine tendrils stretch down from the hood into her head, like fungal roots infiltrating a log. I grab the pieces of haphood and try to yank it free, grimacing at the resistance. The long strands come out reluctantly, pulling skin and hair with them. I scramble wildly to finish removing it, but then Brand screams, the first sound she's made the entire time. The cry fills the air, guttural, animalistic, and her back arches against the ground, heels drumming frantically. The stink of ozone fills the air, and then she goes limp.

I look down at her face, and it's all I can do not to vomit. Her eyes are burst open, ocular fluids running messily down the sides of her cheeks like melted wax. Blood flows from her ears and mouth, matting her tangled auburn hair, staining it a darker shade of red. I push myself away from the corpse, into a squat, breathing heavily.

Psych-sec, think of it as a psych-sec, it's not one of your closest friends, it's just a psych-sec, hold it together, Ash, finish the job, it's just a psych-sec.

I look over at the haphood box, cardboard corner dented from the fall. Numbly, I pick up my knife and slice open the packaging, revealing a dark gray half-helm nestled in protective padding. It looks identical to the broken unit attached to Brand.

Why do the gummies want this? What happened to Brand? What the fuck *was she doing on this boat?*

Without realizing it, my footsteps lead me to the tranqed body of the first guard I shot. I reach down and pull his infsuit hood off, somehow already knowing what I'll find. A dark gray haphood nestles above his freckled face. When I try to pull it off, clinging friction keeps it in place, like a leech stuck to flesh, and I let it fall back. I repeat the process with the second guard, then turn back to the fallen body of my friend. Stomach heaving, I lean down next to her and gather the cruelly broken parts that killed her into my hands.

I don't know who did this to you, or why, but I'll find out, Brand. I promise.

Back in the dinghy, the nameless grayhat silently accepts the unopened box and rifle from me, then hands over a first aid kit and turns the boat toward Ditchtown. I dab antibiotics on my wounds, the cold sea air numbing my exposed skin. The grisly debris at my side numbs my racing mind.

One of my only friends is dead, and I killed her.

7

[The Devil's Own Playground]

"Hey Ash, how're you—"

Jase's voice trails off as he registers my ragged appearance, hair still damp from ocean spray. The gash down my back is hidden by my hoodie, antibiotics and gauze covering the still-aching cut, but I'm sure my expression is ferocious beneath the AR glasses. I feel like shit warmed twice over. Outside, the first stirrings of early morning passersby in the corridors sing their lonely song outside Johnny's.

"Got some questions, Jase."

"Ash, you know I love your streams, and you're practically my sister, but answering questions has never really been—"

I stab my blade into the countertop, tip driven nearly three centimeters into the polymer surface, the metal quivering with a low thrum. It's bad for the weapon, but I'm past caring.

"Got some questions, Jase, and I'm gonna want some answers."

Jase swallows, the first time I've ever seen him nervous.

"Well, ahhh, discretion *is* one of the main services we proviurghhhkkk—"

The counter slides beneath my legs, a barrier that might as

well not exist. I can feel Jase's pulse in my forearm, his skinny neck trapped in the crook of my elbow.

"Ran into a friend on that boat, Jase. Bra—"

My throat momentarily tightens, probably just as tight as Jase's. Saying her name out loud . . . that makes it real. One of my best friends. Murdered. By me.

". . . Brand. She shouldn't have been there. Now she's dead. What did the gummies want with that shipment?"

"Hrghhh . . . I don't . . . know . . . Ash . . . swear . . . standard contract . . ."

Wisps of hair waving on bloody chunks of skull.

"Who gave it to you?"

"Don't . . . know . . . hnghhh . . . Sawyer . . . it was Sawyer . . . drone courier . . ."

Sightless eyes weeping ocular fluid from ruined sockets.

"Sawyer? The head spook himself? Okay. I've dealt with him before. We'll have a . . . talk."

Jase flinches, and I loosen my grip a bit. I don't want to take my anger at Sawyer out on him.

"Need you to examine some tech. We cool?"

He twitches frantically, head jerking up and down in my arms.

Unmoving hands, nails neatly polished in pink and gold.

"Cool."

I let him go and he falls forward, gasping for breath, arms shaking against the counter. Johnny keeps shuffling woks at the stove, up early for the late-night crowd. The smell of noodles hits my nose, setting off hunger pangs that almost double me over. I can feel the adrenaline shakes threatening to rise, and I force my voice steady by pure will alone.

"Johnny, gimme a bowl, yeah? A big one?"

A primordial mass of noodles emerges from the bustling chaos, steam rising from it like the aftermath of an eruption.

A pair of miniature megaspire chopsticks juts out from the tangle of garlic-covered strands.

"Thanks. After you, Jase."

Jase rubs his neck and scowls at Johnny, then walks over to a blue door marked "Storage." He pulls it open, revealing a cramped storeroom, barely four meters long by two meters wide, stuffed with boxes of ingredients and cookware on thin wire shelves. Shuffling past several piles of cleaning supplies, he pauses for an instant, like he's catching his breath.

"Wouldn't recommend it, son."

Johnny's voice seems almost amused, but deadly experience lurks in his baritone.

"Girl's quicker'n you. Besides, she's got a right. Op went sour, friend's dead. Time for answers."

Jase snorts, then takes a last step to the shelf in the back.

"Bah. I wasn't going to do anything. Go back to your cooking, old man."

Johnny chuckles and continues his endless culinary ballet. I wrench my blade from the counter and sheathe it, then follow Jase into the storeroom, slurping down noodles in huge bites. Passing the shelf he stopped at, I glance over, and start giggling, unable to control my emotions.

"Oh, Jase, really? Pepper spray? That's, like, one of the first psych-secs in endgame. Heck, they have nonlethals in Candyland."

I squirt a dab onto my noodles to spice them up, not that Johnny's noodles need it, but more for the appearance of things. Jase scowls, then swings the shelving unit out on noiseless hinges. A large room filled with tables, electronics in various states of disarray on them, lies beyond.

"This isn't the Game, Ash; you tried to choke me! What the hell happened on that boat?"

He slouches into a chair and fiddles with a microboard.

I walk into the room, closing the shelving door behind me, shoving more noodles into my mouth. I wish I could taste them through my anger.

"I wasn't going to kill you, you idiot. You know me better than that. You're like my second little brother."

"Tell that to my trachea," he sulks. I ignore it. I know exactly how much pressure is required to crush Jase's trachea, and I wasn't even close.

"Tell me straight. You swear it was a standard contract? Nothing alt?"

"On my life, Ash. Sawyer sent me a drone, said they needed a box from the silkies, left an intel stick. You know everything I do." He laughs bitterly. "Probably more."

Sounds like typical Sawyer. He loves his fucking spook games. Must be why the gummies put him in charge of their intel branch.

"Had to be sure. Sorry. You ever seen anything like this before?"

I pull the shattered haphood out from underneath my hoodie and hand it to him, outer shell held together by the web of circuitry beneath. He turns it around in his hands, a spark of interest flaring in his eyes.

"That's the new Golgbank haphood. Well, what's left of one. They've been advertising it everywhere. Supposed to have the best fidelity on the market, true one-to-one for every sense, something to do with accessing nerve clusters in a new way. Ship date isn't for another week or two; most places are already preordered out of stock."

"Yeah, well, looks like they've been shipping some out early. It doesn't make any sense, Jase, Brand being on that boat. She's been missing from the Game for over two weeks, and she doesn't run gray ops. I would've known. She tried to kill me. Never said a word. She was wearing one of those."

Jase frowns.

"She didn't recognize you? Like, at all?"

I put my empty bowl down on one of the tables and shiver, hugging myself.

"It was inside her *mind*, Jase. Little tendrils, burrowing into her head. It was like she never even saw me, the entire time she was trying to cut my throat. I kept calling her name but . . . nothing. *Nothing*."

"That's pretty fucking weird. Their ads don't mention anything about mind control. I think I'd remember *that* disclaimer."

"Focus, Jase. I met Brand a couple times before, in the real. She *knew* me."

I pause, thinking back to lunch on a sunny day, wandering a gummy mall, laughing with her at what was considered "style." What it felt like to be normal, even if it was just for a couple hours, even if it was only as normal as a brown kid in a dryburb could ever feel.

"She was nice, lived up the coast a bit. Inland, with the burbies. Her parents had no idea she was a top-tier Gamer, they just thought she was really into tech and staying fit, studying for their Missionary. They wanted her to become a Preacher's assistant, wear one of those stupid lightrobes and sensor halos." My voice cracks, but I ignore it. "I was one of the only people who knew who she really was. There's no way she would've attacked me without talking, and there's absolutely no way she'd be working for silkies on an op."

I shiver again.

"I tried to disable her, Jase. Threw her against a wall, to knock her out. It broke whatever was controlling her. Broke her too. I watched her die in front of me."

"Damn, Ash, I'm sorry. Believe me, I had no idea."

"I know . . . and I'm sorry about earlier. It's just . . . fuck . . . Her eyes . . ."

I turn away, not wanting to Jase to see me cry, see my weakness. The room falls silent. Eventually, I compose myself and turn back around.

"I want to know what's in that hood, Jase, and you're the only person I trust who might be good enough to tell me."

The ghost of a grin flashes across his face, reddening his cheeks, and I'm reminded again of just how young he really is.

"Well, you busted this thing up pretty good, but the central memory clusters look fairly intact. Let's see what Golgbank has tucked away in here." He flips on a pair of custom AR work glasses festooned with strange circuit boards, almost like a digital tribal mask. His dreads stick out every which way behind the hacked-together asynchrony of his glass, and he grabs a multitool, flipping out a screwdriver. "You might want to go snag some more food. This could take a bit of time, depending on how good their IP protection is."

"Thanks, Jase."

He nods and starts dismantling the outer shell of the haphood, multitool moving dexterously from point to point on the crazed surface. I get up and wander back out into the main room. Johnny motions me over to the counter next to him, and points at a stack of small cartons. Their cheap cardboard sides are emblazoned with garish red lettering. I pick one up, and he immediately dumps it full of noodles, flipping the empty wok into the sink. It lands with a small crash.

"For your mom."

He nods at another one, and we repeat the process.

"For you. You doing okay?"

I want to tell him no, let out the grief and rage, but this is Ditchtown, so I nod back.

"I'll manage."

Johnny's eyes go distant, lost in memory.

"You remind me of her. Before." He snaps back to focus, a switch flipping. "Go see her. Kid'll be busy for a while."

"How much do I owe you?"

"Same as always. Tell her hello. Miss her."

"Will do. 'Preciate it, Johnny."

I duck through the bead doorway, noodles in hand, and make my way through lightly populated corridors out of the Brown, heading for Highrise. My senses are on high alert, but no one tries to jump me during the fifteen-minute walk. Lucky for them. I'm not in a tolerant mood today. A message flashes in my vision, Wind and Slend wondering why I'm not logging in for dailies. I tap back a quick response, let them know something's come up in the real. Go on without me. Try to contact Kiro, but the message bounces back. Temporary block. Little shit.

The duty nurse, Raquel, waves at me when I walk in to the clinic, and I nod briefly at her through the clear plastic barrier covering the top of the desk.

"Hey, Ash. You're in early today."

"Had a late night. How's she doing?"

"Seems to be stable so far. Woke up nice and happy. Noodles in the scanner, knife in the box."

"'K."

I place the still-warm containers on a conveyor belt that disappears beneath a rectangular metal hood, then unstrap my leg sheath and lay it in a scuffed box with a hinged lid. Raquel locks the lid and hands me the key.

"Make sure you give it to the attendant to hold before you go in."

"Yeah, yeah, I know the drill."

I approach the clinic's security station, two orderlies in dark blue jumpsuits, shocksticks dangling from their hips, flanking a circular body scanner like a low budget dryburb checkpoint. The one on the right waves me inside. The body scanner hums briefly around my body, and then I'm through to the other side of the barrier.

"Clean. Don't forget your noodles."

"Thanks."

The noodles emerge from their x-ray interrogation box, slightly more cancerous than before. I grab the cartons and walk down the hallway to my left. Walls painted with pastel colors and nature scenes on viewscreens stretch out in front of me, a soothing corridor of calm. Small bulges in the ceiling every few feet destroy the illusion, but only if one knows their contents. I stop at a door with cartoonish rabbits frolicking on its surface and knock. It slides open with a slight hiss.

A young man with close-cropped orange hair and a freckled face greets me, an infectious smile lighting up his face. A small tag on his white coat reads DOCTOR FREDERICK O'SHEA. He sits at a small desk in front of a large window, an antiquated viewscreen filled with charts and graphs blinking over the desk. In the chamber beyond, a woman in a loose-fitting green gown is gradually moving through martial stances, corded muscles lining her slender frame. A small bed is the only other object in that portion of the room.

"Hey, Ash. What's new?"

"Not much, Freddie. Just checking on the old lady before I get back to work. Raquel said she's doing well."

"She is. Remarkably calm today. Took her meds all by herself."

"Any chance I can go in and see her?"

Freddie purses his lips, then nods.

"I don't see why not. She seems to be responding well to the latest treatments, and I know she misses you. Your waiver up-to-date?"

"Yeah. Oh, here's the locker key."

"Thanks. I'll buzz you through. She'll have to use her fingers for the noodles, though, sorry. Regulations."

"I understand. Thanks, Freddie."

Freddie nods again and taps a button on the old-fashioned keyboard on the desk in front of him. A clear revolving hatch next to the window spins open, large enough for five people, and I step inside. Another button press, and it cycles me into the room, like an airlock. I step out and lean against one of the padded gray walls, waiting for Mom to finish her katas, her mirrored reflection slightly warped in the one-way observation window.

Her movements have the slow inevitability of a glacier advancing down a mountainside, incredible amounts of tension and pressure hidden beneath a placid surface. Each circling block, each gently lifted foot placed in precisely the right spot almost without thought. One of the few things left to her. Weathered creases on her face look like wear lines in ancient oiled leather, scars etched into her dark skin, hazel eyes staring at nothing.

About five minutes later, after another series of motions, she exhales deeply and drops out of her stance. She looks at me and grins, features suddenly ten years younger.

"Thank you for waiting, Ashley. Those noodles smell delicious. Johnny's?"

"Yeah, Mom. He says hi. How're you doing?"

"Good, good." Her face turns uncertain. "At least that's what they tell me. Some days, I'm . . . not sure. My memory's been a bit fuzzy. Where's Kiroda, my baby boy? I haven't seen him in so long. He never visits anymore."

A stab in my heart. Kiro hasn't visited in over two years, not since I had to leave Greentower. I hate the Game sometimes.

"Sorry, Mom, he's busy today, couldn't make it. Hopefully next time."

I walk over and hand her a carton of noodles, then sit cross-legged on the floor. She perches on the edge of her bed and opens the thin cardboard container, inhaling the steam with a delighted expression. Suddenly, her eyes go distant, face drooping, like someone flicked a switch and turned part of her off. I swear under my breath.

"Ahh, that brings me back. Johnny was the best squadmate I ever had during the Dubs. Hell of a shot with a rifle, and the best damn cook in the entire force. Man could make prime rib out of synthetic boot leather."

"Mom, we don't have to talk about the Water Wars. Let's just eat Johnny's noodles and talk about something else, okay? Have I told you about my latest Game encounter? I did really well, you'd be proud. Soloed a—"

She interrupts me.

"Game? The Water Wars weren't a game, Ashley. The things we did . . ."

"Mom, just let it—"

She looks at me, not seeing me, her eyes blazing, and the words die in my mouth. Dammit. No stopping the storm now. Only question left is if it can be weathered or not. My stomach growls, and I grab a handful of noodles from my carton, their heat not quite burning my fingers, and put them in my mouth. Might as well eat them before things go to shit. She continues talking, voice soft, her gaze on the cardboard carton in her hands.

"There was one night, right after the Split. We'd been fighting for a little over a year. Us, the Han, Euroleague, UPC, everyone fighting everyone else for water, foreign and domestic. We were bunkered in a town in Kanshoma, using it as a base to run our hapdrones."

She puts a fistful of noodles in her mouth and chews mechanically, eyes lost.

"Johnny'd just finished making a curry, god knows where he got the ingredients. Smelled delicious. Most of us were lining up to grab a bowl. That's when the silkies hit us. Bastards snuck a squadron past our sensors—antipersonnel models. Fléchette launchers, firebombs, monofil, all the stuff that only works on soft targets. Human targets. Old rules said that kind of ordnance was banned, but no one cared about any sort of rules at that point. Take out the meat to get to the metal."

She scoops in another clump.

"Over half the squad died before we made it to the armory. They went hard. Flesh doesn't hold up well against steel and circuits. Bought the rest of us time to make it, though, and then we grabbed some guns. Went hunting. Didn't have any other choice. Lost a third of those left taking out the drones, and most of the town was leveled. Firebombs spread quick when folks are fighting over water."

A bead of moisture rolls from the corner of her eye, following the path of a wrinkle. It drips into the noodles, unseen. She takes another handful.

"Was the damndest thing. Whole town smelled like barbecue. Stomach kept telling my brain that it was hungry. Didn't get a chance to grab any curry before the drones hit. So many dead, and all I could think of was getting something to eat. 'Never skip a chance to eat,' they always told us. I found Johnny lying on a street, half his side missing. Barely stabilized him in time."

She finishes the carton and stares into its empty shell.

"Found the silkie hapsquad responsible, later on, operating out of New Rado as part of a larger force. They were sloppy on comms discipline. Cocky. I waited until they settled in for the night, then locked in their coordinates and sent my own set of drones. Stole a combat group from the armory when no one was looking."

The carton drops, unnoticed, cardboard corner denting inward.

"Took my time, did it right. Suicided the last one into their regiment HQ. Battery overload. Command threw a royal shit-fit about losing materiel on an unauthorized mission, but I ended up wiping out an entire twenty-man shock unit, along with forty-seven supporting personnel and three of their top commanders, so they couldn't discharge me. I was the best they had left."

She laughs, but it's devoid of anything resembling joy.

"They had to give me a medal, if you can believe that. Then I got transferred to one of the guerrilla squads."

Her eyes narrow, and I scramble to my feet.

"Mom. Mom! It's over, Mom, you're not there anymore. Mom!"

"We were tasked with psyops, 'breaking morale' they called it. Sixteen hours a day in a hapsuit in an armored truck, moving from town to town, sending out the drones again and again and again. I spent so much time in them, started losing track of what was real. A game? It seemed like a game at times. Like the devil's own playground. Erase another set of targets, rack up another high score, pop back up if I ever went down. After all, it's not like I was really there. Just a drone, doing what drones do. Going for the highest score of them all."

She looks up at me, but her eyes are clouded, trapped in memory. The green gown sways gently as she stands from the bed.

"Then they gave us the special mission. The one to end it all. I didn't know. I didn't know! None of us knew!"

"Mom, snap out of it, please."

"Who are you?"

"I'm Ash, Mom, your daughter. Ashley."

Her face tightens.

"How do I know this isn't an interrogation trick? How do I know I'm not in a hapsuit right now? You could be anyone! Tell me where my family is! Where's my husband? My children? I'm not telling you anything more!"

"Mom. Please . . ."

Freddie's voice sounds from a small speaker in the corner of the room.

"Ash, you need to clear the room. Her vitals are spiking."

"Mom!"

Bare feet shift into a combat stance, and she screams at me.

"Get away! You're not my daughter! Where's my son?!"

"Please . . ."

"Clear the room, Ash!"

A blurring fist launches at my face and I parry it to the side, stepping over the followup leg sweep, my wrist aching from the power of her strike, shoulder muscles screaming from my earlier wound. Momentum brings her back upright and she tries to grab my arm, but I use her energy to spin her into the bed, momentarily tangling her in the sheets.

A move she taught me.

Quickly, I step back into the airlock. The clear polymer rotates in front of me, and then she's there, beating on the transparent material, fists gradually bloodying, her face snarling in madness. Red smears on the plastic start to obscure her features, and I step through the airlock as it cycles to the observation room, my eyes on her the entire time.

I can't stop the tears from falling.

"Close call there, Ash. I'm sorry."

I turn and face Freddie.

"I . . . she's never had that reaction to the noodles before . . ."

Freddie frowns, and taps several more keys.

"Unfortunately, that's one of the dangers of the therapy.

We're trying to rewire her memories, primarily through haptic reinforcement in a fully immersive chamber, much like your Game, but as you know, it's still very experimental. Sometimes we make strides in one area only to see a setback in another. Smell is linked very tightly to memory, and it appears this set off a bad one." He cocks an eyebrow. "Do you know what she was talking about at the end there? I don't have anything about a 'special mission' on file."

I think about lessons learned in school on brilliant pinpricks of light, stars born where no star should ever exist, a country tearing itself apart. Lessons learned once school was a luxury, half-screamed memories pouring incoherently out of a broken woman in a battered room, a child witnessing a parent reduced to less than nothing.

"She was talking about war, Freddie. War never changes, but it sure as hell changes us."

Freddie looks at me, uncomprehending, but I've said all I'm going to say. Three large orderlies enter the room, dressed in close-fitting body armor over darker blue jumpsuits. One carries a syringe filled with clear liquid. Freddie turns to them.

"Careful, gentlemen," he warns. "The patient is in a volatile state. Try to avoid getting injured."

They nod, expressions tight-lipped and serious, and all three file into the airlock. In the room beyond, Mom is tearing at the bedsheets, ripping them into long strips. The airlock cycles into the room, and the orderlies spread out, two with their hands out in nonthreatening poses. The third carries the syringe behind his back. They tower over her.

Sudden motion from the bed, a cloth strip looping around an orderly's wrist and dragging him facedown into the floor. Another loop wraps around his neck, and he starts clawing at the sheet constricting his airway. The second orderly charges into a kick to the chest, dropping him momentarily to his hands and knees, gasping for breath. The third orderly approaches cautiously, shuffling his feet forward, hand still behind his back. A cloth loop extends out at him, but he sidesteps it, then lunges in, syringe outstretched. It clatters to the floor, his arm trapped against my mom's chest, and Freddie swears, finger poised over another button. Mom twists, forcing the orderly onto his tiptoes, and then the second orderly whips his hand up from the floor and plunges the syringe into her thigh. He collapses to the floor, wheezing for breath. Mom topples onto the bed, dragging the burly orderly with her, but then her grip loosens and her body falls limp. Freddie wipes a hand across his brow, fingers trembling.

"She's . . . going to be okay?" I glance at him. In the room, the orderlies struggle to their feet, wincing.

"Physically, yeah. It's just a fast-acting sedative. We'll keep her under for a bit, then try and figure out what triggered her." He sighs. "Mentally, I don't know. They did some fucked-up shit to your mom, Ash. We're doing our best, but I won't lie. It'll be a long time before she's back to anything approaching normal, assuming it can even be done. You don't put someone through what she went through and expect them to come out the other side unscathed."

You have no idea, Freddie, and hopefully you never learn.

His face darkens, an uncharacteristic scowl settling into place.

"By all rights, she should be at a veteran's hospital. Gummies made this mess, they should be the ones to clean it up. Not some barely graduated hack like me."

"She lost her benefits when she chose not to live in a dry-burb, Freddie. No healthcare out here. This clinic is all I could find, and you were top of your class before they tried to run you out. I trust you."

"Thanks, Ash, but it still pisses me off. To send someone

into that hell and then abandon them afterward. It's not right."

I push my AR glasses up and rub my face, gray hoodie sleeve coming away wet and slightly darker.

"Okay, Freddie, just . . . keep doing what you can. I'll make sure the bills get paid."

"I hate to ask that of you, Ash, but the medications and equipment we're using aren't cheap, especially out here. I think they'll work, eventually, but rebuilding someone's psyche isn't easy." He runs a hand through his hair. "Especially when I have to make up most of this as I go."

"It's okay. I know we'll get there. See you next time."

He nods, face intent on his faded viewscreen, and I make my way back to the reception area to collect my things.

What a shitty day.

8

[Feels and Reals]

Outside the clinic, an incoming message flashes in my glasses. Jase. I tap my acceptance, and a small static picture of his face appears in the corner of my vision.

"Watcha got, Jase?"

"Nothing I want to talk about over the 'Net. You heading back?"

"Yeah, be there in fifteenish."

His face disappears, and I frown. Jase's voice sounded . . . frightened, something I've never heard from him before. Calm, angry, irritated, tense, yes, but never frightened. Great.

My glasses blink again. It's Wind, voice this time. I open it.

"What's up?"

"Slend and I just overheard some boardshits in Arthuria. They were talking about you. Making jokes about the ladder coming down, whores falling hard, 'Humpty Dumpty' cracking apart. Nastier than their usual crap."

"Any specifics?"

"We tried to press them on it, but they logged. Be careful, Ash. Something felt off."

"Okay, thanks, Wind. I'll keep an eye out."

I close the connection and set out from Highrise, pushing

my way through the midday lunch crowds, hands in my hoodie pockets, thoughts drifting back to Mom's latest breakdown.

She tried to kill *me. Just like Brand. That punch would have shattered my sternum. Ahhh, Mom, why can't you be the way you were before?*

Memories from when I was a kid come rushing in, threatening to overwhelm me.

Mom and Dad laughing on the couch, Kiro toddling around in nothing but a diaper.

Late afternoon sun streaming through our apartment's broad windows, green vertical-farm tomato vines swaying in the wind, the smells of Dad cooking needlefish wafting from the kitchen.

Mom slowly walking me through her katas, adjusting my childish legs and arms into the proper positioning.

Stop. You know where this leads.

Dad trying not to cry as Mom walked into the troop carrier, my hand clutching his, Kiro in his other arm.

Long nights at home, lips dry and cracked from water rationing, but pushing my body through the katas, my talisman to bring her back.

Losing myself in hapworlds, alternate realities, escaping Dad's clenched lips at the nightly casualty reports on the viewscreen news, his attention locked on the crumbling death of everything normal. The day the atomics went off, jolting a semblance of sanity back into the world.

Joy at Mom finally being back home, confusion at the darkness in her eyes when she'd retreat into the bedroom with a bottle of alcohol. The small box hidden in a dresser, stuffed full of medals—a treasure chest of poisoned gold.

Let it go. You have to let it go.

Arguments that only grew louder and angrier, until one day Dad wasn't there anymore.

Mom arrested for assault, two gummie security officers in critical condition, another three dead. No mention of a trial. Whispers of "attempted morality violations."

Visiting the mental confinement ward, all bare walls and flickering lighting, a thrashing body strapped to a bed. Doctors who clearly didn't want to waste their time on a broken relic of the past. Kiro retreating deeper and deeper into hap, refusing to come out of his shell.

Fleeing the dryburbs, Mom fooling the tests long enough to get herself released.

I can't let it go.

Another breakdown, secdrones smashing down our megaspire apartment door in the middle of the night to drag her to another confinement ward after ten bodies ended up in the blue, one a relative of the Theocrophant.

Ghosting to pay the rent for a shitty room, whittling myself away, fifteen minutes at a time, all to keep my family alive.

Visiting a three-by-five in the Rust, Mom covered in her own filth, eyes wild, teeth bared like a cornered animal, living in a world no one else could see.

Putting all my rage and anger into Infinite Game, the only escape I had, hate and pain thrown back as I climbed the leaderboards—the audacity of a woman daring to conquer a man's world . . .

Snap out of it. You can't change the past. You can only try to fix the now.

I pause in the middle of a skyway connecting Highrise to the Brown, one of the newer concrete types, motionless spheres between the fluorescent panels shining overhead. My instincts are screaming at me, like when the lava exploded under my feet during the encounter with Hammer.

Something isn't right here . . .

It hits me. There aren't any people on the bridge, and it's

the middle of the day. This skyway should be packed with bodies. I look up to the end of the bridge, hands dropping out of my hoodie to my sides, but it's just as empty as my palms. I step forward, seeking the safety of the Brown, then halt, rocking on one foot. As if in a nightmare, five heavily muscled men step around the corner, blocking off my exit. They take a step forward, moving as a group.

I spin around, the mundane sound of the climate control like a rushing waterfall in my ears, and another group materializes, closer this time. A line of seven more men in form-fitting clothing stand at the other end of the bridge back to Highrise, massive arms crossed beneath bulging pecs. One of them is slightly in front of the others, his short blond hair spiked up over bronze skin, black-faceted AR glasses covering his face like an insect's eyes. His nose is purple and swollen, like he ran into a wall face-first, and he holds himself stiffly. I look over my shoulder. The other cluster of five still block the far end, slowly creeping closer. I tap a quick command, but my AR glasses return only static. Short range comm jamming. My heart begins to pound, adrenaline offering its familiar embrace.

The one in front speaks, his voice dripping with malice. "Hey, Ash. Fancy meeting you here, all alone like this."

"Mikelas. How's the nose? And the nuts? You borrowing a new pair from these idiots? What did it cost you to clear the skyway?"

He flushes, bruised tissue going a darker shade of purple.

"See, it's attitude like that that makes me enjoy what's about to happen to your cunty little face." He raises a hand, and the group behind him starts walking slowly toward me, their arms now swinging loosely at their sides, empty smiles under their dead eyes. "You've been atop the leaderboard too long, Ash. Gotten a little too cocky. Me and the boys want to fix that. Give someone else a chance in the spotlight next league. It's only fair. And lucky for us, we met someone last night who had *lots* to say about you."

No . . .

Mikelas nods.

"That's right, Ash. Seems your baby brother isn't too happy about how you've been treating him, and we were *real* sympathetic. Lent him quite the ear, me and the boys. Heard all about your daily routine, what it's like to be the world's greatest Gamer."

Goddammit, Kiro.

My hand falls to my blade.

"If your 'boys' take another step toward me, I'm going to neuter every last one of you. I am *not* in the mood for this shit right now, Mikelas. You want to send me gore-porn messages? Fine. Psych-sec. You want to come at me in the Game? Whatever. You know what'll happen there. I'll take your gear and scrap it for fun. You keep coming at me in the real, try to track me down, *and* you trick my brother?" The blade slides into my hand. "You already lost your looks. This time it's your nuts. You and your *boys*. Walk. Away."

Mikelas laughs, an ugly sound.

"Looks like you've forgotten how to count, princess. This isn't some Game encounter, and your guildies ain't here. There's twelve of us, and one of you. We're gonna fuck you up, in every sense of the word. Everyone knows Hammer let you win that fight. No one solos a dragon. We had to ditch the encounter, and we're the best guild in the Game."

My knuckles whiten on the hilt, and he laughs again. The group in front is almost twenty meters away now, several putting on brass knuckles, others pulling telescopic clubs out of their pockets.

"Aww, did I hurt your feels with that one, Ash? You sweet on Hammer? You *have* been fucking your way up the leaderboard, haven't you? Hell knows you never would've made it on top on your own, not without being on top of someone else."

"Last chance, Mikelas. You don't deserve it, but I'm putting it out there anyway. Walk away, never come back, and we keep this in the Game."

"The only thing you're going to be putting out is your pussy, you black bitch. Looks like this bridge is suffering a cam malfunction right now. Not everyone in the Brown thinks your shit smells like the Theocrophant's roses." He sneers, then motions to his companions. "Take her down."

I exhale slowly, hands and feet sliding into combat stance. Twelve top-tier players, perfectly comfortable coordinating in groups of four, their bodies honed by years of one-to-one fidelity in the Game, their capacity for violence now second nature. Most likely planning to disarm me, rape me, then kill me. And for what, because I'm better than them at a *game*? Because I hurt their precious *egos*? And my brother *led them to me*?

. . .

The air seems to splinter into jagged crystal, or maybe that's just my mind.

Mom is broken, Brand is *dead,* and I am *done* putting up with stupid shits like Mikelas. They want an encounter in the real? They'll get one.

"You say the cams aren't working, Mikelas?"

The front group of seven pauses, now five meters away, caught off guard by my question.

"Good."

I charge, smiling, my target a pale teenager with a crooked nose on the left side of the line. His eyes widen at my expression. Three steps bring me in range, and I duck under his wild swing, brass knuckles glinting over my head. I dip my blade in and twist it out, sidestepping a descending telescopic rod.

He collapses, hands clutching his ruined groin, wanting to deny the suddenly undeniable. Another rod sweeps at me and I step into the blow, locking my hand around a thick wrist covered in coarse black hair, absorbing the glancing strike on my shoulder. A quick turn and pivot, and he goes crashing to the ground. My blade dips again, a high-pitched squealing sound erupting from the body now writhing on the concrete.

I flip the rod up in the air with my foot and catch it in my free hand, spinning past a fist covered in metal. It clips my chin, but I ignore the pain. I've taken worse in the Game.

Another gentle touch, another bloom of former vitality, another trimming slice to the gene pool. I dive over a round-house kick, then roll past muscular legs, shockingly pale where bare skin lies unrevealed. A quick thrust, and bright red paints the pale canvas. He collapses to the ground, hands instinctively going to violated flesh. A thin keening whistles past his clenched teeth, but I'm beyond caring.

The fifth goon's eyes go wide with fright, and I break his arm with my appropriated club. Brass knuckles clang to the ground, and then he joins them, crimson pooling from his crotch, a once-in-a-lifetime menstruation. The sixth one turns to run; I whip the rod at his legs, bending his right knee awkwardly and sending him to the floor. My blade dips in and out once more, and then I'm running at Mikelas, blade swept back, its dull side pressed against my forearm, my form exactly the same as twenty-four hours ago, only this is no dragon, just a dick about to lose one. He puts his hands out in front of himself, desperately backpedaling, feet stumbling in a mockery of grace.

"No, wait, pl—"

My palm slams into his jaw, the impact stinging my arm. His teeth smash together, cracking several, severing the tip of his tongue. The still-wriggling piece of flesh flies past my head in a shower of blood and spit. I hook his legs and push on his face, following him down to the ground. His nose splatters beneath my hand when we hit, the cartilage grinding and splintering even more, and I kneel into his sternum, ripping off his stupid tinted glasses.

"Pweesh," he burbles, blood bubbling from his ruined nose, slurring his words. "Pweesh."

"You stupid little maggot," I breathe, voice trembling in rage, "you couldn't just leave me alone, could you? Couldn't believe that I might actually be this good at something, because I'm a *girl*."

"Pweesh!" His eyes roll madly.

"No. I told you what would happen if you brought this into the real. Fuck you, Mikelas. You thought your dick made you a man? You'll never be a *man* again."

My blade dips one last time, and I slowly twist it through an entire revolution. He screams, a piercing sound, then passes out. I stand up to face the five hulking figures running from the other side of the bridge, and point my dagger at them. Blood drips off the edge in a steady patter. They stumble to a halt ten meters away, normally dead eyes now filled with an emotion they never thought to experience in themselves, only inflict on others.

Fear.

"Walk. The fuck. Away."

Their weapons hit the concrete in a clattering rush, and then they're gone. I wipe my blade on Mikelas's shirt and sheathe it with a steady hand, then walk off the bridge, calm and collected, until I round the corner and the adrenaline fades. Half staggering, half sprinting, I find a bathroom, barely making it inside before puking. One of the sinks turns on, some sort of malfunction, but I'm not going to complain. Maybe the free water can wash away the sickness inside my mouth, my stomach, the warring sensations of guilt and pleasure.

I force my shaking hands back to stillness. I don't have time to be weak. I can't afford it.

Just another encounter.

Time to have a chat with Kiro.

9

[People Getting Disappeared]

"What the *fuck*, bro?"

Kiro's face shrinks back in my glasses, the tidy neatness of his room visible in the background. He finally decided to answer after the fourth message request, and the waiting's only made me more pissed. I continue my storming march through the corridors toward Johnny's, avoiding a white-robed Preacher haranguing a gathered crowd. The last thing I need right now is to deal with *that* particular brand of sanctimonious bullshit.

"What . . . what's wrong, Ash?"

"You told Mikelas and his group of shits where to find me, *that's* what's wrong. What the *fuck* were you thinking?"

People in the hallway look at me, but I snarl at them and they quickly turn away. I'm sure the bloodstains on the front of my hoodie help stanch their curiosity.

"They . . . they were just asking questions, Ash. Wanted to know more about me." He picks a box up from his bed. "Look, they gave me this neat new piece of tech—"

"Kiro, you . . . you *dumbass*. What the hell do you think they were asking those questions for?"

"I don't kn—"

"They just tried to rape me, Kiro. Twelve of them. On a skyway. Thanks to *you*."

His expression hardens, and he puts the box back down.

"I . . . How is it *my* fault, Ash? How do you know that's what they were going to do?"

"Because they told me, idiot!"

His tone turns dismissive.

"They were probably just trying to scare you. They wouldn't have actually done anything."

I want to scream. How can he be so dense? I've told him a million times what life is like for me online.

His eyes widen.

"Is . . . is that blood on you, Ash?"

I reach up and rub my cheek, feeling sticky wetness. Must have gotten splattered worse than I thought.

"Yes, Kiro. That's what happens when someone tries to rape me. I fight back."

Kiro's face turns furious.

"Every time, Ash! Every time I make some new friends, *you* have to screw it up. Always overreacting, playing the drama queen. Everything always has to be about you. Now they're going to hate me."

I pause, dumbfounded. People swirl around me, shifting glances and mutters trailing in their wake.

"Seriously? I tell you that I was just almost *raped* and your response is to blame me for ruining *your* life? What the *fuck*, Kiro?"

He paces in and out of frame, his fists clenched.

"No, Ash, you listen to *me* for once. You always complain about how hard you have it, how difficult things are—"

I can't control it any longer.

"*Shut. Up.*" The intensity of the words feels like it should tear out my vocal cords. "You haven't visited Mom in over two years—always making excuses about how you don't have the time, but I always see you in the Game. You say you love her, but you abandoned her, and now you're abandoning me. Just like Dad. IonSeal and Mikelas? They're *monsters*, Kiro, and you waltzed right over to them and served me up on a silver platter."

". . . Fuck you."

The connection goes dead, the ugly red light of a block symbol flashing in front of my eyes, and it's all I can do not to punch the wall. Instead, I stalk into a nearby restroom, close the door to a stall, and scream for ten seconds, all the rage I can't show the world. Then I punch the wall and walk out.

"You're late."

I glare at Jase, but he doesn't notice. He's too intent on the disassembled haphood scattered over the table in front of him, broken edges carefully splayed out in an autopsy fan. I close the door behind me, cutting off the sounds of Johnny cooking.

"I had to deal with some shit," I respond, as evenly as possible.

"Anything I should know or care about?"

I think about the last thirty minutes of my life.

"Yeah, don't bet on IonSeal to maintain their ladder position next league. I just castrated a quarter of their guild."

"Castrated?"

One of Jase's rickety chairs nearly collapses when I slouch into it.

"Yeah, castrated. I sliced their dicks off with a knife. Look it up."

Jase pushes his glasses up onto his forehead and gives me a strange look, finally noticing the bloodstains.

"I know what 'castrated' means, Ash. It seems a little excessive, though, even for Ditchtown. This is the real, not the Game. They're not gonna respawn."

I look back at him, expression flat.

"Mikelas and his little band of boardshits were planning to rape me in broad daylight, middle of a skyway, and I gave them the option to walk. They got everything they deserved."

Jase stares at me in silence. The seconds stretch on, and I wonder if I've lost another man in my life by sticking up for myself, but then he swallows heavily and shrugs.

"If you say so. I'm just a little worried about you, Ash. That's pretty barbaric. Gummies might come looking. They don't give a shit about the murder rates out here, but if they feel like you're threatening their manhood, even by proxy, they might do something about it."

"Barbaric?" I try not to take my anger out on Jase, but it's hard. "Threatening their *manhood*? Maybe they should try getting threatened with murder and rape every *day; their* rules targeting women that *they* put in place. Twelve Gamers assaulted me, Jase, fully coordinated, and there wasn't a fucking gummie in sight to try and stop it. Lemme know if that changes your viewpoint on what's 'civilized' and what's 'barbaric.' Fuck the gummies. If they want to come after me, they know where to find me, apparently along with the rest of this damn city. I'm done apologizing for being attacked."

Jase slides his glasses back down.

"Okay, okay, you know your life better than I do. Peace. And yeah, this place fucking blows." He beckons me over. "Anyway, come take a look at this hood. Whoever made it stuffed it full of IP traps, but I managed to get it open without frying the insides. Or myself."

I lean down next to his shoulder, our ears almost touching, adrenaline aftereffects still churning my insides.

"What, exactly, am I looking at?"

He points slowly at what looks like a tangle of fine metal spaghetti in the middle of the dissected hood, nestled deep within the other components.

"This right here."

"Jase. If you don't explain what 'this' is, I swear . . ."

"Easy there, tiger. Oh, that's right, your glasses aren't synced. Here, ride my feed."

A small icon appears in my vision, and I tap it open. Technical diagrams and links to the 'Net appear, overlaying the scattered mess of circuits, memory boards, and polymer casing. I focus in on the cluster of metal, eye trackers in my glasses bringing the pertinent information into sharp clarity.

"A graphene quantum computer? That doesn't make sense. No one's cracked Q-dots yet."

Jase's voice is sober.

"Apparently the silkies did. Ash, this is some heavy shit. Like, 'people getting disappeared' heavy."

"Why? What does it do?"

"Well, I took a look at the internal coding of the non-impossible-computer parts, the ones still working, and near as I can tell, based on your description of what happened with Brand, these things are designed to infiltrate people's minds. More specifically, the mind of anyone who wears them for longer than six hours, at which point it can start giving them instructions."

"What? Mind control? Are you kidding me?"

"Nope. Sounds like sci-fi crap, but it's sitting right there in front of us."

". . . Wow. How does it do it?"

"I'm not totally sure, but it looks like the hood extrudes carbon nanotubes that make their way through the skull to infiltrate synaptic junctions. That's the initial data harvest. The quantum computer builds up a profile, figures out which neuron triggers what, and once it has enough, it starts altering their perceptions by jolting specific clusters. I don't know where the instructions are coming from yet, but I have a couple guesses on how to look."

"What's it changing? In the brain?"

"I was hoping you could tell me. I was able to retrieve the last few seconds of visual display—take a look."

A window expands in my vision, first person perspective of the past. Wooden decking beneath my feet, weathered crates surrounding me in the dark, my hand flashing toward a lean shape, blurry motion, then nothing. I frown and play it back, slowing everything down, focusing on the shape.

It appears to be an old-time pirate, captain of a sailing ship, dressed in flamboyant silks. A red fist insignia is visible on the left breast, a thin blade held swept back in its right hand. As my viewpoint lunges forward, the blade falls and the figure locks its hands around my outstretched wrist. The last frame is of a crate filling my vision.

Cold sweat prickles my spine.

"But that . . . that doesn't make any sense."

Jase shrugs.

"You're telling me. What the hell is a pirate doing in the memory banks of your friend's haphood?"

"No, you don't understand. I *know* that encounter. It's from the Game. High Seas facet."

"She was in the Game?"

"No, she was on the ship. With me. That move the pirate made, that's what I did to try and disable her."

I run a hand over my face, mind racing.

"You're saying this was the last thing she saw?"

He nods.

"Then that means she saw me as part of the Game . . . only she was in the real . . ."

It hits me like a lightning bolt. A second later, Jase stiffens in his chair, the same horrible revelation burning through his brain. He stares at me, eyes panicky.

"Holy fuck. Those hoods. They make you think you're still in the Game."

I let out a low whistle.

"Sure seems like it. But why?"

I start pacing the room, trying to put the pieces together. Jase gasps, then slides his glasses up once more and rubs his eyes. He sounds exhausted.

"Ash. I'm pretty sure I have the answer. I'm also pretty sure you won't like it." He glances over at me. "Conservatively, how many top-tier Gamers do you think there are? People who dedicate their lives to being the very best at Infinite Game?"

I mull it over.

"Conservatively, probably a couple hundred thousand or so. It takes a pretty significant time and resource investment, and you have to want it. Bad. Most endgame guilds are forty to eighty people, and there's five thousand slots on the ladder. If you make it onto the ladder, you're pretty damn good, considering the Game is worldwide. We have quite a few here in Ditchtown, since the gummies don't leave us much else to do other than rot, and it's either find something to do or riot. There are guilds all over the planet though."

"And what is it you do in the Game, Ash?"

"We defeat encounters, and we fight each other. Whatever the devs think up to throw at us, we adapt and figure out ways to beat it. When we're waiting for new encounters, we have PvP tournaments, regional first, then global. Both PvP and encounters are weighted fairly equally in terms of ladder standing."

"And you're doing all this at a one-to-one fidelity with human reactions and abilities, right? Using modern-equivalent weaponry within the Game, lo-tech and hi-tech? Coordinating in four-person squads, with the ability to link squads together for larger encounters? Every day, honing your skills in this make-believe world?"

"Well, yeah, you gotta practice if you want to be good."

"Ash, do you think any other Gamers could do what you do as an operative for the grayhats? Maybe not at your level, but close enough?"

My stomach drops.

"Fuck. Fuck fuck *fuck*."

I kick a shelf against the wall, sending a light rain of disassembled technology clattering to the floor. Jase winces, but stays silent. Smart kid.

"We're all fucking *soldiers*. We've trained ourselves into a goddamned army."

I kick the shelf again, harder. There's no other outlet for the rage and fear pouring through me, thoughts of Mom and Brand ripping through my mind like Dead Zone tornadoes.

"Tell me I'm wrong, Jase. Please."

Jase slowly shakes his head.

"You're not wrong. And if you think you're in the Game, you'll do whatever you normally do to defeat the encounter, right? Push yourself to the edge and beyond, on the off chance that it just might work? Dive down a dragon's throat?"

I want to puke. Brand never had a chance. Never even knew she could die, that there weren't any respawns left. Jase shakes his head sorrowfully.

"Yeah. I'm also pretty sure I know who was controlling Brand. I recognized some of the coding fingerprints—they're pure silkie."

"Assholes. What the hell are they doing?"

I kneel down to start cleaning up the pieces of Jase's tech from the floor, and it hits me. The answer's obvious.

"Of course. The silkies want to hit the gummies just as bad as the gummies want to hit the silkies."

I deposit a handful of circuit boards back on the shelf, most still intact. Not worried about the ones that aren't.

"They still hate each other, tech zealots versus religious zealots. Only, both sides are bound by the treaty. They can't move against each other openly, nothing obvious, nothing that leads to radiation like the way the Dubs ended."

Jase looks at me, not yet understanding, and I scoop up another handful of microprocessors, like tiny silver spiders. A brief shudder runs through my spine.

"It's war, Jase. They think they can start it up again, and what better way to do that than with an army no one knows exists? One already forged in countless hours of combat, trained in every possible weapon and scenario you could ever hope to encounter? One willing to take ridiculous risks because their minds are conditioned to believe death is just a minor setback?"

Jase's mouth slowly opens, and I let the microprocessors fall through my fingers.

"Generals would kill for a force like that. They *will* kill for a force like that. And silkie versus gummie is just the start. The Game is worldwide—*everyone* plays it. Once the silkies take out the gummies, what's to stop them from doing it to Han, or Industan, or, hell, whoever they want? Gamers live in those countries too, and silkie shipping boats go everywhere."

I stumble over to a seat, mind reeling. The color leaches from Jase's face.

"But that's . . . someone would notice . . . people going missing . . ."

"Did I notice? When Brand went missing?" I punch my thigh, angry. "No, of course I didn't. I thought she got caught up with something in the real, couldn't make our scheduled raids. Why would I expect something like this? It sounds insane."

My voice drops into leaden tones.

"Except it's not insane. It's fucking brilliant. No one is going to miss the absence of a Gamer except another Gamer, and even then the thought will be, 'Oh, she's just away from world for a bit.' Until it gets too big to notice. Then the party favors pop off again, only this time everyone's invited."

"But how did this happen to her? To Brand? Why was she wearing the hood in the first place? They're not even supposed to be out yet."

I lean back against the wall, closing my eyes, trying not to think of my dead friend.

"I don't know. I wish I did. Then maybe I'd have been able to save her."

The room falls silent, the only sound Jase tapping his finger against the table. I hear his clothes rustle as he straightens up.

"Maybe we can find out. What's her avatar code?" I rattle off a sixteen-digit number to him, almost as familiar as my own. Jase pulls on a pair of hapgloves. "Okay, one sec, this is going to be a bit fiddly." His hands start twitching on the table surface like he's having a seizure. A minute later, they fall still.

". . . and we're in."

"Into what?"

"Her avatar account, root level."

I open my eyes.

"Isn't that illegal?"

"Yep. Not supposed to be easy to do either, but like most people's, her security sucked. Also, I'm pretty good."

"*What*? Brand was super careful about her accounts. She had them linked biometrically."

"Biometrics isn't foolproof. Vendors have to ensure a non-biometric backup in case your gear goes down and you need to recover your info. Weak point in the system. Ran a back-trace on all her socials, put that through a trends algorithm to pin down her place of residence and interests, and then it was just a matter of educated guessing. Really shouldn't make your emergency password your first pet's name if you're a dog enthusiast on the 'Net."

A new icon appears in my glasses, and I tap my fingers to open it. Brand's portal opens before me, the inside of a comfortable plantation-style house with sunlight streaming through the windows. Chairs and sofas with green upholstery dot each bookshelf-lined room. Wooden fans creak lazily overhead. The shelves hold a mishmash of books, trinkets, painted miniatures, and more—digital representations of what Brand considered important enough to save as a memory. It looks like the inside of a teenager's room from an emodrama, the girl with a quirky personality but still the cherished daughter—like stepping back into a history show or a dryburb, a home before the Split and the Dubs. Dogs bark outside, the joyous woofs of animals playing. It's not full hap, but it's still engrossing.

"What are we looking for?" I ask quietly.

I direct my viewpoint to approach a bookshelf and pick up a small figure of a fighter jet, the haptic feedback in my gloves making it feel like I'm holding the real thing. Root access allows us to handle any of Brand's data without triggering security measures—to the portal, Jase and I might as well be Brand. Our encounter in the Clancery facet starts replaying in front of me—Slend, Wind, Brand, and myself, each in the cockpit of a latest-generation fighter, clearing a path for a landing force of hapdrones, other guilds in formation around us. Missiles streak from anti-air emplacements, tracers burn against the daytime sky, but we're swooping and diving like falcons, taking out battery after battery with bombs and gunfire, outperforming everyone else easily. Golden sigils fill the background, viewers riding our eyes. The memory ends with us parachuting down, hair whipping from the back of our helmets, or, in Wind's case, all over her entire body, triumphant music echoing from the heavens.

"Something corporate," Jase responds. "A sponsorship offer or something. A way for them to get the hood to her before they release it to the public."

I put the fighter jet miniature back down and look at the shelf—the next item is a photo of us in an obsolete tank, all smiles and thumbs-up under a desert sun, goggles pushed up on sand weathered foreheads. MilHist facet. Another is a music box, four figures in ballroom gowns slowly twirling inside—the Court of Roses intrigue encounter, in the nonviolent Masquerade facet. Where I first met Ham. I reach toward it, but then force my fingers to fall. We're not here for memories. I glance around the room, then head for an old rolltop desk set against one wall. It's the only item that seems not to fit, somehow. I flip back the hood and wince.

"It's probably in here, Jase. Come help me wade through this crap."

Giant rats, their sable fur bristling, glare up at me with beady red eyes. They bare fangs like small knives and hiss. There seems to be no end of them, the desk extending back much farther than the wall it's up against. I pick one of the rats up—a rape threat from an IonSeal member scrolls out in front of me, full of vileness and spite. I grimace, and dash the rat to the ground. It disappears, message deleted.

"What *is* all this?"

I see invisible hands pick up another rat, then throw it to the ground as well.

"Her hate mail. She must not have had a deletion program

like I did, so she stored it all in here, going through it when she could to keep from getting charged. I wish she'd said something to me."

I flip through four more snarling messages. Jase sounds shocked.

"I knew it was bad, but I never realized it was *this* bad. What these people are saying . . . fuck."

Another rat hits the floor.

"Yeah, welcome to life as a target, and she didn't even have to deal with the race part. Not a whole lot of fun over here."

"I'm seeing that. Your skyway scrotum massacre is starting to make a lot more sense."

I scowl at Jace.

"Yeah, because god forbid you just took my word for it. Thanks. You should let Kiro know about your revelation the next time you see him."

Jase backs up a bit.

"Duly noted. Sorry. Maybe she kept it in a different drawer?"

"Might have. I'll take the right side, you take the left."

I lower the rolltop back down, trapping the seething mass of rats once more, and pull open a small wooden drawer lower on the desk, revealing shining keys resting on red velvet. Passwords to sensitive information, most likely. I close the drawer and pull open the next. Small gems and coins wink up at me. I pick one up—a financial statement from her bank, deposits from GameCore.

"This looks promising. Brand always did have a thing for organization."

Jase joins me, the view from his glasses showing him staring at the same drawer. Jewels and coins dart through the air, his digital hands lightning quick.

"Okay, let's see what we have . . . got it. A no-strings sponsorship offer from a Golgbank subsidiary, giving her the hood in exchange for consideration on her viewstream. Comes across as big fans—these guys did their research."

"Fuck. She wouldn't have had any reason to suspect anything. I get offers like that all the time."

"Check your messages."

"One sec."

I tap out of Brand's portal and bring up my own, grabbing the battered toy cat to access my private messages.

"Looking . . . There. Fucking hell, they sent me one too, about two weeks ago; same company and everything. Must have been dumb luck that I didn't read it, I usually put sponsorship stuff off until the beginning of each month." I notice something on the address line and curse, my heart sinking.

"What is it?" Jase asks.

"Wind and Slend's portals are in the recipient line also. They sent it to all of us. Shit, I gotta tell them."

A couple quick twitches and I'm pinging their avatars. *C'mon, answer, you two.* Slend's goes to her portal, and I leave her a quick message warning about the haphoods. Wind's continues to buzz, then her avatar shifts from a static representation to dynamic motion. I ping Jase to ride my feed.

". . . Yeah, Ash?" Wind sounds like she's breathing hard. "Now's not the best time. COVER FIRE, SLEND. Unless you're planning on joining us."

"Are you with Slend right now?"

"Yeah—HAHA SUCK IT YOU LITTLE SHIT—we're doing some peeveepee practice. Battlefield's Call facet, two on ten survival mode. TELL YOUR MOM TO TEACH YOU HOW TO SHOOT STRAIGHT, YOU GOAT-FELLATING TAINT SNORTER. Other team's not bad with tactics, but they can't aim for crap. Lemme patch her in."

Slend's avatar reappears in my vision.

"Ash. Missed you. Busy."

"Wind told me. Did either of you get a sponsor offer for a new model of haphood from Golgbank?"

"Yeah, just got the hood today, as a matter of fact. Putting it through the paces now. This thing is amazing, Ash. The fidelity is—DO YOU JACK IT WITH THOSE TREMBLING HANDS, DICKFINGERS?—unbelievable."

"Good gear," Slend chimes in laconically.

"Shit. How long have you been wearing them?"

"Uhh, maybe two hours so far? We were gonna work on some psych-sec training in Freudia after we finish killing these TRASHFIRE BABOON BABIES. Shouldn't take more than another fifteen minutes, tops. Why?"

"I need you two to log out of the Game, right now, and get those hoods off."

"Whaaaat? Ash, we're in the middle of a match. This'll hit—GO BACK TO CANDYLAND, YOU CHODES—our ladder standing if we bail."

"Wind, I need you to listen. Those hoods are dangerous. We already clinched. The ladder isn't important right n—"

A door crashing open interrupts me. I pull my attention away from my portal and back to the real. Framed in Jase's narrow doorway is the headless, gleaming metallic bulk of a hapdrone in riot control configuration, boxy immobilization spray nozzles on both sides of oddly jointed arms, long legs hinged backward, like a bird's. A voice booms out from a speaker beneath the sensor cluster on its chest.

"PUT YOUR HANDS IN THE AIR. RESISTANCE WILL BE MET WITH FORCE."

"Shit. Wind, I gotta go, just please get those damn hoods off."

Without waiting for her response, I close the connection and slowly raise my hands in the air. I could *probably* take a hapdrone in the open, with room to maneuver, but not in a situation like this. Next to me, Jase raises his hands as well.

"ACCOMPANY US OUTSIDE. RESISTANCE WILL BE MET WITH FORCE."

I can't help myself.

"Yeah, yeah, I got it. Lay on, Macduff. Take us to your leader. Terminate. Whatever."

"SARCASM WILL ALSO BE MET WITH FORCE. FOLLOW."

The hapdrone collects the battered hood on the table with a curiously delicate touch, storing it in an exterior compartment on its body, then backs away on stilted legs, neatly avoiding the boxes on the ground. We emerge into the restaurant, where two other drones have Johnny covered at the stove, his hands in the air. He looks at me, a question in his eyes, but I shake my head the barest fraction, as if I were flicking hair from my face. He blinks once, soberly. The lead drone walks backward through the bead curtain, suppression weapons still aimed directly at us, and the other two drones fall in behind, legs bending and reforming into segmented wheels. They click on the tile floor like falling bones.

We make our way through the dim hallways of the Brown to an access hatch, the corridors empty, cleared out by yet more drones standing guard at intersections, cameras above shifting blindly as powerful jammers cut their vision. *An entire patrol squad, just for us?* I want to ask, but discretion stills my tongue. Our little convoy proceeds in silence, broken only by the clicking of metal wheels molding themselves to floor and stairs.

Multiple descended levels later, the lead drone approaches a warning sign–covered door, and it swings open, revealing the lean yet boxy shape of a gummie littoral cruiser bobbing in the noonday sun, all polymer angles and edges. Eye-bending camo-panels cover its swept back length, seeming to merge with the blue water below. A wobbling gangplank extends from the ship to the megaspire, guard railings sticking up from its sides.

Clacking wheels roll across, followed by our footsteps, weapons still tracking our every move. I walk across into the cool darkness of the ship's hold, Jase behind me, a train of drones behind him.

Inside, the hapdrone says in a normal voice, "We appreciate the restraint. Sawyer only wants to talk. Please strap yourselves in. I *will* have to confiscate your equipment, though." Sighing, I peel off my hapgloves and AR glasses, then my blade, and hand them over. I motion for Jase to do the same. He does, reluctantly. The drone collects them in dextrous motions, then waves us to a pair of comfortable-looking seats bolted to the deck. A lap belt closes across my waist, and the drone leans in closer. Its voice drops to a whisper.

"Also, hell of a show with that dragon. Won me a couple thousand."

The drone straightens back up and rolls over to a gap in the wall, placing the confiscated haphood and our gear into a small hatch, then folds in on itself until it's a featureless cube almost two meters to a side. The other drones settle in next to it.

"That . . . that whole wall is drones, isn't it?" Jase asks, his voice low.

"Yeah," I respond, talking normally, "and I wouldn't bother whispering. There are sensors everywhere. Don't try to hack them either, when we get our stuff back. That'll end . . . badly."

"What the hell is going on, Ash?" Jase sounds like he might throw up.

I grin, but there's nothing approaching humor in my expression.

"We've been disappeared. Hopefully they put us back."

10

[Spook Games]

"Ashley, it's good to see you again. How's your mother?"

The bulky man behind the desk has close-cropped white hair above an almond-skinned face; not the white of age, but of stress. A loosely tailored green and brown uniform doesn't quite conceal his muscular chest and arms, sleeves rolled up to the elbows, and his neck strains against the fabric of the buttoned collar. A small name patch is the only insignia on the uniform, and a sleek pair of military-style augmented glasses rest atop his overlarge nose. A small picture frame, contents invisible from this angle, is the only item on the desk aside from our confiscated gear.

I glare at him, and then take a seat across the desk, grabbing my glasses and hapgloves from its surface. My blade's still missing. Guess they don't trust me with it this close to Sawyer. Jase silently joins me, clutching his gear like a talisman. Being blackbagged for however many hours we were in the ship seems to have shaken him. We could be anywhere right now, and he knows it.

Me, I took the opportunity to get some sleep.

Just another psych-sec.

Just another encounter.

"Spare me the concern, Sawyer. You know how she is; broken, and I get to try and fix her. Still playing spook games, huh?"

He laughs genially, but it never reaches his eyes.

"And we're almost as good as you are, Ashley. The offer still stands. Whenever you want to join, there's a rig waiting for you."

"Same answer as before, Sawyer. I saw what happened to Mom. How you used her up and spit her out."

"And you think it's not already happening to you? You're turning into quite the little savage, my dear. Normally you need a license to neuter animals."

Of course he knows what happened in the skyway. I hate Sawyer, hate everything he represents, his emotionless fucking guts, but he's good at what he does.

No.

He's the best at what he does, or the gummies would've replaced him a long time ago. It's not gonna keep him alive, though, if I learn he's responsible for what happened to Brand.

"Maybe if any of *your* people gave a fuck about us, I wouldn't have been in that position, and Mom wouldn't be broken. Let's cut the crap, Sawyer—*what* do you *want*?"

He leans forward, elbows on the desk.

"I *want*"—he points at Jase—"to know what Jason Tanner here knows. More specifically, what he knows about that piece of silkie tech, seven thousand units of which are sitting onboard a cargo ship currently tied up in a customs dispute I manufactured out of thin air, burning a significant amount of political capital to do so." Sawyer points at Jase again, harder, jabbing his finger like a bayonet. "I *also* want to know how he managed to open one of those damn things up when my scientists keep exploding them. I know a lot about what we're dealing with, but I don't know *exactly* what we're dealing with. *He* does."

Jase gulps, color draining from his face. He's probably wondering how Sawyer knew his real name.

"Then," he continues, pointing at me, "I want *you* to do something about it." Jase looks over at me, eyes wide, and Sawyer laughs. It's not a pleasant sound. "Relax, kid, you're fine. You've done good work for us in the past, and I don't forget that. I want her to do something about the tech, not you."

I lean back in the chair, crossing my arms in front of my chest. We need to take care of the important business first.

"Did you know one of my guildies was going to be opfor on that run?"

"No." The word comes out flat, tired, dead. "If I'd known, I would've used another asset. I can't afford to lose your capabilities."

Sawyer's a good liar, but he's not that good. Looks like he's just as much in the dark as I am regarding Brand, but he's still dangerous. Soothing words to Jase notwithstanding, he'll burn us quicker than a midsummer wildfire, and leave behind less than ashes.

"What's in it for us?"

"Ummm, Ash?"

Jase's whisper is low, nervous.

"You mean other than your lives?" Sawyer asks conversationally, leaning backward, murder gleaming in his eyes. "Isn't that enough?"

"I said cut the bullshit. You want me to do something for you, fine. I'll do it. I'm not stupid. You're gonna pay for my time, though, because if you're blackbagging us, sending an entire squad to pick us up, it means you've got no other choice, and that's time away from the Game, time I could be spending making money for Mom." I uncross my arms and lean forward, fixing my eyes on his. "And since you fuckers have made it perfectly clear you're willing to see her rot, I'm not feeling particularly generous with my time these days. Especially for something big like this. Whatever it is you want, my price is her treatment. For however long it takes."

Jase's eyes dart back and forth between us, whites clearly visible, a newbie suddenly thrust into an endgame he didn't even know existed. Sawyer's voice goes soft, and he leans back in.

"What makes you think you're in any position to bargain with me, Ashley Akachi? With you disappeared, and seven aggravated assault charges waiting for me to make them a reality?"

My voice drops as well, and I let my anger, the simmering tension that comes from having to deal with this fucked-up world on a daily basis, finally show.

"Because I know what's in those haphoods, and I know you're shitting yourself thinking about what happens when the silkies activate them. A fifth column, composed of the most lethal members of your society, rampaging through dryburbs across the entire Eastern Board? You can't intercept them all—not if you want to keep a low profile, prevent this from turning into all-out war. The riots are getting worse, the economy's in the shitter again, and people are looking for blood. You think they won't go after the Theocrophant with a nice silkie push? Got any Gamers in the drone forces, Sawyer?"

His nostrils flare, and muscles tense on his arms. For a second, I feel like I may have pushed him too far, but I don't care. I'm tired of these manipulations, of these stupid boys thinking they can shove me around like a pawn. If Sawyer wants to play stupid spook games, then let's play.

"I also know what Mom did for you all. Back in the Dubs.

She's the only reason you're here today, and you know it. She did your dirty work, the work no one else could, and you abandoned her. Left her screaming her lungs out in a three-by-five in Ditchtown, rotting in the water and rust. Left her pieces for me to find."

I lean the slightest bit farther forward, a deliberate motion, putting myself into his space, letting the words come out in a whisper, adrenaline singing its arpeggio across nerves and sinew and blood.

"Lastly, *you're in front of me.* You say you saw what I did to the boardshits, Sawyer? Then let's go, round two, pick your fucking tune. I *love* to dance."

Tension fills the air.

". . . Fine. We'll put her in a hospice."

"No. She's already getting care, and you know she's never coming back to the dryburbs. That life isn't for her, not anymore. Never really was. You pay for where she's at. Whatever they ask. Until she's better."

Sawyer's brown eyes glint dangerously, but he nods.

"Very well. In return, you report directly to me on this op, and you're in it for the duration. Until those hoods are dealt with, your ass is mine."

Bristling, I nod back at him.

"I want full autonomy for my squad, though. We decide our tactics. Oh, and they get paid too."

"Of course."

"What about Jase?"

"If he helps us figure out how these things work, *and* he keeps his mouth shut for the rest of his life, I'll let him go when it's done, along with, say, fifty thousand. Unless he wants a job."

I lean over to Jase, white eyes wide in his pale-brown face, jaw unconsciously slack.

"I wouldn't recommend getting into spook games, but that's probably the best you're going to get."

"Ye-yeah, that's fine. Fifty thousand is fine."

Fifty thousand is more creds than Jase has seen his entire life. Sawyer stands abruptly.

"Good. Both of you, follow me."

Jase scrambles to his feet, pushing his chair back across the metal. Taking my time, I join him. Sawyer may have me cornered, but I'll be damned if I'm going to nip at his heels like a grateful stray. He looks at me coolly, but doesn't say anything. We step out into a deserted hallway, harsh bulbs dangling bare from rusted metal beams. The smell of brine fills the air.

Sawyer leads us past several unmarked doors, integrated biosecurity pads at waist level, augmented reality identifiers refusing to coalesce in front of our unclassified vision. I'm sure Sawyer can see them just fine. I try to access the 'Net, but there's no connection. Eventually, he stops in front of a door that looks like all the rest. It slides open at his touch on the sensor.

Inside, several older men in spotless white coats over traditional dryburb robes cluster around a polymer table, painfully bright lights highlighting its entire surface. On it is the disassembled haphood, technical-looking instruments scattered around in various states of disarray. Their animated discussion cuts off when they realize Sawyer is standing behind them. One, older than the rest, blond hair slicked back like it's painted on his head, turns to him, pushing sleek AR glasses up with a hapgloved hand.

"Sir, we're still examining the device. We wo—"

"I know, Davis," Sawyer interrupts. "This young man has been recruited to assist you. He's the one who opened it. Something I believe you said was 'impossible.'"

"H-he did?" The blond-haired man gawps at Jase. "But he barely looks fourteen. And he's from the Squalor."

"I'm sixteen, and we call it 'Ditchtown,' thanks," Jase replies, a little of his old swagger reappearing. "Apparently my school's a better teacher than whatever crap you got in the dryburbs."

"'Necessity is the mother of all invention, and the street finds strange uses,'" Sawyer murmurs, almost to himself. Louder, he continues. "There will be no animosity. That is an order. We need to understand the precise nature of this weapon. Quickly. If you cannot work with him, Davis, the Theocrophant will hear about it." Davis gulps, Jase smirking at him. Sawyer turns around. "And if you needlessly antagonize my scientists, our deal is void. My patience is not limitless." Jase's smirk disappears, and Sawyer nods. "Good. I'm glad we understand each other. Get to work."

Jase warily approaches the scientist, then sticks out a skinny arm, his hapgloved hand open at the end. Davis stares at it, uncomprehending.

"It's called shaking hands. Supposed to be polite. I'm Jase."

"We transfer introductions through AR in the Enclaves," he responds stiffly. "Physical contact with outsiders can introduce unwanted diseases."

"Yeah, well, I'm not on your 'Net, we're not in the dryburbs, and she told me not to hack your stuff, sooooo?"

Davis continues staring at Jase, who shakes his head and lets his hand fall.

"Fucking burbies. I've had my vaccines. You gonna give me access or what?"

Davis looks over at Sawyer, who inclines his head slightly and twitches a finger. A smile spreads across Jase's face, and he pushes past Davis to the table.

"Daaaaaamn, look at those transfer rates. Okay, let's see what you got . . . yeah . . . mmm . . . so the issue with the array switches here is . . ."

As Jase descends into incomprehensible techspeak, the other scientists stare at him, then cautiously approach the table, Davis holding his nose up like he just ate a slice of rotten nee-dlefish. The expression quickly disappears, though, and soon they're all deep into the muttered half conversations of techies everywhere, nonsense words interspersed with hapgloved ges-tures bringing pertinent bits of info to each others' glasses. Sawyer looks at Jase with a curious expression, his gaze oddly paternal, then he motions to me. I follow him out of the room.

"That kid's smart, Ash. Smarter than I thought. Reminds me of someone I knew a long time ago." He stares at me. "You sure you want him going back to Ditchtown, wasting his life on grayhat crap? I could give him a chance here."

"You leave Jase out of this," I tell him fiercely. "He doesn't need to get sucked into your shit. You'll burn him out, and you know it."

"Undoubtedly true," Sawyer responds. "My masters are not nearly as patient as I am. However, he would be well taken care of while his flame lasted."

"No. He's free, or I don't play your games."

"Very well."

We walk in silence for a bit, boots ringing off the metal grates of the floor, until I can't hold it in anymore. The ques-tion rots me from the inside, like it always does.

"Why'd you do it, Sawyer? Why'd you abandon her? After everything she did?"

Wordlessly, he opens another door, revealing a spacious room packed with viewscreens and whispered conversations, camo-clad figures sitting in padded chairs with integrated hap-glove armrests. A floor-to-ceiling glass window sits at the far end, overlooking a huge open chamber. Twelve spheres, four meters in diameter, sit inside skeletal scaffolding like caged silver marbles, the farthest surrounded by more camo-draped shapes working on its opened surface. Sawyer turns to look at me, still ignoring my previous question.

"This will be your home until the op is finished." My glasses flash to life, a small map appearing. "Barracks for you and your squad are here." A doorway highlights in the room below, set in the side wall. "Canteen is here." Another doorway highlights. "We've isolated this area. Do not attempt to interact with the other soldiers, do not attempt to leave your assigned quarters when you're not running ops, and above all, do not make me regret this. You'll be briefed on the first target after you meet your squad. Stairs are over there."

I slam to a stop. "You said we were autonomous. How do *you* know who I want on *my* squad? I don't trust your people."

Sawyer grins mockingly, his eyes slivers of ice.

"Who else would Ashura the Terrible, champion of Infinite Game, want other than her SunJewel Warriors? The briefing is in ten. I suggest you hurry."

11

[Ghosting the Metal]

"Ash!"

A bubbly voice meets my entrance into the room, followed closely by a pair of arms squeezing me into a crushing bear hug. The owner of the arms is about twenty centimeters shorter than me, her long black hair tickling my chin where it pulls loose from its braid, a Hajj burka draping her body and shoulders. Gummie anonymity restrictions prevent the wearing of full head covers except for extremely specific religious observances. Somehow, none of the Hajj rituals seem to qualify—another drop of intolerance in a vast ocean. I hug her back and smile.

"Ooof. Heya, Wind. Slend. Good to see you both."

A pale-faced woman with close-cropped blue hair, a deep purple bruise spreading from her left eye under the green octagonal lenses of her glasses, nods at me from the corner of the room. She dwarfs the chair she's sitting in, muscles rolling underneath her matching blue tank top when she shifts back and forth. Thin gray gloves cling to her hands and cargo shorts barely contain her thick legs. A viewscreen covers the wall next to her, its surface the dull black of inactive pixels.

Wind hugs me again, then pushes herself back, folding her

own gloved hands into her robes. A feeling of energy radiates from her, as if she's constantly restraining herself from dancing side to side. She looks up at me through her sleek winged glasses, angular facets trailing back almost to her ears.

"They grabbed me right after you called. I'd barely gotten back from the hapchamber, after you told us to get those hoods off. Scared the shit out of my parents. They thought it was fundie stuff, another crackdown. My dad about had a heart attack, especially when they told him to keep quiet or it was my life. Mom wanted to argue, but . . ."

She shrugs, and I pull her into another quick hug.

"Yeah, I know. No chance anyone's gonna listen to a Hajj, especially right now. Fucking gummies."

"Yup. Slend says they picked her up at the same time."

A grunt from the corner.

"Broke a drone. Was being rude."

I laugh in spite of myself.

"That explains the war wound. You two doing okay?"

Wind starts pacing around the room.

"Yeah, we're fine, just a little confused. They didn't tell us anything. Textbook blackbagging. What's going on, Ash? Is Brand coming?"

My stomach clenches, like a punch to the gut.

They don't know yet.

"Brand's dead, Wind. She's one of the reasons we're here."

Wind drops back into a chair, her body going still. Over in the corner, a thunderous expression appears on Slend's face.

"Mikelas? Boardshits?"

"No. It . . . was my fault." Quickly, I explain the encounter on the cargo ship, fighting an unresponsive Brand, the haphood frying her brain. By the end, tears are rolling down my cheeks. "I couldn't save her. I didn't even know she needed saving. That fucking hood . . ."

I find a chair of my own and collapse into it, head in my hands. Wind whistles, long and low, then walks over and wraps her arms around me.

"Shit, Ash. Just . . . shit. That's beyond fucked up. And it's not your fault. What are we gonna do?"

"Dunno," I reply, voice muffled by her sleeve covering my mouth. "Sawyer wants us to figure out who's behind it, but I don't have much. Got a silkie corp that sent Brand her hood, but that's it."

"Name?" Slend's voice is intense.

"Golgbank subsidiary by the name of Unlimited Holdings Limited. Found the message in her portal."

"That's the same corp that sent mine," Wind says, subdued. Slend nods once, sharply.

"And that's your first target."

The voice coming through hidden speakers in the room shatters the illusion of normalcy. I gently disengage from Wind's embrace, looking for the cameras, but they're not immediately obvious. They're probably in the lights. Wind sits down next to me, and I address the viewscreen—as good an option as any.

"Thanks, Sawyer. Good to know your spook shit extends everywhere."

"Spare me the crocodile tears, Ashley. You're in *my* world now. I'm watching everything."

The viewscreen on the wall next to Slend lights up, Golgbank's rainbow logo spinning in the middle. Sawyer continues talking.

"We've isolated the primary staging facility for the hoods. Production center on the outskirts of Industan, owned by Golgbank through four proxies. We haven't been able to pierce the corporate veil surrounding Golgbank and find out which of the Big Three controls it yet. That's your job. A carrier will be in position within an hour. You three are ghosting the metal."

A small icon appears in my glasses, access to the local cloud, and I tap it open in a quarantined subsection. The three dimensional representation of a building appears, featureless walls extending up in a two-story rectangle, similar buildings appearing as shadowed masses on either side. Barbed wire fence surrounds each one, a two-meter gap between metal mesh and concrete wall, deviating only where an access road splits off from the main expressway, leading into a wide loading bay with space for multiple heavy lifters. A truck slowly pulls away from one of the loading docks, sensor dome on the roof of its forward motor unit spinning into position to automatically guide it to its destination. The truck passes through a metal barricade, gates quickly swinging open and shut, then merges seamlessly with the thronging hordes of automatic vehicles filling the streets outside. Trash blows in heavy drifts, stooped figures occasionally stumbling through it like ancient Arctic explorers.

"Realtime feed?"

"Yes. We shifted one of our surveillance sats from the Han border. Also pulled the building's grid data for the last three months."

"Bodies?"

"Infdrones, low profile. Functionally identical to Clancery facet scouts in your 'Game.' You're all rated master-class on them. I checked. Our inputs might be slightly more . . . intense than what you're used to, though."

"Hate riding scouts," Wind mutters. "Stupid things always run out of ammo when the shit hits the rotor, and the shit *always* hits the rotor."

I shush her, trying not to think about the implications of Game assets that are copies of mil-spec drones in the real, and what Sawyer means by "intense." I'll have to think about it later, but not now. There's an encounter to defeat. I feel myself dropping even deeper into strat mode. Several finger twitches open submenus, overlaying the building with its electrical grid, network configuration, and current floorplan.

"Latency?"

"Low fifties. We have a fib-optic repeater nearby to anchor the carrier."

"Loadout?"

"Standard interface tools. Limited combat capabilities. You'll have ten projectile rounds—twenty-two caliber—three shock-darts, and slightly augmented close quarters. Try not to get into a shootout."

"A shootout with ten deuces? Fuck you, Sawyer. What are we running against?"

"Visual sensor lattice outside. Three roaming platforms inside. Cheap models—they only cover visual spectrum on a one-twenty field of vision. Sensors and platforms are coordinated at a command node on the south side of the building, auto turrets throughout the building trigger off their input. Two corp personnel in the room at all times, cycling every eight hours. They're mainly there to fix any breakdowns in the assemblers. Mostly they hump each other or sleep."

A room on the rotating building in my glasses lights up, the infdrone specs settling into place on the right side of my vision. Orange lines trace the guard drones' semi-random patrol pattern through the interior and exterior, a tangled mess of twists and turns. The majority of the building is taken up by a large open section—the main production floor, filled with the squid-like shapes of the assembler bots, conveyer belts stretching between them. Small ancillary rooms dot the edges, most the same size as the closet I call home.

"What's our target?"

Another room lights up in the northeast portion, orange spaghetti patrol routes coiling tightly around it.

"Shipping records. We need to know which parts of Golgbank are involved in manufacturing these things. That should allow us to pierce the corporate veil. The infdrones have a fifty-terabyte capacity for data storage, and appropriate transfer protocols."

"Hack Golgbank," Slend suggests, her eyes narrowed.

"We've tried," Sawyer's disembodied voice responds. "Still trying, for that matter. They're a major subsidiary of one of the Big Three. They didn't survive by being careless with infosec, and they're too big for us to do a blanket infiltration op."

"Yet you think shipping manifests are going to be in this shitty warehouse in Industan?" I shake my head.

"There's a difference between infosec and a megacorp's lawyers covering its ass," he replies drily. "Records are the lifeblood of any institution. They'll be there. Then we can build a trail."

"If you say so. What's our deniability?"

"None." Sawyer's tone is deadly. "There can be no evidence left behind that we were involved. If you lose a drone, if you leave even a lingering fart, your bodies will be dropped with appropriate silkie gear nearby, and you'll be written off as operators from a rival corp."

"Seems extreme."

"So are atomics. Industan is not on the best of terms with us right now."

Wind's face turns bleak, and my anger rises again.

"I wonder why. Maybe you shouldn't let rioters kill people because of a book."

"Not my department. I take care of external threats. Internal policies are up to the Theocrophant."

"Fuck the Theocrophant."

"I'll pretend I didn't just hear you say that."

"Whatever. It's not like we can say no, is it?"

"No. You've got your team, you've got your price. This isn't a game anymore, Ashley."

"It never was, Sawyer. Just ask Mom."

The hidden voice falls silent. I turn to Wind and Slend.

"You two okay with this? I've gotta do it, but I can find someone else if you want."

"Idiot," Slend says. "Already blackbagged. Only way out is forward."

"Yeah, Slend's right," Wind replies slowly. "We're in it for real now. Besides, we owe it to Brand. Whoever's behind this needs to be stopped." She pauses, face falling once more. "And not just for Brand. If those hoods go off, it's gonna provoke more riots. You know it will. You know who they'll blame. Who they always blame."

I want to tell her it'll be fine, that her family will be okay, but I can't lie to one of my few remaining friends. Instead, I clasp her hand, our gloved fingers intertwining.

"Then we need to make sure they don't go off. It's not like we haven't dealt with permadeath encounters before," I add, trying to draw her back to her usual jubilant self. "Remember Lovecraftia?"

Wind grimaces, but gradually it turns into a smile.

"Pretty sure I'd rather take the eldritch horrors, to be honest. What's the strat, boss?"

I let my hand fall away, fingers twitching open a planning schematic. Wind and Slend both trigger their own glasses, sharing my feed, and I highlight the electrical grid.

"I'm thinking safety dance. They've got one drone at that room all the time, except when the power goes. Check out this junction here. . . ."

12

[Frogging]

"Go."

My voice is quiet, even though the only people who can hear me are Wind and Slend on the commlink. Oh, and Sawyer, of course. No way he's not going to babysit this op, but I made it clear I don't want to hear him—no matter what. We'll live or die on our own skills, and I don't need him second-guessing in my ear in real time. It's going to be hard enough focusing on ghosting the scout.

Scouts aren't particularly complex hapdrones, meter-long low-profile eggs with six segmented legs that can traverse most terrains. Two small domes on the front house the sensor suite and uplink channel, and a thin tube juts slightly out between them—an acoustic-dampened projectile launcher, currently armed with minimal weaponry. Always thought of scouts as a mix between a retro sci-fi spaceship and a cockroach.

Learning how to manipulate a scout through the hapchamber was a complete pain in the ass, though. Turns out recalibrating normal motor functions to operate a nonhuman skin feels kind of like learning to play the piano with one foot and your nose, but it was part of mastering the Game, so I considered it time well spent. Unbidden, my thoughts drift back to the encounter with Hammer, his lethal control of the dragon. What would it be like to wear one of *those* as a skin? What kind of practice did that take?

Focus.

My field of vision is split into three separate images—the first, and largest, my primary sensor feed, the shadowed mass of the Golgbank distribution center rising past a chain-link fence in front of me. It's one of five such buildings facing the street, each a minimally designed box built to keep the outside off of whatever lies within. In the upper corners of my vision are Wind and Slend's feeds, shifting with their movements, a triumvirate I imagine would be incredibly disorienting to anyone not used to running hapdrones in the Game. *Or the military,* I realize belatedly.

Naturally, everything feels like an extension of my body, in a very literal sense, but I'm used to that. I can feel myself sinking into the little scout, my formerly watery skin hardening and smoothing, its electronics my eyes, my muscles its nerves. Slowly, I realize there's something *off* about this compared to the Game. Sensations are coming in a little too hot, wavelengths a frequency band too bright. I'm settling into my new skin too easily, like I've always lived there.

Is this what Sawyer meant by intense?

My thoughts . . . shift.

Slend's feed shows her vantage point atop one of the neighboring buildings with significantly less security, automated vehicles racing along the crowded and dimly lit road, their bumpers inches from each other, weaving through the industrial park. Communication and collision beams flicker out from their sensor clusters, ghostly fingers tangling in an invisible band. I have her up there because she's the clumsiest in this form, perhaps a result of how strongly she's worked on her shell in the real. For this op, she won't need to move much.

Hopefully.

A red targeting bracket floats, then settles on an approaching heavy lifter, stacked container pallets rising from its dented bed. I can hear it query the local satnav for position updates, a petulant whine.

"Three."

Slend's voice is just as quiet as mine.

"Two. One. Firing."

Her body gives a gentle burp, no louder than a cough. Through her eyes, I see the front right tire of the truck shred apart, causing it to careen to the side and into an electrical pole, deuce round instantly crushed by the weight of the lifter, just another piece of scrap. Metal and wood collide, the wood giving way in a splintering crack, bulky transformers exploding in fountaining sparks. Containers slide and tumble across the expressway, bringing movement to a screeching halt. Lights along the entire block go dark.

Perfect.

"Sixty seconds until reboot. Moving."

Just another encounter.

Wind and I smoothly unfold from beneath our carrier, a nondescript delivery vehicle parked across a side street from our target. Servo-assisted limbs propel us easily over the barbed wire fence at the back of the building. Blinded surveillance domes fail to witness our brief flight, their electric lifeblood momentarily cut. Both of us hit the side of the wall almost halfway up, driving our piton-like digits into the concrete in grinding crunches, adding a few more divots to the already acid rain–pitted surface. Quickly, we scrabble up to the roof, mechanical spiders defying gravity.

"Ugh. Comp assist is so *boring*."

Wind, on the other hand, could probably ghost anything.

"Focus, Wind. Forty-five."

"Yeah, yeah." The tip of one of her hands peels back, revealing a small multitool. "Opening vent cover." A small whine sounds, barely louder than a mosquito. "Moving."

Wind climbs through the now-open roof vent, her vision switching to the greenish tinge of active nightvision, and quietly lowers herself into the ducts. I follow right behind.

"Twenty-five."

After a quick scamper, Wind pulls up another vent grate, revealing the factory floor below. Assemblers lie quiescent, their normally frantically twitching limbs drooping like unwatered ferns, ghostly luminescence limning all.

"All you, Ash."

"Moving. Ten."

I drop fifteen meters to the hard concrete below, landing on all six legs, servos absorbing the impact almost noiselessly. Instantly I'm running for the nearest assembler, trying not to notice the pieces of splayed-open hoods lying on the conveyor belt.

They look like the one on Brand . . . after I broke her . . .

No. Focus. Finish the encounter.

I jump up between one of the assemblers and the wall, setting a disposable eye against the peeling paint with my right middle foot. It adheres, then disappears, camo panels activating. It'll melt itself down when we're done, more scrap for the dusty corners. A fourth feed appears in my vision, distorted fish-eye perspective covering the entire factory floor, including all three doors leading in. I drop down and crouch behind the assembler.

"Three. Two. One."

I turn off my nightvision, and block all nonstandard visual frequencies so I can concentrate. Lights blaze forth overhead, the smartgrid finally patching around the momentary blockage we created, and assemblers spring back into motion, spindly limbs running through diagnostic routines with jerking clicks. Satisfied that all is well, they smoothly swing back over the conveyor belt, and it rumbles into motion, insect arms dipping down to do their unthinking work. I continue to wait, watching through my third eye's twisted panorama.

Half a minute later, one of the doors slides open, and a squat shape rolls through. It looks like someone put a saltshaker on wheels. A small red light blinks in the dome covering its top, and it slowly makes its way toward the assembly line.

"Careful, Ash. Don't get exterminated."

"*Focus,* Wind."

The commlink goes silent after her giggle. I resist the urge to shake my sensors and keep watching. Another door opens, then a third, each one admitting a surveillance drone. They spread out among the darting limbs of the assemblers, rolling from one to the next, mobile sentries with deadly sight. I take a deep breath, surprised it doesn't flex my metal thorax.

"Time to go frogging. On the move."

Still watching through the fish-eye, I make my third-perspective body move from its hiding space in a scuttling run, sliding between two of the sentries while their backs are turned. I end up behind another assembler, this one closer to the rear door of the factory floor. The drones pirouette, wheels squealing on the smooth concrete floor, and sweep another area. Once more I move, dancing through their blind spots with silent metal feet, combining different angles of vision effortlessly. Another assembler shields me from view, nearly completed haphoods sliding past its whirring bulk. I ready myself for the last push.

Sentry tires squeal through a turn, and I'm racing to the door, front left manipulator closing on the scratched nickel handle, watching myself standing on two legs, three more legs braced for balance, a sixth extended while the drones stare out at the factory floor separated from my back by no more than five centimeters. If either were to spin even the slightest, to break their protocols with a burst of initiative . . .

A quick twist, both of hand and body, and I'm in the hallway, door quietly shutting behind. I let my vision fade from the assembler floor, and sprint to the highlighted door, third on the left. Twist again, and steal inside.

"I'm in. Wind, you're on sensors. Slend, anything outside?"

"Repair crew's here. Normal."

"Accessing servers."

The tip of my rearmost right leg splits open, physical input jack waiting for an entry point. I scan the server, and find one underneath. The jack slides in without a hitch. Data streams down one side of my view, an endless waterfall of incomprehensible bytes. I shift to a different mouth, reaching out for another listener.

"Jase, you getting this?"

"Yeah. Standard two fifty-six encryption, nothing I can't handle. Gimme a few."

I leave him to his cracking and switch back over to the main group.

"Anything on sensors, Wind?"

"No. Relax, Ash. We got this."

I notice vitals are elevated, pulse twenty beats higher than normal back in the shell.

". . . Sorry. Used to having a fourth."

"Miss Brand," Slend rumbles.

"Yeah, I miss her too," I whisper back. A quick buzz in my ear draws my attention away. Jase.

"What's up?"

"We're in. Going through the shipping lists now. Hoooweee, I didn't know Golgbank was running tech for the Polers. Arctic might melt entirely once they get their hands on that heat."

"They're a bank, Jase, they'll fuck anyone for a profit. Where are we in terms of the hoods?"

"Looking . . . There. Got it. Looks like the original plans came from a silkie hub in Calgon. Big arco, lots of upper shell corps. Downloading exact coordinates now . . ."

Another buzz.

"What is it, Slend?"

"Trouble. Response team. Two tanks and a bird. Spinning up now, ETA three minutes."

"Shit," Wind squawks. "There's no reason for a response team to get here this quick."

"Unless they anticipated a follow-up," I reply. "Golgbank probably got word that their shipment into Ditchtown got hit. Figured someone might try and backtrace them. They couldn't have been sure, though, otherwise they would've had them already here. How are we looking on exfil?"

"Interior bots are still on auto. Patterns haven't changed. If that bird gets above the facility, though, getting out's gonna suck. Sawyer says they're Herc and Raven equivs."

"Fucking dick. Of course there're Game equivs. Fine. We'll burn that bridge when we get to it. Let me know if anything changes."

I switch back over to Jase.

"Jase, do we have what we need?"

"Yeah, I got the location, but I still want to poke around. There's all sorts of interesting stuff in he—"

"No time. A Golgbank crisis team is going to be here in less than two and a half minutes. If they catch us, we're all dead."

"Shit. What should I do?"

"Unless you can take down a hardened recon drone and two mainline battletanks, stay quiet and don't distract me."

"What model is it?"

"What?"

"The recon drone. What model is it?"

I roll my sensor cluster. While I'm sure Jase wants to help, we've been doing this a long time. No one hacks into a Raven without cheats, and this isn't the Game.

"Recon Autonomous Vehicle edition nine, aka Raven. Built by Appho Technologies, a silkie mil-hardware sub, commonly sourced to larger corps and govs. Cruising altitude twenty-five thousand feet, loiter time thirty-six hours, infgathering in radar, lidar, infrared, and fifteen hundred different patents pending, though I don't think that's pertinent. Oh, and it also fires missiles. Fast ones. They'll kill us before you can blink."

"K. Gimme a sec."

"Wait, *what?*"

Another buzz. I curse, and flip back over to the group.

"Talk to me."

"Twenty-second warning on exfil." Slend's voice is calm, unhurried. If I didn't know how to listen, hadn't put my ass on the line with her for the past ten years, I'd never notice the thread of fear hiding in the background of her frequency.

"Shit. Okay, how are we looking on the inside, Wind?"

"Same as before. You'll be able to frogger the drones, but there's no way we're making it out before that Raven gets overhead. Once it does, if it sees us, the Hercs aren't far behind, and good luck dropping *those* with deuces."

"One step at a time. Slend, time?"

"Three. Two. One. Go."

I slide out of the door, senses taut. To my left, a drone trundles down the hallway, scanning the motionless walls. I step in behind it, my feet drifting across the floor like falling leaves. At the end of the hallway, I dart into another room, quickly shutting the door with a steady hand.

"Time?"

"Three. Two. One. Go."

I open the door and slide back out, a different drone passing behind me. I ignore it and sprint around the corner, sensors focused on a cooling vent in the ceiling. Screws twist in their frames, as if by magic, and the grate swings down, a hand from above holding it into place. I leap for the opening, driving the servos in my legs almost past their thresholds in order to generate enough upward velocity, then tuck myself into a streamlined ovoid, hoping I calculated the arc correctly. The edges of the vent vanish behind, my belly scraping to a halt, legs tucked tight to my body, and Wind quickly swings the grate back into position, her hands already tightening the screws. The last one slots into place as another drone rounds the corner, salt shaker body scanning the hallway with a triangular beam of red light. No alarm sounds.

"Yesssss!" Wind crows over the command channel. "That's what I'm talking about. Fucking *perfectly* executed frogger. Wait until the boardshits see—"

"Focus, Wind," I snap, tapping her front. "We're not out yet, and this is still the real. We can't afford to fuck up."

"Sorry, sorry," she mumbles. "Got caught up in the moment."

"How're we looking outside, Slend?"

"Not good. Hercs're here, one front, one behind. Raven's overhead, full eyes. I move, it probably shoots. Local meat squad'll be here in ten."

"Shit. Any brilliant ideas on how to get from here to the truck?"

"Disable the Herc in front. Kill its sensors. Hope the Raven's not looking."

"That's not gonna help," Wind interjects. "They find our slugs in the Herc, they'll know it was an op, and then game over, man. It's gotta look like an accident."

I share Slend's vision. A Hercules class mainline battletank, stubby HV turret swiveling atop four articulated tread legs, secondary fléchette launchers bristling from each side of its body like spines, stands in front of the building, its left sensor suite covering our path to the carrier, its right painting the street it half straddles in strobes of infrared. Behind the building, another Herc scans the scrap-littered area. Above, a speck circles in a tight hourglass, sensor beams constantly probing in deadly sunbeam shafts.

Shit. Between the tanks and the bird, all routes out are covered. I groan.

"Well, crap. I know how to disable the front Herc, but unless we can hit that Raven, it doesn't mean shit. We might be proper fucked this time, ladies."

Sawyer doesn't say a word, at least not to me, but then again, he won't until the op is either over or truly busted. We're not dead yet, but it doesn't look good.

My ear buzzes *again*.

"What *is* it, Jase?"

"Uh, I have control of the Raven. If you can clear the front tank, you should probably be able to get out."

I feel my eyes widening, an unfamiliar sensation itching at their corners, not like any of the sensor data I'm used to interpreting.

"What?"

"Well, turns out one of the VPs of Appho really likes old bootleg yaoi vids, and she, uh, happens to live in one of the dryburbs nearby, orbital commutes to Neo Frisco, and, uh, I may have cracked her comms while she was in Ditchtown waiting for m—for a grayhat to build her a bypass crack, kind of surprising, really, that someone in charge of a corp like that lives here, not to mention such shitty opsec, but her avatar codes were just sitting right there, and it's not like—"

"Jase, I swear, I don't know if I want to kiss you or kill you. Can you blind it?"

"Sure, I've got root through Appho's proprietary update kit. Just say the word and I'll reboot the sensors. Takes them about five seconds to boot back up. Is that enough time? I'll only be able to do it once without letting them know I'm there, their self-diagnostics are pretty hardcore."

"Kiss you it is. When I tell you, start the reboot, *exactly* on my mark. Got it?"

"G-got it."

I switch over to the command channel.

"Slend, on my mark, I want you to sever the middle power line with your deuce. Third pole juncture. Think you can make that shot?"

"In my sleep."

"Good. Exfil after you do. Wind, when she drops the Herc, we've got five seconds to get across the street and into the carrier. Can you keep up?"

"Hah. You better try and keep up with *me*, Ash. Last one inside pays for next month's Game subs."

"Sounds good. Slend, in three . . . two . . . one . . . mark!"

The word has barely left my mouth when I'm already switching over to Jase.

"Boot it!"

I don't wait for acknowledgment, but follow Wind out the exterior vent, hoping that Jase won't let us down. We spend one precious second attached to the wall, screwing the vent back into place, then another launching ourselves at the alley where our carrier awaits. From Slend's eyes, I can see the Herc guarding the front twitching in electronic agony at the power line draped across its sensor suite, fat blue sparks arcing into the air in loud crackles, the street draped in darkness once again. Then she's descending in a swooping rush, the bulk of the carrier enfolding her almost instantly.

Wind and I hit the ground, our segmented legs absorbing the impact with minor complaints, and we streak toward the nondescript delivery hauler parked beneath a burnt-out streetlight. Two seconds. Due to the absence of hellfire raining down on us from above, I'm assuming Jase fulfilled his end of the bargain, but I don't have time to worry about that because all I can focus on is getting to safety before my timer ticks down to zero.

One second. Gritty asphalt beneath my feet/hands, carefully adjusting weight tolerances so I don't carve out telltale gouges from the road.

Half a second. An orange warning symbol pops up, a servo/muscle on the verge of seizing up, but I ignore it. No time to worry about anything but the run.

Tenth of a second. Articulated appendages retract beneath my gleaming ovoid body, and I'm skidding/sliding/diving toward the waiting shelter of the carrier, its bulk looming overhead, Wind by my side.

Zero. We're underneath the hauler, popping ourselves up into its briefly open belly, snug in the magnetic cradles as hatch covers slide beneath us, the Raven's deadly sight sweeping the street once more—but there's nothing to witness except a silently spasming tank. Wind's howls of triumph split the commlink, an ululating cry of victory that pierces my polymer bones.

Fuck.

That was *intense*.

13

[Put On a Smile]

I clumsily pull myself out of the hapsphere, goggles pushed back, white-suited technicians already rushing past to service the delicate components. I didn't ride it as hard as Sarah's, what seems like forever ago, but I can't fault them their diligence. My legs wobble and I squat down, one knee flat on the rusted metal deck, arms braced against the other. It's hard to get used to having four limbs again, harder than normal. Not quite perfectly filtered air caresses my eyes, a hint of brine riding its edges, and the touch of salt hits me with its physical weight, causing my eyes to water. I peel my hood back, feeling sweat in my hair, dead keratin strands on a fleshy shell. Wind lurches up next to me, her gait unsteady, followed shortly by Slend.

"That . . . wow. *Wow.* That was fucking epic, Ash. *We* were fucking *epic.*"

She sprawls out on her back, gasping.

"But *fuck* ghosting scouts."

"Fuck scouts," Slend grunts in agreement, then turns away and vomits a thin stream of bile. I can't blame her. My stomach feels like it's caught in a malfunctioning autowasher, spin cycle set to "adrenaline crash," and my brain's not doing much better. Running nonhuman forms properly takes a toll, and once again I wonder how Hammer felt in the dragon's skin. Wonder if his comedown is the same as this.

Booted footsteps sound from behind, a steady staccato pace. Wearily, I push myself upright, still on one knee.

"Sawyer."

"Ashley. Good work. Your mother would've been impressed."

"Mom isn't allowed to handle anything more dangerous than noodles because of what you did to her, Sawyer. What the hell was going on with those scout senses? That didn't feel at all like the Game."

"I told you it was going to be intense. Our gear gives you *all* the input, Ashley."

I shiver, still not fully myself. If that's what it's like every time . . .

"Was the op a success?"

"Yes. We're going over the data now. You and your team should get some rest."

"Piss off. You don't tell us what to do."

My stomach growls, energy burn overtaking the adrenaline, squashing the body displacement. I pretend like I didn't hear it. Sawyer, to his credit, does likewise. I creak into a standing position.

"We're gonna get some food. You better have a worthwhile kitchen here. C'mon, ladies, let's hit the showers first."

Slend and I offer a hand to Wind, pulling her upright, all of us leaning on each other, hot water our only goal.

Sawyer doesn't say anything as we stumble off, and I almost begin to think he might have a heart. Then I remember Mom, how many walks she must have made like this, losing a little bit more of herself after each ghost, and suddenly it's all I can do not to add my vomit on the floor next to Slend's.

The other two feel me tense up, and shift so they're supporting more of my weight.

"Something wrong, Ash?" Wind whispers, her head touching mine.

"Let's just get to those showers," I croak back. I can't talk about this. Not so soon after an op. Not without water and food, without something to make me feel human again.

Mercifully, they both remain silent, Slend bumping the locker room door open with a shaking elbow. A pile of towels sits on one of the splintering wooden benches, brown, shapeless robes next to them, wireframe lockers stretching along the walls, but other than that the room is empty, no sign of any gummie presence.

"Of course. Can't contaminate their precious 'purity,'" I hiss, tearing my suit off in agonizing slow motion, letting it crumple to the floor. I snatch a towel and stagger over to a shower, violently wrenching the knob. Water jets from the small spout above, cool at first, then warm, then painfully hot, steam misting into the white-tiled room and obscuring the walls. I hear Wind and Slend join me, adding their own splashing groans to the clouding soup.

I lose myself for a while, letting the beating spray wash away my sweat and pain, my thoughts and memories. I am nothing but the pressure of wet heat, a shapeless mote in an unending sea. Floating on a cumulus of nonexistence, gray currents swirling my—

". . . sh. Ash. *Ash.*"

Reality snaps back in, along with Wind's voice. I sigh.

"What is it, Wind?"

"We going to talk about what set you off out there? I've never seen you like that. I thought you were gonna try and delete Sawyer."

"Looked bad," Slend opines.

I reach for the soap, nothing more than a thin bar of fat and lye, rubbed smooth by countless hands before me. Lather spreads over my body. I examine the shower room, but between the water and steam, we should be safe from eavesdroppers.

"That run. Did anything about it feel . . . *wrong* to you?"

"I was a bit more disoriented than usual coming out of the scout, but other than that it was great," Wind chirps, scrubbing under her armpits. "Felt like I was really in control, in the groove."

Slend nods.

"Run was good. *After* sucked."

I lean back under the water, rinsing the soap off, trying to feel clean.

"It didn't feel . . . different? Compared to the Game? Like you were getting sucked into the drone? Like it was weird coming back out into a different body?"

Slend frowns.

". . . Yeah. Don't like scouts."

Wind raises an eyebrow, water sluicing down her dark skin.

"Now that you mention it, yeah. When I was in, I was *in*. Thought it was just because of the circumstances, but . . . yeah. Why?"

"It . . . made me think of Mom. When we were walking away from Sawyer. Of what she had to go through during the Dubs." I gently pound a fist against the wall. "We were only ghosting for half an hour. They had her running sixteen-hour days, weeks at a time. Months. Assault drones, recon drones, terror drones, anything they could shove her into. I found her service record when she first came back, before she junked everything. Before she finished breaking."

I don't mention the things that weren't in her record, words the gummies didn't want committed to paper.

Wind turns her water off and grabs a towel, shivering.

"That sucks, Ash. Ultra sucks. You think it's going to happen to us?"

"Don't know. But we sure as shit shouldn't trust Sawyer. We need to figure a way out of this *quick*."

"Jailbreak?" Slend asks, turning her own water off.

"Not yet. Still have to secure a way back to Ditchtown. Based on the sights and smells, plus how Sawyer got me and Jase here, we're on some kind of petro rig, probably methclath, which means we need a boat. Let's recon first. Figure out how many are on board, what our options are. Then we can move if we need to."

"Sounds good. Food first?"

"Yeah. Be there in a sec."

I twist the water off, my other arm leaning against the gritty tile wall. The shower helped a little bit. Maybe some food will help a little more. I towel myself dry and walk back into the changing room, then try to stifle my laughter. Wind is practically swimming in her robe, its arms and legs ending a good half a meter past her hands and feet, extra fabric twisted around her head in a crude covering. Slend is the exact opposite, brown fabric straining to close in front of her chest and waist, elbows and knees clearly visible, other parts nearly so.

"Why—" I cough, still laughing. "—why don't you two switch robes?"

Wind's jaw juts out from beneath her makeshift burka.

"I like this one."

Slend crosses her arms, causing several seams to split.

"Same."

I shake my head, some cheer returning to my heart. If they want to make the gummies uncomfortable, well, we all fight back in our own ways, and I'm certainly not the one to stop them. With a quick pull, I rip the sleeves off the remaining robe, then put it on, using one of the torn off pieces as a crude bandanna for my still-wet hair, bare arms tingling in the cool air. Hapgloves and glasses slide into place, though I still feel naked without my blade. I motion to my friends.

"Okay, let's go get some food. Eyes on everything."

Several minutes later we're seated at a rickety metal table in a dingy cafeteria, low-energy glowstrips buzzing across the ceiling, multiple trays of food from the printer in front of each of us. The selection wasn't terrible, but neither was it top of the line. Functional food, designed to keep soldiers functional. We begin the process of refueling, pushing blandly inoffensive proteins and carbohydrates into our guts, the room silent except for our lip-smacking gulps.

At the other tables, uniformed gummie soldiers gawk in our direction, their own food forgotten. All twenty-five of them are male.

Fucking Sawyer. He said we'd be isolated. This another spook game?

I let loose a loud belch, trying to push the discomfort level even higher. Across from me, Slend shifts her weight to one side, then rips a fart that sounds like a machine gun going off. Someone drops a fork. It lands with a tinny clang. Wind nonchalantly tosses a chunk of protein in the air and skewers it with her knife, then nibbles the edges daintily. A chair scrapes across the floor, and a shadow falls over our table.

I look up into the face of a young gummie officer, all rounded curves and pale skin, dull camo not quite loose enough for his softly muscular form. Hesitantly, he lifts a hand in greeting.

"Are . . . are you . . ." he stammers, suddenly nervous, eyes darting side to side behind his standard-issue military AR glasses. I stare at him dispassionately, chewing a mouthful of meat and beans, waiting for the questions, the abuse. *Are you supposed to be here? What's wrong with your clothes? How dare you sully our pure space? When will you convert to righteousness?* I wait for him to make his move, to force me to put him in his place.

"Are you . . . Ashura? From the Game? Leader of SunJewel? Sorry if this is weird, I found a picture of you in the real, I know that sounds like stalking, but I *love* you guys!"

I almost choke, neurons crackling and short-circuting in my brain, food seizing the opportunity to go down the wrong tube. A coughing fit ensues. Wind slaps me on the back, giggling under her breath.

"That's—" I dislodge a particularly irksome piece of faux-steak in a racking wheeze. "Yeah, that's me."

He slides into the seat next to Slend, eyes shining, glancing back and forth at all of us. Slend continues eating, unperturbed, arm muscles flexing with every lift of her fork. The muted hum of conversations starts up throughout the cafeteria.

"Then *you* must be Wind, and *you* must be Slend! I stream you guys all the time! Oh man, when that dragon popped up, and I saw it was Hammer, I thought you were screw—" He looks around hastily, then resumes. "Excuse my language . . . thought you were in big trouble for sure. What a fight! My friends were *so* mad they missed the livestream."

"You're . . . a fan?" I ask. He nods eagerly.

"Ever since you guys took down Neo-Cthulhu-Ultra in the Kaiju facet. I was in basic then, learning how to ghost. Been watching ever since. Not much to do out here between patrols, and your streams rock. Best teamwork on the ladder."

"They let you watch our streams?"

"Let us? Heck, they're practically required lessons by some of the instructors at officer's school. We spent four days dissecting your tactics during the Mittani event on CCP. The way you were able to split IonSeal's defensive fortifications without taking a single casualty . . . it was incredible. I don't know if it would work in the real the same way, but it was amazing to watch."

I take a drink of water, still trying to wrap my mind around this unexpected conversation. He smacks his forehead with an open palm.

"Oh, but here I am being rude; I haven't even introduced myself. I'm Skyler Chaddington the Third, first lieutenant, BP second company. We're off-shift, just finished up a patrol. Nailed a couple silkie auto-smugglers, chock full of contraband. It was my team's recon drones that spotted them. Call me Sky."

His earnest, stupid name, combined with his earnest, stupid nature, loosens something inside me I didn't even know was compressed. *This kid's a burbie through and through, serving on the Wall, and he . . . likes us?* I offer my hand across the table.

"Ash. Nice to meet you, Skyler. Sky."

He shakes my hand gingerly, as if unable to believe it's actually happening. I make sure not to crush his fingers.

"W-wow. I never thought I'd get a chance to meet *the* Ashura herself, along with her team." He pulls his hand free, looking at it in wonder.

"Make sure you wash that at some point," Wind says, still smiling. "You don't know where she's been."

"Wind!" Damn irreverent Hajj girl.

Skyler laughs nervously, as if unsure whether he's allowed to or not, then looks at the three of us.

"So, what is it you're doing here? Didn't you guys just clinch the ladder? Oh, and can I get a selfie for my socials? My friends'll never believe me otherwise."

Oh, crap. Sawyer said we weren't supposed to talk to anyone.

"Uhhh, well, we were—"

A hand falls on my shoulder.

"Ashley and her friends were on a private boating cruise, celebrating their victory, and unfortunately their vessel foundered," Sawyer says in a friendly tone, like a paternal uncle dropping in on a conversation. Laugh lines surrounding his eyes back up the lie, though not his irises. The void lurks within those merciless orbs. "Luckily, one of our esteemed Border Patrol ships was close enough to pick up the distress call, and brought them back here to recuperate. After all, it would be a tragedy to lose the inestimable SunJewel Warriors, champions of Infinite Game, bringers of glory to the Theocrophant, right after their most recent triumph."

"General Sawyer, sir!" Skyler shoots to his feet, hand flashing up in a razor-sharp salute. "Apologies, sir! I did not notice you enter the room, sir!"

"At ease, Lieutenant." Sawyer waves a hand. "You are a Game afficionado, correct? On your first deployment?"

"Sir, yes sir!"

"Then it's only natural you would want to meet these three, whom you so quickly recognized." Sawyer's lips tighten the barest fraction. "Though I must confess, I thought your squad was scheduled to eat in the southwest cafeteria today."

Somehow, Skyler stands even straighter.

"Printer malfunction in the southwest cafeteria, sir! Just came off patrol, and regulations state that all troops must replenish physical reserves as quickly as possible in case of emergency, sir! I checked the duty board and saw this cafeteria was empty, sir!"

"Excellent initiative," Sawyer murmers, his fingers twitching inside his hapgloves, and Skyler relaxes. I don't. I get a feeling the young lieutenant might end up another "training accident" statistic, but there's nothing to be done right now. No reason to worry Skyler about anything more than not embarrassing himself in front of the general. Sawyer puts a hand on the kid's shoulder. "Why don't you take a memory with the ladies, with proper filters, of course, and then I'm afraid I'm going to have to take them to get some rest before their trip back to the mainland."

"Sir, yes sir!" Skyler beams, then scrambles to put himself in a position where his glasses, now in hand, can catch all four of us. One smiling selfie later, he bounds off, like an overeager puppy. I pop a last chunk of kelp-bread into my mouth, then stand, Wind and Slend following suit. We trail Sawyer out of the cafeteria and back to the hapsphere chamber. Technicians continue their scurrying dance around the dull gray globes, various arcane instruments appearing and vanishing from dented toolboxes.

"I told you not to talk to anyone."

"He started it," I reply, folding my arms. "Your troops, your problem. Why'd you let him take a picture?"

"Because if I hadn't, he would've posted to his socials anyway, and that would look even more suspicious. No plan survives—"

"Contact with the enemy, yeah, I've read von Moltke too. Didn't know your own troops were the enemy, though. What's the plan now?"

Sawyer walks up a battered flight of stairs and ushers us into a room. Our clothes lie on a table inside.

"Information is the enemy, Ashley, information we do not want our enemies to consider meaningful. You and your team in a top-of-the-line drone station with worldwide linkups is meaningful to a select group of very dangerous people, and Lieutenant Chaddington does not keep his socials scrubbed quite so thoroughly as I would like. There is a trail, miniscule, but existing, that can be followed back here."

He points toward the clothes, then turns his back. Slend rolls her eyes and we start changing.

"I've already sunk a small craft several kilometers from Ditchtown, an off-the-books asset, in case one of the Big Three or Industan come looking. Han is undoubtedly already looking, but they snoop everywhere. I'm sending the three of you back—I wanted to keep you here for the duration of the op, but that looks to be impossible now. Instead, we will assume that the story of your boat capsizing is the truth, and you are fortunate to have survived long enough to be picked up by an automated Border Patrol cruiser."

"What about Jase?" The ice in my voice matches his own.

"Consider him . . . necessary to our efforts here. He will be treated well, and he'll help our scientists tease the secrets out of that piece of tech."

"A hostage."

"Yes. That too. Keep an eye on your messages. I'll send you further instructions once we've gathered enough info on the next target. In the meantime, I expect you to act normally. Log in to the Game for your dailies, make note on your socials of how embarrassing losing the boat was, how fortunate you were to be *briefly* rescued by the Border Patrol, and above all, do *not* let anyone so much as even *smell* a hint of what happened in Industan, or things will end very badly. For all of us."

"Put on a smile and lie for our lives?" Wind asks sarcastically, fitting her burkha around her shoulders.

"Another day in Ditchtown," Slend responds, eyes tight behind her glasses. Idly she clenches her hands, muscles popping up and down her arms.

"Exactly." Sawyer's voice reveals no hint of emotion. "Play the role you're required to play, and we might just make it out of this alive."

"There's a difference between making it out *alive*, and making it out *intact*, Sawyer." I strap the sheath onto my leg and slide the blade home.

"Yes. There is. Now go, the LC is waiting. I'll be in touch."

In deference to the fact he still has Jase, I wait until he's out the door before I call him an asshole.

I make sure he can still hear me, though.

14

[Knots]

I step off the gangplank and into the Brown, waiting for my eyes to adjust from the flash of dazzling late afternoon sunlight outside. Wind and Slend were dropped off earlier—Wind near her parents' place in Westspire, Slend in the Rust. I don't know why Slend chooses to live there, especially after our continued success in the Game, but then again, who am I to judge, stuffed in my three-by-five closet.

Icons blink to life in my view, overlaying the dim halls, connection to the Web and regional 'Net reestablished. Lots of public messages on the socials, couple private ones just for me. I skim the socials first—fans glad I made it off the boat before it sank; boardshits wishing we'd all gone down with it; global news of more "hostilities" in Industan, just one of the many slow burn wars constantly churning in the background; another silkie corp merger and "rebranding" between two subsidiaries of the Big Three, a quieter sort of war than drones and bombs but just as deadly. Fashion news from the UPC style algorithms, this season's wear incorporating lots of curves and the old maple flag, reds on whites. Blood on snow in the Arctic, a Han hauler raided by Polers as it made its way through one of the shipping lanes topping the world, refugees doing whatever it takes to survive. Local news from Ditchtown, a medical ward in the Rust burned down, looting and small riots in Northspire, a rise in missing persons postings.

I wave the socials away. Just the everyday noise of too many people sharing too small a room. A quick finger tap opens my private messages. The first one's from Johnny, a terse two words.

"Doin' okay?"

I realize my feet are already walking the route toward his shop, weaving through the maze of corridors with a mind of their own. I need to let him know what happened, where Jase is at. I dash off a quick text reply letting him know I'll be there shortly. The next message offers me an unbelievable deal on all-natural male enhancement, guaranteed to add length *and* girth. Straight to junk, and a spam filter update. The third one's from Hammer, wanting to get together and talk, sending the usual stupid grin across my face. I make a mental note to message him as soon as I'm done at Johnny's.

I enter, the beads rattling in counterpoint to the sounds of sizzling noodles and shifting woks. Johnny fills a bowl and places it on the counter. Gratefully, I grab it and a pair of chopsticks, but don't take my accustomed place on one of the battered stools.

"You got a minute—private?"

Without a word, he hits a button on the stove, turning the electric coils off, and dumps the rest of the noodles in a bowl for himself. Another button drops a latticed metal barricade across the entrance—I know from memory that the AR sign on its front reads BUSY, BACK WHENEVER. We walk through the storage closet and into Jase's workroom, still in the same state of disrepair as when the drones dragged us out . . . shit, a little more than half a day ago. It feels like half a year. I slide into a chair, bowl warm in my hands. Johnny leans against a workbench.

"Some heavy stuff went down." In between bites of noodles, I describe what Jase and I found in the haphood, the raid in Industan, Sawyer keeping Jase on the rig. Johnny's eyes narrow imperceptibly at Sawyer's name, but other than that he doesn't say a word.

". . . and that's about the gist of it. Sawyer said he'd let us know when it's time for the next op, that we need to act normal until then, but I don't like it. I don't want Jase getting sucked into that world, and running those scouts felt . . . wrong. Like they were taking something away."

Johnny taps his index finger against his leg, almost like he's triggering a firing stud.

"Rig sounds well defended. Got a location on it?"

"No," I reply, trying not to sound frustrated. "Other than that Border Patrol squad showing up in the cafeteria, Sawyer's opsec was superb. They kept us in the cruiser for almost four hours each way, and it made way too many course changes to keep track of, especially without my gear up and running. That rig could be right offshore, or halfway up the coast. If we hadn't run into that squad, we'd still be there."

"Have to get back to it, then."

"Yeah, but that means we're going there under Saywer's terms. Again."

"Can't always get what you want, kid."

"Seems to run in the family," I grumble, pushing some noodles into my mouth.

"Seems to." Johnny inclines his head. "Be careful with those drones. Hate to see Sawyer do to you what he did to Naomi. I still owe her."

I try not to frown. Johnny's used Mom's name twice in the

many years that I've known him, and each time it was when things were as serious as a heart attack. Not a good sign for where he thinks this adventure is headed.

"I'll do my best. I don't plan to be in them a second longer than necessary."

"Wise. Let me know if I can help."

"Will do, Johnny, thanks. Appreciate the noodles—I'll let you know what comes up . . . ?"

He nods, and I exit the workroom, placing my bowl on the counter. The grate clatters back up into the ceiling and I return to the Brown, heading for my room. The trip passes uneventfully, couriers making their usual rounds through the stairwells, wizened old techheads stretching their legs and playing mah-jongg under fitful lamps, the bustling flow of hidden people working hidden lives. It doesn't feel like home, but it feels . . . alive. A place struggling for a living, not one waiting to die.

I latch my door behind me and sprawl, as much as sprawling is possible, onto my mattress, fingers already plugging in the jammer and opening up a channel.

<<Ham. You there?>>

<< . . . Ash! It's good to hear from you, I was starting to worry. You haven't been on for a while.>>

I chuckle, thinking about how being gone from the Game for less than a day was enough to make Hammer concerned. *What does that say about my playing habits?* Though, to be fair, normally after an encounter like the one with the dragon we'd be tearing through the rest of the content nonstop, so I can see where he's coming from.

<<Sorry, some stuff came up I had to deal with. You wanted to chat?>>

<<Yeah. Usual spot?>>

<<Sounds good.>>

I close the channel and open up a link to the crypto-room, not bothering with my full hapsuit, only the hood, and of course my gloves. I'm not really in the mood to get physical, not with all this other crap hanging overhead. The gatekeeper, this time wearing the skin of a giant ant in a tophat and monocle, checks my code, then passes me through. Seconds later, Hammer sits across from me, the endless tables stretching out around us.

"So what's up with my favorite dev?" I try to keep my voice light.

"I . . ." Hammer pauses, then stops. Odd. This kind of reticence isn't like him.

"I wanted to make sure you were okay. Out there."

"What, you mean the boat thing? It was just a little water, Ham. Embarrassing, for sure, but nothing more. Didn't even get any needlefish bites."

I hate lying to him, but the fewer who know the truth, the better. Johnny, I trust with my life. Hammer, I trust with my heart, but that's not the same.

"It's . . . more than that. Ash, do you remember when we first met?"

"Yeah, of course. Masquerade facet, the Midsummer Ball, couple years ago. You tried to lure me away from the objective, as I recall."

His lips turn up into a half smile.

"And I almost had you too. Ten more seconds and you would have missed your chance at the duke."

"I almost let you. That's why I came back after I poisoned his wine. The conversation was far more interesting than whatever that plotline was supposed to be. Finally someone other than the girls I could talk the Game with. Like, *really* talk."

Hammer laughs.

"I'll never forget the look on all the other players' faces

when he keeled over, right in the middle of a waltz. They couldn't believe there was a vulnerability window that early. Most of them packed up and went back to Candyland for the night."

"Whereas we"—I take his hand—"spent it dancing. Which was lovely."

"It was." He sighs, smile disappearing. "Ash, I have to tell you something, and you're probably not going to like it. No, you're definitely not going to like it."

My heart pounds. *He's going to give up on us, he doesn't want to deal with my bullshit, I'm going to lose him, fuck fuck fu—*

"I've been tracking you since two days ago, when you told me about Mikelas. I thought he might try something. I saw what happened on the bridge. I . . . understand why you did what you did, but I'm worried about you. What's really going on, Ash?"

Fuck. He's right. I don't like it. I don't like being caught in the lie, don't like that Hammer might get involved, that he's good enough to track me without a single indicator popping up in the Web. No one should have been able to track me, not with Jase's upgrades and the programs I bought. Anger starts its familiar march through my chest.

"Why were you following me? I told you I had it under control. *How* did you follow me?"

He holds up a placating hand.

"I was worried, and I . . . see the 'Nets a bit differently than you do."

"What the fuck does *that* mean?"

"I'll get to that, I promise. As to why I was following you, I know it's creepy, but after what you told me the other day, I was worried what Mikelas might try and do to you. What he *did* try and do to you. So I wrote a little script to notify me if anything looked . . . off."

He laughs, bitterly.

"For all the good it did. Damn thing didn't notify me until they'd already closed in on you. It's a good thing you handled it, Ash, because all I could do was watch. I had no way of helping, nothing that would get there in time. I've never felt so fucking useless in my life. I thought about breaking into your comms, but by the time I noticed what was going on, it was already too late and I didn't want to distract you."

"At least you're smarter than Kiro," I mutter. He looks at me questioningly, and I motion for him to go on, a curt gesture.

"I promise, if I thought I could've made a difference, I would've done anything. *Anything*. I can't even imagine what that was like for you."

"It was pretty shitty, yeah. You know what else is shitty? Having your boyfriend spy on you. When else have you been watching me?" I ask, angrily. "And why didn't you tell me before this? Something like that could get you into deep trouble, even with the silkies."

"Never before that, I promise. I know privacy's important to you. Hell, it's important to me too. Everyone needs a space where they can be someone else." His expression grows distant. "Everyone."

"And what about after? You said you never spied on me before, but what about after?"

He shifts guiltily, eyes downcast.

"I kept watching after you took care of the boardshits, to make sure you were okay. The, uh, the sink, that was me."

"And after that?"

Ham looks up at me, gaze piercing.

"And after that. Which is what I'm most worried about. Ash, a gummie drone squad disappeared you and your friend for half a day, and when you got back, it was only you. What's going on?"

Shit. Shit shit shit.

"Have you told anyone? Please tell me you haven't told anyone."

"No, of course not. Ash, whatever it is you're tangled up in, I can help. I *want* to help. I have . . . some resources. I know what it's like to be alone—and I don't want you to feel that way, facing . . . whatever this is."

"I'm not alone," I say absentmindedly. "I have my team." My voice firms. "I don't want you involved—I want to know you're safe. This is my business. I'll take care of it." I stare back, not letting him look away. "Also, you didn't answer my other question. How did you follow me? What's with 'I see the 'Nets differently'?"

Hammer shifts in his seat, brow wrinkling.

"I, ahh, wasn't entirely honest with you, Ash. Back when we first met."

I arch an eyebrow.

"Oh, really? About what?"

"I told you my dad was involved with the Game, that he helped get me my position as a dev. Remember?"

"Yeah, I remember. So what? A little nepotism isn't anything out of the ordinary in this day and age. Cost of business; silkies, gummies, Han, hell, everyone does it."

"My dad's the executive VP in charge of research and development for WGSK. They own the sub-corp that makes the Game. GameCore. He's actually one of the original developers."

I feel my jaw drop, trying to process the absurdity of his statement. He can't be serious.

"Your dad. Is the executive VP. In charge of research and development. For WGSK. And they own. GameCore. Which he built."

He nods, looking miserable.

"Your *dad*. Is in *charge*. Of research and development for *one of the Big Three*?! Fucking fuck, Ham, what the fuck am I supposed to do with that? That seems like a *pretty big fucking deal,* maybe *something you mention* to the girl you're sleeping with, a girl who happens to live in a *gummie fucking protectorate* that's literally a hairsbreadth from war with the fucking *silkies* on any given day!"

I'm almost shouting by the time I finish, and I have to resist the urge to reach across the table and start strangling him. My beautiful, intelligent, *idiot* lover. What the *shit*. Why can't I just have a normal fucking relationship for *once* in my goddamn life?

I force myself to take some deep breaths, calm down as best I can.

"Why didn't you tell me earlier? Also, what does that have to do with tracking me?"

He looks down at the table, then slides a picture over to me.

"What's this?"

"Open it."

I tap it open, not sure at first what I'm looking at. It seems to be some sort of holding tank in a dark room, filled with a clear liquid. Wires stretch through its interior, connected to a shriveled and pallid form, limbs waving gently in response to unseen currents. Control panels blink steadily along its length, incomprehensible charts and graphs tracking data I assume is important. A tall man with pale hair, an expensive-looking suit covering his thin frame, comes in and lays a hand on the outside of the tank, then turns to the readouts. He scans them for several minutes, then leaves. I turn my attention back to Hammer.

"I don't get it."

"That's me."

"Nice suit. What's in the tank?"

"Me. It's where I'll be for the rest of my life."

It hits me. Hammer isn't the man in the suit. The person I've known these past two years, the lover I've shared so much with—touched, slept with—the other half of my soul is . . . *this*. A broken shape twisting in a tube. He raises his hand with that preternatural grace, and all of a sudden it's too much. The lies, both his and mine. The memories that never seem to go away, no matter how deeply I bury them. My anger shifts to pain, ghostly grips of other men haunting my skin, and I have to run, escape, be anywhere else but here.

"I . . . I'm sorry . . . I can't do this right now . . ."

"Ash!"

His cry fades with the room and once again I'm sitting in my tiny closet, walls seeming to press in around me. Sweat drips down my body and I tear the goggles off in a rush. I have to leave, move, do something, go somewhere, be someone else, if not forever, then at least for now. My feet trace a path through the corridors that my eyes don't see, mind whirling in on itself, and then a familiar voice sounds.

"Hey, Ash, everything okay?"

I look up into Sarah's smiling face, her hands busy locking the entrance to her hapspheres, done for the day. Something in my heart jumps.

". . . No, Sare. It's not. Want to grab a drink?"

"With you, honey? Any time. C'mon, we can hit up the Acid Burn, should still be early enough to grab a seat."

She links her arm through mine, gently pulling me through the bustling nighttime corridor, and the physicalness of her contact sends a jolt of electricity through my skin. It feels exactly the same as a hapsuit, but in my mind I know it's different. We don't say anything as she leads our way through Highrise, groups of people in brightly colored outfits eagerly making their way to various clubs and diversions, their happy chatter bouncing off the tiled walls, and I'm grateful for her silence. I want . . . something. Anything.

Sarah, arm still linked with my own, halts outside a doorway with a gaudy AR sign, the words ACID BURN dissolving letter by letter and then roaring back into flames. She nods at the bouncer, a burly guy in tight clothing who I could drop in my sleep, and he motions us through. Inside, the heavy chatter of a busy bar fills the air, muted lights providing just enough light to not trip over the scattered chairs and couches, the clink of glasses like a swaying chandelier. Sarah snags two stools at the bar, a dark expanse of wood, and motions me into one. I sit and lean my head into my hands, dimly aware of her putting an order in with the bartender. Gently, her hand falls on my shoulder.

"So, what's the deal, girl?"

A pair of glass tumblers arrive in front of us, mild yellow liquid filled with intense swirls of red, and I slam mine back, a burning trail of ice that expands through my stomach in a familiar sting. With a soft burp, I place the tumbler back on the bar. Sarah laughs.

"Okay, that's a hell of an answer, even though you're supposed to sip those, but if it's going to be that kind of night . . ."

She slams hers back and coughs, then motions to the bartender again.

"Next round's on you. What're you buying us?"

"Same thing," I mumble, tapping over some creds. The bartender vanishes back into the chaos of drink-making, and I straighten up a bit, facing Sarah. "Same thing every damn time, in this same shitty world. Trying to survive, Sare, and no one making it any easier." I run a hand through my hair and lean back, not quite tipping over the stool. "Especially not me."

Another pair of drinks arrive in front of us, but this time I take a small sip. Can't afford to get too drunk and perform poorly in the Game tomorrow. Sarah matches my sip, and looks at me over the top of her glass.

"Now this is *definitely* not the Ash that I know, wallowing in self-pity and shit. Hell, I just saw that girl solo a dragon a couple days ago, and *everyone* knows that's impossible."

I take another sip, feeling the warm glow spreading through my body.

"Some things are tougher than dragons, Sare."

"Yeah? Like what?"

Like my brother jumping in bed with boardshits. Like my boyfriend revealing he's stuck in a test tube for the rest of his life. Like the end of the goddamn world.

"Like figuring out what this is. Between us. I have a boyfriend, Sare."

"Lots of people have boyfriends. Lots of people have girlfriends too. All I know is . . ." She takes another sip. "I like the way you don't give a fuck about what other people want you to do. You do what *you* want to do."

I sigh.

"Do I?"

She chuckles.

"Oh, honey. You have no idea. You know that word's already gotten around about what happened on that bridge, right?"

I tense, but she pats me on the hand.

"Relax, Ash. Every woman in this miserable place probably wants to buy you a drink for what you did to that fucker, and probably most of the men. Hell, I wish I could have done it myself. Back when he used to frequent my place . . ." She trails off, eyes hardening, then shakes her head and takes another drink. "But that's a long story. You're the one who went and did something about it, even when everything was against you." Sarah gives me a smoldering look. "And yeah, I want to get into your pants. I'd say that's been pretty obvious."

I flush, heart lurching, covering my heated cheeks with another sip of the increasingly tasty drink. Sarah laughs, a peal of merriment.

"Oh, Ash, I'm not going to do anything you don't want to do. If you're not interested, just say so. It's not going to hurt my feelings. There are plenty of fish in the sea."

"It's . . . it's not that, Sare . . . it's just . . ."

It's just Hamlin will never be able to give me this kind of contact in the real. He'll never hold my hand, not without a hapsuit between us.

"I think we could have fun, Ash." Sarah's tongue darts out, moistening her lips, and I watch, entranced, as she leans in. "I think we could have a *lot* of fun." Suddenly, we're kissing, her tongue brushing against mine, her lips hot and firm on my own. Just as suddenly, we're apart, her eyes locked on mine, a sad smile dancing at the corners of her mouth.

"But I don't think you want only fun. I think you want something real, something that anchors you to someone else. And that's something I don't think I can give you."

What do I want? Hamlin can never cheat on me in the real. He can hold my hand as anything, be anyone. I'm the one with power in this relationship, maybe my only relationship where that's ever been true.

I stare at her, my mind and body reeling, emotions on overload. The physical sensation, the rawness, so different than my life before, so different than ghosting to make ends meet with Ryeen, so different than the enormity of what I now realize is Ham, even though this contact is one we'll never be able to share, but what does that matter in the face of everything else we can?

That's what I want. That's what I've always wanted. Hamlin.

I pull her in for another kiss, savoring one last moment, then push myself away and finish my drink.

"Thank you, Sare."

She tips her tumbler at me in a salute.

"Of course, Ash. Now go. You've got someone I think you need to talk to. I'll see you tomorrow?"

"Of course, Sare." I grin. "Same time, same place."

She blows a kiss at me and I stride out of the bar, knots of happy people lighting the way back to my room.

"Hamlin . . ."

We're back in the crypto-room, his response to my request almost instant. He looks up at me, face tense. Guarded. Like he's expecting me to hit him, use my perfectly honed muscles to smash his carefully crafted visage. Like I can't see the pain in his eyes. Before I can say anything, he's talking, words tumbling out, eyes flicking back down to the table, away from my own.

"I'm sorry, Ash. I'm so sorry. It's why I didn't tell you who my dad was. Who I am. I was born paralyzed, polio mutation. Apparently it first showed up when they stopped vaxxing. Virus finally figured out how to nullify maternal antibodies. My mom wanted to abort, but my dad wouldn't—he made her carry me. Couldn't lose his precious heir, and obviously the laws are what they are, even in the west. They divorced a year later. I don't talk to either of them that much. Mom's just . . . yeah. Dad's too obsessed with trying to regain his place on the corp track. The board'll overlook a divorce or two, but no one wants a cripple in position to inherit."

I feel his words wash over me, the baring of his soul, and I let my anger go. I've made my choice, and it was no choice at all.

"Shit, I'm . . . I don't . . ." I suck in a breath, then release it. "That sucks."

He shrugs, shoulders still tight.

"I'm luckier than a lot of other people. Death rate was in the hundreds of thousands before they figured out another vaxx. They stuck most of those affected in camps to die. No profit in curing them back then. My dad had the creds to hook me up with a state-of-the-art life-support system, and before I was old enough to talk, he'd used his exile to the 'games' division to focus on building the tech to allow me to interface with the 'Nets. Bunch of contacts in my brain, even better than haptics, not that I'm ever outside to know the difference.

"You want to know how I followed you? I grew up on the 'Nets, Ash. I grew up in the Game. This—" He waves a hand, encompassing everything around us. "—is where I live. It's my house, my backyard, my dreams and my nightmares. I'll never be anything outside, but in here, I can fly. Taking control of some spyeyes in the Brown is like breathing." He laughs, grim. "Not that I can do that on my own either."

I reach across the table and take his hand. Startled, he looks up at me.

"But why didn't you just tell me? I'm not going to pretend this is easy, but . . . shit, Ham, I love you. Ever since that first day we met. You know that. You *listen* to me, the only person who ever has."

"You say that you love me, but that's in here. In the Game. You can't love what I am in the real."

The bitterness in his voice is startling.

"This body is a lie, Ash." He gestures to himself. "Oh, I've earned my abilities, but not like you. Nothing I have translates. In the real, I'll never hold you in my arms, never walk with you on a beach, never give you kids, never *touch* you. Hell, I don't even know what a beach really feels like. I think even to my own father I'm not much more than a continuation of his work with the corp, a way to vindicate his career, give himself a *real* legacy the board can't ignore. He only visits once a year, and it's to lecture me on my responsibilities, wearing his haphood like it physically hurts him. Like *I* physically hurt him, just by reminding him what I am in the real. He keeps talking about his plans for me, how he wants me to experience everything the world has to offer, but he can barely even look at me."

I squeeze his hand, wondering what my own dad thinks when he thinks of me—if he ever does. Wondering if this is the right choice, this anchor I've chosen for myself. Ham and I, both shattered in our separate ways, terrified of admitting how much we need each other.

"I was scared to tell you, Ash. Scared that you'd leave. Find someone . . . real, someone who can do what we do here out there . . . I'm nothing outside of the Game, outside of the 'Nets. Who can love nothing?"

I think back to Sarah, our brief moment earlier. A moment of connection, yet minuscule compared to all the moments I've shared with Ham.

"You're not nothing, Ham. You're so much more than that. Who you are in here is all I've ever known—and all I've wanted to know. That's who I fell for. Did you ever wonder why I never pushed for a meeting in the real? I was afraid too—afraid you'd see my messed-up family, the shitty box I live in. Afraid it might distract you from what we have, what I already love about you."

I look around at the dark calmness of the crypto-room, an ocean of universes never quite touching.

"I wish we could just stay here forever, me and you."

"R-really? Be honest, Ash."

The eyes in his beautiful face are dark with uncertainty.

"Really, Ham. I'm not happy you didn't tell me earlier, because *wow* is this a monumental adjustment." I shake my head. "And now is sort of a fucked-up time to learn it. But I've kept my own secrets too, and the latest round of crap in my life is pretty spectacular, not going to lie. I need you—this place—you're my haven."

His tears match my own.

"Thanks, Ash. It's been sitting in my stomach like a damn gravity bomb. I was scared shitless you were going to leave me when I finally told you, and every day I delayed made it worse." He squeezes my hand back, the other wiping his eyes. "So what exactly is the 'latest round of crap' in your life?"

I take a deep breath, then exhale. Fuck it. If Ham wants to know . . . it's not like Sawyer can do anything to the son of a Big Three EVP. I quickly bring him up to speed on everything that's happened. Brand dying, the hood controlling her, our raid in Industan, Sawyer's suspicion that one of the Big Three is behind it all, Jase trapped on the rig, Gamers possibly starting another hot war. At the end of it, he looks shell-shocked.

"God*damn*, Ash. I'm almost regretting asking you about this now."

"Really?"

I start to pull my hand away, but he holds on.

"I said almost." He smiles. "Look, I'm stuck in a tube, and you're stuck in a gummie protectorate with a bunch of troglodytes, but we can do this. I don't want to see war in the real any more than you do. And hey, we can work on the same side for once. Dragon and dragonslayer together, saving the world!"

I smile back at him, my heart lifting.

"See? That's why I'm not going anywhere. Bodies are a

credit a dozen. Hearts and minds are a lot rarer. Trust me, if I wanted a slab of beefcake, there's no shortage of dickpics in my socials."

"If you say so. Also, yuck."

"Yep. Okay, strat time. The way I see it, our first order of business is to figure out where Sawyer's base is, in case I need to spring Jase. After that, we can track down who's responsible for Brand's death. Once we find them, assuming Sawyer doesn't get there first, me and the girls will pay them a visit."

"Works for me. I'll start looking into offshore base locations as soon as possible. The Game execs . . . my dad . . . have me alpha testing some interesting new encounters right now—not ghosting anything yet, just overseeing, but the AI looks like it's pretty intense." He winks at me. "I think you'll find it an interesting challenge."

I mock punch him.

"No hints!"

Ham laughs.

"Fine, fine, you're right. I'll try and sneak into my dad's avatar when I get a chance, see if he's heard anything about all this. The EVPs tend to keep tabs on everyone and everything—perils of corp life." He rolls his eyes. "What a future to look forward to, huh?"

"Thanks, Ham. Just . . . be careful, okay? I already lost Brand. I don't want to lose anyone else."

"Careful is my middle name." He startles, as if pinched. "Whoops, gotta go. Time to test another encounter. I'll let you know when I find something."

"Sounds good. Love you."

"Love you too."

We lean across to kiss, our lips meeting, his chiseled body fading away to nothing until all I'm left with is the memory of his tongue on mine, and the new awareness that only in this place is that even possible. The whispered hush of a million unintelligible conversations ebbs and flows around me, and I rest my head on my hands, wanting to stay in this hidden sanctuary forever. Safe from all the pressure, all the demands . . .

My eyebrow twitches.

Fuck it. If I wanted to live a boring life, I'd have stayed in Candyland.

I log off, and seconds later, I'm asleep.

15

[Dailies]

Shapeless forms running at me, their muscles bulging and distorting grotesquely. Heads splitting open, gray tendrils creeping forth from their shattered jaws, stretching for my face. Slend's lifeless corpse, Wind lying next to her, Kiro vanished, Hammer dying . . .

Gasping, I pull myself awake, sweat cooling across my body. What a horrible fucking dream. I pull my glasses off of their recharge station to check the time.

Ugh. It's too early to be awake. No messages, so Sawyer hasn't pinned anything down yet, and Kiro still has me blocked. Just the ever-present torrent of socials. Groaning, I push myself upright, reaching for my toothbrush, and delete another deluge of abuse. Looks like the boardshits are going with bestiality today. Necrobestiality.

Throw on a baggy sweatshirt that hangs to my knees and head out into the corridor to the communal faucet, sliding into line behind the old techheads and grannies; the only ones up at this hour. Decide to browse the intelligible parts of my feed while I wait for my few drops of water, another rationing stricture instituted overnight by the gummies. My blade hangs comfortably against my thigh.

Flare-ups in northern Han, former Siberians still not accept-
ing their new overlords. Pictures of smoldering craters half
a kilometer across, burned-out shells of drones, mangled remains of bodies crumpled beneath flattened megaspires. The
insurgents have heart, but that doesn't mean much against a
battlegroup with orbital support. One drone dies, they send
in another, along with some tungsten. Takes way more time to
grow new insurgents than it does to pump out another drone
or kinetic, and the Han gave up caring about collateral damage a long time ago. Just like everyone else.

Another currency collapse in the Euroleague, third one this
month. Lots of speeches from weak-chinned officials, spout-
ing the same stiff-upper-lip shit as the last two times, but nothing's changed. No one's in the market for past glories, just
for bread, but without access to arable land, all they can do
is starve. The Confederation of African States doesn't seem
that interested in helping either, no doubt remembering tales
passed down from their ancestors. A lumpy, pale-faced woman
asks why no one cares about the starving. Tag that one under
irony.

Closer to home, more riots in Ditchtown, this time in
Southspire, nominally the headquarters of our gummie task-
masters. Couple security stations burned, armaments looted,
nobody quite sure how or why it was done. Typical. I dribble
some water onto the toothbrush, watch my water account
dip down. Still enough to survive on. Stick the brush into my
mouth and head back to the room.

I slip back inside, not bothering with the locks because
I'm leaving shortly, and down a pouch of protein. It hits my
mouth with the same disgusting sensation as always, because
for some reason the corps can't figure out how to make a
protein pack that doesn't have the consistency of jizz, but
it'll keep me moving, which is all that matters. Throw on

my everyday wear—cargo pants, thin T-shirt, leather jacket, surplus tacboots—and head back out, locking the door behind me.

The Brown is quiet at this hour, younger misfits either still buried in their coding, red eyes twitching, or passed out from another all-nighter, their bodies refusing to press any further no matter how many stimulants zip through their veins. Stairwells yawn empty, free from the couriers' tread. Mah-jongg boards sit in solitude, awaiting their relics, and the only sounds are those delivered by my staccato steps.

I make my way through the lower levels of the Brown and over to Sarah's in Highrise, enjoying the illusion of peacefulness, the delusion that I'm the only living being in this honeycombed hive, free to wander where I wish. Tap off a message with my hapgloves to Wind and Slend, letting them know where we're starting.

"Hey, Ash."

Sarah greets me at the front door, switching her sign over from CLOSED to NOT CLOSED. Not nearly as welcoming as OPEN, but this is Ditchtown.

"Hey, Sare. How was the rest of the night?"

She chuckles, throwing an arm around my shoulder, walking me inside. I can feel her hips rubbing against me, the side of her chest against mine, and wonder if maybe I made a mistake.

No. Focus.

"It was fun. Found a spicy little number after you left, and what that girl could do with her tongue . . . ooooohhhh."

She mock shivers, and I smile.

"Glad to hear it. Meant to mention it before, but sorry for not coming back in after we killed the dragon. Might have cost you some business."

Sarah laughs, and plants a light kiss on my cheek before heading behind the reception desk.

"Ash, honey, I've been booked solid since you took that thing down. Everyone in Ditchtown wanted to use the same gear Ashura the Terrible was riding when she made history. Hoped some of your magic might rub off on their sorry Candy-land asses."

"Did it?"

"Not a chance. As much as I love my spheres, it's the player that makes the stream, not the gear. You're one of a kind, Ash, and as long as you want to keep coming here, I'll always have a sphere set aside." Sarah pauses, then winks at me. "Of course, you're still paying for petro. A girl's gotta make a liv-ing somehow."

I smile and flip my hand at her.

"Never change, Sare. Never change. Which one am I in today?"

"C-5." Sarah gives me one of her looks. "She'll handle any-thing you want to throw at her."

I flush and walk toward the door, feet moving slightly faster than normal.

"Thanks, um, Sare, but it'll only be dailies today. Just, um, keeping in shape."

I flush again and her airy laughter trails me into the locker room, echoing in my head as I pull off my clothes. Looks like she's not planning on stopping the flirting anytime soon, but a part of me is glad about that.

Why can't I have both? Ham won't care. What's he going to do about it anyway?

The unwanted thought creeps through my mind like poi-son, and I rub my hands against my face. Great. What a way to start off the morning—thinking about how to betray the one person absolutely devoted to me by taking advantage of the one thing he'll never have. What the hell is wrong with me?

No. I love him. He loves me. That's enough. It has to be.

Several contorted minutes later, I close up the molecular lock on my hapsuit, and grab my goggles. A short walk down the halls, and I'm at the scaffolding surrounding hapsphere C-5, dimly lit by a single bulb hanging from the sparse room's ceiling. I tap open a commlink.

"Ready when you are, Sare."

"I'm always ready, sweetie."

I half smile and shake my head, a section of the sphere flowing aside to make an entrance. I climb inside and center myself on the floor, a dim glow of light filtering in from outside.

"Ready for diagnostics."

"Diagnostics initiated."

Sarah's voice shifts to cool professionalism, and the sphere rotates under my feet, the opening sliding shut and plunging me into darkness. I snap my goggles into place and watch a wireframe grid form in front of me—the bare-bones visuals of syncing. The landscape starts to move, and I keep pace with the sphere's rolling gait, slapping my hands against pillars that form at my sides, their dull gray bulk falling away at my touch, until everything falls still once more.

"Five by five across the board. You ready?"

I slide my goggles up, taking in the utter blackness surrounding me, then push them back down and wedge the scent emitters into my nose. Just me and my circular tomb.

"Let's do it."

Green fields unfold in front of me, thick grass underfoot. Wildflowers burst from the earth in multicolored sprays. Puffy clouds dot the perfect sky, and trills of birdsong drift on the wind. A jocular rabbit in a tuxedo bounds up to me, his overlarge eyes glistening with saccharine glee.

"Welcome to Cand—"

Wordlessly, I clench my fist, and obliterate the rabbit's head in a massive punch. Pink and gray brain matter sprays across the gentle field, and then the sky pulls down tight, blue shifting to red, clouds warping into swirling vortices. A thunderous voice booms from above.

"Welcome to endgame, Ashura. Incognito mode is currently enabled. Please select a facet."

The whirlpool clouds resolve into static images, one for each of the visible endgame shards. There are hidden ones as well, for players who know how to look, but I don't need to access those for dailies. I point my finger at the picture of a spiral galaxy, and pull like I'm caressing the trigger of a gun. Suddenly, I'm drawn into the picture, perspective warping and distorting in smeared blotches. Clarity snaps back into focus, and I'm standing inside a space station, suited crew members bustling off to various tasks around me. A handsome spacer, laspistol dangling at his belt, slides to a halt in front of me.

"Excuse me, miss, but co—"

I cut off the NPC dialogue and head straight for the hangar bay. I already know what I need to do in the CCP facet, since I've done it hundreds of times before. It's fun to listen to quest descriptions for dailies the first few times, interact with the NPCs, but after that, it's simply not efficient. A quick series of finger twitches and I'm broadcasting to the 'Net, my stream numbers already shooting up into the thousands. Don't ask me why, but people love to watch, even when it's something as mundane as digital chores.

Quick climb into the cockpit, the canopy hissing shut around me. I punch in my confirmation code to activate the X-Cross spacefighter, a nimble antipiracy craft armed with quad-lasers, six proton torpedoes, and as much attitude as a pilot wants to bring. I could paint mine gold, but I like keeping it low-key, so the default skin remains. Seconds later, the launch catapult vaults me out into space. It's not true zero-G, of course, no hapsphere can create that, but the illusion is pretty damn close, faux-acceleration pushing me back into my seat. I toggle open a private comm channel.

"Wind, Slend, you here?"

Two more fighters swoop in next to me, light blue ion streams trailing away from their engines, stubby proton torpedoes hanging under their bellies.

"Another day in paradise, boss. Let's light some fuckers up!"

Slend only grunts, and I grin.

Nothing better than farming with friends.

I press a red button on the side of my throttle, boosting into tunneldrive. The stars turn into streaks of light, a massive weight squeezes against my chest, and even though I know, *I know* it's just the actuators inside my hapsphere mimicking the crush of acceleration against my suit, I can't stop the smile from spreading ear to ear, because *holy shit* does it feel good. Swimming the stars, twisting through the void like a darting bird, freed at last from the constricting chains of gravity, the universe my playground . . .

Dailies in CCP never get old.

I check my nav panel while the fighter rumbles through tunnelspace, the Game's equivalent of an old loading screen. Their servers are good, real good, but even the best hardware still needs some time to load a full haptic suite. Looks to be an easy daily today, simple smash-and-grab attempt, fixed number of attackers and defenders, primary objective a cargo ship carrying medical supplies to a besieged asylum world. The numbers on each side push me into another grin, smaller than before, but no less delighted.

In this daily, most Gamers favor the attacking side, because the secondary award for blowing up the cargo ship is almost as much as the primary award for seizing its supplies, whereas the defenders have to get the ship safely to the planet to get anything. Basic game theory favors the attackers, not just because they have an easier objective, but because that easier objective makes it far more likely players will join that side, compared to the uncertain payoff of a defender.

On the other hand, long odds are how we make our money.

I slot us onto the defending team, and open a public tac channel between me, Wind, and Slend. If the poor newbies with us want to join in, as long as they're polite, I'm more than happy to help them learn. A second later, two more icons blink into existence—xXx420AshuraREALxXx and Steve. Neither has more than a hundred hours logged in endgame.

"We're fucking fucked. Five vee fucking twenty? Fuck that. Let's suicide quick so we can try again."

xXx420AshuraREALxXx sounds like a ten-year-old boy with his balls in a vise. I roll my eyes. Fucking burbie parents never supervise their fucking kids.

"You'll be fine. Just try your best to stay alive. Do a barrel roll."

"You sound like a girl are you a girl do you want to meet up we should meet up my dad he can drop me off at—"

Fucking. Burbies. I slap a ten-second mute on xXx420-AshuraREALxXx, one of the perks of being the best. The higher up the ladder you go, the more control you get over chat. Speaking is a privilege in endgame, not a right, and guilds have split over mutedramas before.

"Uhh, I hate to throw a game, but our odds really don't look good. Maybe the kid has a point? It'll be faster than waiting through the quitter queue. I only have a couple hours left tonight."

Steve has the voice of a middle-management corp drone, a guy with a drone wife, two drone kids, three times a year drone exit pass to class single-A restricted territories but only with bond of security and don't you dare think about staying a day over or at any unsanctioned lodgings. I briefly wonder if he's ever had sex in anything other than the missionary position.

"Oh *please,* Ash, *please please please* let me tell them. *Pleeeeeeeeease.*"

Wind sounds like she's salivating. Who knows, she very well could be. I don't want her to spoil it yet, though. Gotta tease the stream a bit.

"Wait, please. You know it's best if we spring it when they're just about to attack."

"Awwww, Ash, you're no fun."

". . . Ash? Why is she calling you Ash? Your tag just says 'Player One.' What are you talking about?"

Poor Steve. He has no idea.

"Focus, Steve. The QQ isn't an option. We're going to be outnumbered four to one, and that means you're already in trouble. Now listen, when the battle starts, I want you to—"

"—two girls you're both girls wow do you think we could maybe get some drugs or hav—"

Another ten-second mute.

"—I want you to focus on staying alive, Steve. Reshunt all your power from weapons into shields and engines, and stay away from combat as much as possible."

"But . . . that makes the odds five to one. There's no one that can take five to one. Not unless you're legendary, and everyone knows that legendaries always run with their own people."

Steve doesn't sound convinced of our skills.

"It's actually gonna be more like six to one, Steve, but that's okay. We'll handle it. Trust me."

The weight on my chest drops away, tunnelspace breaking

into the panorama of an oncoming planet. Bands of white clouds slide across its red-and-green surface, the shining bulk of a ten-megaton cargo hauler gleaming below us, harsh blue light from the system sun making razor-edged shadows along its length. Red brackets pop up through my cockpit—enemy forces. I flick my weapons to active, and nudge the throttle forward. Pressure settles against my body again, but it's nothing compared to what these combat maneuvers are about to demand.

"—ucking Christ look at how many of those fucking fa—"

Fifteen-second mute this time, with a ban warning. It probably won't stop him, but it's worth a shot. I assign initial targets to Wind and Slend, and highlight an evasive route for Steve. A chatter of conversation comes over the public band, the other team close enough now to try to run psych-sec.

"Haha look at these losers, outnum—"

"Go home, scrubs. Nothing for you here but de—"

"Fucking bitch nigg—"

I perma-mute that one, an action that might give away who I am, but based on their straightforward approach, I doubt they're smart enough to figure it out in the time remaining. The numbers on my stream keep climbing, everyone waiting to watch us do the impossible. Red and blue dots close in on each other on my nav plot, the giant yellow of the hauler crawling beneath us.

"Wind. I think it's time to do the honors."

"Oh, *finally,* thank you thank you *thank you.*"

Wind drops our incognito cloaks. Normally, players have to operate under their actual username, but there's an endgame item that allows players to hide themselves for a twelve-hour period, and I've always considered it one of the more elegant aspects of Infinite Game. If you're not in endgame, you don't need the item, because no one cares who you are, but if you're good enough to stockpile it, you're good enough to need to hide when you're interacting with everyone else.

We have enough incogs to last a decade.

On the nav plot, Ashura the Terrible, Alhazred's Wailing Wind, and Slenderwoman suddenly burst into existence, the burning green emblem of the SunJewel Warriors searing above our ships. Together, we've accounted for over ninety thousand kills in this facet alone. My stream erupts into an excited chatter of laughter, betting, and reaction memes, which I ignore with the ease of long practice. The other team responds immediately.

Two ships simply vanish, willing to drop out and pay the quitter queue penalty. One was an initial target for Slend, but I trust her to pick another.

"THAT'S RIGHT, FUCKERS, YOU BETTER QUEUE QUEUE," Wind screams on the public channel, firing off a full spread of three proton torpedoes. Three other enemy ships fall out of formation, turning as if to flee, even though there's nowhere to go. This encounter's locked and loaded.

Slend and I fire our own blast of torpedoes, initial salvos away. Five ships puff out of existence, but a wall of destruction streaks back at us. Our countermeasures spew forth—jamming devices, cartwheeling mini-mine chaff, decoy beacons mimicking the signature of an actual fighter. We corkscrew out and away to confuse target lock.

"—oly shit it's Ashura what the fuck what the fuck what the—"

xXx420AshuraREALxXx is blessedly vaporized by a proton torpedo, comms silenced on death, but at least he ate up six torpedoes that might otherwise have targeted someone who matters. Steve doesn't waste any time on talking, a good sign, and spins into a clumsy roll. Thunderous blasts engulf his ship, but luckily for him, he listened, and diverted all power to shields and engines. The four of us flash across the stars, and then the cooldowns finish resetting. Time for round two.

Another flight of torpedoes blossoms out, me and Slend and Wind dumping the rest of our ordnance. Four more ships disappear, but another tsunami of death sweeps in. Explosions rattle my body, and warning signs puff into fitful existence across the cockpit.

"Shields at thirty." Wind's voice is calm.

"Left engine out." Slend sounds bored.

"Sensors at fifteen." My nav plot hashes and jiggers, static reducing it to an indecipherable wreck. "Let's fucking do it."

I match velocity with Slend and pull in front of Wind, utilizing our still-functional shields to keep her safe from the swiftly approaching laser volleys. Slend's voice is a constant hum in my ear, feeding me updated enemy positions. Together, we advance on the remaining fighters, Steve fluttering behind us in wobbly arcs, the distance between us spreading.

The three hostiles that initially fled circle around toward Steve, sensing a weaker target they might be able to gang up on. That leaves six for us. His panicked voice finally fills the comms again, drowning out Slend.

"Oh shit oh shit oh shiiiiiit, what do I do what do I do there're three of the—"

"Steve!"

I'm not angry, just loud. Cutting through his adrenaline, his fear. He falls silent.

"Breathe. All you have to do is keep your distance and dodge. This is endgame. Now grow a fucking pair, and pull some pilot shit!"

I hit him with a thirty-second mute just in case, and turn my focus back to Wind and Slend. Two-to-one odds are better than what we faced before, but they're still not great, especially not when I'll be knifefighting blind. I focus on Slend's voice.

"Two at one. Two at twelve. Two at eleven. Twelve cutting below. One cutting right. Eleven cutting above."

Laser blasts start impacting my shields, shaking the cockpit. I put more energy from my engines into the shields, since we're stuck at Slend's pace and I've got power to spare. Both of us make sure to keep between Wind and the hostiles.

"Twelve low five clicks. Eleven high three clicks. One high right three clicks."

My targeting systems start picking up faint returns, dancing red ghosts in my vision. I need to get closer to use what's left of my sensors.

"Wind, take twelve. Slend, cover me, I'll take eleven first. Is Steve still alive?"

"Yup. Three on him. At eight. Nice jukes." Slend sounds surprised. I can't blame her.

"Okay, well, keep it up, Steve. Good job."

"—WOOOOOO DID YOU SEE HOW CLOSE THAT LASER WAS HOLY SH—"

I mute him again.

"Wind, break on my mark."

More laser fire rattles my shields, but they're holding. Barely.

"Mark!"

"TIME TO DIE YOU PISSBABY FU—"

Five-second personal mute for Wind. I love her, but I need to concentrate.

I yank my stick back and slam the throttle forward, trusting Slend to point me in the right direction. A second later, two red brackets appear in the middle of my viewscreen. My lips peel away, a tiger's smile, and I pull the firing trigger. Streams of coherent light spit out, and one of the brackets disappears. I throw my ship into a looping roll, dancing around the shots I know are already reaching to embrace me. Deadly particles sleet by, and I fire again. The other bracket vanishes.

"One at mid four, two clicks. Overboosting . . . firing . . . got him. Other engine's out. One at five high. Circling behind."

I flip end over end, more gravity squeezing my bones. Gray creeps in to the edges of my vision, but I force myself to ignore it, clenching my teeth and muscles. Another burst of acceleration and a red bracket appears in front of me once again. I stab my finger home, and the hostile fighter joins its brethren in oblivion, seconds away from vaporizing Slend.

"Wind, talk to me."

"Psh. They never knew what hit 'em. Both down, along with my shields."

"Steve, how're you doing over there?"

"HOLY CRAP WE WON THEY'RE RUNNING WE WON I'M ALIVE W—"

I frown. Not having sensors sucks.

"Slend, where are they going?"

Slend draws in a breath, then grunts again. She sounds annoyed.

"Found some brains. Inc three to hauler."

"Shit. They have any torpedoes left?"

"Ten. Two'll crack it."

"—OOOOO WE FUCKING WON THAT WAS AMA—"

"Double shit. How long?"

"Minute and a half, max."

"—ZING THERE'S NO WA—"

I mute Steve and take a second to think, try to figure a way out. If those last three fighters hit the hauler, then we'll lose our rewards for this daily. We've already clinched the ladder, so in the grand scheme of things it doesn't mean much other than some wasted time, but I *hate* losing. Unfortunately, Wind and I won't be able to reach the incoming fighters in time, our battle splitting us off to the opposite side of the hauler, and Slend's engines are shot. If Wind could get there, normally she'd be able to stop the torpedoes with her shields and lasers, but that strat's tough to implement with no shields. I have the shields and guns, but I can't target the torpedoes anymore, and Steve is, well . . . yeah. He's already contributed plenty as a distraction, and even though he hasn't used any of his torpedoes, I doubt he's experienced enough to take down anyone but another Candylander. Against three endgamers, he's an explosion waiting to happen.

Time to do the impossible.

Just another encounter.

"Wind, target the one in front. Assume a least time intercept on the hauler's engine core. Don't worry about shields, he'll be busy by the time you get to him."

"Got it."

She jets off, beginning her long-distance attack run.

"Slend, I'm gonna micro hop. How far are they?"

"Thirty-seven kay clicks, two mid. Closing at five hundred clicks per. You sure?"

I do some quick math in my head. Doable.

"Yup. All power to sensors. Be ready to give me updates. Steve. You still with us?"

"Y-yeah. I'm here."

"Good. You know how to switch friendly fire off?"

"Um, yeah. Why?"

"When I tell you to, I want you to launch a full salvo at the back fighter. After I wipe the middle one, I want you to launch a full salvo at me."

"At . . . you?"

"Yes, Steve. At me. Don't worry, I'm not going to report you for griefing."

"O-okay. How are you going to kill the middle one?"

"You'll see. Launch your torps."

I hope Steve doesn't freeze, and turn my ship to line up with the incoming fighters. There's no way to train for what I'm about to try to do, just instincts and luck. My thumb hits the button for tunneldrive.

In CCP, players use tunneldrive to travel between star systems, crossing trillions of kilometers in seconds from one fixed point to another, and for ninety-nine point nine percent of them, that's all they'll ever know. Tunneling out of a system through anything other than an established route vaporizes a ship—devs not wanting to waste resources rendering literally everything. What most people don't realize, though, is that the restriction only applies to travel *outside* of a system.

As long as I stay within the bounds of the local star, the Game won't murder my ship. Of course, to stay within the bounds of the local star, I have to get this exactly right. Too soon, and the drive won't spin up enough, dumping me right back where I started. Too late, and I'll find myself a million clicks away from the enemy ships, entirely too far away to accomplish anything more than a temper tantrum, something that would also be highly embarrassing from a streaming perspective. My margin of error is less than razor thin.

Impossible to be the best playing it safe.

Starlight streaks form around me, and just as quickly, I hit the button again, dropping myself back into realspace, Slend's voice immediately sounding over my comms.

"Eight high relative. Ten clicks back. Four gees to close at max."

Nailed it.

I roll my control yoke over, Slend's terse words letting me know I'm above and behind the left side of the last three ships, and that catching them is gonna hurt a bit. I shunt half the power from my weapons to engines and crank the throttle. Four gravities' worth of force punch me in the everywhere, nothing but blank space and scrambled sensors in front.

"Steve. Talk."

Speaking's not fun, but it's necessary.

"Uh, wow. That . . . uh . . ."

"Did. Torps. Hit."

Two red brackets appear in front of me, one slightly behind the other. I adjust to center the rearmost in my aiming reticule.

"Y-yes! I got one!"

"Good. Launch. At. Me."

"Oh yeah, sorry, forgot. Firing!"

I tap a code to access the tertiary power panels, part of the ship hardly anyone uses, because hardly anyone wants to play at that level of fidelity in their hapsphere, deal with the pain it potentially brings. Another couple of taps and all power drops from life support, shunted into weapons. Bitter cold quickly envelops me. Groaning, I squeeze the firing trigger. An overcharged spurt of eradicating light turns my vision purple, ripping through the blackness like an earthquake, doubling the range at which my lasers can normally strike. Red bracket turns to black space.

A new voice sounds on the public comms, the last pilot. I recognize his guild seal, one of the feeder guilds funneling into IonSeal. One popular with the boardshits.

"So, you're Ashura? You're good. Real fucking good. I thought those other losers were gonna be enough to wipe this cakewalk. 'Specially twenty vee five."

"Wiped. Your. Asses. Like. Toilet. Paper. You're. Next."

He laughs, an unpleasant sound, like a hyena.

"Yeah, you got the trash, but it doesn't matter. I'm still gonna win. You can't stop my torps, not from there. Especially not if I overcharge."

Slend's voice sounds again.

"Ultra launch. Engine core. Six vamps inbound."

The pressure on my face doesn't let me smile, as much as I want to, and my toes feel like they're encased in blocks of ice. *Perfect. He got scared, and launched them all at once.*

I shunt all power to engines. I'm not aiming at anything visible, just a combination of guesswork and hope. Six more gees join the weight on my chest, eyesight narrowing down to a thin tube, more frost enveloping my limbs. Warnings sound all over the cockpit, the Game's way of telling me I'm nearing the limits of what they'll allow, but I don't care. It's just me and the encounter. The timing on this is going to be thinner than a molyblade. I blow past the hostile bracket in a blur, its stunned handler unable to handle his weapons in time to catch me.

Something in my stomach tightens. I slam all power into the shields of my horrendously overstressed fighter, blowing out every circuit to create a momentarily impenetrable barrier, acceleration dropping to zero. The weight on my chest turns from a steady pressure to nothing to a heaving ocean of kinetic force, buffeting me from every possible angle, Steve's torpedoes detonating their massive payloads, seeking to crush my life from existence, but in doing so massacring the six torpedoes not half a click away in an orgy of mutual destruction, their sensors fixated on the hauler. Life support slowly rumbles back online, abacus beads prolonging my existence a few slides more.

"No fucking way!"

"Vamps down."

Slend's voice arrives nearly simultaneously with the other pilot's. I'm too tired to grin. My ship tumbles helplessly, everything used up in my insane burst of speed to catch up with the torpedoes, then survive the impact of Steve's salvo. I open a link to the public comm. I'm helpless, but I still need a couple more seconds. Luckily, this jackass probably sucks at psych-sec.

"Gee gee, well played, better luck next time. Torps are vulnerable to fratricide. You should've ripple fired. You only needed to get two through. You'll never make IonSeal with that level of scrubness."

"Ggrraaaaghhhhh! You stupid . . . you stupid *bitch*! You fucking cheated!"

"Losers make excuses. Winners fuck the prom king. Not my fault you played like shit. Get good."

"Oh that's fucking it. That's fucking *IT*! I don't give a fuck *who* you are, I've still got lasers, and I'm gonna blow your cun—"

"SAY HELLO TO MY LITTLE FRIEND, YOU REJECTED SPERM SAMPLE."

Wind's blasts cut his angry ranting short, her ship screaming in from below, bare to even the slightest of return fire, and this time I quirk the corner of my mouth up. My stream goes wild.

"Good timing."

"Nice psych-sec. Thought for sure he was going to see me coming in."

"Nah. Tunnel vision. Takes a long time to break that, and his tag shows less than a thousand in endgame. Gee gee, Slend."

"Yup."

"Good job, Steve. Couldn't have done it without you."

"That. Was. Fucking. AWESOME! SunJewel rocks!"

"You got it, Steve."

My ship stops spinning, perspective shifting to the "Mission Accomplished!" screen. Heat rushes back into my body, the hapsphere readjusting, and with the tingling return of sensation I realize just how close I pushed the safety limits. Another couple seconds and the Game would've booted me back to login, biomonitor signs hitting hardcoded thresholds. No one tries to hack the threshold limits, not unless they have a death wish. Hapspheres do everything they're told.

Everything.

A glowing treasure chest puffs into existence in front of me—our loot. As the highest-ranked player, I get first dibs on the after-action spoils, and in a five versus twenty match, playing as defenders, the spoils are very good indeed.

I shift over to our private channel.

"Hey. What do you think the odds are Steve has a golden X'er?"

"None."

"That drone? Slend's right, ze-fucking-ro. He'll never even sniff a legendary ship."

"Wanna pass it to him?"

"K."

"Hahaha, you bet your ass. He's prolly gonna have a heart attack."

I tap my finger on a stack of top-tier crafting ingredients, one of the guaranteed rewards for winning as a defender, and the whole reason why we're running this daily. They spiral down into my pocket, this facet's version of a belt pouch. The twinkling gold spacefighter, limned in an aurora of pale orange light, drops back into the loot box. It's a one in ten million drop for this specific encounter (modified by outnumbered odds and mission objectives, of course), but Wind and

Slend follow my lead. It's obvious when Steve opens the box, because his voice sounds like he's found religion.

"That. That's. That's a golden. A golden X'er."

"—at the shit ohmigod ohmigod pleeeeeeease dude pleeeeeeease pass it to me my friends will be so jea—"

Another thirty second mute for xXx420AshuraREALxXx.

"All yours if you want it, Steve. We've got plenty. Good work out there."

"I. Thank you. *Thank you.* This is unbelievable. A golden X'er. I just. Thank you. Oh man, the guys at the office aren't gonna *believe* this."

Wind's laughter echoes over our private link, loud and pure. Slend's chuckles join her, and it's a struggle to keep my voice from cracking.

"No problemo. Stay frosty, Steve."

I drop us back to facet selection before I have to listen to xXx420AshuraREALxXx whine about how he *really* needed that ship and *totally* deserved the loot, despite all evidence to the contrary. Steve's reaction to what, for us, is nothing more than a bauble was totally worth tryharding the encounter, and judging by the amount of donations popping up on the stream, most everyone watching seems to agree. It's not featured creds, but my share will be enough to cover petro for Sarah and my food packets for the next few weeks. Better than losing.

I tap open the next daily facet, Wind and Slend my shadows, the streamers trailing in our wake.

Clancery facet. Escheria facet. Harlequin facet. Daily after daily after daily, each one testing a different skill, each one necessary to prep for the edges of endgame. Some give crafting ingredients, like our first mission in CCP, required to create the wards and weapons we need to survive the fringe. Others give hints of information, clues to the upcoming season and encounters, corners of a puzzle whose pieces aren't even in the box yet. A few are simply for our personal pleasure, stomping out dens of boardshits, trashing their carefully hoarded gear, sending them crying back to Candyland, wilted digital dicks in hand.

Another sobbing boardshit disappears, winking out of existence from his supine position on the arena floor in the Duello facet, blood leaking across his body, and an alert appears in my vision. Time to go see Mom. Next to it, stats from my stream pop up, numbers slowly dropping over the past four hours. That's not what the alert is about, though. View dropping is perfectly normal during dailies, and all the excitement happened early on in CCP. I sheathe my rapier, waving to Wind and Slend, both leaning against the wooden barrier surrounding the massive fighting pit, an axe at Slend's waist, a barbed whip at Wind's.

"Gotta go. Take care of the rest?"

"Gosh, *finally.* I was getting bored over here, Ash."

Slend inclines her head, thumb running along the edge of her axe, following Wind down to the sandy floor. The duelists waiting on the other side actually flinch back when the two of them bare their teeth in a mockery of a smile.

"Thanks. I'll be in touch."

I shut the stream down, putting out my standard message of thanks for watching, and log out to the real.

Darkness envelops me, the unlit interior of the hapsphere quickly broken by a rectangle of light—Sarah, alert as always. I walk over to the doorway.

"Nice trick with the fighter, Ash. Though I'm pretty sure I remember hearing you say you were going to take it easy today. Petro charge is gonna be a little pricey."

I shrug.

"What can I say. Losing sucks. I'd rather win."

"Hah, you and me both, girl. You and me both." She hops inside, prying up a panel. "You coming back later?"

"Maybe. Depends how it goes with Mom." Thinking of her brings up another thought, a newer, more recent wound. "You seen Kiro around?"

Sarah looks up from the cluster of microprocessors she's working on.

"Not since your last run. Why, you want me to ask around?"

"Yeah. I'd appreciate it. He's not answering his messages, and I'm worried he might be starting to roll with the wrong crowd."

"K. I'll hit up the other operators, see what turns up. If he's used a sphere, I'll find him."

"Thanks, Sare."

"Sure thing, hot stuff. See you around."

"Cya."

I change out of my suit and take a quick shower, the thin stream of water almost insignificant after the pounding excess available onboard Sawyer's rig. It's barely enough to bring me back to reality. I slip back into my camouflage.

Slide out of Sarah's side door, less of a crowd gathered around the front this time. To be fair, today was only dailies, not a featured encounter, but there's always a crowd for Ashura the Terrible. Only this crowd is a bit older, a bit more filled with swagger, rough edges clearly visible in the midday light of glowstrips.

I pull my hood over my head and set off for the Brown, cutting a path through the bustle of humanity. More Preachers

out today in their pristine robes, their perfect teeth spitting out stained words. Fewer Hajj, those visible walking in
tight groups, eyes wary. Undercurrents of fear, hate, and pain
rumbling beneath it all like the first tremors of a petroquake,
nothing shifting off the shelves just yet, but sharper jolts on
their way.

Gonna be riots soon.

I swing by Johnny's, grab some noodles, shake my head
at his unspoken question. No word from Sawyer. Make my
way through discontented corridors, the few tourists visible
hidden behind anti-crowd fields, dispersion levels set to max.
Won't help them if there's an actual riot, fields can only handle
so much kinetic load, but at least it gives them the illusion of
safety. A better reality would be to leave, but they're not smart
enough to realize they have that choice.

Thick mass of angry protestors chanting outside Southspire,
demanding to know when service offices are going to reopen,
help them find work, food, water. I shake my head. Gummies
are more likely to send assault drones than aid. Salvation or
starvation, no in betweens.

Pass back through to Highrise, its upper corridors quiet,
but not the good quiet of sleeping or work. No, these corridors are the hot, dirty quiet of barricades behind doors, knives
dripping in the dark, the static gloom before a superstorm
crashes down like an orbital blast. I check my socials, see if
there's any local alerts.

Nothing for Highrise, but a riot's definitely brewing in
the Rust. Folks pissed about losing their medical care. Hope
Slend's okay, but knowing her, she'll probably be leading it by
nightfall. I angrily wait for a mandatory ad to finish autoplaying,
some stupid plutocrat service with orbital hoppers skimming
them from coast to coast in less than half an hour. As if anyone
here could afford that. Check some deeper holes the usual

boardshit suspects gather on, but there's not a trace of trouble from them. Not much of anything, actually, which is surprising. Maybe word about Mikelas got around.

A message pings from Ham. I tap it open.

<<Been looking, nothing yet. Have a few more tricks I want to try. He's got a partition I can't crack, might have what we need.>>

<<Be careful.>>

<<You too. Talk to you later.>>

<<Later.>>

Walk into Mom's clinic, the guards out front nervously checking their stunners, hands never far from their belts. One waves me through without really looking, her eyes constantly scanning the corridor. Plop the noodles down on the belt, pass over my knife, and I'm through to the cheerfully painted hallways and gaily disguised turrets, muted screams echoing from behind some of the doors. A pair of orderlies pass by in hushed conversation, shoulders tense.

I step into Mom's outer room.

"Hey, Ash."

"Hey, Freddie. How is she?"

"Stable. I think we managed to pin down a couple of the more traumatic incidents."

"Two down, infinity more to go?"

"Something like that."

"Here. Brought you some noodles."

"Thanks. You heading in?"

"Yup."

I step into the airlock, leaving Freddie behind to enjoy his noodles. I'll grab a protein pack later, and I don't want to risk setting Mom off again. The circular chamber cycles through, and I walk into the inner room, where I lean against a wall and wait for Mom to finish her katas. Several minutes pass and then she finally comes to a halt.

"Hey, Mom."

"Ashley, dear, how are you?"

She walks over and gives me a hug, all outward appearances normal. I hug her back, then lead her to the bed.

"Sit, Mom, sit. I'm good. How are you doing?"

"I . . . think I'm doing better. Did you bring Kiro with you?"

"Not today, Mom. He's busy with some stuff."

"Okay, well, next time you see him, let him know he should stop by. I miss him, Ashley. He reminds me so much of your father."

I try to keep my face blank.

Mom, the last time you saw Kiro, he was maybe fifty-five kilos soaking wet. Now he's pushing a hundred and ten and raging with adolescent hormones. I doubt you'd even recognize him.

"Of course, Mom. I'll let him know."

"Thank you, dear. How are your friends, in that game of yours? What were their names . . . Wind, Brand, and Slend, was it? Oh, and Johnny's boy, Jason! How are they?"

Brand's dead, Mom. I killed her. Watched her eyes melt from the inside out. Wind and Slend might end up with her, if I can't pull off this job for Sawyer, and Jase is stuck on a gummie drone rig who knows where, probably scared out of his mind. He's not used to spook shit like I am. Like we are.

"The girls are good, Mom. We took down a dragon the other day, was a great fight. Wish you could have seen it. Jase is busy with his tech stuff, you know how he is."

She laughs, a throaty peal of sound.

"That boy and his electronics, I swear. I'll never forget when Johnny came back to camp with him, some squalling, dirty little thing he'd found in the rubble somewhere. I thought he was crazy, trying to rescue some poor refugee baby in the middle of the Dubs, but he went and did it, regs be damned.

Told me, 'What was I supposed to do, Naomi, just leave him there?' Managed to whip up some formula out of mud, sticks, and leftovers, and gave him an old tablet to keep him busy until we finished the deployment. By the time we got back to base, the kid had already figured out how to bypass the child filters."

Another fit of giggling.

"His first two words were 'access denied,' and you should've seen Johnny's face. I think he was hoping for 'dada.'"

I let a smile creep across my lips.

"Sounds like Jase, all right. He still loves taking things apart. He's even figured how to put some of them back together by now."

"Is Johnny still in that tiny shop? I told him he should be a gourmet chef in one of those fancy enclave restaurants, but he never listens. He's always had the knack for it."

He stayed here to keep an eye on you, and me, and Kiro, and Jase, Mom. He's never going to leave unless it's all of us together.

"Same place as always, Mom. Pretty sure he's happier with his woks than with some uptight burbies."

"You're probably right. And you, Ashley?" I feel her hand on my shoulder, thin, but strong as iron. "How's my baby girl?"

Drowning, my lifejacket packed with lead. Falling, but my chute's gone missing. Trapped in a sphere I can't log out of, and it's spinning a step too fast.

"I'm fine, Mom. Just doing what it takes, one foot in front of the other, surviving. Making my way forward."

"One foot in front of the other, huh? I have some experience with that, Ashley." Her voice turns soft. "Just make sure you know what road it is you're walking, and where it ends, okay?"

I look over, meet her hazel eyes, shining bright with warmth and intelligence, surrounded by the cracks of age.

Dammit, Mom. Why can't you be like this all the time? Why can't we just be normal?

"I'll be fine, Mom. But thanks. I appreciate it."

"Of course, dear. You know you can talk to me about anything. Anything at all."

An alert pings in my glasses. A message, from Sawyer, hovering in front of my mother's face, but I'm the only one in the room who can see it.

"I know, Mom." I push myself to my feet. "Look, I gotta go, work keeping me busy, you know? It was great talking to you. Keep doing what Freddie tells you to, okay?"

She stands up as well, and pulls me into another hug.

"I love you, Ashley. My beautiful girl. Love you so much. Don't forget to tell Kiro to visit! It's been so long since I've had a chance to talk with him."

My arms wrap around her.

"I love you too, Mom. Be well."

I pull away and head for the airlock, trying not to cry, or scream at my selfish brother, or wonder if this is the last time I'll ever see my mother. The airlock cycles me back into the outer room, Freddie smiling at his desk.

"Good session, Ash. I really think we're gonna get this thing."

"Right, Freddie. See you next time."

Some dailies really suck.

16

[The Weight of an Avalanche]

"Sawyer."

"Ashley. Assorted others."

I'm leaning back in a battered couch, booted feet propped up on an even more battered table, the very picture of at-fucking-ease. Nowhere I'd rather be, no sir, this is the barest minimum of my attention I feel this worthless matter deserves.

And don't you just wish that wasn't a big-ass lie.

Jase is at the other end of the couch, his fingers nervously twining and untwining, like a tiny nest of cobras. I've never seen him this scared, not even when he backed down a pissed-off Han Triad goon, not even when I dragged him out of a dryburb pedohouse, doorframe still smoking from the shaped charges I managed to scrounge up, his kidnappers trussed and barely alive, moaning how they hadn't even had time to do anything. Wind and Slend each have their own chair, their positions as fauxchalant as mine, all of us in a semicircle facing a viewscreen, Sawyer's face staring back. We're on the mysterious rig again, Sawyer's terse message summoning us to return on another interminable boat ride. He finally speaks.

"It's time. Mr. Tanner, fill them in, please."

Jase clears his throat.

"Well, uh, we backtraced the, uh, shipping manifest you guys pulled out of Industan, and, uh, after cracking through some shell corps, we found the parent corp. That's, uh, that's the good news."

I blow a tuft of blue hair out of my eyes. Need to trim my bangs soon.

"Good news means there's also bad news. Let's have it."

Jase replaces Sawyer's face with a massive schematic, wire-frame lines crossing like a bowl of Johnny's tastiest.

"Bad news is, uh, the parent corp trail dead-ends in this arcology. Neo Frisco."

I suck on my lower lip. Neo Frisco isn't one of the biggest arcos in silkie territory, but it's not some small corp park either, and, more importantly, it's one of the oldest, built around the still-glowing craters of the former silkie holy ground, Norcal Bay, which means it's going to be *heavily* defended. Scouts aren't going to stand a chance. This can't be what has Jase so worked up.

"Specfuckingtacular. Probably an entire battalion of corp private security guarding that arco. Guess we're done here." I stand up. "Have fun starting a war, Sawyer, because it's going to take a battlegroup to break into *that*."

"Not so fast, Ashley."

Sawyer doesn't sound amused.

"We, and by that I mean *I*, need to know if the trail ends here, or if it extends all the way to one of the Big Three, and if so, how deep. You and your team, whether you realize it or not, have been training for this your entire lives. There is a reason we allow Ditchtown its autonomy. I am calling in the marker. This mission cannot fail. To that end, the Theocrophant has approved the use of additional materiel."

The spaghetti tangle schematic disappears, replaced by a rapidly expanding list of drones, blue outlines surrounding them. The last two glow red. Slend's low whistle is the only sound in the silence. What feels like an hour later, I pick my jaw up off the floor and sink back into the sofa, trying to process.

"What the *shit*, Sawyer. This isn't 'additional materiel,' this is a fucking 'pocalypse."

Wind's voice is low, awestruck as she reads down the list.

"That's two full companies of Hercs, a squadron of Ravens, an entire complement of Shredders, three EM platforms, an offshore railgun cruiser with assorted screens, and, and, and . . ."

She trails off, coming to the last item in the list. I can feel my heart beating in my chest, low, steady, and I have to moisten my suddenly dry lips.

"That's . . . that's an orbital, Sawyer. Those are *kinetics*."

"Correct." His voice is dry, inflectionless.

"What the *hell* is going on?"

"Mr. Tanner, please explain to the team why such resources have been made available."

Jase swallows, his throat bobbing, sweat now visible on his forehead. Suddenly, he looks his age, and I remember just how young he is. How young we all are.

"Last night, a team of eight Gamers in the new haphoods assaulted the, uh, Theocrophant's residence. The Gamers started unarmed. The, uh, the Theocrophant and, uh, the, uh, the—"

Sawyer cuts in.

"The Theocrophant and two guards made it out, all heavily wounded. The detail for his residence was over a hundred of our best security personnel, along with local swift-reaction drone forces."

A brief clip of shadowy violence unfolds, uniformed figures threshed before reapers, suddenly materializing blood a constant motif. Sawyer continues.

"We were utterly outclassed, and only the last-ditch sacrifice

of the guard leader, a Captain Banks, thwarted the final at-
tacker, allowing the Theocrophant to escape. Preliminary autopsy analysis puts all eight assailants as members of the Game
guild IonSeal. None seemed aware that they were fighting in
the real at any point in time. Their losses were total, but not
before inflicting more than thirteen times their number of fa-
talities against the finest soldiers we have to offer."

I clench my fist.

"And why isn't this all over the socials?"

"Don't be naive, Ashley. You think we would let something
like an almost successful assassination on the Theocrophant
get out?"

"God*dammit*, Sawyer! You're talking about warshit! We
didn't sign up for this!"

"And yet here you are." Cold, so cold, that voice. "My re-
sponsibility is to protect the Church of Christ Ascendant, the
'gummies' as you so brashly call them, from *all* foreign threats,
and I will do *anything* to meet that goal, because if I don't,
then we will *die*." A brief silence. "Yes, Ashley Akachi, this *is*
war, but right now, it is still a *small* war, it is still a *conventional*
war, and it is our job to ensure it *stays* that way."

"With *kinetics*?" Wind squawks.

"Correct, Fatima bint al-Hajj. Preferably with conventional
drone forces disguised as a rival corp we can plausibly deny.
If necessary, with a railgun and orbital kinetics that will likely
cost me my position. Ultimately, without atomics."

The room falls still, all of us remembering the lessons from
school, the news reports, those terrible pinpricks of starlight
broadcast across a burning planet. The Green Mountains, the
Bowl of Ash, the Pits; Dead Zones littering the length and
breadth of the continent. The burnt black shadows engraved
across concrete walls; the hairless withered dead, curled in on
themselves like spiders, silkie and gummie alike; red skies

beneath dirty brown clouds. A moment when it seemed everything must fall apart, everyone breathlessly waiting to see if other countries would follow our lead and end it all.

Unbidden, my mind drifts to a wooden box filled with medals, tortured sobs from a broken woman, a grimy three-by-five covered in filth.

A hushed voice breaks the silence. I realize it's mine.

"But won't the silkies escalate even further? If we hit an arco? With kinetics?"

"There is a significant chance, yes, but it's one we're now forced to take. We can negotiate if it turns out this was a rogue effort from beneath C-Level in the Big Three, some overeager executive making a power grab, but we *must* bring a stop to these haphoods before this turns into something unstoppable. As it is, it took a considerable effort to talk the Theocrophant down from the nuclear option. He was fairly hysterical."

I catch something in Sawyer's voice in that last sentence, a hitch on the faintest edges of hearing.

Is he . . . afraid? *Is it just as hard for him to confront this as it is for us? With everything he's done, that he made Mom do?*

"Therefore, Ashley, Fatima, Brynn, Jason, it falls on you to bring me back my answers. You will have the support of an entire battlegroup, all tasked with ensuring you achieve your goal. Command them as you see fit."

"Why us?" I whisper.

"Why you? Why *you*?"

Sawyer's laugh coughs out like a death rattle.

"I have no drone pilots better, no scientists smarter, no one I can turn to in this terrible hour more useful than you; you children who've gloried in strife for over ten years and proven yourselves the greatest warriors on the planet. You think we don't force our people to play the Game, and other countries the same? You think it's a coincidence that Game assets are functionally identical to the most widely used military equipment across the world? The Game is what we use to train our *elites*, it's what *everyone* uses to train their elites, and none of them *ever* make it to the endgame ladder because they aren't *obsessed*.

"Why you? *You* are the magic bullet I'm conjuring out of thin air, my deus ex machina, the only ones who have a chance to keep this planet from plunging into a catastrophe even worse than the Water Wars. *You*."

I thought I knew who Sawyer was. I thought I knew the depths of his pragmatism, the extent to which he'd sacrifice himself and others. I thought that beneath it all, there might still be an ounce of humanity, a flicker of warmth.

I was wrong. The coldness of his voice makes that more than clear.

"Do. Not. Fuck. This. Up."

17

[Kobayashi]

"Eyes overhead. Passives only."

Wind's voice is soft, softer than I've ever heard. I can't blame her. This doesn't feel at all like the Game, no matter how similar the interface, no matter how much we're trying to treat it like just another encounter. I've put her in charge of recon, since she's actually our best coordinator, Slend's efforts in the dailies notwithstanding, but I can feel her jumpiness. I'm jumpy too. It's been a long day, and not looking to get any shorter.

"We're fucked if we launch those kinetics, Ash. There's no way the silkies don't come back from that with nukes. Not on an arco. They can explain away drones as another corp, some railgun shots as a targeting algorithm glitch, but not kinetics. Everyone can track orbitals."

"Fucked anyway," Slend says, her attention on the Hercs moving into position to the south and east of the target, still outside the arco walls, moonlight dappling their camo panels. "Too many defenders. Even with kinetics. Total Kobayashi."

I split my attention away from the Shredders I'm maneuvering—fast, highly mobile four-limbed drones with molyblade edges on the inside of each leg. Good for killing things long after the ammunition runs out.

"Then we better hope we can cheat a way out. Jase, you doing okay?"

"Y-yup."

For some reason, I flash back to earlier in the day. Steve the pilot.

"It'll be fine, Jase. You know what to do. Remember the plan. Just be ready for my signal."

I flip from command view to strategic, taking in the entirety of the battlefield. The southeast quadrant of the arcology unfolds beneath me, a sprawling mass of interlinked office towers, apartment complexes, and vertical malls radiating outward from the huge domed manufacturing complex in the middle, purveyor of trinkets and knickknacks to all the drones swarming within. Massive conduits snake through the buildings like hideous metal veins, shunting people, cargo, food—anything and everything anywhere and everywhere so long as it never has to leave the arco.

It looks like a distended pimple, waiting to burst.

Our target is an eighty-story tower located halfway to the manufacturing complex, bordering one of the smaller outer neighborhoods. On the forty-sixth floor is the main office for Unlimited Holdings Limited, as far up the corporate shell as Jase could pierce, and the primary server cluster for the corp. If we can get one of the Shredders inside, it should be able to pull out any information related to the hoods and bounce it back through the haplink.

Getting a Shredder inside without starting a war is going to be the trick.

"Wind, Slend, in position?"

I flex my fingers to bring me back to command view, making

sure my squads of Shredders are in position along the east wall. I'm going to be ghosting those drones soon enough, and I'm not really looking forward to another dive into Sawyer's wartech depths. Mom still hasn't made it out.

"In the box."

"Yup."

Wind's controlling the Ravens, recon and fast fire support, her natural role. Slend's on the Hercs, our heavy hitters and main tanks. I'm on the Shredders, and . . . the other two. I try not to shiver, looking at the gently blinking icons for the offshore cruiser and the orbital. Using those won't just result in some ones and zeros shifting around in a Game server, but I may not have a choice. Sawyer made it clear that failing this encounter isn't an option.

All the drones are slaved to rudimentary combat algorithms, allowing us to broadly direct them from command view, but the algorithms don't offer much tactical flexibility. For that, we have to jump into an individual unit, give it a more personal touch. Wargame encounters in endgame normally involve anywhere from fifteen to fifty units per player, and the best players know exactly when to take over a drone for maximum effect, constantly swapping among individual control, command view, and strategic view. Luckily I'll only be controlling twenty Shredders, so multitasking will be a breeze.

Just another encounter.

"Wind, let's see what we're up against."

"Raven one, going hot."

Wind flips one of her circling drones' sensors to active, bathing the area below in strobing sweeps of radar, lidar, infrared and ultrasound. Threat icons splash into existence across the map.

Slend is right. We don't have a chance.

Three security stations, each packed with more than two

hundred rapid-response drones, lie between us and the tower, their defensive emplacements already cycling up. Almost fifty Hercs patrol the empty ground-level streets, guarding against corporate espionage and sabotage from any discontented arco residents. A hangar in the upper left, near the manufacturing dome, starts spitting out interceptors, swarms of deadly anti-air drones capable of dropping a Raven in one pass. There's no way we're making it through all of that without using kinetics.

Well, maybe one way.

"Scenario three. Slend, take us in."

Slend's Hercs rip out a volley of high-velocity rounds, aiming at the same spot on the thirty-foot-high wall surrounding the arco. Massive divots appear across its concrete surface, then a segment of wall simply vaporizes, loosened stone collapsing to either side of the gap in a geyser of dust and debris. My Shredders are already flowing through, the Hercs not far behind. We're met with counterfire almost immediately, HV rounds and cluster bombs spraying back from the nearest arco Hercs. Two Shredders disintegrate, caught on the edge of the blast zone, and one of Slend's Hercs loses a leg, but her counterfire obliterates the closest threats in a flurry of violence. Flames and smoke lick up into the night sky, highlighting the underbelly of the arco. Cracked asphalt flows beneath my feet, alarms wailing from behind shattered glass windows, and we make our way forward.

My senses fall into the peculiar rhythm of battle, time slowing down and speeding up simultaneously, attention flicking from Shredder to command view to strategic view to Shredder like a hummingbird with attention deficit disorder, each slice lasting a lifetime, then gone in less than a second.

Wind's Ravens stooping and screaming across the sky, missiles streaking in whipcrack lines, clouds of interceptors chasing them like angry wasps.

Slend and I smashing our way through a cluster of riot drones, chrome and polymer pinwheeling out of explosive impacts, one of the Hercs going down to concentrated micro missiles.

Shadowed megaspire canyons linking the occasional noon-bright intersection, buzzing yellow sodium lights flitting past like falling stars, a brief lull amidst the chaos.

The flaming wreckage of a Raven slamming into the upper floor of a megaspire, debris raining from above in deadly molten drops, crippled interceptors plummeting in hailstone impacts.

Our forces slowly dwindling, whittled down by a nonstop onslaught, but pushing inward, our target creeping closer and closer.

The innocuous red icons waiting for me to unleash their atmosphere-rending screams.

Shit. We're not going to make it through with just the drones.

"Wind, Slend. Gonna backdoor. Wind, you're on the Shredders."

I transfer control of all but one of my Shredders to Wind, leaving her to juggle them with her four remaining Ravens, keeping them darting around our flanks. Slend continues to press forward with the Hercs, a solid nucleus. I commit fully to the one Shredder I kept for myself, feeling the metal close in around me, through me, becoming me, and split off at a tangent, arrowing away from the others.

My senses expand, sharpen, the taste of the battle raw on my tongue, like the copper bite of fresh blood, streams of energy rippling across electromagnetic spectrums. My limbs flicker like clockwork, driving me forward in bounding surges, scuttling across conduit pipes and through alleyways. Polymer flesh settles around my metal bones, my union with the drone once again driving away all awareness of my biological shell back in the hapsphere.

A riot drone appears around a corner, wargear festooning its spindly limbs. I flick my wrist and its control module separates into four equal pieces, gutted insides sparking, chunky body toppling like a felled tree. I push my pace higher.

"Massive concentration between us and the target, Ash. No way to avoid. Contact in fifty."

Fifty seconds to make the impossible possible, my desperate throw of the dice. If this doesn't work, I'll have no choice but to engage with my last two options. No choice but to usher in Armageddon.

No fucking pressure. Thanks, Sawyer.

Another two riot drones appear, a Herc behind them. I cartwheel to the side, predicting the first HV round. It slashes past, obliterating the lower floor of a megaspire, contrails corkscrewing in its passing, vacuum pressure trying to drag me back. The riot drones fire, chattering bursts of puncturing lead, seeking my body. I dance the stuttering steps of death, never predictable, never still, closing in until my legs kick out and eviscerate their innards.

Something slams into my side, an explosive round from the Herc's close-defense system. One of my limbs disintegrates, fluid leaking from the jagged stump, but three limbs are plenty to deal with a Herc. I engulf it in my whirlwind, and wreckage trails the wake. I push my pace higher.

"Contact in forty-five."

I crash through a ground-floor glass window, wireframe schematics unfolding in my mind, my destination within reach. Pry the lift-bank doors open with a squealing wrench, delicately balanced on one leg, and scuttle up the shaft, floor numbers whizzing past.

"Forty."

Carve open the doors on floor twenty-three, catapulting myself into the corridor beyond. APPHO INDUSTRIES blazes above a set of double doors. Glowing metal trails my entrance.

"Thirty-five."

Dart down a lushly carpeted hallway, abstract paintings dotting its walls. Left. Right. Right again. Left. Reduce another door to scrap.

"Thirty."

The ambient temperature drops significantly, cooling units keeping server clusters at peak efficiency. An interface socket extends from my body, and I mate with the appropriate server jack.

"Jase, you're up."

"Twenty-five."

"Uh, okay. Going."

I pull out of the Shredder with an almost painful effort, shifting my attention back to command view, watching our forces close in on a lurid red mass of enemies. The two deadly icons glow seductively, beckoning. I take a breath, ready to resume controls of the Shredders from Wind, when my vision wavers, then explodes. Rank upon rank of jagged barricades appear, an impossible obstacle of firewalls, flensing protocols ready to neuter any intruder.

Dammit, I'm still linked to the Shredder somehow. Fucking Sawy—

"Twenty."

"Hah! Idiots didn't update their credentials yet!"

The barriers pop like soap bubbles and data shudders into solid existence around me, a supernova of information, overwhelming in its intensity. Helpless, I watch my viewpoint twist and turn through the infinite depths, flicking from point to

point almost faster than thought. Logic structures loom overhead in convoluted Escherian knots, subdirectories draw me
toward them with a singularity's irresistible pull, partitions
paint the multidimensional space in colors that defy description, but still I'm dragged onward, delving through what
seems to be the very fabric of the world.

"Fifteen."

"Gimme a sec . . . okay, we're in. Grabbing admin."

My view distorts, shifting out, the blinding information
cloud falling away until it's a single star in an entire galaxy.
Twinkling jewels lie below me, a goddess's view of a digital
firmament, and suddenly I'm plummeting back in, uncontrol-
lably descending toward another mote.

"Ten."

"Looking, looking . . ."

The supernova engulfs me again, this one a darker flavor,
deeper, vaster. Entire civilizations' worth of data flow past, corp
archives dating back to before the Split, before the Dubs, before the rising seas and choking winds and murderous storms
pinwheeled across the world like razorblade tops.

"Five."

"Almost there . . ."

Names, faces, dates, words, projects, numbers. They slam
into me, a firehose of data gushing its contents across my brain,
and I feel like I should be screaming. Maybe I am.

"Three."

"Almost . . ."

The endless ocean narrows into a discrete point, a single
drop, infinitesimal. It might as well not even exist.

"Two."

"Got it! I've got it! I'm out!"

My mind returns to me, command view reestablishing its

normality over the fever dream in which I lay trapped. The orbital icon is close enough to touch, a whisper away from activation.

"One."

Speaking feels like too much, entirely too much, but I am Ashura the Terrible, Ashura, Ash, Ashley, and it is either speak, or let the world die.

"Fall back," I croak. "Max speed. Let's get the hell out of here."

Our forces bleed away from the red, Wind and Slend hopping between drones to cover the retreat, and it takes everything I have not to puke, hot bile stinging my throat.

18

[Just Another Encounter]

The lights are too bright. The darkness is overwhelming. My clothes are a second skin, fire racing through my nerve endings. My skin is an alien artifact, draped across pretender's bones, a usurper squatting atop a throne. The air is suffocating hot heavy damp can't breathe thinning out now crystal shards slicing lungs with its absence of where did the sound go no deafening roars of force smash—

"Ash!"

The world snaps back into focus, like a low-res pic that finally finishes buffering. I realize I'm sprawled out on my back, arms and legs gently twitching. Wind stares down at me, haphood peeled back, concern etched across her dark features, techs hurrying around her to service the spheres. Slend stumbles up next to her, wiping a hand across her mouth.

"Boss?"

It takes a second. To remember. Who I am.

". . . Yeah. Just another encounter. That's all."

I push myself to my feet, ignoring throbbing actuators. The pain will pass.

"C'mon, let's clean up. See what Jase managed to grab."

Neither of them asks any further questions, and I'm grateful.

I don't want to think about anything right now. We shamble off to the locker room in undead lurches, unsteady feet dragging us across the treacherous floor. Maybe some hot water will make me feel human again.

"Excellent work, Ashley. You and your team both." Sawyer gazes out at us from the viewscreen, tucked away in some office somewhere on the rig.

I rub at my head with one of the scratchy towels, trying to convince my hair that it's dry. Beside me, Wind stares at the ceiling sprawled along the couch, arms spread wide. Slend straddles a chair and squirts another stream of water into her mouth. Jase nervously taps his fingers on a side table, gaze distant, lost. At least Sawyer let us keep our own clothes this time.

"We didn't fuck it up."

Sawyer's mouth tilts up the tiniest fraction.

"No. No, you most definitely did not. I must confess, I did not think we would find ourselves in this position. I was fully prepared to be mounting a full-scale territorial defense at this very moment."

I wave my hand tiredly.

"Yeah, that's us, the SunJewel Warriors, overachievers extraordinaire, bringers of world peace. Just another show for the stream. Cut the shit, Sawyer. What's going on?"

Sawyer resumes his normal flinty expression.

"Very well. Since you didn't activate the cruiser or orbital assets, a tenuous peace is holding along our borders with the Silicon Zone Egalitare—the 'silkies.' The Big Three suspect we might have attacked the New Frisco arcology, but each of them suspects the other two just as much. This gives us a window in which to act."

"Gives *us* a window to act? We've done enough, Sawyer." I slump back next to Wind on the battered couch, and pretend that my next words have nothing to do with my experiences in the drones. "Use your military people. That's what they're there for. We found what you wanted."

"You're done when I say you're done," Sawyer snaps back. "Those hoods are still out there, or have you forgotten about your friend so easily?"

Brand's face flashes through my mind, and I tense.

"*Fuck* you, Sawyer. We've more than earned our creds on this. You've got your target. You pull the fucking trigger this time."

". . . I can't."

"What do you mean, 'you can't'? That's *bullshit*, Sawyer. We're a fucking Game guild. You're the government. *You* collect the fucking taxes, *you* deal with the existential crisis."

"The target is not accessible by drone."

"What?"

Sawyer runs a hand through his bristly hair.

"In his brief time in the New Frisco cloud, your friend Jason secured essential information. Information identifying the individual behind these hoods."

"So? Why are you telling us this?"

"The individual in question is an EVP for one of the Big Three, the ultracorp WGSK. He lives in a compound covered by concentrically smaller domes, each laced with a Faraday shield, and all his connections are through shielded underground tunnels. No signals get in or out, and the sort of sustained bombardment required to breach a gap would prove . . . prohibitive. It's quite an elegant setup, actually."

"Again. Why do we care? If the drones can't get in, use a commando squad or whatever you call it. Send one of them."

"Oh, but I am. The best one I have, experts all." An ugly light enters Sawyer's eyes. "You."

I sit bolt upright.

"No fucking way, Sawyer. You forced us to ghost, not invade some silkie's fortress in the real. We're Gamers, not soldiers."

"You seem to be laboring under the misapprehension that you have a choice, Ashley. You aren't just doing this for me, or the Church, or to prevent the party favors from popping off once more."

His voice drops.

"You're doing it for Fatima bint al-Hajj's parents and extended family, surrounded by the dispossessed who are all too prone to riots." Wind's eyes narrow. "You're doing it for Brynn Murphey's brother, serving five years in prison for inciting revolt, guarded by a warden who views a dead inmate as another profitable empty bed."

Slend's mouth becomes a razor line.

"You're doing it for your mother, Naomi Akachi, practicing katas in her cell of mind and body, desperate to escape both."

Somehow I'm standing, fists clenched at my sides.

"If you even think about going after her I will fucking *end* you, Sawyer."

"I'm just pointing out realities, Ashley. Realities that everyone must acknowledge, and for you, that means—"

His eyes widen in shock.

"Ta—"

The world flips upside down, something smashing an iron fist into my cheek and nose, my legs flopping over the couch. Darkness cuts down with guillotine swiftness, the overhead lights blanked. Ringing echoes fill my ears, a failed processor shrieking malfunction.

Wha . . .

Red light sputters sullenly into existence, emergency generators coming online. I can feel my brain doing the same, the ringing slowly fading. Clarity kicks open the door of concussion, citing necessity. Groaning, I peel myself off the floor, snowblind static fuzzing my vision. I fumble off my broken glasses and stick them in a pocket.

Just. Another encounter.

"Wind," I croak. "Slend. Brand." I can feel blood dripping off the side of my face in slow trickles.

"Guh. The . . . fuck was . . . that?"

Wind sounds groggy, confused. She tries to push herself up, but tips back over after regaining a knee and sprawls out on her stomach. She must have hit her head harder than I did.

". . . Explosion. Close."

Slend is a little more coherent. I hear her spit. Something clatters on the metal. Sounds like a tooth. She drags Wind upright, holding her close, stabilizing her with a heavily muscled arm. I press a hand to my brow, trying to stanch the flow of blood.

"Brand?"

Noisy puking.

"Good, you're still alive. Let's figure out who the fuck just tried to blow us up."

Never mind how close they came to succeeding.

Just another. Encounter.

I take a step toward the exit and almost fall, the room spinning around me in nausea-inducing dips and whirls. I suck in a deep breath. Must have hit my head harder than I thought, but there's no time to be weak, not right now. The others need me. I force my vision to stabilize, then will my feet to move. The other three follow behind, Wind still leaning against Slend's side.

The same sullen red light illuminates the hapsphere chamber, draping the scaffolds in eerie shadows. Muffled pops sound in the distance, a sort of irregular staccato clapping that slowly gets louder. When recognition finally dawns, I swear, and lurch into cover beneath one of the scaffolds, motioning the others to join me.

"Someone's shooting at something," I hiss.

Slend raises an eyebrow.

"Hostiles?"

"I doubt they're here with fucking fruitbaskets."

"Fair. Plan?"

"Take 'em out."

She nods, and hands Wind over to . . .

Who is that? That's not Brand. What happened t—

. . . Jase, both of them leaning back against the sphere's base. I put a hand on his shoulder, trying to center myself. Trying to rid my brain of the accusatory eyeless stare of my dead friend, to shake away the concussive fog warping my thoughts.

"Jase, Wind's out of it right now, so you're gonna have to be her legs, okay?"

He looks back at me, pale moon sclerae wide under his glasses. Another burst of shots chatters in the distance, even louder this time, and he flinches.

"Wha-what do I do?"

"For right now, hide here. Slend and I are going to scout the area. Once it's clear, we'll come back and grab you two. We need to find Sawyer, figure out what the hell's going on."

"You're . . . you're not going to leave us, right? Ash?"

I stare at him, trying to understand. *Why would Brand ask . . . Oh yeah. He's probably still in shock. Not used to this kind of endgame shit.*

"No, stupid. We're not going to leave you. We're all getting off this stupid rig. Together."

Jase nods, lower lip tucked between his teeth, Wind's head lolling against his shoulder. I grab his hand and squeeze.

"Together. I promise. Just keep breathing, Brand. Slend, let's find the doors."

We creep away from the hapsphere, scuttling from shadow to shadow, listening to the gunfire grow louder. Screams start adding their counterpoint, quickly silenced by kinetic teeth, and I wish this was just a psych-sec, another test in the Game, not real not final not like Mikelas on the bridge that was just everyday life in Ditchtown but this is something that might snuff out every last one of us kill me and Wind and Slend and Jase and Johnny and Mom just like I killed Brand and—

Just another encounter.

I force air through my nose and mouth, force my panicky mind back under control, following the advice I gave Jase scant minutes ago. More echoing shots, more screams, more tight silences, drawing closer every time. A rough beast slouching our direction with the ponderous inevitability of a gummie Preacher, a swarm of wardrones, a cat-six supercell, nothing left but to find a corner and pray that terrible gaze sweeps by uninterested. All I can do is trust my instincts, carrying me through the shadows like a second skin, a dance I've done in so many terrifying slices of make-believe but never like this, never in the real.

Just another encounter.

Finally, we reach the blank metal door leading out of the sphere chamber, a red emergency light glowing fitfully atop it. I point my finger to the other side and Slend glides over, the two of us flanking the archway, our nostrils flaring, our eyes wide. My skin feels stretched too tight, numb, tingling, some primordial part of the brain stem flaring chemical surges my body *cannot* avoid. I see everything. I see nothing. The seconds fall with heartbeat crashes.

Just another encounter.

An eruption of noise, harsh cracks sounding like a devil's whip.

Just another encounter.

A gurgling moan.

Just another encounter.

Fingers claw at the other side of the door, scraping down the paint-flaked surface. The barest tremor of feet kicking on iron, tiny vibrations the last ordered energy a life will ever construct. Silence.

Just another encounter.

A gentle creak, the door swinging back into the corridor. A beast at the threshold, pawing its way in with talons of lead. Nothing moves.

Just another encounter.

The thin barrel of a rifle pokes through, malignant matte black snout yawning wide. My heart hammers a war rhythm in my chest.

Just another encounter.

I wait for a few more inches to clear, then wrap my hands around the metal and *pull.* Thunder erupts next to my face, bullets spraying off the floor and into the distance, a pale finger clenched on the trigger, off-balance body following behind. Heat sears my palms, but letting go means death, so I ride the pain, pushing it to the back of my mind, all my attention on keeping the gun pointed away from those of us still living. A meaty thunk, then silence. The hand falls limp, flopping to the ground, and I pull the weapon free, immediately swinging it into a ready position to cover the corridor.

Nothing moves.

"Ash. Look."

I glance over at Slend, searching the sprawled body she knocked senseless, confiscated pistol in one hand. She toggles the pistol's underbarrel light and aims it at our assailant's head. Wisps of blond hair frame elfin features, peeking out from beneath a thin gray covering.

"Shit. That's one of those hoods."

A momentary surge of vile nausea, Brand's face floating in

front of me. I clear the sour spit from my mouth, hearing it splat against the deck in a phlegmy lump. The Gamer's chest slowly rises and falls below, his breathing ragged.

"Plan?"

"Go back and get the others," I respond. "We can't afford to let someone stumble over them."

Slend nods and hurries off, one more shadow amidst the red. I keep an eye on the corridor and rummage through the Gamer's odd mix of clothing—a web of tactical harnesses overlaying rumpled casual wear, hapsuit underneath, like he tried to dress himself while still in the Game. Not much useful on him, just some extra ammo magazines in curved metal shells. I pocket them, their weight heavy against my legs.

A quick check of my appropriated rifle shows it's a gummie top-of-the-line riot response model, capable of semiauto, burst, and full-auto modes of fire. I would have preferred one of the stubbier Han bullpup variants, but in the Game you learn to use whatever's available. Current magazine at half, fifteen shots remaining, normally fires rubber rounds but not today. I flick the fire selector to "burst" with a chipped thumbnail.

Slend whistles behind me, letting me know that she's approaching. I keep my sights trained on the passageway out, not relaxing for an instant. A light tap on my shoulder, Jase and Wind's ragged breathing nearby.

"I'll take point." A thought occurs to me. It should have occurred five minutes ago. Still not fully functional yet. "Jase, are you hooked in to the rig's cloud?"

"Uh, lemme check . . . yeah, but barely anything's active."

"Can you pull up a schematic?"

"If that was an option, I'd have done it when we first got here. All I've got are local data transfer protocols, and even if there was something to transfer, none of you have working glasses."

"Damn. Guess we're going in blind. I know Sawyer's office is a couple flights above us. Slend, standard leapfrog. Jase, stay behind us, stay in cover. Let's go."

Just another encounter.

I slip into the corridor, stepping over the corpse of one of the sphere techs, blood inching away from her in a slowly expanding pool. My boots squelch lightly as I pass through. Psych-sec. Ignore it. I try to make my senses expand, take in the entirety of this unfamiliar environment, breathe in the threat vectors and exhale our counters. Water drips fitfully from a ruptured pipe, and the low whoop of alarms strobes monotonously. Half-heard, half-felt gunfire tattoos its presence in intermittent bursts. The rifle's sights feel like an extension of my own eyes, tracking everywhere I look.

The door at the end of corridor hangs open, a large space beyond. I duck my head through for a quick look. A food printer sparks in the corner, highlighting toppled chairs and several overturned tables. Bodies litter the floor, all but one in the dull camo of the Border Patrol. I make three quick hand gestures at Slend—moving in to the right, come in after and clear left. Deep breath. Inhale. Exhale.

I dash through the doorway, staying low, neck crawling with the anticipation of incoming shots tearing me apart, scanning the right side of the room, corners first, watching for movement, sights smoothly circling until I'm crouched behind a table, bullet holes dotting its thin metal length, a woefully insufficient barricade.

Silence.

"Clear."

"Clear."

I motion Jase and Wind into the room, and move up to a doorway on the far wall—if I remember correctly, it should lead us to a stairwell. Pause on the way there to check the bodies for ammo—nothing. Bad luck. The sounds of shooting grow louder. Slend takes position across from me and raises an eyebrow, red light painting her face. I nod and kick open the door. A dark shape at the end of the hallway, gun already rising, finger pulling back. Three quick kicks against my shoulder, and the shadow falls, my ears ringing once more.

I sprint forward, element of surprise gone, but no one else appears, and then I'm at the stairwell. More gunfire echoes from above, harsher, longer, angrier bursts, the uncontrolled spraying of novice operators. I slap a new magazine into the rifle, old one clattering behind, trying not to think about the dead boy with three craters in his chest, eyes blank, body tossed like a rag doll. Slend can upgrade her weapon now, more loot for the group.

Slowly ascend the stairway, Slend next to me, rolling my boots onto the wireframe metal steps, staying as silent as possible, my sights scanning the spaces above. The echoing gunfire increases in intensity, nearly on top of us. I round the first landing—nothing. Continue our slow creep. Second landing— two figures lying on the stairs, maintaining the smallest profile possible, backs to us, firing out in economical bursts, slapdash clothes thrown on over black hapsuits. A constant deluge of bullets whines and spangs into the walls around them, none seeming particularly aimed. Neither of the figures flinches, or even makes a sound.

I take out the one on the left, Slend the one on the right, a brief twitch their only recognition of death, our shots blending in with the general racket. I ignore the stench of voided bowels, the tang of fresh blood, the heavy way Slend's throat moves as she swallows. We deftly frisk them, pocketing several full magazines, not meeting each other's eyes.

Just another encounter.

Gradually, with no return fire, the wild shooting up top halts. A couple of short cheers echo down the stairwell.

"Hey!" I call out, taking a chance. "Who's there?"

The self-congratulating stops. A nervous voice responds.

"CCA Border Patrol! Who're you?"

"Friendlies, under Sawyer."

". . . Miss Ashura?"

". . . Lieutenant Chaddington?"

I move to the second landing, carefully peering around the corner. A bloodied group of BP soldiers stares back at me from around the edges of the hallway doorframes, maybe eight in total, gun barrels all aimed in my direction, most twitching in spasmodic jerks.

Please don't fucking grief me.

No one shoots, and I release a breath, taking in the rest of the scene. Several bodies lie out in the open, twisted in the origami of violent death, long stains on the walls a deeper shade of crimson. One of the soldiers steps out and waves, pistol in hand, directing the others to lower their weapons.

"It *is* you! Where'd you learn how to use a gun?"

I roll my eyes and motion for Slend to stay put, keep watch on the stairs, and then I walk over to the lieutenant. We duck inside what looks like a small classroom.

"Yes, Sky, it's me. What's the situation?"

He fumbles to check his pistol's ammo, then slides the magazine back home. I wonder if he even saw it, his adrenaline-enlarged eyes never leaving my face.

"Someone suicided a fucking—excuse my language—plane into us. Took out the command uplink. Our entire cloud's offline! You know as much as I do at this point."

"Sawyer?"

"Dunno. We were on our way to check when we got pinned

down here. I lost—" His throat bobs, posture momentarily stiffening. "—lost five of my people. We got ambushed coming from the armory, got trapped in this hallway. It was a shooting range for them."

"Is the armory still secure?"

"Was when we left, but who knows now." He shakes his head. "What the hell is going on? Those don't look like silkie troops. And what are *you* doing here again?"

I think about trying to explain to him that he's fighting local Gamers, trapped in a quasi-reality they think is just another encounter, commanded by an as yet unknown force lurking within the corporate veil of WGSK, which may or may not lead the entire planet into another radioactive war, and that my Game guild has been dragooned into foiling their nefarious plans by his government's unofficial spymaster.

Yeah, no.

"We need to find Sawyer. What's the quickest way to his office?"

He twitches his hapgloved fingers like he's summoning a waypoint, then scowls.

"Of course. Cloud's down. It's . . . up another two flights, left at the end of the hallway, one of the doors on the right."

"Thanks."

I turn to leave. He grabs my sleeve. I suppress my initial reaction to drop him.

"Wait, you're just going by yourself? Miss Ashura, it's dangerous out there. I can't let you do that. This isn't like the Game."

No, you idiot, it's exactly like the Game, and that's the problem.

"It's just another encounter."

Skyler looks at me.

"What was that?"

Stop thinking with your dick and get out of my way.

"If it makes you feel better, your squad can take point. Have they trained in CQB? Room clearing? Dynamic entry? Studied Fairbairn at all?"

He lets go and fiddles with his pistol.

"We had some lessons in basic. All of us here are mainly in charge of surveillance drones, though."

I try not to sigh. Surveillance drones, while requiring a high degree of skill to operate effectively, don't translate their inputs to much more than patience and an occasional vigorous wrist roll, and Sky's "lessons" were likely forgotten as soon as he graduated, no matter how keen he is on following regulations.

Fucking newbies.

"I'm sure it'll all come back to you. C'mon, let's go. We've gotta keep moving."

I leave him behind to get his people ready and head back to Slend and the others.

"Plan?"

"This group's gonna show us where Sawyer's at. Odds are good they'll shit themselves again if there's another encounter. Stay in the back, stay low."

"Meatshields."

I'm about to nod when I realize what we're actually saying. Slend arrives at the same understanding a second later. We stare at each other for a long moment.

"Shit."

"Yeah. No respawns this time. Do your best to cover them if you can. I'll take right side."

"Yup."

"Hey, Jase?"

He looks up at me from the lower landing, Wind still leaning on his shoulder.

"Yeah?"

"We're gonna be moving up, following a group of soldiers. Stay behind us, and don't leave cover unless we tell you to."

"So exactly what I've already been doing. Thanks, Sun Tzu."

"Just trying to keep you alive. You're welcome."

He flips a rude gesture at me, and I hold down a grin. We're in a bad spot, but Brand never liked being told what to do either.

Keep it together. Brand's dead, and you could easily be next.

Lieutenant Chaddington and his people come clattering into the stairwell, bunching up behind each other, some trying to look in all directions at once, others tunneling in to a single spot with fevered intensity. My lips tighten. Sky gets them into two ragged lines and they funnel up to the next landing, gun barrels bristling like a frightened porcupine's quills, frequently crossing each other's field of fire. I shake my head and follow, Slend on my left hip.

No one shoots at us, and up they go again, an ungainly centipede. I motion to Slend, pointing at the corridor they didn't bother clearing. She nods, and kneels behind the wall, rifle steady, both of us covering our rear. I beckon for Jase—he starts climbing, Wind stumbling after, and then everything happens all at once.

Screams and gunfire erupt from above, some of the former mercilessly cut short by the latter. A sudden figure at the end of the hallway, loping toward us, angular shape raised to its shoulder. I squint down my sights—is it wearing a uniform? My own finger tightening on the trigger, slowly, not yet at the hair's width separating life and death.

A swarm of murderous insects buzzes my ear, and I close the circuit. A brief rattle, echoed from beside me, and the figure flips onto its back. Unmoving.

Just another encounter.

I turn my attention to the upper landing, one pincer of the trap hopefully dismantled. Jase stares at me, mouth gaping.

"Are . . . are you okay, Ash?"

Stinging hotness drips from my jaw, a new line of red flowing over the dried blood from earlier. I reach a hand up and touch ragged tears in my flesh.

"It's just an ear. Mostly intact. Wait here."

I take the stairs two at a time, stopping just below the next landing, beside Lieutenant Chaddington. He's crouched beside the doorframe, an unmoving body sprawled halfway through. The lieutenant blindly sticks his pistol around the frame and fires until his trigger clicks, then leans back, breath heavy, helmet slightly askew. The body's glassy eyes give me an inscrutable examination, no thoughts left to move them.

"Situation?"

Lieutenant Chaddington flinches, like someone stuck a jolter to his ass.

"Oh jeez, you scared me! Someone ambushed us, we were almost through and then, just . . . shit! Hazelton and Berkshire are down. The rest took cover in the room on the left. There was a lot of shooting. Hey, did you know your ear's bleeding?"

No, I totally missed the part where a bullet tore through it, a couple centimeters from killing me, and oh yeah, the pain isn't excruciating at all.

"Does the room have any exits?"

He pats at his pockets, searching for something.

"Uhh, no, I don't think so."

"Why isn't your squad shooting?"

"They were before."

He keeps patting at his pockets, becoming more and more frantic, gaze shifting like he's forgotten something important and sheer willpower can change reality itself. Finally, he looks up at me.

"Do you have any ammo?"

I can't help it. I put my palm over my face. A couple bullets zip through the doorway, just enough to let us know someone's still watching.

"Holy. Shit. You forgot to grab extra ammo from the armory. That's, like, *literally* lesson one of endgame. Let me guess, you each took the standard service weapon and two bundled mags from a ready locker, right?"

He nods miserably.

"Which, based on the volume of shots earlier, means the rest of your group is probably out of ammo as well, and trapped in a room with one way out. Gee fucking gee. How many attackers?"

"One? Maybe? It all happened so fast. This isn't like basic at all."

"For fuck's sake. You didn't even *count?*"

"It was dark, and there were people running, and, and and—"

". . . Fine. It's . . . Jesus. Fine. I'll deal with it. Somehow."

I pop my head out in a darting motion, then retract just as fast. A bullet whips past almost instantly, but I'm already back in cover. I note the impact mark. Good reflexes, good aim. Great. Probably one of the upper-tier guilds.

Fuck.

Hopefully not someone I know.

Focus. Wide corridor. Second body crumpled maybe a step out, reachable. Small alcoves equally spaced, alternating left and right. Enough room to shelter in, with an open door. Shooting gallery if the door's closed. Gun barrel peeking around the far left corner of the hallway's end, hugging the floor. Prone target.

I take a second to think, see the clues, the options. Another bullet hits the far wall, our unseen shooter prudent with pinning fire, the bullet pinging away with the higher pitch of a lighter caliber. My eyes fall on the corpse. It stares at me, not quite accusatory, not quite Brand's empty sockets, but almost as if it knows what I'm considering. I give a mental shrug. No other way out that I can see.

"Pull that body over here."

Lieutenant Chaddington looks at me like I told him to fuck his mother. With a needlefish. He's obviously never had to deal with a psych-sec before.

"But that's Berkshire!"

"It's a corpse is what it is. Pull it over. There's another one on top of its legs, you'll need to make sure it gets pulled in too." I don't give him time to respond. "Slend. Up here. Jase, bring Wind."

Slend kneels next to me, the other two a step lower, Jase starting to hyperventilate, Wind pawing at his chest.

Dammit, that's right, she gets grabby when she's drunk. Concussion's hitting her the same way. She needs to recover soon, start contributing to the group. No time to deal with Jase learning about the birds and the pollination drones. I focus on Slend.

"You remember what we did in Gothica? In the Marquis's castle?"

Skyler interrupts, grunting as he pulls on an arm.

"Oh, I remember that stream! You couldn't use metal because of the Marquis's anti–earth element barrier, but he had all those archers, so you . . . strapped dead goblins . . . to . . . as armor . . ."

The sounds of puking fill the stairwell, punctuated by another pinging impact on the wall. I ignore them, not relevant.

None of the ricochets have hit us yet, so the random number generator's still on our side. Slend nods.

"Good. You shield up. Once you're ready, I'll bounce across first, draw initial aggro. After the first shot, tank it. Stick to the right side, shooter's on the left. As soon as you're out, I'm firing. Take the doorway on the right and clear that room, it's about four meters up the hall. Probably empty, but best to make sure. Once you're in, if I've missed, take some shots."

"Don't miss."

"I don't plan to." I turn back to the lieutenant. "How are we doing on those bodies?"

"I've . . ." He heaves, but nothing comes out. "I've got most of Berkshire over. I . . . it's just . . . Berkshire. Hazelton. They're heavy."

"Yeah, no shit, it's called dead weight for a reason. Here, move down with Jase and Wind, let Slend handle it."

The lieutenant stumbles down the stairs, eyes red and unfocused. Slend lets her rifle hang from its strap, and grabs the body's wrists. Grunting, she drags the corpse across the corrugated floor, cloth sliding over iron, her muscles dancing. A second head appears, half of its jaw missing, its arm draped over the first body's boot. Slend pulls that one in as well, accompanied by another suppressing shot. We check both for ammo—empty—before rolling them facedown. Slend squats between them, gathering a fistful of fabric below their necks, and stands, her face tensing with effort, surging biceps lifting limp marionettes, their swaying forms awaiting the puppetmaster's command.

"Moving."

Just another encounter.

I sprint across the doorway, a shot pinging behind. Drop flat on my stomach, Slend charging out into the hall, more shots sounding off like popcorn. Bodies twitch and dance to kinetic tunes, sodden thumps and flying gore a grisly ballet, but Slend keeps her shields tight, and the flesh being ruined no longer has a mind to care. I sight down the hallway, tracking muzzle flashes through the three pairs of shifting feet, Slend twisting to shoulder open the door, bullets still pouring into the mangled lumps she holds, and I begin my exhale.

Triple crack. Triple crack.

Finish exhale.

The firing at the end of the hall stops, and I scan for movement. Nothing. Slend's voice calls out from the room on the right.

"Clear."

"Tango down," I call back, still scanning the hallway. It remains static. Slend reappears in the doorway, her rifle ready. Movement at my side. The lieutenant.

"I . . . my squad . . . is everyone okay?" The last words rise in volume, calling to the room, and he walks out into the corridor. The door opens and a head peeks out.

"Barty's gone. The rest of us are still alive. Do you have any ammo?"

They file out into a clump around the lieutenant, babbling questions, gesturing at their rifles, blocking my firing lane. I draw in a breath to yell at them to take cover, we still don't know if this level is clear or not, when a flicker of motion appears through the forest of legs. Metal clinks on metal, once, twice.

"Grenade!"

I roll behind the doorframe wall in time with my words, and a thunderclap of sound punches me in the ears again, squeezing my temples in a vise. All I can hear is ringing, a tin harmony to the hot orchestra of pain throbbing my perforated ear. Push my way up to a sitting position, back against the wall, trying to put myself together yet again, rifle resting on my lap. Quickly glance out to survey, an all too familiar move at this point. Dripping chunks of flesh paint the walls, dark smears under dead ruby light.

"Slend? You still here?"

Coughing, then an answer.

"Yeah."

Something tickles my nose, an acrid, scorched scent, different from the grenade's explosive residue, different from the usual scent of gunfire. I look over to check on Jase and Wind, both slumped against the wall, still breathing, and notice a slight haze in the air. Great. I call out to Slend again.

"Rig's on fire. We gotta find Sawyer. Still at least one hostile out there."

"Plan?"

"Quick and dirty. I'll take point. Sawyer's office is to the left at the end of the hall. Cover fire on my go, bounce up and clear."

"Got it."

A sudden burst of gunfire nearby, sharp rifle cracks interspersed with the heavier boom of a high-caliber pistol. Sounds like it came from . . . around the hallway to the left. I rise to a kneeling position.

"Go."

I move out into the hallway, rifle snugged to my shoulder, sights steady, Slend suppressing from the right. Nothing moves except for the slow trickles of blood down the wall and my cheek. My boots pull with every step, the floor sticky and grasping. Kick in a door, gory bootprint staining the thin plastic, hating to waste the time, but an uncleared room is a potential bullet in the back.

"Clear."

I post up in the doorway, covering Slend's advance. She

enters the next room on the right, the last before the hallway's T-junction terminus.

"Clear."

"Jase, move up to Slend."

Jase scampers past, dragging Wind by an arm. She giggles as they slip past Slend into the just-cleared room. Still non-functional. I move out, hugging the left wall, Slend joining me on the right. Halt before the junction. Pop my head around for a quick look, then back into cover. Nothing except a wall of twisted debris twenty meters down. Look at Slend. She shakes her head—same. Hold up a hand with three extended fingers.

Two.

One.

Swing around the corner, Slend walking backward behind me, covering the other direction, dirty red light our only illumination. Nothing but distant gunfire, steadily growing fainter. Stop next to an open entrance, the last before the mass of tangled wreckage, one hand reaching back to halt Slend. A layer of smoke gently drifts along the ceiling, and flickering shadows reach out from the doorway.

"Sawyer?"

"Ashley . . ."

The voice is low, thready, barely reaching my battered ears, a far cry from Sawyer's usual clipped precision. I risk a quick look into the room, but it's impossible to see anything other than a chaotic mess, one lone failing light flickering intermittently in strobing pulses.

"Sawyer, is the room clear?"

". . . clear . . . Ashley . . . need . . ."

He trails off again. I tap Slend's shoulder twice, pause, then once more. Going in. Stay here and cover. She taps back once—understood. I take a deep breath, then spin into the room, trying to see everything at once.

Flashes of red light, shadows looming from floor to ceiling, corners clear, a shape crumpled in front of me, unmoving, half its head missing underneath a shattered hood, another sprawled behind a desk, hand twitching, pistol nearby. I sight in, inhale, focus. It's the unpattern of standard gummie camouflage. Let my finger relax, then exhale.

"Clear."

I kneel down next to Sawyer, trying not to wince at the girder lying atop his crushed legs or the blood pooling from his stomach, sodden hands futilely attempting to stanch the upwelling. A broken picture frame lies near his head, three figures from the past trapped in a shattered web. His eyes flutter behind his glasses, and he coughs liquidly, a thin trickle leaking from his mouth.

"Ashley. Glasses . . . open. Take. Data. Plan . . . op."

My fingers clench against the rifle's knobby grip.

"No . . . no. You can't ask this. We've done enough. This isn't our fight."

"Have to. Only one . . . trust. To succeed. To stop. War."

"Why? *Why*, damn you? Why me? *Why me?*"

"Like . . . mother . . . like . . . daughter. Do what . . . needs . . . doing. No matter . . . cost. Please."

Goddammit, Sawyer. You fucking asshole.

"Jase! Get in here."

Sawyer coughs again, a harsher spasm this time, more blood seeping around his fingers, lips pulling back in a snarl of pain. Jase hurries in, then stops, shocked.

"Is—is that . . . ?"

"Yes," I respond tonelessly. "Scrape everything you can off his glasses."

"But . . . he's, shouldn't we—"

"Just do it! Quickly, while his biometrics are still active."

Jase flinches, then squats down next to me, fingers twitching inside his gloves. Seconds pass, the only sounds Sawyer's pained breaths and the ongoing background destruction of the rig, Wind babbling nonsense words in the hallway. A million thoughts chase each other through my mind, a million scraps of emptiness, void of meaning or form. I stare at the picture frame, trying not to see the smiling faces of Mom, Johnny, Sawyer, arms draped around each other's shoulders, unit insignia visible over their fatigues.

". . . done. I made a full backup."

Sawyer groans again, his breathing changing to sharp pants.

"Thank . . . you. Minisub . . . escape. Wish . . . tell . . . Naomi . . ."

A sound disappears from the discordant medley surrounding us, a small sound, hardly worth noticing, there one instant, then gone, an absence aching like a missing tooth. I reach down and slide Sawyer's eyes shut.

Just another encounter.

"Is . . . is he . . . ?"

I stand up, turning back to the door.

"Yes, Jase. He's dead. Look through his data, see where that sub's hidden and where we're at."

"It's . . . a couple levels down. Through some hidden passages. We're a couple kilometers south of Ditchtown. Ash . . ."

The voice fades away to inconsequentiality. I glide out into the hallway, rifle at my cheek, hoping someone fills its hungry sights. Smoke trails wave their grasping tendrils above, harbingers of what will soon be a funeral pyre.

"Let's go."

Just another encounter.

19

[Sounds of Home]

Liquid waves embrace splintered wooden pilings, their starlight surfaces vanishing beneath the shadows of the pier. A darker shape, rounded and snub, vanishes with them, air bubbles trailing from its open hatch. All around us, the towering spires of Ditchtown rise like blazing spears piercing the night sky, a forest of dirty life. The creak of windfarms drifts in on the mild ocean breeze.

Home.

I set off along the dock, a ramshackle structure crudely attached to the shattered windows of this towering megaspire's lower floor, unfinished skeleton girders clawing up to the distant moon. The Rust. Rotting wood crunches beneath my weight, Wind, Slend, and Jase's footsteps trailing. My hands feel curiously empty without a weapon, my hip lighter than I'm comfortable with, blade lost on the rig, rifle lost beneath the waves. Too many surveillance spheres inside to carry firearms openly, and even though we have Sawyer's data, we've lost his protection. My stomach growls, counterpoint to my throbbing ear.

"Ughhh, dammit, Ash. My head is fucking *killing* me."

"Yeah, Wind, that's what happens when you get a concussion.

Takes your brain a while to stitch itself back together. Some parts never do."

"Gee, thanks for that uplifting response. I feel better already. I mean, I would, except for the brain damage and my stomach trying to eat itself."

I pull open an access door, rusted hinges squealing in protest.

"We're all hungry. Just be happy you didn't have to deal with that shit on the rig . . . Shhh!"

Instead of the normal welcoming hum of a megaspire, gunfire echoes from above, the sharp cracks of projectile rounds mixing with the deeper thuds of drone-fired suppression grenades. A low buzz underlies it all, the anger of a disturbed hive. I pull everyone into a huddle on the stairs.

"Sounds like a riot," I say in a low voice, fingers itching for the hilt of my blade.

"I swear we just left this exact scenario," Jase grumps, folding his arms over his chest. His fingers tap against his scrawny biceps. "Checking local socials. Looks like it's centered around Southspire and the Rust." His face tightens. "The nexus of each one looks like a group of Gamers, Ash. Tight clothing, big muscles, moving way too quick. Gamers not responding to much of anything."

"Because of course the frying pan leads to the fire." I snort. "Why would we expect anything else?"

"Plan?"

Always to the point, our Slend. I glance over at Jase, the only one of us with working glasses.

"How bad are the riots?"

"Bad. Almost every floor on the Rust is reporting something. Southspire is a little cleaner, but not by much. They've got drones everywhere. Looks like they're sweeping from the top down."

"Well, at least there's a small piece of luck. If we hurry, we can still make it out before whoever's under those hoods hits the cordon."

"And then what?" Wind asks. "Sawyer's dead, right? Along with the rig? Call me intolerant, but I don't think the Theocrophant is going to give a single shit about *us*." She tugs angrily at her burka. "Not like we owe them a damn thing anyway."

I pat her on the shoulder. Sometimes leading is knowing when to defuse a bomb instead of accelerating its countdown.

"Let's just make it out of here, get to Johnny's, and get some food. We can try to figure out everything else after that."

She tugs at her burka again, then lets her hand fall and nods. I turn my attention elsewhere.

"Slend, you take point. This is your turf. I'll cover the rear. Wind, eyes everywhere. Jase, what's our quickest route to safety?"

"There's a couple smaller spires we could pass through, then cut through the edge of Southspire."

"Bad idea," Slend says. "Boardshit turf."

"Yeah, they'd probably be just as happy to break us as some windows. Anything else, Jase?"

"We can head up to Eastspire, but there are a *lot* of socials coming out of the area between us and the skyway. Snaps of busted stores, trash fires, anti-Hajj graffiti, fights with the drones. Typical riot stuff. Gummies have a moderate blockade on the bridge—socials say they're letting through people who weren't actively tagged by the suppression drones—but getting there means going through the thick of it."

"Great. Just once, I'd like to have a non-shitty choice of options. Just to see how it feels. Slend?"

"Eastspire. Boardshits have lookouts in Southspire. Weapons. Coordinated. Too many."

"Eastspire it is. Keep your head down, Jase, and keep up. Let's move."

We push into the depths of the Rust, Slend leading the way up battered stairwells and through cramped utility passages. Sounds of fighting grow louder the higher we ascend, the maddening hum ebbing and flowing in heavy waves. Eventually, Slend pauses in front of a grimy door.

"Main atrium. Dangerous. Necessary."

"Can't we circle around?" Jase asks. "Schematics show—"

"No. Blocked. Rust changes. People add, remove."

"She's the one who lives here, Jase," I murmur. He shrugs, clearly unhappy. I ignore it. "Take us in, Slend."

She gently pushes the door open, the din of madness now seeming to echo right beside us. A quick look, and then she's trotting in, Wind on her heels. I give Jase a shove to get him moving, and he stumbles into line. I follow him out, straight into a gummie Preacher's hell.

We're on a walkway running a complete circuit along the wall, nearly five meters wide, various doors leading to outer portions of the Rust, a waist-high barrier on the inner edge. It overlooks a vast open space, the center of the building—this atrium's floor is five stories below, its ceiling six stories up. The Rust was originally designed to have twenty such atriums, each stacked atop the other, each highlighting a different architectural style, but the builders only made it to atrium twelve before shutting the project down, another victim of the Dubs.

This atrium is all concrete slabs and straight lines, a brutal assault on the senses, about as inviting as a fist to the face. Scattered glow panels provide feeble illumination, nearly overwhelmed by a reddish-orange glow from the empty middle. I sneak a look over the railing while we run, staying low—giant piles of trash dot the atrium floor, some smoldering fitfully, others belching sheets of flame upward. Groups of skulking figures weave in and out of sight on the other levels, most with makeshift weapons, some chased by stalking drones, suppression grenades erupting from spindly arms toward their prey, choking chemical fog mushroom-puffing around thrashing bodies.

The noise level suddenly triples, a massive press of bodies surging out of doors on the top level. Screams and shouts intermingle with gunfire and suppression grenades, the mob brought to bay by an unstoppable wall of remote-controlled metal pressing down like a trash compactor. Several figures topple over the railings, screaming as they fall, shrill cries filled with animal terror, and I swallow heavily when they abruptly cut off. The rest of the seething mass roils along the walkway like an overturned ant nest, slamming into and through doorways, a marching wall of drones driving them on.

Slend picks up the pace, not quite an outright run, but close. Jase gulps down air in panting heaves—he's not prepared for this at all. I'm impressed he's made it this far. We barrel into another stairwell, legs churning up its steps two at a time. One level passes, then another. Slend kicks open a narrow utility door, an oddly pristine cleaning supply hallway beyond, and then we're back into the atrium. The bedlam is a wall of sound, close to the threshold of physical pain. Footsteps thud over our heads while more despairing shrieks Doppler past.

Our run turns into a full-on sprint, leaping over unmoving bodies, blood pooling beneath several. Scattered pieces of a shattered drone nearly trip up Jase, and I haul him back upright.

"Thanks," he gasps.

"Just keep running," I shout back, eyes scanning constantly for threats. Based on our relationship to the atrium, we must be nearly halfway across the megaspire by now. Slend crashes through another door, Wind right behind her. I push Jase after them, into a twisting residential hallway, bodies and beaded curtains dotting its length.

The wailing screams of a baby chase us, then fade, replaced by the steady slap of flesh on flesh, sex or death, no way to tell, no way to stop, eventually covered by chanting prayers, a nasal hum of indeterminate words. Slend charges through corridor after corridor, weaving a path along the guts of the Rust, and the roar of the mob grows louder and louder. We duck through yet another door and I almost slam into Jase, his body pressed up against Wind, gasping on her shoulder.

Across from us, a towering man with matted dreadlocks and the flattened nose of a fighter faces Slend, hefting a length of metal pipe in one hand. Rastafarian colors cover his loose pants, and a logo for one of the grimier techie bars adorns his sleeveless shirt. Six more hulking figures stand behind him, in two loose ranks. He points the pipe at her.

"And what're you doin' back in Terrell's turf? Told you before, this is my piece of the Rust."

Slend walks up to him, arms loose at her sides, putting herself directly into his personal space. A centimeter closer and they'd be touching. Her forehead barely comes to his chin.

"Terrell. Move."

He tilts his head back and laughs.

"Oh ho, boys, the ogre thinks she can tell a man what—"

Slend's fist cracks across his jaw like a meteor strike, and he topples bonelessly, pipe clattering away, face smashing into the thinly carpeted floor. She immediately walks up to the group, positioning herself in front of the first rank's middle figure, a fleshy man with a poofy mass of curls. He stares at her, eyes widening, trying to lean away.

"Move."

"Wait, why di—"

She uppercuts him, his front teeth smashing together, one flying out, his eyes rolling back as he falls. The other men flinch back toward the walls of the corridor, leaving only the middle one between us and escape. Slend steps over the twitching body, directly in front of the last of Terrell's toadies, a heavily muscled bald man with tattoos covering his face in swirling designs. He takes a step back, and she matches it instantly. Behind, the howling gale of the mob sounds like it's almost on top of us.

"Move."

He scrambles out of the way until his quivering spine flattens up against the wall, and Slend nods.

"Let's go."

Wind, Jase, and I jog through the human tunnel, their eyes looking anywhere but at us, expressions stunned. After we're through, Slend takes the lead once again, pushing us up into a sprint, more hallways flashing by.

"Damn, Slend, that was pretty badass," Wind crows over the roar of chaos, her feet seeming to barely touch the ground. "I thought we were goners for sure when you pasted that first one."

"Bullies. Hit once, they fold. Lots in Rust. History with Terrell."

"Is that why you live here? Kick some ass, take some names, get some workouts in the real?"

"Cheap. Lawyers aren't."

"Oh." Wind's response is subdued. "Yeah, that's true."

She falls silent, and Slend pushes open another door, this one covered in "emergency exit" warnings and scratched graffiti. I can hear individual footsteps not far behind, the quicker members of the mob mere seconds away. We emerge into a large corridor, horrors of the atrium to our left, its hellish glow stretching out like streamers, a gleaming army of drones to our right, the arching bridge of the skyway beyond them. Exhausted, we stumble up to the closest one. It's the first time I've ever been happy to see a riot drone.

"Please, let us out, we're trying to get somewhere safe."

"HALT. PREPARE FOR FACIAL SCAN."

"Yes, fine, whatever," I snap tiredly, "just let us out before we're crushed."

"SCANNING. APPROVED. STAY PEACEFUL, CITIZENS. Nice job on that dragon."

"Thanks."

We push our way through the serried ranks of drones, roaring screams chasing our heels, until we finally emerge onto the empty safety of the skyway. Jase promptly falls to his knees and starts puking, Slend and Wind continuing on to Eastspire. I let him have a minute to try to get his body under control, and turn around to watch the Rust. Force myself to witness.

Scattered figures dart around the corner from the atrium, and then the full boiling mass appears, incoherent screams heralding its arrival. The drones respond with a volley of at least a hundred suppression grenades, choking gas and incapacitating flashes engulfing the swarm, a fireworks crescendo of pain. Bodies fall beneath trampling feet, then disappear behind yellow-tinged clouds. Electrified nets add a buzzing crackle to the mayhem, arcing current arching backs and clenching jaws, while rubber bullets slam into those somehow still upright, pinballing them back into the maelstrom. It's pandemonium, a relentless assault on those trapped between the sets of drone forces, and I turn away, sickened. The casualty rate is already catastrophic, but the drones never stop their mechanical rhythm, a brutal meat grinder to the rioters' flesh. Most will survive, but they'll wish they hadn't. I pull Jase to his feet.

"Come on. We need to get out of here. There's still a chance it might get worse."

Jase wipes a hand across his mouth, and stumbles into a ragged pace next to me. Behind us, the sounds of home continue unabated.

20

[How the World Ends]

Eastspire's entrance stretches in front of us like a gummie chapel. Vaulting corridors lead away from the chaos in the Rust, their steady lightpanel glow calm and soothing, a balm from above. No one is visible, inhabitants driven inside by the riots, leaving nothing to disturb the hush. It feels like sanctuary.

Or damnation.

The buzz-saw hum of riots still vibrates through the floor, a physical sensation felt rather than heard. The air itself is hot and sticky, pregnant with potential outbreaks of mayhem. Our footfalls seem to echo unnaturally, marking us as intruders in this urban jungle. I feel like we're crossing a megaspire's roof in the middle of a cat-six.

As if by instinct, we draw closer together, moving through the oppressively silent halls in a cautious trot. Wind's footsteps are even less perceptible than usual, Slend's hands clenching and unclenching in a regular rhythm, Jase tapping in midair, a flood of socials drowning his mind. I twitch my wrist, and frown at the lack of blade in my palm, same as the last five times I tried. Around us, the marks of violence pass by.

A crimson handprint on a wall, dragging to a spotlessly gleaming shut door.

A left-footed boot, tipped over on its side, a pair of glasses lying next to it, one lens cracked.

A muffled sound creeping out from a corridor, guttural grunts and moans, halting in irregular pauses.

"This," Wind whispers, floor-to-ceiling anti-Hajj slurs creeping past, paint dripping in slow-motion bloodstains, "is the *worst* fucking psych-sec I've *ever* fucking seen. Muhammad *wept*."

"We're almost there," I respond tiredly. "We'll be fine once we reach Johnny's."

"Doutbful," Slend rumbles, and I'm hard-pressed to disagree. Wind is right. We've all seen riots before, but this is fucking *awful*.

"We're almost there. C'mon." I pick up the pace, leading us over another skybridge and finally into the Brown. The smothering atmosphere burns away like midday fog, banished by reliably flickering glowpanels. "Jase, have you contacted the old man?"

Jase startles at the sound of his name.

"Wha— Johnny?" He bites his lower lip, the dimmer lighting of the Brown shrouding his face. "Yeah, I've been trying, but the gummies have the 'Net on total lockdown now. No socials, no private comms, nothing but upbeat messages about how great our life is and will be after this minor inconvenience finishes resolving. Can't even get a sniff of what's going on with the burbies."

"Shit. If they're using war tactics, that means things are really bad. Some of the enclaves probably got hit. They must be panicking." I bring us to a halt and bang on the rusted metal shutters, the sharp raps echoing a little too loudly. "Johnny! Open up! It's Ash!"

Seconds pass, then the thin slats rattle upward, just enough for us to duck under, uncomfortably low. I give a grim smile.

Johnny's still got traces of the Dubs in his system, just like Mom.

I squat my way underneath, vulnerable to a strike from above, hands out to my sides, clearly empty. When I stand, Johnny's leaning against the wall, one hand picking at his hair, the other holding a medium-caliber handgun at his side, thumb switching the safety on. He nods at me, and I nod back. The others follow me in, and Johnny's eyes widen fractionally when Jase ducks through, but he taps a finger and the shutters rattle back down. When he speaks, his voice is a little huskier than normal.

"It's good to see you, son. Didn't know if I'd get the chance to say that."

"It's . . ." Jase pauses, looking every inch his sixteen years in age. "It's good. To be back. Dad. There. There was. The rig. It was—"

Johnny steps forward, pulling him into a hug, pistol hand patting him on the back. Jase melts into muffled sobs, shuddering against Johnny's chest, and I wish I could join him. This isn't the Game, no matter how similar the encounters feel. This is the real.

"I understand, son. I understand. I can't promise it'll get better in time, but you'll find a way. To come back to those who need you. Even if it breaks you."

He says the last words staring at me, his eyes tight in his dark face, and it's almost more than I can bear.

Mom.

Almost. I am Ashley, Ash, Ashura, Ashura the Terrible, and if ever there was a time to don that mantle, it's now. Do the job, because there's no one else to do it, and you find a way, even if it breaks you.

Just another encounter.

I pat Jase on the shoulder and take a seat on one of the stools.

"He did good, Johnny. Real good. Any chance we can get some noodles? It's been a long day."

Johnny hugs Jase close one more time, rubbing his head, then walks behind the counter, sliding the pistol underneath. He hands me a medical kit, motioning toward my ear.

"Sure thing, Ash. I'm going to want to hear that story, though."

The familiar clang of metal wok on porcelain stove fills the air, oil sizzling above the heat.

"Oh, don't worry," I groan, forcing my muscles to finally relax, "you're going to get to hear how the world ends. Whether you like it or not."

Three bowls of Johnny's finest and a hastily applied first aid dressing later, I slump back on my stool and belch contentedly. Slend leans against the wall on her corner seat, idly sipping on a cup of water, while Wind digs into her fourth bowl, chopsticks flashing from food to face and back. Jase stares at the wall with his chin on his hand, not seeing anything other than unwanted memories of the past twenty-four hours. Johnny tilts his chair back, boots propped on a shelf underneath the counter, hands folded across his stomach, toothpick bobbing up and down in time with his words.

"Hell of a story, Ash. Hell of a story."

I wipe my mouth with a napkin, feeling the tingle of garlic and spice against my lips.

"So, we've got Sawyer's data, but, it's just, I don't know, Johnny. That asshole was an asshole's asshole, and I know you and Mom had history with him, but . . . shit. What if he was right? What if we *are* the only ones who can stop this?"

Johnny rolls the toothpick to the other side of his mouth.

"Hate to say it, but he was right. Getting some socials from old friends, ones who took the Enclave package."

"What," Jase squawks, his interest momentarily piqued. "How are you getting info from the global 'Net right now?"

Johnny barks out a laugh.

"Did you forget who taught you how to put those things you broke back together, son? I may not have been born with an aptitude for much more than cooking, but if you were going to learn tech, then I'd be a poor father if I couldn't guide your hands. I've got some back doors I don't want you using until you fully understand the risks."

Jase's eyes regain their thousand-yard stare, and Johnny nods.

"Reckon you might be just about ready to understand those risks." He looks at me. "It's not looking good, Ash. South 'Lanta's mostly gone, along with Missansas. Seems like the local defense squadrons got overrun by unknown assailants, garrisons wiped to a man, and gummies insist on keeping mainline battletanks for 'peacekeeping.' Not much that's going to stop a squad of heavies in the middle of an Enclave once they get rolling. Gummies ended up shifting an orbital over."

"On their own cities? They used kinetics on the *dryburbs?*"

My voice is awed, almost disbelieving at first. Then I think back to Sawyer's scorn for the Theocrophant, and reconsider what lengths I might imagine the gummies capable of going to if sufficiently frightened.

"Seems they felt like there was no other choice," Johnny replies slowly. "Nothing more dangerous than a true fanatic with nothing left to lose. Sawyer knew that. Naomi too."

"That's . . ." Wind's voice trails off. "That's insane. Their own people." She looks over at me. "What are we going to do, Ash? What *can* we do?"

I drum my fingers on the countertop.

"Let's look at what Sawyer gave us first. Jase?"

Jase looks over at me, eyes regaining their focus.

"Yeah . . . yeah. Old man. You got a projector?"

Johnny pulls a small half-sphere from beneath the counter and slides it over. Jase taps a couple buttons on its underside, then puts it down. A display appears on the wall behind me and I swivel my stool around, leaning back on my elbows. Jase starts moving his fingers, accessing Sawyer's data. Words and charts flicker across the wall in bursts of light, too quick to follow.

"Okay, there should be an overview in here somewhere . . . got it."

A stark document appears, three lines of text on an official-looking page, each branching out with links to other portions of Sawyer's trove. Slend gives a low whistle, and my eyes widen.

"Fuck me."

Wind reads the terse sentences hanging in front of us out loud.

"*Threat level—catastrophic. Utilize Operation Dragonslayer. All measures authorized.* Signed by the Theocrophant."

I pinch the bridge of my nose.

"Jase, what's in that 'All measures authorized' section?"

Half the screen fills with a list of military assets. Most glow an ominous red. Wind nearly chokes on a mouthful of noodles.

"Holy shit, Ash. Those are nukes. Sawyer was going to use *nukes*."

"Yeah," I respond grimly. "He was. Jase, what was he going to use them on?"

The laundry list of death shrinks away, replaced by satellite images of a circular dome surrounded by forest, a winding road leading away from its western flank. A small scale at the bottom right puts the dome at nearly a kilometer in diameter. Basic wireframe grids overlay it, architectural plans of what's underneath, each stamped with "LAST KNOWN DATA. LIKELY INCORRECT." They paint the picture of a sprawling compound composed of multiple buildings all jammed together, a seething hive of corporate scheming. A list of security forces scrolls by on the left, an estimated company of silkie ex-military forces with support elements.

"So there's the 'what.' A fucking WGSK fortress. Now the question is 'why?' Jase, you find anything?"

He gulps and nods.

"It's bad, Ash. You know how the shipping schedule for those hoods put their release date in a couple weeks?"

"Yeah."

"They're already shipped and distributed. There's going to be a surprise announcement tomorrow. Anyone who pre-ordered one likely already has it. Worldwide. That's why the silkies were willing to take a loss on those boats."

I sit upright.

"What about the shipment Sawyer interdicted?"

Jase looks miserable.

"That was the fifth shipment to Ditchtown. The other four went through customs with no incident, and most of our Game stores break embargo all the time. The dryburbs obviously proscribe silkie tech, but there's nothing stopping any burbies from coming out here to buy one. Other than the fact that they hate us, but they still come."

"Shit. Shit shit shit. That's what's driving the riots, and why we got attacked on the rig. They're already taking over the top-tier Gamers. Still, though, that doesn't explain why this one particular facility is so important."

Another page flashes across the projector.

"Looks like Sawyer's people thought this might be the central control hub for whatever's behind the hoods. When I was working with his scientists, we tracked a lot of unusual data patterns converging through the global 'Net, but you'd have to know they were there to find them. I figured you'd need a control protocol that was similar to the Game, but not quite the same." He swallows. "I guess they isolated it before they died."

Johnny raises his voice.

"Sawyer always had something hidden, least when I knew him. Check for additional files."

Jase's hapgloved fingers take flight again, and then a new graphic appears on the wall.

"Huh. Right again, old man. Ash, check this out. Sawyer thought the silkies were planning on using this tech to subliminally influence other countries once they wiped out the gummies."

I run a hand through my hair, trying to think.

"What was Sawyer's plan?"

Jase pulls up more documents, and almost chokes.

"Send the three of you in to take out whatever was inside, with whatever resources you needed. If . . . if you failed . . . nuke it. You . . . you would have been . . . carrying one . . . deadman's switch . . ."

He looks like he wants to throw up. I can't blame him.

Don't pretend like you wouldn't have hit that button if it got bad enough and you thought it would solve things. Sawyer knew exactly who you are. How do you think Mom ended up in that room?

Wind pushes her bowl away in a screeching slide, her face pale.

"This is crazy, Ash. Yeah, we're good at the Game, but we're not commandos. I mean, at least I'm not. My parents expect me to go back to school soon. Slend's trying to get her brother out of prison. You're taking care of your mom. We didn't sign up for something like this."

"No, we didn't." I grimace. "We should run the fuck away, but there's nowhere to go, Wind. It's not like we can hide somewhere—everyone across the world plays the Game. The only way I see this thing ending is with WGSK in control of *everything*, or the planet irradiated. Unless someone stops them."

"Yeah, but why us? Why does it have to be *us*?"

"I don't know!" I lower myself back down to my seat, my fist aching where I just punched the countertop. "I don't know. You're right, Wind. This is bullshit. But who else is going to do it? Who else knows it needs to be done?"

"Only us." Slend's voice is tired. "Always. Impossible ladder fights? Only us. Standing up to boardshits? Only us. Save the world?" She laughs angrily, her arms tensing like she wants to tear the world apart. "Only us. Fuck."

I cover my face, elbows on my knees. It's been a long day in a longer week.

"Yup. I don't even know how the hell we would do it. Sawyer was the one with all the gear, and now he's dead." My hands fall away, shoulders slumping. "I don't have a plan. I don't know what to do. Maybe this is how the world ends, all of us hoping it would've been different, stuck waiting to die."

Silence drags through the room. Eventually, Johnny clears his throat.

"I don't know much about the world ending, but I do know exhaustion. You all need to get some rest. Boy's about to pass out on his feet." He cocks a brow at Jase, who's visibly swaying, and I realize my eyelids are drooping. "Why don't you all catch some sleep—here, if you need to."

I push myself upright, finally noticing the time display on the projector.

"Thanks, Johnny. You're right, it's almost midnight. Let's try again in the morning, take a fresh look. That sound workable to everyone?"

Wind and Slend nod, Wind's eyes and lips tight. Slend looks over at Johnny.

"Cot?"

"Boy has one back in his workroom. He can take my bed upstairs. Here, I'll show you."

Johnny ambles off, Slend and Jase in tow. I put a hand on Wind's shoulder.

"I'll walk you back home. I'm sure your parents are worried."

She brushes it off. When she speaks, her voice is low.

"I can make it on my own. I just . . . I don't know, Ash. I don't know. What if I want it all to burn? What if I want all those bigoted pieces of shit who make fun of my parents and splash pig blood on our door and look down their noses at me every single fucking day of my life to get what they deserve? What if I don't care about saving the world if it means saving them?"

I take a deep breath, then another. I'm so goddamned tired.

"I get that, Wind. Look at the color of my skin and what the boardshits say, and tell me I don't. Just . . . get some rest, okay? We can talk about it more tomorrow."

She turns toward the door, pulling her burka up and folding it around her head. A quick button press brings the safety grill rattling up, and she pauses, not looking back at me.

"Tell me the truth, Ash. Are we doing this for everyone else? Or are we doing it because you don't want to lose, no matter what it costs?"

I . . . don't know. I wish I did.

". . . We're doing it for everyone, Wind. We're all that's left."

". . . Sure."

She ducks under the metal grill. I call after her.

"Stay safe, Wind. I'll see you in the morning?"

She lifts a hand but doesn't respond, then disappears into the hallway. I sigh, and walk over to the entrance. Johnny's voice sounds behind me.

"You need a cot too, Ash?"

"I'm good, thanks. Have to go grab another set of glasses, then check on Mom and Kiro. I'll see you in the morning."

"Good hunting." He reaches out and grabs Jase, keeping him from falling over. "Come on, boy, up you go. There's a bed with your name on it, but we're both too old for me to carry you up the stairs these days."

I duck out beneath the grill, and set off for my room. Rusted metal clatters shut behind my heels.

The backup pair of glasses slides over my face and begins its synchronizing procedure, a slowly spinning wheel in the upper left. I strap my second-favorite blade to my wrist and shut the door behind me, heading back out into the Brown, my destination Highrise and the clinic. The heavy silence persists, thunderstorm weight almost tangible beneath the failed glow-strips. It matches the pressure in my head, thoughts starting to fuzz and blur, heat throbbing from the missing chunk of my ear. The only people I pass are a group of couriers, their normally exuberant footsteps subdued and careful.

Highrise is slightly more active, huddled groups quickly making their way from one destination to another, but no one meets each other's eyes, or stops to chat. I check in through the clinic's security, still heavy despite the late hour.

"How's she doing, Freddie?"

"Sleeping. You okay, Ash? You don't look so great. What happened to your ear?"

"Been a long day, Freddie. A long day. Hey, I need you to do me a favor."

"What is it?"

"If it starts getting bad, the riots, whatever, let her out? Please?"

Freddie swivels his chair to look at me, concerned.

"I don't know if I can ethically do that, Ash. Your mom needs treatment, and our facility is very secure. I think it would be better for her to stay in here if things become troubled."

"Please. If it gets bad. I don't want her dying in a cage. At least give her a chance."

"I . . ."

"Thanks, Freddie. Tell her I love her when she wakes up. I gotta go."

"Be safe, Ash."

I reclaim my blade and exit the clinic. A small ding alerts me that my glasses have finished updating. I set off toward Kiro's last address, hoping he hasn't moved. I've given him space, even though he's given nothing in return.

A tsunami of message alerts floods my vision. One from Sarah, the rest from Ham. I open Sarah's.

<<Your brother's been playing at Vlad's. Thought you should know.>>

Shit. Vlad's is IonSeal's turf. Kiro, what the hell are you doing?

Swipe it closed, open the first message from Ham.

<<Hey, give me a buzz when you get this. We have to talk. Regarding our previous conversation. I've learned some things.>>

Swipe to the next one.

<<Need to talk to you please. It's urgent.>>

A faster hand motion.

<<Message me.>>

Brushing messages away like cobwebs.

<<need talk. now. brand's killers. rig.>>

<<ash. hoods. dad. not right.>>

<<ash trapped help>>

<<as19KLW #(72.2;1$@>>

The rest are indecipherable gibberish, a mishmash of text and symbols, each growing progressively shorter. I tap in Ham's contact code, a private line through the global 'Net. Dangerous to use without a jammer, but there's no choice. A connection opens.

<<>>

<<Ham?>>

I continue walking to Kiro's address in Greentower, passing through deserted corridors. I ignore the moonlit spectacle of Glassbridge at midnight, like walking in a crystal tunnel between pillars of fire.

<<Ham!>>

My feet fall faster, boots clicking on the fish-patterned floor of Northspire. Inside the hoodie pockets, my fingers twitch nervously, uselessly.

<< . . . ash>>

The message flutters into vision like a wounded animal. I round a corner into Greentower, hanging agfarms draping the balconies outside in shrouds of mossy leaves, and take the stairs two at a time, leaden acid twisting my guts. My arms churn, fingers punching symbols into the uncaring air.

<<Ham! What's going on?>>

<<help. dad. hoods. tried. warn. stop him>>

I round a corner and almost fall, his scattered words hitting me like gunshots. Steady myself against the railing, then keep climbing.

<<WHAT?! Stop who? What about the hoods? Are you okay?>>

<<dad. controlled. brand. gamecore.>>

<<Ham. Ham, answer me, are you okay?>>

<<forced. encounter. game.>>

I barrel out through the stairwell exit, almost sprinting down the hall toward Kiro's room.

<<Ham!>>

<<ash help>>

Knock on his door, softly at first, then urgent, desperate, pounding, rattling the frame.

<<HAM!>>

I lean back and slam my foot against the door, once, twice, not caring how much noise I make. On the third kick, it crashes inward, hinges torn and ruined. I step over it and into Kiro's room. Nothing moves.

<<Ham.>>

<<>>

I brush past the neatly organized desk, meticulously pruned bonsai tree trays squared up to its edges, dried needles carpeting their bases. Step over the row of free weights lining one wall, arranged in ascending order, the faintest layer of dust covering their bulging ends. All I can see is the carefully made bed, a small box sitting on its foot.

<<Ham . . . >>

The connection times out, signal lost. I reach down and pick up the cardboard container, refusing to acknowledge the all-too-familiar images of a gray haphood on its sides, cheerful marketing phrases encased in quotes underneath each graphic, its lid torn along the center line where cheap packing tape ripped the flap edges. I pull it open, knowing that the padded interior will be empty, yet feeling my knees buckle just the same. Cardboard bounces dully. The mattress is cool against my back, firm, the ceiling above dotted with carefully placed luminescent stars re-creating the constellations overhead.

My brother always loved the stars, ever since he was old enough to point up at them and laugh.

Frantically, I start searching the 'Net, using every trick I know, but it's no use. He's gone, both of them are gone, and I should let the girls know or Johnny or Jase but I'm so tired. . . .

The stars whirl above me.

Time passes.

I guess this is how the world ends. A broken connection, a casually opened package, a heart ripped out of your chest. I let my eyes slip shut.

21

[Penetration]

An insistent chirping. Sunlight beaming down overhead. Kiro toddling toward Dad on unsteady feet, laughing the whole time, treacherous drifts of sand threatening to topple him at every step. Gulls circle and dive into the rolling breakers, sometimes emerging with a needlefish, sometimes not. Mom waves from her stomach, stretched out on a faded towel. I wave back, feeling the salty breeze on my fingers. Windfarms creak in the distance, counterpoint to the jabbering birds.

The soaring cries grow harsher, shriller, Dad sweeping Kiro up into his arms and spinning him around, smiles on their faces outshining the sun, Mom laughing, high and pure, the gulls calling louder and louder—

". . . sh! Ash!"

Reality slams back down around me, Kiro's ceiling visible through my glasses, Jase's voice in my ear, my body stiff and sore from sleeping half on the bed, half on the floor. Jase sounds terrified.

"Wha . . . what is it, Jase?"

"Oh jeez, I finally got through, you're alive. Ash, where are you? Is everything okay?"

I drag a hand across my face.

"Am I . . . yes, Jase, I'm fine. I'm at Kiro's." Last night's memories intrude, a gut punch of unwanted terror. Kiro. Ham. I force myself up. "Actually, I'm not fine. What's the problem?"

"We thought you were dead. It's almost noon, everyone's at Johnny's, we tried messaging you but you never answered and so I went to your room and tried your door and it wasn't locked and you always leave it locked and you weren't in there and—"

Of all the nights to forget to lock my door.

"It's okay, Jase. It's okay. I'll be at Johnny's in a few. I'll meet you there. Let the others know. Sorry."

I cut off the connection and look around blearily. The shell of my brother's room surrounds me, his bonsai trees shedding another layer of dried needle carpet. The empty box yawns on the floor, and I drag my eyes away from it. Door's still open—I'm lucky no one came in during the night. I check the time—11:57 a.m. This floor of Greentower must be relatively peaceful, my forcible entry aside. Probably why Kiro chose to live here. He never did like conflict.

I push myself off the bed and stagger out through the wreckage of the door, wedging it shut as best I can. It doesn't feel like I got any sleep at all. My eyes feel scratchy, hot, pounding drumbeats of pulsing blood echoing through my skull, the bandage on my ear crusty with dried gore. Nothing to do but move forward. I put one foot in front of the other, making my way across the bridge connecting Greentower to Northspire. Pause.

Crowds of people fill the far end of the bridge, a strident voice piercing from their depths. I keep walking, nudging my way through. Need to get to Johnny's. The voice grows louder.

". . . mnation and hellfire! Brought to us from a loving

God, eager to set His children back on their rightful path, free from the sins of their fathers! Free from the sins of whores!"

The voice is right next to me. I look up, realize I'm in the middle of a clear space, gummie Preacher staring at me, his arm outstretched, meaty finger pointing like an accusatory nail.

Goddammit. I'm on my way to figure out how to save your ass, and this is the thanks I get?

"Filthy whores," he shrieks, spittle flying from his lips, AR emitters echoing his words in a belated choir, "tempting us to eternal damnation! Tempting us to forsake our loving Father! How else can we explain these ill omens, these signs of wroth, these demons in our midst, dark of thought? Surely He demands repentance! Who will pay His price? Who will bring us salvation?"

I try to push my way back into the crowd, but no one seems interested in clearing a path now. Eyes shift and dance, refusing to meet my own, refusing to meet his, but drifting ever so slowly in that direction. Soft murmurs rise up like the first chop before a cat-six.

God. Fucking. Dammit.

I spin back around to the Preacher, marching up to his face. He glares at me behind the glow of his cross, fat cheeks red, spotless robes white and pristine.

Psych-sec. Just another fucking psych-sec. Disarm the crowd. They're not burbies. They're just scared.

I pitch my voice to carry.

"Salvation. You ever wonder if your guy, what's his name, Jesus, you ever wonder how he took his shits?" The Preacher's eyes widen at the apparent non sequitur, but I don't give him a chance to respond. "I mean, here's the son of God, put here to save us all, according to you, wandering through a preindustrial society for thirty-some-odd years, yeah? With the camels and the slaves and fuck-all else? But still human, right? Still had to eat? In order to bring salvation?"

I turn toward the crowd, walking a circle around him, forcing him to spin to keep me in sight, forcing him to react to me, to make me the center of attention.

"See, I think about that, and then I think about basic biology, you know, the kind even your type allow us to study, and then I think there's no way he's using a toilet, mainly because they hadn't been introduced yet in that neck of the desert." I snap my fingers, pretending to look confused. "But here, here's where I really start to have questions, here's where I really need some guidance, mister *preacher* man, because if you *really* stop to think about it, he had to have diarrhea at least once or twice during that time he spent guiding the lost and curing the sick. Not the easy kind, the squeeze and wipe and make sure you grab some more vegetables if any happen to be available, but the bad kind, like when you get a piece of needlefish out of the printer that doesn't smell quite right, and you spend the next six hours hoping you won't have to flush more than once because you're not sure if your water credits for the day will cover a second."

Scattered laughter, faces rapt. The Preacher draws in breath, and I ride over him again.

"Salvation. So here we have this messiah, this prophet, this son of God, holiest of holies, robes hitched over his hips, spraying filthy ass-juice all over the nearest thornbush, unless he's unlucky and has to save that to wipe, and yet every time I see one of you, you're telling everyone that everything that's not *pure,* that's not *pristine,* that's not *spotlessly white,* must be full of sin. That *salvation* comes from a perfectly sculpted figure looking sorrowfully down from a fucking artisanally crafted torture device while red-cheeked cherubs sing hosannahs about clouds or some stupid shit. Do I have that right?"

More laughter, people in the front few rows trying to cover their smiles.

"You—you—"

"Yeah, yeah, filthy whore, we got that the first time, but let's get back to the point. See, I think of your guy painting the desert brown, bereft of anything more technologically advanced than the wheel, son of God wandering the barren sands, dispensing salvation, and I start wondering how you, in your *shiny* white robe and *shiny* golden cross and *shiny* AR halo, sitting in your dry and comfortable Enclave on solid ground, eating actual non-printed food and non-rotten needlefish that won't leave you swearing on top of a half-busted hole in the wall that charges you for your own hygiene as another cramp tries to turn your body inside out while you try not to scream because someone might see it as a sign of weakness and come take what little you have left, I wonder how you can even possibly grasp the tiniest part of that filthy desert nomad's message. Salvation."

Even more laughter, an undertone of ugliness threading its depths, and the Preacher shifts back and forth nervously.

"That's—that's not—"

"Because, you see, this man, this pissing, crapping, malnourished, dirt-covered, matted-hair scraggly-bearded *son* of *God* who spent all his time caring for the poor and curing the sick, bringing them *salvation,* I wonder how he would react to someone like you, all shiny and clean and well-fed, descending forth from your temple on the mount of the wreckage of the world, wreckage you helped create by preaching your *certainty* that the waters will never rise, your *certainty* that enough money can buy forgiveness, your *certainty* that others suffer while you squander because what use are the riches of earth compared to the riches of heaven?"

I pull his sleeve away from his arm and let my blade fall into my hand. Quickly, neatly, I slice a strip off. The crowd watches, expressions stony. Beaten down. Weathered by day after day after week after month after year in Ditchtown. I roll the fabric between my fingers, and he trembles.

"I wonder what that man would say if he found you covered in silk, berating a crowd in third-rate printed polymer, surrounded by the tattered remnants of the past, not perfect, no, but not this pit of despair, witnessing their community burn yet again, driven to yet more violence against each other. I wonder what *he* might think of your *salvation*." I let the scrap of cloth fall, fluttering down to the grimy floor, and sheathe my blade. "How do *you* shit, mister preacher man?"

His mouth gapes like a landed fish, but nothing comes out. I turn my back and walk into the crowd. A gap opens for me, bodies slowly shifting aside, then closing back in, pressing toward the middle of the circle. Toward the cowering man in white and gold, shining like a beacon in the middle of a wasteland. I leave them to their questions and continue on into Northspire, clenched fists shaking at my sides.

Several minutes of walking sees me out of Northspire, leaving its anti-Hajj graffiti-scarred walls behind, and into Highrise, where the tourist crowds are a fraction of their normal size, no doubt scared away by the ongoing riots. I make a small detour past Sarah's, but her CLOSED sign is up and blinking steadily—no Gaming today. Probably a good idea. I send a message wishing her well, even though I know it's just a hollow gesture, and continue through Glassbridge into the Brown. Knock on Johnny's rusted metal shutters.

"It's Ash," I call out wearily. "Open up."

The shutters jerk upward, and I duck through, straight into a crushing embrace from Slend, her thick arms wrapping around me like steel bars.

"Scared us. No time for soloing."

I lean into her, feeling the pressure on my mind ease the slightest amount. Another pair of arms wraps around us both.

"Don't ever do that again, Ash," Wind says, her voice catching the tiniest bit. "Not after a day like yesterday. Promise you won't leave us like that again."

Another bit of pressure crumbles away, and suddenly it's like a dam bursting. It's all too much, even for Ashura the Terrible, entirely too much weight for one person to bear. Brand dead, Kiro missing, Ham frightened and lost, the world crashing into ruins once again. Tears roll from my eyes into Slend's thin shirt, Wind's cloth-shrouded head. I cling to the two of them like life preservers.

"I . . . I didn't . . . I didn't warn him. We fought, and then everything started happening so fast . . . I forgot. I forgot and now he's gone."

"Who's gone? What're you talking about, Ash?"

Jase hovers nearby awkwardly, twisting his hands together. The words tumble from my mouth.

"Kiro. He had a package for one of those haphoods in his room. It looked like he hadn't been there for a couple days. He's . . ."

"Shhh, shhh." Wind rubs my back. "It'll be okay. We'll find him."

I keep talking, keep forcing the pain out.

"It's not just him. Ham . . . Hamlin. He's in trouble too, and I wasn't there when he needed me. I don't know if I can save him."

"Hamlin?" Slend sounds confused. Of course. I never told them. To protect them. To protect me.

"Hammer," I reply tiredly. "I've been dating Hammer for the last two years. We're pretty serious. We didn't want to tell anyone because . . . well, you've seen what's happened before, what the boardshits have done. I'm sorry. I should have trusted you."

Wind leans back and looks at me for a long, silent moment, arching an eyebrow above stress-bruised sockets.

"Hammer, huh?" she says at last. "Well, he's probably the only person with a chance of keeping up with you. What's he like? You know, when he's not trying to kill us. Is he as good in bed as he is at the Game?"

"Wind!" In spite of myself, I blush.

"C'mon, Ash, it's an honest question. You can't just mention you're dating the best dev in the Game and expect it to slide by. We wanna know more, right, Slend?"

"No. Prefer imagination. Never disappointed."

Slend's deadpan rumble makes me hiccup, and the shaking sobs in my chest slowly transform to laughter. I wrap my arms around them tighter,

"You two, I swear, you're the worst." I let go of the embrace and take a step back. "It's . . . complicated. Between me and Hammer. He's stuck in some sort of immersion pod, totally paralyzed in the real. He actually lives in the Game. Before I lost contact with him, he mentioned something about trying to stop his dad, some high-level VP at WGSK. I'm pretty sure that means Ham's dad is our target."

Jase frowns, tapping his fingers.

"I don't think you're entirely correct, Ash."

"About what?"

"About Hammer's dad being your target. From what we were able to decipher from that hood you captured, it seems like they're controlling the wearers in real time. The hoods can revert to a basic set of preprogrammed instructions if they lose connection, essentially playing out whatever the scenario was on autopilot, but they're designed to have someone in charge. I don't think a single person could handle that amount of info.

They have to have a team—maybe a lot of teams—somewhere in there."

"Either way, Ham thinks his dad is in charge, so if we capture him, we should be able to convince him to shut it all down whether he is or not. As an EVP, he can snap his fingers and get shit done."

Johnny clears his throat.

"I don't think it's going to play out that way. Doesn't sound like a silkie op. Not . . . corporate enough."

"Any suggestions?" I ask him. He shakes his head.

"Then we'll proceed under the assumption that Ham's dad is the prime target for now, and improvise when we need to. No other choice."

Slend cracks her knuckles.

"Breach?"

"Yeah, that's the tricky part. I have no idea how we're going to get in there without Sawyer's backing. Anyone got any ideas?"

"Orbital strike?"

"That's what Sawyer had planned, but it's gonna be tough without an orbital, Wind."

"Then we're fucked. Too much security, too many chokepoints for a frontal assault. Even we're not that good."

"Fucked." Slend grunts her agreement.

I sigh.

"Fucked indeed. Not to mention, we still have to get there in the first place. This place is on the other side of the continent. Not like we can hop into a shuttle and bounce right . . . over . . ."

The audacity of the plan hits me like a headshot. Maybe there is a way. I tap open a connection, hoping she answers.

<<Yeah?>>

<<Ryeen. I need a favor.>>

<<Say the word.>>

<<It's a big favor. It'll burn both our names. Like, scorched-earth burn.>>

<<Was getting tired of this one anyway. What are you looking to do?>>

<<You mentioned a couple days ago you could get some rich clients to send an orbital hopper if they thought it was going to be an encounter in the real. Offer still on the table?>>

<<Of course. Why the concern?>>

<<Need to steal the hopper.>>

<<Bold. I like it. What for?>>

<<Better you don't know. I'll tell you if you want, though.>>

<<It's fine. You always did right by me, Ash. When do you want it?>>

<<One sec.>>

I turn my attention back to the room.

"Jase, any chance you can lay your hands on some high-altitude suits? Preferably by today?"

He sucks on his lower lip.

"I can try, but I'm not sure my contacts deal in that kind of stuff, Ash. They're more on the digital side of things than the real."

"I'll talk to some people," Johnny interrupts, putting his hand on Jase's shoulder. "Got some old friends, old favors. Seems as good a time as any to cash 'em in. Might not be much left to use 'em on if I don't."

"Thanks, Johnny. What time do you think we'll have them?"

"Seventeen hundred by the latest."

<<Ryeen, can they get the hopper here at eighteen hundred local time?>>

<<Eighteen . . . six o'clock? For you, in the real, these people would walk naked through a Dead Zone. Yeah, it'll be there.>>

<<Thanks, Ryeen. Be safe.>>

<<You too. These johns have teeth. I'll send you the details in a sec.>>

I look at Wind and Slend.

"Okay, we have a way in."

"If it involves high-altitude suits, I'm sure it's entirely safe and sane," Wind responds.

"You'll love it. We're going to disguise ourselves as sex slaves for depraved billionaires, knock out or otherwise disable an unknown number of guards, most likely armed and dangerous, hijack an orbital hopper, reprogram the nav system into going terminal at the WGSK facility, bail out on initial descent while we're almost one hundred kilometers above the planet, then charge through the smoldering crater of a front door the impact will create for us, whereupon we'll assault an entire Big Three compound filled with highly trained security forces shooting to kill who outnumber us at least ten to one. After all *that*, we'll overpower a WGSK executive vice president and somehow force him to undermine his corporation by shutting everything down."

Wind starts giggling.

"The Prophet wept. That's not a plan, Ash, that's the plot to a terrible hap movie. One of those gun-porn pieces Slend loves."

"Lens flares are pretty."

"Look," I reply, "it's not the best plan, but it's the only one I can think of in the time we have left that has even a chance of working." I drop my voice. "Speaking of which, are you two sure you want to do this? I can't back out, not anymore, but that doesn't mean you have to join me. This is probably a one-way run with no rezzes."

Slend puts her hand on my shoulder, a comforting grip.

"Gotta stick together. Only ever us. Wish Brand was here. Always wanted to save the world."

I pat her hand, hot prickling pushing its way to my eyes.

"Thanks, Slend. I wish she was here too. Wind? You can probably get your parents out if you move quick."

She smacks me in the other arm, then curses, waving her hand.

"Of course I'm staying, you granite-bicepped idiot. We're a team, right? SunJewel Warriors? Masters of the Game and all that? Slend's right—we have to stick together."

"It's just, last night. You were pretty upset."

"Yeah, well, I talked with my parents, and they said that the true measure of one's faith isn't kneeling when times are good, but standing when times are hard. Then my dad shook his finger at me; you know how he is. 'You help those who help you, Fatimah. Go. Your mother and I trust you to do the right thing.' What was I supposed to do after that, be the asshole who *didn't* help her friends protect the planet?"

I grab her into another hug, crushing her against my side.

"Well, I appreciate it, and I'm sure Slend does too." Slend nods, and I wipe the moisture from my eyes. "Ok. Let's figure out some strats. The way I see it, our primary needs are gear to assault the compound, and something to reroute the shuttle."

"Might be the boy and I can help you out a bit there," Johnny says. "Think you can reprogram an orbital shuttle by remote, son?" Jase nods once, firmly. "Good." He waves us to join him behind the counter. "Follow me."

Bemused, I watch Johnny roll back the rubber floor covering, spotted with spilled grease and trampled noodle bits, to reveal a crude hatch set into the floor, ragged edges rounded in the curving flows of arc-burned metal. He punches in a code on the heavy-looking lock, then pulls the hatch open, revealing a short ladder leading down, lights flicking on to banish the darkness. I look over at Jase, but he seems just as confused as I am. Johnny climbs down the ladder, and we follow.

At the bottom is an armory.

The room is long and thin, one wall covered in various projectile-launching devices ranging from pistols to what looks to be a crew-serviced heavy machine gun. A counter runs along the other wall, tools and printers neatly arrayed along its surface, carefully labeled cases of ammo stacked underneath between scattered pallets of grenades and flashbangs. Suits of body armor hang against the far end, like a war fashionista's dressing room.

"Now it's *definitely* a gun-porn movie," Wind whispers, her voice awed. "Look at all this stuff."

Jase's eyes are three sizes too big for his head, dreadlocks whipping back and forth across his face as he scans the room. I get the sense he's having difficulty reconciling who a parent really is compared to who he thought they were. I should know.

"Damn, Johnny." I run my hand over the polymer grip of a vintage Water Wars pistol. A red warning light blinks gently on, internal processor not recognizing my biometrics. "Never took you for a collector." I take my hand off, and the light fades away. Johnny stops next to a battered assault rifle located in the exact center of the wall, an older model, the only piece in the room that looks less than perfect.

"Got caught without a weapon, once. Wouldn't have made it out by myself." He raises his hand, as if he's going to lay it on the rifle, but then lets it fall and turns to face us. "More accurate to call me a lender than a collector, though. Sometimes someone needs a little extra oomph. Take down a couple sentries on a cargo ship, bust a synthetics dealer, maybe blow open the door of a pedohouse." He inclines his head at me. "Helps keep the bills paid."

Slend grunts from behind.

"Heavy. Like it."

She's holding the crew-serviced machine gun, muscles not quite visibly straining.

"You and your big guns," Wind scoffs. "Don't ask me to carry that for you. And don't blame me when you crater—we have to jump out of a shuttle, remember?"

"Taking it anyway."

"Don't say I didn't warn you. How are you even going to carry ammo for that beast? Seems a little awkward to use as a club."

Slend scowls, and Johnny hitches a thumb at the back wall.

"Should be a mecha frame under the flak vests. See if it fits."

"How . . . how do you have a *mecha*, Pops?" Jase sounds stunned. "The Han don't let *anyone* have mechas. They're designed to self-destruct when the user dies or has one removed without a password, and no one's ever cracked their manufacturing facility."

"Knew a razorgirl, once. Helped her with some problems. She let me keep it as a souvenir."

I feel my jaw slowly drop open. I knew Johnny was capable, but this is something else. He laughs, a long, deep rumble.

"I was in your mother's unit for a reason, Ashley. I may not have been on her level—hell, none of us were, not even Sawyer—but that didn't mean we sat around with our thumbs up our asses either. Once I got out, I had to make ends meet, feed a hungry kid, and that meant doing the work that needed doing." His laughter dies down, and the smile vanishes from his eyes. "No matter what the job was. That life's behind me now, but I still lived it. Every second."

Silence fills the room, finally broken by a small cough from Wind.

"Got anything suited more for someone my size? Something lightweight? With fur, maybe?"

Johnny nods, a little bit of the tightness banished from his face.

"I don't know about the fur, but there are some SMGs over here that you might like. Come take a look."

Wind and Johnny walk farther down the wall, debating the merits of various types of ammunition. Slend pushes past them to scrounge up the mecha, leaving Jase and me standing next to each other. I nudge him with my elbow.

"You doing okay?"

He tugs on a handful of his hair.

"I . . . it's just . . . the old man, I've never seen him do anything other than make noodles all day. I knew he fought in the Dubs, hell, that's where he found me, but all this . . ." Jase sighs. "Shit. I dunno, Ash. Every time I think I have a handle on the world, it flips upside down again."

I clap him on the back.

"You're not alone, Jase. You're definitely not alone. Parents are a pain in the ass."

I leave him to his thoughts and amble along the room, mentally cataloging the various weapon systems. A familiar bullpup rifle on the wall catches my eye, and I take a closer look. A neat line of stitching, nearly invisible, scars the otherwise immaculate shoulder strap. I turn away, trying not to think about Brand, searching for something else to consume my mind. A pair of shapes above the workbench, slender and slightly curved, one longer than the other, draw me forward with hypnotic intensity. I stop in front of them, rapt.

"Go ahead."

Johnny's voice is soft. Soundlessly, I reach up and grasp the larger shape, polished lacquer smooth under my hand. I grip the tightly wrapped leather hilt and pull the blade out several centimeters. Bright steel gleams under the armory lights, a wavy, almost incandescent line millimeters thick separating the lighter cutting edge from the darker spine of the sword. Air seems to hiss past the exposed edge.

"It's . . . beautiful."

"The Honjo." Johnny's voice is nearly as reverent as mine. "One of the Shinji's national treasures, before they were absorbed by the Han. Thought about giving it back, but was never sure if there was anyone left who would appreciate it."

"How did you get it?"

"Long story. Lots of people turn up in Ditchtown."

I slide the blade back home and return the scabbard to its place on the wall. Johnny hands me the smaller sheath, a lesser curve nearly seventy-five centimeters long. The instant my hand touches the hilt, it feels like a part of my body. I bare the length of metal fully, revealing a shadowed stretch of steel that almost seems to drink the light, brilliant highlights dancing across the walls as I twist it under the glare.

"The Musashi."

I take a practice cut, metal gliding through the air like an extension of my arm. It seems to demand a kata, and I refuse, reluctantly. The noise as I slide it back into the scabbard sounds almost disappointed.

"Take it."

I look up at Johnny, stunned. He nods.

"That one's a fighter, not a looker. You fit each other. Not sure what use it'll be against guns, but it's better than collecting dust in here."

I look around. There's not a speck of dust to be seen.

"Are you sure, Johnny? This is a work of art."

"Absolutely. Weapons are made to be used. Even if we wish they weren't."

I loop the cloth straps around my waist, but it doesn't feel quite right, scabbard threatening to knock against the walls. Shift it to my back. Perfect.

"Sword-porn too, huh?"

Wind grins at me, her hands busy reassembling a boxy-looking submachine gun, a second one in front of her, and I grin back.

"Sword-porn too. If we're going to do the impossible, might as well do it in style. How's the mecha, Slend?"

Slend gives us a thumbs up, the mecha's angular contours framing her legs and arms like a matte gray exoskeleton. She spins her heavy machine gun through a full revolution like a baton, her already formidable strength amplified by the mechanical servos, then starts disassembling it to fit into a duffel bag, boxes of ammo already stacked neatly inside.

I turn to the wall, and the bullpup rifle snags my attention once more. I force myself to grab it, to confront that nearly invisible scar. The weight is solid in my hands, reassuring. Check the action. Smooth and steady, just like the last time I used it, only now it's chambered for live rounds, not tranq darts. I run my fingers over the raised line of stitching, the only physical remnant of my friend.

For you, Brand. I wish I'd known sooner. I'm sorry.

I grab a duffel bag of my own and start loading it—plenty of extra magazines, body armor, several grenades and flash-bangs, a basic first aid kit. All the normal tools of the trade. Shrug off the sword and lay it on top—it barely fits inside. Run the zipper shut with a quick tug, metallic teeth smoothly catching each other.

"Wind, Slend, you two ready?"

"Lock stock and ready to rock."

"Yup."

"Good. Jase, make sure you're up-to-date on that shuttle. Johnny, we'll be back in a bit. We're going shopping."

22

==

[Sonic]

The autocab glides to a halt, wheels gripping faintly cracked concrete, and I peer out heavily tinted windows. The decayed ruins of an old airport surround us, broken windows gaping like missing teeth, collapsed boarding bridges tilting drunkenly down to the ground. Early evening twilight blazes orange above the distant treeline, the sun not quite beginning its disappearing act for the day. Shadows stretch out in elongated shapes, harbingers of the coming night.

A sleek orbital shuttle sits on the runway, upswept wings black with ceramic heat reflector tiles, three engine nozzles protruding below its tail fin. The passenger hatch swings open and a mobile stair cart trundles up, attaching itself to the side of the shuttle. Two burly men in fitted suits and dark glasses walk down the steps, approaching the autocab, pistol bulges not quite concealed by the bespoke tailoring. I tap a message to Johnny and Jase, covering us from the dilapidated airport's roof.

<<Moving out.>>

"Showtime, ladies."

The autocab's door opens, and I watch myself step out, Johnny's rifle scope feeding into the upper right of my glasses.

A darkly muscular leg, bare to my hip, iridescent tattoo coiling up under the sleek purple slit dress that hugs my body like a glove, emerging again in the deep vee front plunging nearly to my belly button, a thin cloth strap around my neck preventing the whole thing from flying away in the snapping breeze. Fingertip-covering purple gloves stretch nearly to my elbows, leaving my palms and underarms bare, and stiletto heels cover my feet. A short black wig envelops my head and ears in a tight curl. Visual hashing makeup shrouds my face in tribal patterns, invisible to normal sight, overwhelming confusion to any surveillance spheres or AR glasses focusing in my direction. I've got enough problems without an angry billionaire chasing my shadow—assuming we survive this. The guards won't care, since I doubt their boss allows them to see anything other than what he deems necessary. His toys aren't in that category.

Behind me, Wind emerges, a flowing yellow gown fluttering behind her like wings, waist-length hair chasing it in streaming lengths, strips of brown skin darting in and out of vision. A pair of designer glasses completes the affair, curling around her eyes in thin rectangles, camouflage coloration marking her face as well. Slend ducks out of the other side of the car, resplendent in a snug black leather halter and pants, aviator-style lenses shrouding her features. She flings opens the trunk, muscles tightening beneath her form-clinging outfit. One of the men nearly trips over his own feet, then catches himself.

Good. Another group that sucks at psych-secs.

I smile and wave at the leading guard.

"Hey there, you our ride?"

"Yeah—" He clears his throat. "Yes, Miss . . . ?"

"Persephone, but you can call me Seph." I let my left hand trail across his cheek, his stubble scraping my skin. "Be a dear and help with the luggage, yes? We're so eager to get on board."

"I, uh, have to check you for, uh, weapons. Sorry."

"Oh it's fine, we're used to . . . touching."

I give him a smoldering look and place one leg forward, pushing down the butterflies in my stomach. This is bringing back a lot of memories I really never wanted to face again, and there's no logging out if it turns bad. His hands close around my ankle, warm and dry, and he runs them up my leg, quickly, professionally, then repeats the process on the other leg. Despite myself, I'm impressed. I was expecting him to linger around my crotch. Beside me, the second guard begins the same process on Wind, who momentarily stumbles, leaning forward. She braces herself by grabbing his neck, the top of his head brushing against her chest, his face in her groin. I want to laugh at the sudden redness in his cheeks, but I force myself to maintain composure.

Seduction is always about composure.

"I'm afraid I'll have to do your upper body next," my guard says apologetically. I wink at him.

"Not a problem, though I'm not sure where I'd be hiding anything. With this dress, I might as well be naked."

He slips behind me, cheeks blushing, and I want to slap my forehead. Why is it that every guy thinks a woman flirting means he's going to get laid? This underling *knows* he's only here to keep his boss safe, yet in his mind, he's imagining us fucking like wild animals. It'd be depressing if it wasn't so useful. I glance over at Wind, who lets her lip drift slightly upward in our prearranged signal. Step one complete.

The guard finishes patting me down and turns to the autocab, heading for Slend, who's busy pulling duffel bags out of the trunk. The other guard finishes with Wind and joins him.

"We're going to get on board if you don't mind," I call out, and they nod absentmindedly, furrowing their brows at the bags. Wind and I set off at a quick walk for the stairs.

"What are these for?" I hear from behind, one of the guards poking at a bag. Slend steps closer to him.

"Tools. To party."

Our heels click up the stairs in staccato pulses.

"Okay, well we'll need to take a look inside. That's a lot of tools."

"Lot of party. Unload first."

The voices fade away, cut off by the shuttle's interior. An open cockpit door to our left reveals a single pilot going through his preflight checklist, hands touching invisible switches and comparing virtual readouts. To the right, a luxurious tube, three plush seats and a couch in close proximity to each other, roof not quite low enough to make me duck. An olive-skinned man clearly used to the luxuries his status affords him lounges on the couch, white robes spilling to either side, bright blue lenses covering his eyes, his expression bored and indolent—likely an Industan petroboy looking to have a good time on daddy's dime. Another guard sits across from him, hapgloved fingers busy with something only he can see, omnipresent pistol bulge under his unbuttoned coat. I caress my right hand across the back of his neck as I pass, coming to a halt in front of the swarthy man. He extends his hand, a languid gesture.

I take it, bending my head as if to kiss his fingers, catching Wind standing behind me in bare feet, her heels kicked off to the side. Good. Everyone's in position. I tap out a message to the others with my free hand.

<<Go.>>

Several things happen at once. The guard convulses, eyes rolling wildly, a cornucopia of drugs boiling into his bloodstream from the dermal patch I placed on his neck, triggered by Johnny's remote command. In my glasses, I see one of the guards outside doing the same, slumped against the autocab, while Slend knocks out the other, his hand just barely clearing his jacket before her fist drives him unconscious, not waiting for the drugs to finish kicking in. Wind dashes into the cockpit, looping her fluttering lengths of dress around the pilot's mouth and throat, choking him into insensibility, and I jerk the petroboy forward, sliding my arm around his neck and bracing it against my other arm, forcing his head to the side, his glasses seeing nothing but the couch. I can feel his pulse jumping beneath my forearm, his panicky breaths hot and scratchy, and then I squeeze until he goes limp, one slippered foot slightly twitching, pulse now weak and thready. Anyone monitoring his biosigns probably thinks he just had the blow-job of his life. I carefully remove his glasses and tuck them into his robes, making sure not to reveal the other guard or myself.

<<Clear.>>

Wind emerges from the cockpit, followed by the sounds of a dragging body.

<<Clear.>>

I kick off my heels and heave the petroboy to the entrance, stacking him on top of the pilot. Below, Slend finishes putting the second guard into the autocab and hustles over with two of the duffel bags and a backpack. She throws the duffels into the cabin, hands me the backpack, and then grabs the last guard in a fireman's carry, taking him back to the autocab. Wind pushes past me and grabs the petroboy by the feet, dragging him down the stairs, giggling as his head thumps on each step. He's going to wake up with one hell of a headache, that's for sure.

I move into the cockpit, pulling out the small box Jase put together in his workshop.

<<Jase, you getting my feed?>>

<<Clear as Glassbridge. Look underneath the central console, there should be a panel there you can pry out.>>

A section of the cockpit highlights red in my vision, and I duck down. Sure enough, there's a small panel with several screws holding it shut. I grab a multitool from the backpack and seconds later it's open, revealing a tangled mass of colored wires. In Johnny's feed I can see Wind and Slend loading the pilot into the autocab and returning with the last piece of gear, a large and sturdy case about the size of a coffin.

<<Okay, now what?>>

<<Strip these three wires and hook them into the appropriate ports.>>

Three of the wires start glowing—orange, blue, and yellow—along with three slots on the box. Three snips of the multitool later, Jase's box is hooked into the shuttle. An amber light appears on its surface, then turns a blinking green.

<<I'm in. You're done here, Ash. Just leave the box somewhere in the console.>>

I shove the small rectangle in among the rest of the wires, then stand up to join Wind and Slend, who are busy changing into combat gear—compression bodysuits first, followed by tactical harnesses, then ballistic panels for body, legs, and arms, tacboots for their feet. I shimmy out of my dress and race to catch up. We should have some time before anyone realizes something's wrong, but there's no reason to waste it.

<<I'm through the firewalls. Isolating navigation protocols. Got it. Rewriting destination. Done. Locking out remote takeover. Done. Ready when you are.>>

A simple-looking red button appears in my glasses. I ignore it for now and finish strapping the last piece of ballistic armor to my shin, then move over to the coffin-sized crate. Wind and Slend are already hauling out pieces of the high-altitude suits: bulky gauntlets, helmets, and boots trailing thin fabric sleeves, a stiff backplated torso with circular connection seals at the hips, shoulders, and neck. The overall impression is of an old deep sea diving suit. We help each other with the connections, then pull out three metal tanks and hook them up to the suit fronts, threading the nozzle connection into the port at the bottom of each helmet. Air hisses into my ears, and the suit slowly puffs out, stopping at one atmosphere. A countdown appears on the inside of the helmet—ninety minutes before tank failure. The final piece is a parachute knapsack screwed into the backplate. I can already feel the sweat starting to drip down my skin.

<<Everything okay, Ash?>>

<<Almost done. Just need to load the gear.>>

We toss the duffels containing our weapons into the crate with clumsy suited hands, then reattach the lid. Slend hits a code on the control panel—assuming no malfunctions, a web of restraining harnesses will keep the contents from moving more than a centimeter or two in any direction. Another code pops out three tethers with hooks on the end, which we quickly lash around the seat stanchions and winch tight. No sense in having a hundred-kilogram pinball bouncing through the cabin on takeoff. Wind and Slend each take a seat, awkwardly wrapping restraining belts around their bulky forms. I waddle up to the cockpit and wedge myself into the pilot's chair, the last rays of the setting sun lancing through the front window.

<<Okay, Jase, we're ready. See you on the other side.>>

<<Good luck, Ash. Be safe.>>

<<You too, Jase. Thanks, Johnny. For everything.>>

<<You got it, Ashley. We do what needs to be done.>>

<<Yeah. Always.>>

I tap the red button. The shuttle rumbles to life, executing Jase's program. Thrusters pop into ignition, then settle into a subsonic thrum. The side door closes, mobile stair cart scurrying away like a frightened mouse. The shuttle's nose slowly turns, lining us up on the runway, and the hum turns into a roar, acceleration force pressing us deep into the seats. With a start, I realize I'm grinning. All those years playing the Game, and now we're finally experiencing it in the real. Space.

The nose lifts, and more acceleration shudders through the shuttle, torching us skyward with ever increasing velocity. Light bursts in intensity, the sun reappearing over the Earth's curve, sky shifting from burnt sunset into lighter blue into ever darker shades of bruised purple, until everything is a strange crystal black, diamonds burning steadily in the distance. My stomach grumbles, unmoored from its familiar gravitational tether, and I want to cry.

Nothing could have prepared me for this. Nothing.

<<One minute to insertion point. Venting interior.>>

Jase's automated warning brings me back to reality, and I watch a swirl of objects rip past—small bits of paper, a dirty pen, fly carcasses—sucked out by the opened side door. The brief hurricane settles down, and I release my belt harness, feeling myself float slightly away from the seat. I pull myself into the main cabin, where Wind and Slend are busy unhooking the cables from the seats, our crate drifting in the vacuum interior. My purple dress waves from its tangled embrace of a seat, somehow still intact, an ethereal wisp of another life. I join the other two, and we each attach a hook to our suits' chest plates. Slend taps one last code into the crate's control panel, setting the parameters for its own chute deployment. Below us, the planet beckons like an azure and emerald gem, white swirls dancing across its facets.

<<This is fucking awesome, Ash.>>

Wind's eyes glow behind her faceplate and glasses, smile lines crinkling their corners. Slend, unsurprisingly, is silent, but I can see her smiling too.

<<Wait until the boardshits learn about this. Fucking outer

space,>> I send back, and we all start giggling, one last calm before the awaiting storm.

A message breaks the moment like a fist hitting a nose.

<<Ash. Jase here. Ahh . . . you should know that the entire board of WGSK just got annihilated. All dead, homes destroyed. Looks like Gamers, but that doesn't make any sense . . . >>

<<And our target? Still there?>>

<<Yeah . . . weird. Shit's getting real tense on the socials. There's talk of Han and Industan regiments on the move. Johnny says . . . He says to stay frosty, Ash.>>

I shiver. Once. That's all I can afford to let myself feel.

<<Got it. Thanks, Jase.>>

With the WGSK board out of the picture, convincing Ham's dad should be easy, at least . . . but then who's running all the Gamers . . . ?

The automated voice sounds, and the splintered calm falls away completely.

<<Fifteen seconds until insertion.>>

I feel time's familiar unwinding, my senses hyperaware, every piece of information processed, analyzed, discarded.

<<Three. Two. One. Beginning descent.>>

<<That's our cue, ladies. Time to do the impossible.>>

We push our way outside of the shuttle, still hanging on to the open door, watching the sleek shape orient itself downward with brief puffs of gas from impulse thrusters. A slight vibration starts shaking the door in our hands, atmospheric drag kicking in. We used the bare minimum of delta-v, so friction heat shouldn't be a problem.

<<Glide path established. Begin separation.>>

We give ourselves the lightest of pushes away from the shuttle, door swinging shut behind us, and assume a diving profile, arms tight against our sides, toes pointed back, keeping pace with our kinetic door knocker. My suit starts shaking harder, atmosphere growing more pronounced, the three of us forming a triangle with our gear crate in the middle.

<<Let's give it some more space.>>

We each extend our arms, legs curled up, and slowly the shuttle moves away from us, continuing its terminal descent almost straight down. A guide path appears in my glasses, mimicked in Slend's and Wind's as well, a series of gold rings we plummet through like arrows. The ground below grows closer, wispy clouds starting to form around us, a larger system below. Blue leaches back into my vision, rapidly growing lighter. Our descent roars around us, the shuttle dwindling to a dot, its streamlined shape auguring down, rockets firing one last time. It vanishes into a puffy white mass, and we plunge after it, water droplets streaking across my faceplate. The air starts buffeting us harder, but we maintain our formation, ring after ring flashing around us. I check the time in my glasses.

<<Shuttle impact in thirty. Chutes in eighty-five.>>

<<Check.>>

<<Check.>>

We emerge into another open space, a lower layer of dark and dangerous clouds looming below. Lightning flickers along their edges, and I hope the random number generator sides with us one last time. More golden rings appear, then disappear, the shuttle now a small green bracket no longer visible to the naked eye. We dive into the storm.

<<Impact in ten. Chutes in sixty-five.>>

<<Check.>>

<<Check.>>

The seconds tick by, rain clouds squalling around us, and then the ground reappears once more. A small mushroom bursts into existence among the green, dirty gray bulges billowing out, our chariot reaching its final resting place in a blaze of kinetic thunder and light. The hooks detach from our chests, cables falling away from the gear crate. I watch an altimeter circle slowly closer to zero.

<<Chutes in three. Two. One.>>

Deceleration slams through my body, the high-performance parachutes crawling up and out of our back-mounted packs, unfolding into low-profile rectangles, shedding velocity in open defiance of gravity, gold rings still guiding our way. Below us, the gear crate deploys its own chute, aiming itself for the edge of the steaming crater now resolving into visibility, a broken scar outside a squat and ugly wart. The ground grows closer, swatches of green shifting into patches of forest, then individual trees; gray lumps transforming into cracked concrete and fire. Updrafts buffet our chutes, but we control them with the ease of long practice. The gear crate touches down, a tumbling skid. We follow it, parachutes flapping away, our feet scrambling across the churned and muddy ground. The upper parts of our suits slip away like molting snakeskins, gloves, torso, helmet, their task complete. Flames hiss weakly in the underbrush at the edge of the crater, raindrops relentlessly assaulting their flickering attempts to grow.

I step out of the bulky high-altitude boots and open up the crate, quickly ripping webbing off our duffels. I pull mine to the side and reach for the scabbard, securing it to my back. The bullpup rifle follows it, scarred strap looping over my shoulder. Small clicks sound from Slend's legs, the mecha forming itself around her, heavy machine gun in her hands, and she feeds a belt of ammo into its hopper, more cases hanging from the mecha's frame. Wind clips one of her submachine guns to her chest, then cocks the other, a bandolier of grenades running across her hips. Our eyes never stop scanning the broken remnants of layers of dome, a seventy-meter hole gouged from the force of the shuttle's impact, secondary fractures radiating outward in jagged tears. Smoke pours out from within, and gradually, shapes appear in its depths. I look over at the other two, and they look back. We nod.

Time to move.

23

[Down the Dragon's Throat]

Gunfire crackles from the indoor park ahead, a concentrated volley of orchestrated death buzzing out from manicured topiaries like swarming wasps. Bullets ricochet wildly off the concrete debris shielding me, windows shattering into tinkling waterfalls of debris. I take the opportunity to reload, staring up at the light panels blanketing the atrium's ceiling. A sudden crump silences the firing, one of Wind's flashbangs, and Slend opens up with her heavy machine gun, mecha-assisted strides putting her into a flanking position far quicker than the defenders expected. I spin over into a prone position and pick off two figures trying to exfiltrate from the killing zone, their arms flailing as they topple like hewn trees.

<<Clear.>>

<<Clear.>>

<<Clear.>>

We push forward through the small park, our third encounter with WGSK's security forces, shattered bodies sprawled in our wake. I don't let myself think about them, not yet. We still have to get deeper into the complex, to what is hopefully the control room, if we've read the blueprints right. The other half of WGSK's army is no doubt on its way.

Straight lines of hedges give way to even straighter lines of corridors, another interminable set of skyscraper connective tissue. I check the map overlay in my glasses—three blinking dots running through a maze of wireframe halls, Sawyer's data the only resource availab—

I'm on my back, gasping for air, pain radiating from my chest where a sledgehammer just flattened me, scabbard digging into my shoulder and spine. Wind's submachine gun chatters noisily, then Slend's face fills my vision, expression concerned. Jamming hashes our comm channel in a static hiss.

"Hit?"

My gasps turn into choking coughs, bruised lungs slowly refilling, a deeper, piercing pain still lingering.

"Armor . . . caught it." I push myself to one knee, wincing. Wind is posted up at the hallway's intersection farther down, a uniformed corpse at her feet, busy scanning for more threats. "Probably a cracked rib or two." I grab my rifle, and force myself into a jog. "C'mon. No time. We gotta keep moving."

Slend nods, the mecha boosting her past me and up next to Wind. They spin around the corner, and I follow. More shots ring out, a cluster of figures hidden behind couches and desks in what looks like a reception lobby, and we dive for cover in the doorways lining the hall. I look over and see Wind hissing with pain, right hand clutching her left bicep, submachine gun dangling loosely from its strap. Blood seeps out between her fingers and drips to the floor below.

"Status?" I yell over the fusillade of gunfire.

"In and out. Stings like a *mother*fucker. I'll be fine. Slend! Head down, 'nade in three!"

The heavier cracks of Slend's machine gun die away, and Wind lets go of her wounded arm, pulling a grenade off her bandolier. Fragmentation this time. A flick of her thumb sends the arming pin spinning out, and then she whips it across the linoleum floor toward the lobby. A second passes, then another, sounds of consternation just beginning to rise before the ringing explosion wipes them away with red splatter smears. I advance out of my alcove, trotting toward the wreckage, hunting for survivors, Slend covering my right. Smoke fills the air, setting off a ringing fire alarm, and my finger twitches once, twice, neutralizing the last threats, their groggy movements giving them away. Water sprays down from overhead sprinklers, cold and clammy on my skin, and we move deeper into the facility.

"Through here and down three flights. Go."

More violence, more encounters, more damage. Slend takes a bullet in her thigh on the first landing, mecha working double time to take the load, but she presses on, lips set in a grim line, heavy machine gun ripping craters from walls and flesh. Wind twists an ankle diving out of the way of a grenade on the second, fragments peppering her back and side, her armor barely absorbing the worst of the deadly kinetic force. A steady stream of curses spills from her mouth as she staggers along, almost too low to hear, but her aim remains true, hands swapping between her submachine guns with automatic ease, flinging blood and grenades until her bandolier is almost empty.

We emerge onto the third landing, panting for breath, and miraculously, nothing attacks us. A long corridor, bare of branches, extends to a set of solid-looking double doors. I glance at the other two.

"How's your ammo?"

Wind pats one of her submachine guns, unclipping the other and letting it fall to the floor, then pulls a last flashbang from her harness.

"Thirty rounds, then I'm dry. One sparkler left. Slend?"

Slend drops her heavy machine gun and pulls out a large pistol, sliding an oversized magazine home.

"Twenty-five. Punching after this."

With the mecha's enhanced strength, her punches should shatter concrete, but that's not much use against a bullet. I check my rifle—fifteen rounds left, no extra mags.

"I've got fifteen and my blade. Let's move."

We set off down the hallway, alert for any traps, but the cheerfully painted walls, swooping and dipping with murals of fantastic creatures and exotic landscapes, remain still. Halfway down, to my shock, it finally penetrates—I recognize almost all of them as encounters from the Game. I look closer. A small figure is barely visible in the background of each one, streak of blue in her hair, dagger brandished aloft. Wind sucks in a breath.

"This is creepy, Ash. Mega creepy."

"Just another psych-sec, Wind. Just another encounter. We're almost there. Map says our target is behind these doors. Slend, if you'll do the honors?"

Slend nods, then delivers a thunderous kick with her mecha-enhanced leg. The doors splinter and crash inward, one falling off its frame entirely. Beyond, a large oval room lies shrouded in twilight gloom, a familiar liquid-filled tank in the middle, consoles surrounding its length, a thrashing body floating in its depths. Scattered ceiling lights shine fitfully, most burnt out and shattered.

"Well, this certainly looks like a boss roo—fucking hell."

My stomach falls with Wind's startled exclamation. Stepping out from behind the tank is a Shredder, molyblade legs tapping gently on the black-and-white patterned floor, streamlined shell rising nearly halfway to the vaulted ceiling overhead. Armored panels spring up around the tank and consoles, fully enclosing the vulnerable occupant, one last spasm briefly visible.

"Hamlin," I whisper, heart sinking. "Oh, Ham, what are they doing to you?"

"Ash!" Wind's voice is urgent. "What do we do? That's fucking wargear!"

The Shredder skitters forward, directly at me, an oversized insect covered in polymer plates. I let off a burst at its central core, but it twists as I fire and the rounds deflect off its armor.

"Scatter and ground it! Aim for the legs!"

Wind and Slend split off to the sides, limping heavily, small salvos from Wind interspersed by single shots from Slend. Bullets whiz and spang through the room, but the Shredder keeps advancing, none of our attacks finding a vital junction. One limb scythes at me, molyblade splitting the greasy air, and I roll to the side, feeling the wind of its passing. I roll again, another limb slamming down with floor-cracking force next to my head. A third leg sweeps at my ankles, and I flip over it, unloading the last of my bullets into the joint, watching it deform and warp, ignoring the stabbing pain from my broken ribs. Wind darts in from the other side, slamming her flashbang into the gap, then pinwheels away, caught by a backhand blow from the second leg. She slams into the wall, head lolling into unconsciousness, and the flashbang explodes, a thunderclap of deafening light and blinding sound leaking out from the joint. The Shredder's wounded leg falls limp and still, actuators severed, and I dodge another molyblade strike seeking to bisect me. My rifle strap splits apart, a ghost of the past, bullpup shape spinning away, momentum sending me tumbling across the floor. Slend appears, grabbing one of the Shredder's legs with mecha-enhanced strength, muscles close to bursting from her skin. Screaming, she pulls, ripping it free in a shower of buzzing sparks and hydraulic fluids, then flies off in the opposite direction from Wind, another Shredder leg slamming across her midsection with a crunching impact, pieces of mecha spiraling away in violent constellations. She hits the ground and curls into a ball, unmoving, blood leaking from her earlier wound, the dismembered leg next to her. The Shredder scrapes its way toward me, disabled hind limbs dragging behind it in a halting screech, front legs striking like pistons.

I reach over my shoulder. Still there. Snarling, I unsheath my blade and stalk toward the drone. It stops moving, lying in wait, and I enter its range, adrenaline fueling my senses. One limb swings diagonally down. I sidestep and lean, feeling the molyblade neatly slice the tips of my bangs, then bring cold steel down in a two-handed grip on the exposed joint. The ancient metal does what it was created to do, and the leg falls limp, actuator fluid spurting like lifeblood. The last limb lashes out, a dying snake's final deadly blow, but it's not fast enough. I duck beneath the thrust and impale the Shredder's control section, polymer splitting beneath the Musashi's chiseled tip, delicate microboards and control chips splintering into ruin. Grinding noises sound from within, and then the Shredder falls still.

I exhale, hands trembling, and that's when the fiery agony of a bullet smashes into the back of my leg, dropping me to the ground.

24

[Maru]

Air whistles between my teeth, the pain from my shattered leg threatening to overtake my entire mind. Sound intrudes, a slow clapping echoing around the room, chased by the clicking tread of dress shoes. Grimacing, I push myself over into a sitting position, leaning against the corpse of the Shredder, blood seeping through my hand. The Musashi juts out beside my head. A tall man with pale hair approaches, still clapping his hands slowly, thin black glasses covering his grim face. Next to him, a dazed-looking figure in a hapsuit and telltale hood holds a pistol aimed at me, his eyes seeing nothing but the Game. I incline my head at the man with pale hair.

"You're . . . Ham's dad. The WGSK exec."

"And you are Ashley Akachi, or 'Ashura the Terrible,' perhaps the greatest player of our little game ever. Imagine my surprise when I discovered my heir was consorting with such . . . filth."

The venom in his voice takes me aback.

"Excuse me?"

Might be tough going convincing him to shut this all down.

He examines his hapgloved hands, then brushes them against his exquisitely tailored suit.

"Don't play coy, Ashley. Or should I say, 'Persephone.'"
I flinch, and he nods. "That's right. When I caught my son
sneaking around in my private messages, I wanted some answers. He tried being stubborn. Eventually, he came around."

"You . . . forced him? To talk about . . . me?"

He takes a step closer, features pinched.

"I built his neural lace, and I ultimately control its inputs.
Sometimes a father must be stern with a wayward child."

"Child—he's not . . . what did you do to him?!"

None of this makes any sense.

"Only what I had to. He'll thank me for it, once he under-
stands the gift he's been given. Once you're gone. Now, more
importantly, why are you here?"

*The rolling deck of a container ship. Melted eyes, running like
wax. A dying man's unspoken wish.*

. . . because I don't fucking lose. To anyone.

". . . I wanted some answers."

"Cute. I confess, when you first rose up the leaderboards, I
found you mildly intriguing, a brown girl determined to succeed in our world, but then I put you from my mind. Enter-
tainers can be found under any rock. They shine, they wither,
they die, and those with power continue on." Another step.
"But then I find my son passing you messages. Acting on your
behalf. *With* you. And then, after some digging, I discover
that you're working with the CCA, those religious zealots.
Tell me, was this part of your plan? Turning my heir from me
in order to please your masters? Using him to save your own
worthless skin? What lies have you fed him?"

I can feel the pain coursing through my leg, warm blood
seeping out in sticky waves.

Great. A fucking monologue.

"I don't know what the fuck your problem is, but I'm no
fanatic, and the gummies know shit-all about Ham. We've

been together for two years, and I only learned who he really was a couple days ago, when he told me. Then he told me he needed my help—to stop you. What the hell are you doing to him?"

"I'm saving him. My *son*."

He laughs, but it sounds more like a sob. His hands clench at his sides.

"He was born incomplete, a cripple. A freak. When he was a baby, a newborn, the doctors said we 'should let him go.' That his life would never be 'anything more than misery.'"

His voice rises, madness lurking in its depths.

"'*Anything more than misery!*' Like he was some kind of . . . of insect! That he meant *nothing*. But they were wrong. *I* proved them wrong, again and again. I've given him the bodies he never had, the life he'd never hold. Now he will finally have the freedom to run, and dance, and laugh. Forever." Moisture gathers at his eyes, but all his attention is on me. "You and your friend, Sawyer, forced me to elevate him to his new position earlier than expected, but Hamlin is adjusting to the demands. To his new life."

I almost want to tell him to stop talking and shoot—he wouldn't last ten seconds in endgame.

"What do you mean, his new life?"

"Surely you understand that much, or you wouldn't be here. Stupid girl. Who do you think is controlling all those hoods?"

A chill run downs my spine.

Teams. It has to be teams. No one person could control all those hoods . . . no . . .

"You're lying. Even if Ham could do that, that's not who he is. He wouldn't start a war, kill innocents. He's a Gamer. Like me."

More laughter, sneering this time.

"'Like me,' you say, after slaughtering how many? 'A Gamer,' an *otaku*, as if that's something to be proud of. A Gamer. Not a contributor, not a creator, no, just another obsessing puppet, dancing on our strings and calling it life."

My lips peel back in a snarl, and he advances again.

"No, this game you play, this *Game* you have *wasted* your life in, is nothing more than a plaything for my heir. I built it just for him—a tool to help him grow, a world to let him touch and feel and learn in ways he never should have been denied, and *you* were just another part of that. A little toy for him to play with, and break, and discard. As I taught him."

Clicking heels come to a halt, bare centimeters away. He looms over me like a wrathful deity.

"I was planning to teach him, guide him gradually, give him scenarios with much less destructive goals, *allow* him the freedom to find himself, understand my plan and embrace it. I was going to let the board think they would always have him on a leash, until we were ready to wield his full power. But you had to interfere, distract him, set him against me . . . you manipulative little *cunt*."

Just another encounter. Another psych-sec. This fucker just has to talk, and that's keeping you alive. For now. Engage him.

He's close enough that I try to swipe my hand at him, hook his heel and drag him down, but he steps out of the way easily, my arm flopping weakly across my lap.

"I caught him sneaking around in my archives, doing your work, looking for hidden secrets in the haphoods *I* designed, designed for *him*. Looking for gummie bases and . . . testing mishaps. Looking for things that would embarrass *me*, give the board another chance to deny me."

He almost screams the last words, glaring at me. I glare back, but his anger shifts suddenly, tone now gloating.

"Thanks to you, though, his snooping attracted my attention. Gave me a chance to act first. I couldn't let the board pull the plug, not when we were so close."

He spits, momentarily distracted.

"They thought they'd control him, pick the targets, declare the attacks. They loved that idea, taking the CCA apart from the inside out, but only if they didn't risk anything—only if they could sell more *trinkets* afterward. Cowards. I made sure he dealt with them once they approved the final stages."

For fuck's sake, either shoot me or give me a tourniquet. That explains Jase's last message though.

"Why would Ham kill off the board? Does he even know them?"

He refocuses on me.

"Right now, my son thinks he's in a Game scenario, one I was forced to design too quickly thanks to the need to rid him of *your* influence. He's under attack by the entire planet. Everyone hates him—but I ensure certain enemies are regarded as more dangerous than others. There is no sanctuary to be had but what he makes himself, and he's fighting to regain control of the scenario. He's already taken care of the board, and a certain petro rig outfitted with hapchambers. You were lucky to escape."

Flashes of blood and fire echo through my mind, a charnel house floating above the poisoned sea. Sawyer, gasping out his last breaths.

I wasn't lucky, I'm the fucking best. Just another encounter. Giving everyone what they want. I feel myself drifting. *Focus. Keep him talking. If he's doing that, he isn't killing you.*

"You fucking animal. You're turning Ham into a monster."

I remember reports of disturbances across the globe, socials going crazy over the past couple days, pieces of a puzzle I didn't know existed finally falling into place.

"Murdering the world, millions of people, and for what?!

You're not saving your son—you're destroying him. Even the gummies and their 'savior' are better than you."

"You little bitch—how dare you question what I've done for my family!"

He gestures with one hand, and another bullet crashes into my leg, barely missing my shin. I hiss at the sudden shock, keeping my screams bottled in. The blank-eyed Gamer gazes dumbly at nothing, pistol steady in his hands.

Shit. He's going over the edge. He's going to kill me slowly . . .

"I have done everything! Sacrificed *everything*! My son *is the future*. I have *made* him the future."

His breath catches, and he turns away. More blood pulses through my hand, hot, wet, sticky. Throbbing counterpoints beat through my veins.

Not good. You're losing a lot of blood. Something has to happen. Make something happen.

"The future? An eternity trapped as your slave?"

He ignores me, gazing into the distance.

"His future is . . . everything."

"Bullshit."

Fanatic eyes snap back onto my own.

"He can ghost anything. Anyone, because he has no body to hold him back anymore. A being of pure intellect, untethered by . . . humanity."

An ugly intensity enters his eyes.

"He, who has never walked, will now be able to stride the entire globe, using any pair of feet he wishes. He, with his withered fingers, will build an empire, a singular concentration of will and desire, all hands working toward one overarching goal. He will be the guiding light to lift everyone else past their petty grievances and stupidity. He will be *perfect*. And he will have any woman he wants."

What an asshole.

I clench my fist.

"I said bullshit. You don't care about the world. You don't care about Ham. He's only *perfect* if he obeys you."

"Watch your mouth, bitch."

So fucking tired of this. So tired of shitty men with shitty dreams.

"Fuck you. He's your lab experiment. Your invention. Your *intellectual property*, a twisted silkie bullshit fantasy if I've ever heard one!"

His face turns red, but I'm not done.

"You never asked him if this was the future he wanted—if he wanted to be something other than your perfect little soldier. You never stopped to listen, to care. To love him for who he is. And when he found someone who *really* does love him, you trapped him in a nightmare, one *you* created. He'll *never* forgive you."

I pound weakly on the dead drone.

"I *saw* the messages he sent me, begging for help, begging me to stop you. I *saw* him, in there, thrashing in that tank. He hates what you're doing, who you are. He *told me*."

"You *whore!*"

He takes a quick step and kicks me in my gunshot leg. I can't help myself. The pain is too much. I scream. The Gamer twitches, an incongruous ripple passing through his entire body, like stone trying to will itself into life.

"You think you know anything?"

Another kick. Another scream. Another twitch.

"My son will have *everything*, and he will *thank* me for it!"

Another kick. My vision grays, and I try not to pass out. Another tremor from the Gamer, feet shuffling minutely side to side.

"I will destroy you . . . no, I will make *him* destroy you, and the instant before you die, you'll realize your 'love' meant *nothing*! That it was *never* real!"

He kicks me one last time, and I lose track of the world for a moment. When I come to, he's standing by the brain-addled Gamer, rage-lines still creasing his face. He places a hand on the Gamer's shoulder.

"You see her? Your greatest rival, the one you were never strong enough to kill? I have made you strong. While she lives, you risk falling to her again. Do what you've always wanted to do. Defeat her."

The Gamer's finger tightens around the trigger, his body almost vibrating.

Is this finally it? My last encounter? Too bad the stakes were so high. I wish I could at least see the others. Wind. Slend. Brand. I wish I believed the gummies. . . .

I wonder if I'll register the bullet before it scrambles my brains. The finger begins to tighten, and I tense.

A message of death screams across the room, a sharp retort echoing harshly from the tiled walls. I flinch, then my brain catches up and I realize I'm still alive. The shot missed.

"What . . . what are . . . hurghh . . . you . . . doing!"

The Gamer has Ham's father in a chokehold, one hand fighting against two to control the gun. Another shot coughs out, painting the Gamer's midsection red, and he falls to the floor, dragging Ham's father with him, tendons standing out on the older man's hands as he tries to wrestle the weapon away. The chokehold never wavers.

"I . . ."

The Gamer's voice sounds rusty, as if he doesn't know how to actually speak.

"I'm . . . sorry . . . Father . . . Love . . . her . . . You never . . . listened . . . Just wanted . . ."

The gun fires again, and again, swift lead eviscerating the Gamer's abdomen, but he only squeezes tighter, turning the pale-haired man's face purple. The gun falls, perfectly manicured nails scrabbling and clawing against the constricting pressure. I start crawling over, nearly weeping at the pain. The pale-haired man's foot twitches, then goes limp. Finally I make it to the Gamer, my hands slipping through the rapidly expanding pool of blood.

"Ham!"

Sightless eyes stare at me.

"Ash . . . still . . . alive . . ."

"I'm here, baby, I'm here. We need to stop this, get you out of there."

". . . can't. He . . . locked me out . . . stuck . . . encounter . . ."

"I'll get Jase to find a way! Stay with me, baby."

". . . no time . . . losing . . . Ash . . . end it . . . please . . ."

"No, no no no, Ham, I can't do that, please don't ask me to do that, please . . ."

The Gamer goes limp in my arms, and I realize he's dead. Shaking, I look around the room. Wind is still unconscious, slumped against the wall, Slend on the floor, unmoving except for the faintest rise and fall of her chest. The armored walls guarding Ham stand like a monolith, marred only by several bullet scuffs and a thin slice where one of the Shredder's molyblades swung through. My rifle, its strap neatly cut in two, lies nearby, the Musashi still piercing the Shredder's heart.

Just another encounter. Just another encounter . . . JUST ANOTHER FUCKING ENCOUNTER . . . Find the clues . . .

I claw my way over to the rifle, then use the strap to lash it around my injured leg as a splint. Suck in several deep breaths, then push myself to my feet, walling off the pain as best I can. Tears roll down my face and my teeth clench tight, but I am

Ashura the Terrible, and I do not lose. Not even when no one is watching. Especially when no one is watching. I yank the Musashi out of the Shredder and toss it over by one corner of the armored core, steel clattering.

I stumble my way to the torn-off Shredder limb, parts of Slend's mecha scattered nearby, my friend's chest rising and falling in shallow waves. No time for friends. Screaming, I lift the meter-and-a-half length off the ground, balancing it on my shoulder like a claymore, inner molyblade edge still exposed, its weight crushing. The room spins around me, blood loss becoming noticeable, but I force it under control.

The walk back to the armored walls is an eternity of pain, each step its own private hell. Time passes. Eventually, the trial ends, vision clearing to reveal the corner where I tossed the Musashi. With another scream, I bring the leg chopping down, an oblique cut shearing off the bottom half of the corner. The Shredder limb thuds to the floor, and I know I won't be able to lift it again, but I don't need to. Panting, I slide to a seated position, wincing when my wound hits the cool tile. I swivel the molyblade leg so it cuts the bottom of the corner, then pick up the Musashi, levering it into the thin cut. Twin thumps sound, the metal sections falling away, leaving just enough of an opening for me to crawl through. A minute later, I'm leaning against Ham's tank, staring at him through the watery glass, blade propped point-down as a crutch. A haphood of unfamiliar design sits in a cradle next to one of the control consoles, a sleek, hard thing, like a chrome beetle. Small tendrils dangle from its interior, almost too fine to see. Gently, I grasp it in both hands, lifting it from its perch. Displays come alive, running through their initial diagnostics.

I slump down, tank cool against my back. Trembling, I

place the hemisphere over my head, linking it to my glasses, and dive into his thoughts.

Vision fades, replaced by nightmare.

Scenes flash in front of my eyes—scattered fragments of surveillance cameras, social streams, and first-person perspectives stitched into terrifying kaleidoscopic wholes.

Frantic soldiers, overwhelmed beneath concentrated fire from haphood-adorned Gamers, armories and vehicle parks broken into across multiple nations and countries. Drone control centers swarmed under and infiltrated, their command pods utilized by blank-eyed men and women coordinating multi-pronged assaults. Madness on a global scale, warning alerts flashing across every 'Net, citizens urged to stay inside, masses of people rioting and fleeing the chaos, the social fabric revealed for the thin facade it's always been.

I feel myself falling deeper, my mind spinning down the whirlpool drain, thoughts subsumed beneath the overwhelming immensity of data. Just when it seems like I'm going to drown, a single viewpoint clarifies.

Three men in a familiar clinic monitoring room, puffy bandages swelling their groins under their tight-fitting clothes, more bandages covering the face of the largest. A red haired man in a doctor's coat huddles in the corner, his face bruised, a deep cut across his lower lip. A window in the wall looks through to an older woman, her movements slow and sure as she glides through her stances.

"Time to have some fun," the bandage-faced man sneers. "That black whore's gonna regret the day she fucked with us. We'll do her mom first, then her."

"Please," the doctor cries. "She's a patient!"

One of them kicks him into silence, and they step through the revolving entrance lock. A short scene of violence unfolds, necks snapped with ruthless efficiency, but only after limbs break and shatter, accompanied by high-pitched shrieks, streaks of blood dripping down the window's inner surface. Sobbing, the doctor taps a command into his hapgloves. The lock revolves back, and the woman steps out. She nods at him.

"Thank you, Freddie. Do you know where my children are?"

"Try . . . try Johnny's. Ash always hangs out there."

"It'll be good to see that old scoundrel again. Be safe, Freddie. Dark times. War times."

She strides out of the room, hospital gown flapping around her brown, bare legs.

Is . . . is that . . . ?

The whirlpool drags me down once more, spitting out another scene.

I'm walking through a plush ballroom, smiling visages of Han emperors beaming down from the walls. Mirrors bounce my reflection back at me, a blank, acne-scarred face, gray haphood covering my head, red-tinted hexagonal glasses my eyes, form-fitting shorts and t-shirt my dark body. The pupils staring back at me don't seem to have anyone home.

A door swings open, two figures striding through.

"Look, Ilya. A noodle shop lump, come creeping into our domain. What should we—"

My hand rises lightning fast, a pistol in it, and I shoot them both in the eye, their coiling tattoos vanishing in a spray of blood and bone and brains. Half unsheathed molyblades slither back to quiescence. I step past and through the door. A terrified man huddles behind a sumptuous wooden desk.

"Look, I'm the ambassador, I can get you whatev—"

His face disappears too, and I walk out, my movements the finely tuned ticking of a precision machine.

No . . . why would he . . .

An older man crouches behind a barricade made of furniture, beckoning to a group of cloth-shrouded figures beneath the rusted shutter of his shop. A teenager, more boy than man, helps them inside, interior already packed and stuffy, where a dark-haired man and a burka-clad woman are organizing food and water, their faces scared yet determined. The maddened hornet buzz of a riot sings through the background, an incoming tsunami ready to break. A surge of people boils around the corner, frothing forms in pure white robes at the front, most bearing crude weapons, some waving signs with anti-Hajj slurs. The older man sighs, and sights down the length of his battered assault rifle, unshakeable relic of a violent past, spare magazines stacked neatly at his feet, then strokes the trigger with metronomic regularity.

Bullets find flesh, the same grisly dance steps he's spent his whole life trying to escape, and though he's not as young as he once was, no hesitation mars his precision. White-robed figures flip and fall, then those with weapons, the steady popping halted imperceptibly by smooth reloads. The bodies trip those behind them, and eventually the mob breaks and runs, leaving their dead where they lie.

He slides the empty magazines behind him, where the teenager scoops them up.

"Try and get 'em filled quick, boy. We need to go check on Glassbridge."

The teenager gulps, but his hands are steady as he reaches for a box of ammunition.

At least . . . Wind's parents . . .

A woman stops in the middle of a glass tunnel, hospital

gown falling still, her eyes wide with wonder at the evening sights. In the distance, sparkling petro rigs merge with enormous windfarms, the running lights of cargo ships sliding beneath the spinning blades, while an illuminated balloon hovers overhead like a second moon. Closer, birds swoop and dive into the murky water, returning with the occasional needlefish thrashing in their mouths. The serried lights of megaspires rise around her like heavenly pillars, stretching upward until it seems like they must touch the very stars themselves, scattered patches of green vertical farms dotting their lengths. She twirls, laughing, and looks out in the other direction, where a distant red glow lights up the bottoms of heavy clouds, dry land barely visible. The sprawled bodies at one end of the bridge don't even appear to register in her eyes.

She drinks in the vista, an ancient smile tugging at one corner of her mouth, then turns and continues over the bridge. A figure at the other end, shape where before lay absence, causes her to halt, then break into a run.

"My baby!"

No . . . Mom . . . don't . . .

I'm watching a woman run toward me, features the finely etched wear of not quite old age mixed with stress, and inside I'm screaming. The weight of a knife sits solidly in my hand, tucked neatly against my forearm, invisible from the front. A killing position. She gets closer, hospital gown flapping incongruously around her lean frame, white teeth visible in an infectious grin that almost seems to burst from her dark face. She calls a name, arms outstretched, and I step into the embrace, hand rising with the ponderous inevitability of an ocean. Arms squeeze me tight, a mother's grip, the blade slides home, an assassin's thrust. I look into her eyes, and she dies, the smile still there.

no no no NO NO NO NO

A battered man, ancient rifle slung over his shoulder, emerges from an armed picket line and stumbles to a halt, tears falling from his eyes. In front of him, a young man stands up from a newly dead corpse, blood dripping from his blade, and stares at him uncomprehendingly, gray hood covering his skull. The older man dashes a hand across his face, smearing the moisture into his cheeks.

"Aww, hell, Naomi. Dammit all to hell."

He fumbles for his rifle, more tears appearing in his eyes, and the younger man springs into a run, knife outstretched. Just as the older man is about to draw a bead, a small shape flashes past him, tendrils of electricity arcing from its tip. It hits the younger man, who stiffens, then falls, arms and legs twitching. From behind, the sound of harsh panting, greedy lungs sucking down air. The older man slowly lowers his rifle, flipping on the safety.

"That . . . was a hell of a throw, son. Jolters aren't the most aerodynamic thing."

"Thanks, Pops. You know she would have never forgiven you if you shot him."

"She's dead, boy."

"I meant both of them."

The older man stands there for a moment, then nods. He grabs one of the still-twitching hands.

"C'mon. You get to help me drag him back."

Jase . . . thank you . . .

Somehow, I surface, mentally gasping for breath, trying to regain myself. Countless shadowed tables surround me, whispered conversations just past the point of intelligibility, small candles gently glowing in their centers. I look across the table I'm at, seat comforting beneath me, atmosphere the same as it always is in the crypto-room.

Ham gazes back at me, sorrow in his eyes.

"How . . . how are we here?"

He reaches across and takes my hand.

"Sometimes I'm able to pull myself out. Escape from my father's prison. The scenario he's locked me into—it's a world forever at war. Victory condition—I'm the only one left standing. He had to build it quick, so there are some rough edges, places where the logic breaks down. Like forcing me to kill the person I love."

"Ham . . ."

"It's getting harder and harder, though, harder to remember that my life is something other than the Game. Harder to remember that I'm an *I*, and not all those other people. You caught a small glimpse of it, but it's so much worse. So much more intense."

I shudder. He's getting drawn into the ghosts, just like me. Just like Mom.

Mom.

"Was . . . was that you . . . Kiro . . . ?"

"Yes. I'm sorry. When I'm under, it's like I'm in a dream, one where I've lost all control. It's just the encounter and subconscious reflex. Please don't blame your brother."

"Can you stop it?"

He shakes his head wordlessly.

"What do we do?"

He smiles wistfully.

"You know what you have to do, Ash. It's a true Kobayashi."

A small picture appears on the surface of the table, me leaning against the tank, venerable blade in my hand, haphood on my head. In the picture, I wobble upright, facing Ham's floating form.

". . . No. No. You can't do this to me, Ham. There has to be another way. There's always another way."

He shakes his head again.

"There isn't, and I don't know if I'm going to be able to make it out again. You have to stop it before it gets worse, Ash. While there's still a real to return to. If it's a choice between me and the world, you have to choose the world."

More pictures appear on the table's surface—pitched battles between tank battalions, dirty mushroom clouds rising from orbital impacts, missile hatches sliding back, ominous red numbers skipping their way to zero. The figure of me raises her blade, and tears drip down both our faces.

"I don't want to lose you. I can't lose you."

He cups my cheek.

"I couldn't leave you if I wanted to. No matter what, I'll be with you."

He smiles.

"This body's only ever been a burden to me anyway. I'll always love you, Ashley."

The clocks continue their countdown, and his body goes stiff. I can see the light fading from his eyes. On the table, my figure tenses, muscles tightening.

"I love you, Hamlin—forever."

The blade plunges down, piercing glass and fluid and skin and flesh and heart and I don't know if it's his hand or mine that guides it. He shudders, then dies, candles winking out all around me.

Please. Let it be just a game.

My world goes black.

25

[Ghosts and Shells]

Wake up. Check my messages. Couple updates from Wind: news from college, telling me about the hot new freshman in her dorm. Smile and dash off a reply, ignoring the small stab in my heart. A brief missive from Slend, appeals court going well, her brother soon to be released, both of them moving north to the UPC once he's free, find a way to live off the grid. Send my congratulations, and an invite to get together if they're ever back down here. He'll probably want a drink or ten—gummie prisons are no joke.

Wander down the hall to brush my teeth, water credits good for the month, switch over to my socials. Quick clips of Han and Industan working together to rebuild the ruins of Central Asia, another limited nuclear exchange leaving its glowing touch on the world, figures in boxy white suits mapping the devastation. Maybe reclaiming farmland will keep them occupied for a while. News of more trade sanctions against the Big Three, spearheaded by the Reformist Movement within the CCA, sober figures in plain suits with black ties denouncing richly attired technocrats flanked by legions of attorneys—the newly appointed board members of WGSK. Seems like everyone but the Big Three are on board, so the sanctions might actually pass. The first wave of Gamers released from treatment, promising stories of redemption and recovery, special events within the Game to celebrate their return. Retrospectives on the Night of Games, solemn accounts interspersed with footage of the moment everything stopped, Gamers halted in their tracks as if they had collectively suffered a massive shock. I try not to bite my toothbrush in two.

Closer to home, more funds allocated to refurbishing the Rust, half its floors burned away during the Night of Games, the occasional body still floating up on the current. Hopefully Slend has rent control—if she ever comes back. Other reconstruction efforts underway in Highrise, the Brown, and Southspire, several dens of Gamers having caused extensive damage there. Pictures of slow, but steady, progress, walls restored, shops revitalized, communities banding together once again. Shells regaining the life within, one three-by-five at a time. Who knows, maybe it'll last more than a couple decades. We can always hope.

Head back to my room and change into my work outfit, a slick shirt and pants combination emblazoned with Johnny's new logo: NOODLES (AND MORE). He's branching out into other cuisines: hummus, shawarma, kebabs, and the like. Lot of families remember what he and Jase did, and they told their friends. These days, it's running me ragged keeping up with the orders. I slide on my tacboots and lace them up. Left leg is feeling pretty good, the pair of bullet wounds reduced to aching moments when a cat-six rolls in. Maybe I'll race some couriers today.

Spend the morning dropping off lunches, crisscrossing my way around Ditchtown. Sunlight gleams through Glassbridge, but despite the sights, I don't linger. I don't think I ever will, not anymore. Too many ghosts. Deliver a couple of cartons to some techies in the Brown, stuffed away in their air-conditioned cells, and take my lunch break, grabbing some more noodles from Johnny. I throw the two containers in my backpack and head toward Highrise.

Greet the guards at the clinic entrance, new faces slowly grown familiar over the past six months. They irradiate my noodles in the scanner, same as the ones before them, then pass me through to the other side. I grab the cartons and head down the pastel colored corridor, scars painted over and gone. Knock on the door and head inside.

"How's it going, Freddie?"

"Good, Ash. Good. He's having a good day today. Responding real well to the treatments."

A small scar tugs at the corner of Freddie's lip, a memento from Mikelas. That and the dark bags under his eyes make him look like he's aged a decade since he watched over Mom.

"That's great, Freddie. Buzz me through?"

"Sure thing."

I enter the revolving lock, and it cycles around me, opening onto a small room with a neatly made bed. Kiro is doing one-handed headstand pushups against the wall, his feet nearly touching the ceiling at full extension. When he sees me, he grins, and pops upright.

"Heya, sis!"

"Heya, bro. How're you doing?"

I pass him a carton of noodles, and he digs in with his fingers, greedily slurping them down. I follow at a more sedate pace, perched on the edge of the bed.

"Good, real good. Freddie said I haven't had an episode in almost a week. I think we're getting close to beating this thing."

I try not to laugh at his upbeat tone, so changed over the past few months.

"Well that's great, Kiro. Glad to hear it."

He gulps down another handful of noodles.

"Yeah, I can't wait to get back to the Game. It's been so long, I hope I haven't lost my skills. I'm trying to stay in shape in here, but it's tough without a real hapchamber, you know?"

My heart sinks. Even though they're finally letting some of those affected by the Night of Games log back in, Freddie's been telling me that of those who do, ten to fifteen percent have some sort of relapse. Nothing nearly as bad as before, but still enough to be worrisome—vacant-eyed Gamers roaming their hapsphere, as if they're searching for something, most eventually snapping out of it when their power supplies fail or someone notices. Some take days to return. I don't want to lose my brother a third time.

"I bet. Tell you what, let's take it a day at a time, see what Freddie thinks is best. You know they're following his treatment protocols all over the world, right? If anyone knows when you'll be ready to leave, it's him."

I reach up and ruffle his hair, and he smiles.

"Sounds good, sis. Hey, tell Jase and Johnny not to be strangers, yeah? I haven't seen them in a while."

"I'll let them know, bro." I stand up, motioning at the lock, trying not to think about the last time Jase and Johnny saw Kiro, charging them over Mom's bloody corpse, knife aimed at their throats. It's a struggle to keep my voice even. "I'll let them know. Hey, I gotta get back to the job. It was good seeing you, Kiro. Keep working, you'll be out of here before you know it."

"You bet, sis." He laughs. "Ladies first, yeah?"

I smile back at him, stepping into the lock.

"Age before beauty."

On the other side, I pause by Freddie's chair, the momentary lightness evaporating.

"How long do you think it's going to be, Freddie?"

He takes a deep breath.

"I don't know, Ash. On his good days, he's good, but on the bad days . . . it's bad. Real bad. We've already had to retire two orderlies for medical reasons. One's lucky he's still alive."

"Is it the same as the others?"

"Yeah, it just seems to be hitting him harder. We're calling it 'fuzzed,' like when you wake from a particularly vivid dream, but you can't quite recall exactly what it was you were doing. It's the word on the tip of your tongue, the utter certitude that you *know*. That you know exactly what something is, only you don't know any of the details." He rubs his chin, frustrated. "Hooking him up to a modified version of the Game helps, but he's lost a part of himself, and I don't know if he'll ever get it back. It's like there's someone else living inside him when it happens."

I pat him on the shoulder.

"Do your best, Freddie. If anyone can bring him back, it's you. I'll make sure the bills get paid."

He lays his hand on top of mine.

"Just . . . stay strong, Ash. Anytime you want to talk, I'm here. Don't feel like you're alone in dealing with this."

"I appreciate that." I slip my hand out from under his. "Gotta go. Food to deliver, creds to earn, you know how it is."

I walk out of the door and exit the clinic, heading back into Highrise. A small symbol glares at me from a wall, one of the new anti-Hajj graffiti tags that have been popping up recently, the boardshits' latest attempt at resurgence. I feel the black mood threatening to devour me, my own personal storm building over the last half a year.

Was any of it even worth it? All that we sacrificed? Sure, the world's still here, but what was the point if the rot's still eating it from below? I flick a rude gesture at the tag and make my way back to Johnny's, passing the ubiquitous midday crowds, anger bubbling in the pit of my stomach. It feels like acid chewing me apart from the inside.

I push through the bead curtain covering Johnny's entrance, and slide past the crowds of people waiting for one of the few seats to open up, loud waves of conversation bouncing off the walls. Behind the counter, Johnny shifts his woks, seemingly oblivious to it all, turning from time to time to shave off some meat or adjust a kebab. Jase waves at me from his spot tending tables, hands clearing off the remnants of a meal and ushering another pair of customers over. I wave back, but my heart's not in it.

"Take the rest of the day off, Ash. Do something fun. Go live."

Johnny's voice seems to cut through the din straight to my ears, and I glare at him. Am I really that transparent? He tilts his head toward the door, and I sigh. I probably am. I head back into the Brown and let my feet drift, following my thoughts. Shabby printed clothes rub past my shoulders, colors in all hues of the rainbow, tourists pointing and jostling, some staring through tablets, most wearing glasses, but I feel like I'm alone, an unmoored ship in this sea of humanity, missing its anchor.

It's an all too familiar feeling lately.

When I look up, I'm standing outside Sarah's door, her sign turned to NOT CLOSED, crowds of people milling at my back. Some carry signs cheering on the current ladder leaders, others hold printed replicas of notable Game treasures, but I ignore them all. My gaze is trapped by the sign, by my memories, the weight of desires in my head, realities in my heart, who it is I really am. Who it is I want to be.

Life's been a featureless blur since Wind dragged us all back on a stolen copter—too busy trying to find a cure for Kiro; rehabbing my mangled leg; making ends meet, one day at a time. Too busy to want to feel, because feeling means facing what happens after your world ends.

The SunJewel Warriors are gone, disappeared to the real . . . or dead. Saw the images of Brand's funeral on my socials while I was still stuck in a bed at the clinic, another injury I'll spend the rest of my life trying to heal. I couldn't even be there for her at the very end. Couldn't even leave a comment, lest the boardshits descend on her grieving family. The memory rises, unwanted.

Endgame. My first steps into a new world. The Gorger dead at my feet, my blade dripping blood, stinging pain in my side from the punch it landed, but victory. My victory. The few followers on my stream chattering about the improbability of my kill, posting to their friends.

A group sneaking out of the shadows, mocking voices, sneering faces, ready to claim the spoils of a fight they were too afraid to face.

"A newbie, all alone. Dunno how you took that Gorger down, but it's ours now."

My victory.

"Looks like she's not moving. Sucks to be her."

My encounter.

"Log out, bitch. Or we'll hurt you. Find who you are in the real. Have some fun."

Tired of running.

"Looks like she wants a fight. Your ass is ours, newbie."

Shapes circling in, closer and closer, weapons bared, my eyes trying to track everything at once but everything moving so fast. Too fast.

Golden light, a presence at my back. Two figures instantly in-cinerated, their gear falling to the forest floor, the rest scrambling over each other in their haste to get away. Turn around on shak-ing legs, all of it too much to take.

"Hey. You doing okay, newbie?"

A smiling face, an outstretched hand, a long fall of auburn hair, like coils of banked flames.

"I'm the Devil's Brand. Silly name, I know, but I came up with it as a kid to piss off my parents and it kind of stuck. You been in endgame long?"

No.

"It shows. You did pretty much everything wrong. Didn't scout the encounter, didn't check for gankers, didn't bring consumables, no teammates—you were pretty terrible."

Story of my life.

"Thing is, you still won. Since you took a tier-three encounter down, you've earned an endgame name—should keep you a little safer from the boardshits. Easiest way to spot a newbie, you've all still got Candyland names. What do you want to be known as?"

Ashura.

"You mean 'Asura'? Jeez, you can't even spell right. You really are terrible."

Ashura the Terrible.

"Hah. I like it. Let me teach you about endgame, Ash . . ."

The memory fades. I wonder if anyone even remembers Ashura the Terrible anymore. The Game still exists, but leaderboards are always temporary.

What am I even doing here? What's the point in caring? None of it lasts.

Something tugs at my sleeve, and I tamp down the familiar combat reflexes, the instinct to spin and slash. A small girl, half her dark hair in neat braids, the other half in frizzy poofs, smiles up at me, the fabric of my hoodie trapped in her dirty fingers.

"Can you sign this? I just need one more, and you're the last. It's for my room."

I look down at an actual hard-copy printout, protected by

a clear sleeve, of four knights on dragonback. Their armor gleams from a setting sun, fantastic swords held high above their impossible mounts, and identical grins stretch across their exposed faces. Silently, I nod and take the proffered marker, adding my sharp signature next to Brand's looping curls, Wind's airy swoops, Slend's compact strokes. The girl smiles even wider, and clutches it to her chest.

"Thanks. You guys were the best. One of these days, I'm gonna beat your records. Bye!"

I watch her disappear into the swarming throngs of people, and try not to scream.

There's always another encounter.

I gesture at the security camera, its gray lens a mirror of my thoughts. The door swings open almost immediately, Sarah beaming on the other side. She gathers me into a rough embrace as the door closes behind us, swiftly shutting off the noise of the crowd. After another squeeze, she leans slightly away, staring at my face.

"It's good to see you, Ash. I didn't know if you were ever going to come back."

"There—" My voice catches, and I clear my throat. Damn ghosts. "There was some heavy shit, Sare. I didn't know if I ever wanted to come back." I think of the psych-secs, the endgame encounters, their beckoning depths in which I can lose myself forever, a dive I might never surface from if I don't want. "I'm back now. Got a sphere for me?"

She tilts her head, examining me, then walks us down the corridor.

"For you, always, Ash." Her arm tightens around my shoulder. "But hey, don't feel like you have to jump right back in. We could always just hang out, get some drinks, talk, you know?"

I feel her hip rubbing against mine, but that's all I feel.

Ham's face rises in front of me, and I shake it away angrily. He's gone, and it's up to me to find a way through my problems.

Story of my fucking life.

"Thanks, Sare, but I think I'll go straight for the sphere. Is my gear still in my locker?"

"Of course. I'll put you in B-3, she's always been one of my steadiest." She grabs my hand, and I halt in front of the locker room entrance, looking back at her. "It's . . ." She shakes her head and turns away. "Never mind. Go get dressed, I'll warm the sphere up."

I know what she wants, and once upon a time it might have been something I wanted too, but those days are dead and gone. I shrug my way into my hapsuit, motions the tiniest bit ragged, hitching in places where some extra weight found its way to my thighs and hips, then run the molecular zipper up my back, tracing the familiar curve from ass to neck, feeling the familiar blandness replace my skin. I want to sink into the numbness, let it silence everything.

Grab my haphood from the shelf, its older style flexible weight comfortable in my palm, trying not to think about rigid gray hemispheres, tendrils waving like clutching hands. I pull the stretchy material over my face, attaching it to the suit, then pick up my immersion viewer. If I'm going to sink, I'm not planning on half-assing it. Pad down the hall to my assigned hapsphere, B-3 shining above the door in a gentle white glow. Push it open and head inside.

The hapsphere sits in the middle of the room, squat, elegant, deadly, open hatch beckoning me with seductive promise. I climb inside and slide my immersion viewer over my eyes and nose, one strap briefly catching on my missing chunk of ear. Sarah's voice rattles in my head.

"Doing okay, Ash?"

"I'm fine. Let's start this up."

"You're the boss, boss."

We run through the preliminary setup routines, hands slapping wireframe pillars, feet jogging loosely across an endless plain, and I struggle to feel anything other than hate. Hate for the sphere, for the Game, for myself. How can I be this person again? *Why* should I be this person again? After all the death, how can I go on living like nothing has changed? What kind of monster am I? Wind and Slend both moved on, escaped from this endless treadmill. Why can't I?

The forever plain offers no answers, and soon brakes to a halt, columns sinking back into the nothing that birthed them.

"Five by five across the board. Ready if you are."

Will I ever be ready for anything again? Will I ever feel more than this empty shell?

"Put me in, Sare."

"Sure thing, Ash. And here. We. Go."

My portal appears, and I gesture past it, ignoring the ever-scrolling socials, the unread messages, the tattered remnants of my life. Perfect fields rise like magic, replacing the homey cavern, wildflowers waving under the noonday sun, a light breeze drifting through my hair, bringing me the scents of small living things and ruffling the grass on the surrounding hills. An ideal, sugar-coated world, where the heroes always win and no one ever dies.

This time I do scream, an explosion of sound across the pristine landscape. On and on it goes, my throat raw and burning, until at some point it must have stopped, because I'm crouching, fingers tangled in the immaculate grass like I can choke the very life from the ground itself.

The tuxedo-clad rabbit hops up, overlarge eyes shiny as always. It doffs a top hat and bows.

"Welcome to Candyland, Ashura the Terrible."

I let go of the grass and stand, feeling old and tired. At

least the rabbit remembers me, its familiar voice saccharine and content.

It stares at me silently, and I stare back, wanting so much. Wanting things to be different, to be the way they were. Wanting the SunJewel Warriors to ride forth once more . . . but things will never be the way they were, Brand will never return, Slend and Wind have left, I'll never see Ham again, and all that's left is to try to escape this reality for as long as possible, no matter the price.

I cock my fist and send it toward the rabbit, seeking the pain of endgame, the violence, the destruction, seeking to bury myself in a spiral that will only end one way, but I need something, anything to get me through the endless days.

The rabbit smiles faintly, then leans to the side, my hand whistling harmlessly past its floppy ear. It winks at me, and I gawk, mouth falling open.

Impossible.

The rabbit's voice sounds again, deepening, darkening, and in that instant, I finally recognize it, a voice I haven't heard in half a year, one I didn't know was so important until I couldn't hear it anymore.

My anchor.

"You'll have to be quicker than that. Eat me, Ashley."

It turns and leaps away, bounding amongst the perfectly green grass, heading deeper into Candyland, never once looking back. Haltingly at first, I stumble after it, away from endgame, my feet gradually moving faster and faster, absent friends at my side. The wind whips past my face, tears streaming from my eyes, and I realize I've found the smile I thought was gone forever.

Acknowledgments

There are a bunch of people I would like to thank for helping make this book a reality. What started out as an internal act of catharsis has, with the assistance of some amazingly talented folks, transformed into something that hopefully inspired and entertained you.

First and foremost, my family—Isabel, Olivia, and Remy. Love you all, and yes, we can go out for sushi. My agent, Rob, who isn't just a tireless worker and promoter, but also a friend. I'm so glad you became a part of my life, and I'll write you those football memoirs someday. I swear. Cynthia Manson, an invaluable help who took my first draft and found all the spots to make it something amazing. I'll get that epic tale of Gilgamesh from you eventually, and it'll be great. Tanya DePass is an awesome woman doing awesome things at I Need Diverse Games (@INeedDivGms on Twitter), and I'm so lucky to know her. If you don't want the boardshits to win, check out what she does (and throw a couple bucks her way). Finally, I'd like to thank Edwin McRae for helping with the initial reads. Appreciate it greatly.

On the Tor side, this is my first time doing a book with them, and I couldn't have asked for a better group—led, of course, by the legend himself, Tom Doherty, who is just as great in person as you would think. A big thanks to my first editor, Brendan Deneen, who believed in the story and helped polish it to a mirror finish. Sad to see you go, but I know you'll keep being awesome. My second editor, Chris Morgan, was a joy to work with and did a great job shepherding us to the finish line. Hoping to do more with you in the future. My copy editor and production editor, Angus Johnston and Melanie Sanders, caught all the little mistakes that one never thinks are there, and I cannot thank you both enough for finding them. The art, by Vault49, is everything I hoped it would be, vibrant and stunning in a way that makes Ash leap off the cover.

And lastly, a special thanks to all the paste-gobbling, poop-socking, alt-right gatekeeping boardshits out there who remind us each and every day that there's still plenty of work to be done cleaning up our misogynist, racist, sexist society. Chapter Eight's for you.